A CONTRIBUTION TO THE HISTORY OF JOY

A CONTRIBUTION TO THE HISTORY OF JOY

RADKA
DENEMARKOVÁ

Translated from the Czech
by Julia and Peter Sherwood

COFFEE HOUSE PRESS

Cover design by Kyle G. Hunter
Book design by Coffee House Press
Author photograph © Karel Cudlín
Typographic swallows © Lucie Zajíčková

Coffee House Press books are available to the trade through our primary distributor, Consortium Book Sales & Distribution, cbsd.com or (800) 283-3572. For personal orders, catalogs, or other information, write to info@coffeehousepress.org.

Coffee House Press is a nonprofit literary publishing house. Support from private foundations, corporate giving programs, government programs, and generous individuals helps make the publication of our books possible. We gratefully acknowledge their support in detail in the back of this book.

Kobayashi Issa haiku trans. David G. Lanoue, https://haikuguy.com/issa/searchenglish2.php.
Ludwig Wittgenstein quote from *Culture and Value*, ed. G. H. Von Wright and H. Nyman, trans. Peter Winch. Oxford: Blackwell, 1980. 46.
Swallows gather on a line © hatheyphotos / Adobe Stock

Library of Congress Cataloging-in-Publication Data
Names: Denemarková, Radka author | Sherwood, Julia translator | Sherwood, P. A. (Peter A.) translator
Title: A contribution to the history of joy / Radka Denemarková ; translated from the Czech by Julia and Peter Sherwood.
Other titles: Příspěvek k dějinám radosti. English
Description: Minneapolis, MN : Coffee House Press, 2026.
Identifiers: LCCN 2026018432 (print) | LCCN 2026018433 (ebook) | ISBN 9781566897662 trade paperback | ISBN 9781566897679 ebook
Subjects: LCGFT: Detective and mystery fiction | Thrillers (Fiction) | Novels
Classification: LCC PG5039.14.E54 P7513 2026 (print) | LCC PG5039.14.E54 (ebook)
LC record available at https://lccn.loc.gov/2026018432
LC ebook record available at https://lccn.loc.gov/2026018433

Printed in the United States.

32 31 30 29 28 27 26 25 1 2 3 4 5 6 7 8

For Ester. For Honza.

For the swallows of Amrum island.

baby swallows in the nest
eyes glued
on the evening sky
KOBAYASHI ISSA

No cry of torment can be greater than the cry of one man.
Or again, no torment can be greater than what a single human being may suffer.
The whole planet cannot be in greater torment than a single soul.
LUDWIG WITTGENSTEIN

There is no ban on old women climbing trees.
ASTRID LINDGREN

TABLE OF CONTENTS

Folk of a feather don't flock together.

My body has been riddled by the wind.

PROLOGUE

A head against a brick wall. A body under horses' hooves. How much is hidden in routine and ritual. They had coffee together a few times. They went for a walk along a murky river. They sat on a bench, drowning in each other's eyes. They went out for dinner. They went to a concert. They held hands. Timidly, he put his arm around her shoulders. Boldly, around her waist. They kissed. They tasted each other. Tonight was the first time they went to the movies together. To see the old British film, *Brief Encounter*. Now they're in a tearoom, and believe they're talking about the movie. But in reality they're talking about themselves, hiding behind the movie's protagonists. The masculine blue and the feminine yellow meld together, paving the way for a spring not affected by the changing of the seasons. The sacred teapot is bubbling away gently. They have touched the deepest recesses of each other's overflowing hearts. They forget about time and time forgets them. They miss the last bus.

It is nighttime. No rickshaws in sight. An unscheduled, half-empty bus slows down. Obligingly it pulls up. The overflowing hearts get onboard. Grateful, they pay the smiling driver. They don't notice that the windows on the bus are blacked out. The future is shrouded in semidarkness. They head for the seats at the back. The bus peels away from the curb. The driver steps on the gas.

Holding hands, they discuss the film. A quiet conversation punctuated by pauses between words and pauses within words. A young man in a seat behind the driver stands up. He is holding a metal bar. He walks toward them. The two young people holding hands after watching a movie together for the first time don't know that they will never touch each other's bodies again, that they will never lock eyes again and that their words will never connect again. Two other young, strong male bodies on the bus get up from their seats. They block the aisle. They are all smiles. What bitter-sweet smiles. A silk moth. *Bombyx mori*. Come and listen to the sound it makes.

From a bird's-eye view, everything is fiendishly simple. Body memory never lies. For centuries, swallows on the wing have talked about the human bodies down below. The reservoir of trust down there is shrinking. It is *only* in flight that the "I" blooms like a yellow tulip as it dives into the calyx, following a trail down a maze of mirrors. Do swallows need courage? They live by their own rules, the only way they know how. No matter how fragile they seem to be.

Forked tails circling a hill. The name of the hill is Petřín. The mound is dotted with couples in love. Its location at the heart of Prague's Old Town lends it a romantic aura. How much is hidden in routine and ritual, my dear.

Walking down the hill, the couples pass an orange-colored house with white windows and a red pantile roof. The house crouches at the foot of Petřín Hill, but there is no smoke coming from its chimney. A non-smoker. A humble beggar, its forehead pressed against the hillside. At night, a slender streetlight illuminates its façade. Reaching into the house, it sticks out its head sensuously. The house itself resembles another streetlamp dropped from the sky by a defiant beetle.

The people living in the apartments of the orange house with a view of the green hill are listening to music with their windows wide open. Couples passing by slow their pace and listen.

The gleaming windows are not covered by curtains. A stray dog, starving, emaciated and in heat, has settled on the cobblestones: a dog that's emaciated is a disgrace to its owner. It sees four identical-looking girl dolls and one boy doll performing identical movements, looking like carbon copies of each other: each with a pair of eyes, ears, legs, and arms, and a single mouth, head, and trunk, all walking on their hind legs. How confusing for the dog

The enamel on the faces of the four girl dolls is yellow, while the enamel on the boy doll's face is blue.

The paint on their faces is flaking off.

The dawn squeaks at the gate. The dog sits up.

The orange walls part. The show is about to begin. The dog is watching a puppet show. It sees a dolls' house, and in it four yellow girl dolls and the shadow of a blue boy doll. The dog sits there with its tongue lolling out. It swallows some fallen leaves. It waits to see which window will toss it a gnawed bone. The dog does not bark or bite. Just like time. Hmm.

Swallows circle overhead, chirruping. They share jokes about men and women. Sex is joy. The same jokes, told for centuries, contributions to the history of joy, collected by the swallows. They encounter a battleground that has never known peace. There is a tacit agreement and a territory that has not yet been liberated and never will be, one that anyone may conquer, where everyone is allowed to do whatever they please. A plowed field. A vast field of black, fertile soil. Its name is the body of the one who is weaker. There's no point reporting the conqueror to the police.

The swallows fly on. Their wisdom feeds *only* on doubt. They will remain true to their nature as long as they live.

A FRAGILE AUTUMN AND THE RESTLESSNESS OF HUMMINGBIRDS

The man is seated with his back against a massive wooden beam. His bowed head is examining his belly; the belly is oblivious of the activity all around. The body is dressed in a tight black vest, fashionable shorts, and a checkered silk pajama top left unbuttoned. The top, bought in Scotland, sports a clan emblem on the front. All that is lacking is a kilt. The man is hatless and barefoot. His legs are stiff and splayed out like those of a wind-up doll. His toes are rounded and smooth. If you tickled the crinkly pink soles of his feet with a feather the toes would curl inward, the bones cracking. The man seems embarrassed by his casual attire. His eyes are lowered.

The place where he is resting is spick and span, well organized and half-empty. The attic, which the owners refer to as the loft, forms part of a new-build family home. It boasts a metal staircase, a long tongue beset by tragedy, and an array of flashy, expensive suitcases, bags and ski boots lounging on the shelves. Downhill skis and cross-country skis and ski poles extend along tall narrow white racks, followed by golf clubs, shoes, and sports bags. The loft bristles with metal laundry stands bolted to the floor. The bristling metal stands are not used for drying laundry; the family uses the dryer in the basement laundry room. The man's hair is gray. It is a firm turf, like a thick and evenly cut brush. The doll's legs are muscular, the biceps on its arms lean, its back broad and masculine.

The well-maintained body is deceiving itself.

In fact, the man is past his prime. Even though he used to swim every weekend to wash away the sins of the work week. A mighty stroke of the arm, an intake of breath, a dive below the surface. The chlorine would wash away the stress and dissolve the importuning of the years. He didn't need to work but he did. He liked to work because he didn't need to.

The loft is a hive of activity. A police detective is kneeling by the man as if about to tickle the soles of his bare feet with a feather or a stalk of grass. Or as if to have a quiet word with the body.

The man doesn't react. He remains silent and unresponsive. Out of the lonely evening of the fall a swallow, its eyes misty with rain, flies into the loft. The assembled men welcome the distraction; the collective laughter of powerful baritone voices startles the delicate bird. Panicking, the swallow keeps hitting its head against the wall, circling around the dormer window until it finds a way out, to freedom. In its little beak it carries a purple Japanese cherry blossom, the kind that doesn't grow in these parts. One swallow most certainly won't make a summer at this time of the year, and only among Japanese cherry blossoms does a silk moth feel truly at home.

As the Detective, waddling duck-like, nears the man's left temple, his trousers bulge out at the knees. The seated man's eyes are lowered to his own chest while the Detective's are lowered toward the man's neck. He crouches down and watches as a young doctor carefully lays the body, dressed in shorts and the silk pajama top, on the floor, palpating it again with his fingers. The man offers no resistance. There is a white noose coiled around his neck. As if the body was stowed here, tethered with a white rope so it wouldn't run away. Like a pet dog hitched to its kennel. An overturned teak chair with a curved lattice back lies by the beam, its indecently spread legs flailing in the air. Three more chairs, tall puritans with latticed backs, stand guard by the wall. They expect visitors to flop down on them and enjoy the puppet show, seated on their squashed rears. A further eight teak chairs, their spitting images, rise proudly from the first floor next to a folding kitchen table. None of the chairs has any doubt that it was suicide.

It was suicide, obviously.

The men pack up their gear.

Compared to the resting body, the Detective is young: he is thirty-seven. He enjoys his work even though he does need to work. He is zealous and his memory serves him, although he's not sure how well. The Detective's body totters as he waddles duck-like to the other side of the face. Hesitantly, like a blind man, his hands feel the face, taking in the skin and the wrinkles. Hesitation is the thief of time; perplexed by a pair of grooves on the man's neck, he ransacks his memory for details of that course on suicide and murder by hanging. One of the grooves is at an angle. That's just as it should be. But there's also another, barely noticeable. And that one is straight. He points this out to the doctor. The doctor waves his hand dismissively, it's obviously a suicide, don't be silly, shush.

The Detective stands up. His knees give a crack. He disturbs some dust and a swallow's feather that was caught on the man's full lips. The Detective looks out of the open window at the rain. Bodies of swallows are lined up along the telegraph wires behind the garden like music notes on a stave. They are a stone's throw away. But is this the time to be casting stones?

It is.

The Detective climbs down the metal staircase to the second floor. There is a wide glass-covered terrace with a view of the city. A small child is playing on a fluffy rug appliquéd with toy motifs. The child steers a toy engine along rail tracks woven into the rug. A young woman on a black leather sofa with metal armrests has now stopped weeping. A mirror on the opposite wall, fashioned from dozens of oval teardrops, multiplies the reflection of her golden hair, tied in a bun, and her pert little nose. In a hushed voice she answers the questions from a capable, plump policewoman who is taking notes with one hand and holding the woman's wrist with the other, to register her panicky pulse. The distance between the weeping body and the body upstairs in the loft spans more than thirty years. She has just returned home from a late summer vacation by the sea. Yes, it was today, yes, this Saturday afternoon. She was taking the empty suitcases up to the loft, my husband likes . . . liked everything to be neat and tidy. Routine and ritual, he used to say, that's the strategy for getting through the day, darling, otherwise life will become hollow or disintegrate.

He wasn't meant to be at home, the tear-choked voice rasps. On Friday he went to . . . was supposed to go hiking, although he was no longer as passionate about mountain-climbing as he once was, but he still went skiing, and in summer and fall he liked to go hiking with friends. No, he isn't . . . wasn't sick . . . he was . . . really fit, even though he was pushing seventy. The Widow breaks down in tears.

The Detective interrupts the two women. He offers a handkerchief to the one who is weeping. The Widow has run out of tissues. The Detective's handkerchief is linen, with an old-fashioned embroidered monogram. The policewoman steps aside. The Detective fires off a fresh battery of questions. Hurt and surprise sweep across the Widow's face. But she's already explained all that, she was taking the empty suitcases to the loft. No, she has no idea why he might have done it. No, they didn't have an argument. In fact, he was bursting with fresh energy after the charges against him were dropped under the presidential amnesty.

The Widow grabs the Detective by the hand. She drags him over to the bedroom like some eager courtesan. There's a piece of paper lying on the bedside table. The Detective's eyes take in the scribbled words: *contact lenses, sunglasses, suntan lotion, lip balm, compression bandage, notes on chapter 86, medication.* The Widow's hips give an exultant wiggle. The wiggle doesn't go unnoticed by the Detective. Neither does the outline of her breasts with their firm nipples and the slim waist and the curvy hips. A vast king-size bed with chubby, plumped-up white pillows winks at him. She taps the paper with a long fingernail painted peach, pecking at individual words. Her husband would always draw up a list before going on a trip, in his boundless joy and anticipation. He always wrote it out in longhand. Whenever he really cared about something and was in a hurry, he would write by hand, something he rarely did otherwise. So why on earth would he have made a list if he'd decided to go instead on his final journey, what would have been the point. How should I know where he was planning to go and why, I have no idea what kind of list he might have drawn up for his final journey and what the point would have been, says the Detective, rebuffing her brusquely. The woman won't give up. But surely he would have scribbled at least a few lines addressed to *her*. The young Widow's eyes glisten. The tears spill over. The three-year-old boy with his toy engine gets under her feet. She isn't weeping, she is *only* staring. No, he had no enemies. Well, a while ago he had been upset by some minor matter relating to his former assistants. But that all turned out to be nonsense. They'd accused him of sexual harassment at work, one even claimed he had raped her, or something of the sort.

The Detective feels ill at ease in the bedroom. He moves next door, to the man's study. The Widow and the little boy dutifully scurry after him. The study's outer wall is also made of glass. Raindrops trickle down the pane. They live in a fishbowl, the Detective thinks. The bodies of swallows on the telegraph wires regroup, composing a new tune echoing the rhythm of the raindrops.

On the corner of a massive, semi-circular desk, a slender water carafe with a crystal embedded within it gleams on the dark-brown surface. A similar crystal, only smaller and with a beveled edge, glitters in the window. It is a teardrop sparkling blue in the pane, shimmering in the double glazing. A teardrop flashing, its reflection redoubled. The other walls are lined with framed photographs, crammed cheek by jowl, a kind of black-and-white wallpaper. Across the wall facing the window run metal rails the same color as the photo frames. The Detective plants a stubby finger on a round button next to the shining carafe of water and looks at the woman. She sniffles, flaring her nostrils: a facial clue of security and trust. She nods by way of approval. He presses the button with his index finger.

The photos begin to slide along the wall, rattling and rolling. The Detective presses the button again. The moving pictures jerk, stop and jiggle as if someone had breathed on them lightly. The Detective's eyes scan the photos. He turns around, his index finger poised to press the button again. The female voice behind him patiently explains that this was her husband's invention. It allowed him to alternate the photos, displaying pictures with his visitors without having to sift through piles of images. Several presidents feature among those pictured with the man. They all share the same thick mop of gray hair. Besuited, seated in a theater auditorium, laughing. Casually attired at a tennis match, all looking in the same direction, following the path of the ball. Besuited, sitting at chess boards.

Wrapped in heavy fur coats, in a group at the North Pole. On a golf course with movie stars. Judging a beauty contest. Drinking Becherovka liqueur at a table laden with food. All the pictures were taken after 1989.

Have a go, the Detective encourages the small boy to press the button, a misshapen beetle. The boy shelters behind his mother's back. This is . . . was strictly forbidden by his father, the Widow explains, somewhat embarrassed. Why aren't there any pictures of you, the Detective asks, looking around the room. The Widow's face, reflected in the window, remains unmoved. The Detective asks more questions, gluing the story together with his saliva like a swallow's nest. The air grows heavy with the unspoken answer as they both ponder the question. The unspoken answer glues them to each other.

Anything else?

No, nothing unusual otherwise. He had handed over the management of his companies to his oldest son from his second marriage many years ago and set up an office here at home, dropping in on the company from time to time to keep an eye on a few special building projects. The Detective rummages through the drawers of the massive desk. He opens the man's journal. And what about the other children, the ones from his previous marriages, I mean. The Widow sighs, his oldest son is the *only* one he got on with, in fact it was the son who got in touch after many years, he had no contact with the other children or ex wives and never discussed them with me, they're finished projects, he used to say.

Finished projects? That's right.

The Detective flips through the journal. A couple of sheets of paper fall out. And a folded newspaper clipping. The Detective spreads out the sheets next to one another. You said he hardly ever wrote by hand. His body is joined by the Widow's. The Detective blinks involuntarily and pulls in his stomach, begins to breathe faster, deep breaths and flared nostrils, a sign of feeling secure and trusting, his body has reacted, he is attracted by the woman's scent. Her husband really hadn't been keen on writing by hand, these are *only* notes for a book he jotted down in pencil, some words are underlined in purple ink, oddly enough. For a book? Yes, he was working on a book about his life, at first he refused to hire a helper but he wasn't making progress so someone recommended a creative writing course taught by Birgit Stadtherr, you know, that weird writer who fled to England after the war, then lived in America or someplace and has recently come back to Prague, she writes in English and *only* about men, that is, kings and statesmen, apparently she is currently writing a book about President Beneš. Well, and this spring she ran a brief course in creative writing *only* for a select group of hand-picked people, the elite, otherwise her husband wouldn't have enrolled. It was expensive, horrendously expensive, don't ask me how much it cost, oof, you can imagine, an American, and of Czech origin to boot, and eventually she pressured him into taking a relaxation therapy course with Diana Adler that was even more expensive. He said he would never finish it otherwise, it was only thanks to her that he made himself write something before each class. She had great influence over him. Both women did. This clipping is of an article by her, you can take it as well. He said he wanted to write a novel about abused men. He was annoyed by what's going on these days. What is it that's going on these days, the Detective asks, glancing over a scathing article signed Birgit Stadtherr. What he reads gives him a jolt in the groin. I don't really know what he meant by it, says the Widow recoiling with a smile. The awareness of a smile on her tanned face horrifies her.

The Detective is sorry to see her body move away. He misses the physical closeness and wishes he could sniff her hair. The Widow's eyes alight on the Detective's middle finger, which sports an engagement ring. Oh this, I inherited it from my grandfather, he replies hastily to the squinting almond eyes. Can I have a look at what your husband has written? You can, but . . . The Widow's delicate face turns pale. But . . .? Well . . . I would like to ask you, well, if I may be so bold, considering this situation, I mean, if it's even possible under the circumstances . . . The Detective clears his throat to encourage her. He is tethered to a sentence that won't end. Ehm, well . . . I mean, could you read it here in this house, in his study? I don't want the computer to go astray, you see, our entire life is wrapped up in it, all the contracts and business deals as well as our recent emails and family photos and accounts, that kind of stuff. Of course, only as long as you don't need to confiscate his notebooks and everything else as exhibits, although . . . it's quite ridiculous. I don't mean you personally or the police, God forbid, but if you wouldn't mind coming here it would make me feel better, and I wouldn't be so scared in this big house all on my own . . . I mean . . . if at all possible.

The Detective's breaths become deeper, accompanied by a quickening in the groin. He agrees even though it's against the rules. State-of-the-art technology watches them mockingly, including the printer, ready to spit out pages covered in writing for the Detective to take away right now, archived in his pocket on a flash drive, or as printed paper in his arms. The bodies of the Detective and the Widow pay no heed to the technology. A state of elusiveness, highly valued.

The Widow sees the Detective to his car. On the threshold she shakes drops of water from a black umbrella. She doesn't look back.

◇

Birgit Stadtherr and her two friends, Diana Adler and Erika Eis, have boarded a flight from Prague, brimming with a chill joy. It takes them just a few days to build their nest in England. Their excuse appears quite mundane at first sight. Diana is going to teach a yoga master class. Birgit is writing a book on Czech President Edvard Beneš and is going to teach a master class in creative writing, though only if some of the girls they *desperately* need to attend actually enroll. The assignments of her prospective students are immediately covered in her comments, written in purple ink: the passages marked with a purple cross are to be deleted, they're dead wood, necrotic tissue, shush. Meanwhile, Erika wanders around town pecking out crumbs of information.

They discuss the movie *Brief Encounter.* Reaching a school, they come to a halt. A pair of brick twins, an elementary school linked to a high school. They check the address against a tangle of capillaries on the map. They plug into the connecting artery. Taking tortoise steps, they trace it from both ends. They chat to street vendors. Buy a few trinkets. The street is bustling, spotlit by a surprisingly bright sun. A Chinese bistro, a Vietnamese convenience store, an Indian, a Thai, and an Italian eatery, a Japanese and a Pakistani, a Lebanese and a Czech, an Arab and a Spanish, a Polish and an Afghani, a German and a Russian, a Nigerian and an American restaurant, and so on, and on and on.

They pick an Uxor-Hiom restaurant.

Their bodies slip through an orange bead curtain into semidarkness. Shining eyes and snow-white teeth bared in smiles greet them on the far side of a brick bar. They find a table in a corner, with a view of the street and the building opposite. It is four P.M. The owner is eager to please. He brings the menu with the day's specials, with many of the dishes crossed out. He is wearing a tight V-neck T-shirt. Birgit moans. She can't believe her own eyes. She puts on her reading glasses just to make sure. But yes, she is seeing right. Such a beautiful man, and yet he is wearing a T-shirt with the image of Arnold Schwarzenegger's body, oh well, what can you do, you can't expect a fairground quack to prescribe real medicine. She remembers how stunned she was, truly stunned, when her ex-husband told her that for his high school graduation exam he'd written an essay on Albert Schweitzer, the German philosopher, doctor, and humanist, founder of a hospital in Lambaréné. She was touched by the maturity of his decision.

But after the first of their three sons was born, she mentioned this one night when Erika came to dinner. Erika's face lit up, why, Schweitzer was also a musicologist, an organ player, and theologian. But Birgit's husband stared at them in incomprehension.

"But I never wrote about . . . about . . . about . . ."

"You said you wrote about Albert Schweitzer."

"I didn't."

"You didn't?"

"No, I didn't. I wrote about Arnold Schwarzenegger."

The name Albert Schweitzer didn't ring any bells. Unfortunately, Arnold Schwarzenegger's name did ring a bell with her. It made her realize that love, in her particular case, was not only blind but also deaf.

Erika gets up. No one pays any attention to her. Least of all Birgit, who is gawping at the restaurant owner's T-shirt as he serves her. She is served by Arnold.

At this time of the day the only other guests hanging around are dark-haired men, their eyes glued to a TV screen or their phones. Uxor-Hiomian music fills the room along with an exquisite and plaintive fragrance: the older men are smoking. Erika checks out the bathroom. Wet, pink toilet paper is snaking around the toilet bowl. A poster has been taped to the body of the brick wall. A

Wonderbra advertisement. Erika looks around. Shot after shot, section by section, each blink of an eye carving up what she sees. She fishes out her own paper tissues from her pocket.

She returns to Birgit with her hands scrubbed. Birgit is trying to work out the lyrics to the song coming through the restaurant speakers. To decipher a language she is not familiar with. Erika sits down, stretching out her crippled leg under the table.

"If I were living with them, they wouldn't as much as give me a sip of water."

Erika watches the men, judging them, as if all men were the same. Her right hand clutches a chain with a golden cross and a ruby. She tugs at the pendant. The chain digs into the wrinkled skin of her neck.

Birgit is silent as bitterness fills her like beer foaming in a pint glass. Why does Erika have to bring up gender all the time. How can the Blessed Erika be sure that a woman would give her a sip of water? Wasn't her Jesus or Buddha or Mohammed or whomever she happens to believe in now, a man too? Manhood is being equated with humankind in general. How monstrous. All those rigid codes of manhood and womanhood and the notion of the female body as second-rate. No sexual revolution has yet taken place. Religions need a sexual revolution. Why can't a swallow be Pope?

They pile a spicy medley onto their forks. Eating perks them up, the mouthfuls packed with chili and curry. The owner puts cups of coffee on the table and sprinkles some cardamom on top.

"Let's hope it's not arsenic," Erika says calmly.

Embarrassment licks Birgit's back. If she could, she would pour arsenic into Erika's coffee herself. She takes a hot mouthful and swallows. Maybe our lives have been too intense. Lovers, sex, and quarterly orgasms are a pleasant form of yoga. The word adultery means nothing to her. She had disconnected from her husband just as she had, for one unhinged moment, disconnected from Diana and Erika when she thought the latter had gotten her act together and stopped careening from Buddhism to Protestantism and from Zen to Orthodox Christianity; feeding the void inside, using her eyes as a camera. Erika also flitted from one *man* to the next, to serve more than one master requires strong willpower. The Prophet disliked the Christian trinity, *four* is the divine number, Islam allows four wives and four pieces of evidence are required as proof of truth. In Diana's life there had been *only* one man. She would have been lost without him and he without her. They ended up grown into one another even though they no longer shared a bedroom.

Birgit's exasperation bubbles up, thickened by a roux of crankiness. Anxiety makes her spin like an out-of-control whirligig. She should go home and write. Writing should be cutting, like a knife. Like scissors sunk into the palm. Like a glass crushed in her hand; others will end up prizing the shards out of *their* flesh. Her body is smashed to smithereens, her saliva is toxic. It was Diana who dreamt up the ploy of training courses, while Birgit resisted, not keen on reams of prosperous and bored scribblers who would be the first to drop out in a crisis, who believe that it's enough to cobble together a few sentences and that's it, pages and pages covered in writing they share with her like leaves of lettuce grown in their own gardens, suitcases full of it, all trash, the slag of soiled pages, of defiled language, people who, instead of mindful writing, are driven *only* by the desire to publish, to have a product, who imitate patterns and kill literature, oh how all this pains Birgit. To wrap oneself in life and suck out words from the shell, like a raw egg.

Birgit gives a slurp and swallows a chili pepper. She is not up to writing today. She has been infected. Contaminated by the writing of others. Her publisher will have to find someone to decipher

Birgit's handwriting. And ask that person to report back, lacerated by her words. To offer their own confused reading of what her body has written. Birgit is implausible. Life is implausible. You'll go out of your mind before too long. I'll go out of my mind before too long, thinks Birgit, adding hot chili to the spicy mixture. She stumbles over so many subjects she ought to cover and so many ways to tackle, vary, and cuddle them, kiss and rape them, recast and assault them, pick at them the way her index finger picks at a wound. Sprinkling the wound with the crumbling life that is sticky and sycophantic, usurping her. Adding some salt, pepper and seasoning. Chopping herself up into slices of lean pink meat and gluing herself into the pages. It's not my fault that I'm high-strung and intense, that I present in so many repugnant and attractive forms, all of them truthful. It's not my fault that I was born with a brain, shouted Marie-Olympe de Gouges in 1793, as she was dragged to the scaffold; she died under the guillotine because she was dangerous. A second-class citizen is supposed to shut up and not write, she inveighed against the Jacobin reign of terror: you have declared war on me, so you shall have war; this war is not over but the one that is over, or the part that has ended, has been largely lost. It's best not to let up. Life is diverse and wild, exuberant and unreadable, and literature is elusive and waits to be born.

Birgit likes the sound of words like silk and moth, *Bombyx mori*. The miracle of words that hatch out. She stumbles over other people's words and over Erika, who is intuitive, fragile, and vulnerable and who wishes she could wake up one morning and be an adult, wouldn't that be wonderful. She stumbles over other people's words. She cleans them. She stumbles over her own body and the bodies of her two friends. Siamese triplets. She should have stayed on her own, uncoupled; she shouldn't have come back.

Now it is too late to go back to quarterly orgasms. Her flesh is dried up and smoked like Norwegian cod.

The atmosphere in the bar has changed. The sun has retreated, making room for a body making an entrance. The body sends the curtain rippling. It is pawed and fondled by the beads. Long hair, long eyelashes, long legs. Everything about this body is long. The snakes of tiny beads cling to the curves, tooth and nail. Hips crammed into skinny jeans ripped at the knees. The wounds in the fabric are straight, the threadlike scars frayed. Firm, round breasts peep out from a white plunging neckline. A laced bra puckered at the edges. A black leather jacket, unbuttoned.

"Wonderbra," says Erika calmly.

"That's not funny."

"It is."

"You're never funny. By the way, we can see you're playing with your cross." Erika's hand recoils. It's been slapped on the wrist.

Birgit is disgruntled, Erika's high spirits have sucked out what's left of her own good humor. The atmosphere changes. The air is heavy with desire and stifled tension. A surge of the girl's sexuality washes over the male bodies. There we go. Having reached the bank of a raging river that divides childhood from womanhood, every girl is caught off guard by her own sexuality. Fierce, hot, vulnerable, exposed, and mighty. With legs spread wide, her mind hovers uncertainly over her own body, which the mind doesn't recognize. It sends the eyes out on a recce toward the mirror. Birgit's eyes shift from the girl's body to the chubby Erika. It's as if we've been obliterated from the female race, she thinks. For eroticism responds to beauty and freshness. Love is a different matter; love doesn't factor into this.

Diana the dompteuse would disagree. Diana speaks *only* of the soul. Even though she has spent her whole life taking care of the body. If Diana were here now, she would simplify everything by shifting attention to svadhistana, the sacral chakra she believes enhances passion and sexuality—she would say that these kinds of young women absorb and emanate orange light, that they glow orange, or that their chakra is blocked. Birgit becomes increasingly irritated; she is fed up with Diana's and Erika's drivel and baloney. And she is fed up with the droves of immature individuals who call themselves educated adults; instead of devoting five minutes to some soul-searching, getting it together and working on themselves, which *is* hard work, they look for a simple recipe or instruction manual, switching between coaches, goddesses, and gods, sins and punishments, indulgences, TV competitions, exotic countries, expensive sessions with confessionals and witches, astrologists and psychics, and paying through the nose to attend seminars on how to *achieve happiness in one hour* and *communicate your wishes under angelic guidance.* And once the seminar is over, they go home and have a bit of fun abusing their partners, children, and underlings. So, tell me, Blessed Erika, what route does the simple, straight, and unconditional path of love take to another human being? Birgit would like to place a sacrament of withering words on their tongues. And make them swallow it. Words such as kindness and goodness, respect for one another and empathy. For instance. No one wants these words, no one likes their taste, they cost nothing.

The girl is beautiful. As beautiful as a statue, as a doll, as a child, an exquisite child that has grown up too soon, she looks around, poised on the threshold where the freshness of morning dissipates and afternoon arrives; the delicate spiderwebs of femininity have begun to gather. It is one minute to noon.

Skin the color of honey.

But the beauty is cheapened by some inherent coarseness. She is aware, only too aware of her beauty. If she were not, she would be an elusive weapon that would be impossible to tame, a loose cannon, indestructible because of her naïveté. But this is no longer innocence crying out to be defiled. She knows. And she is calculating. All around the room, glistening male eyes are fixed on her, the bodies taut, the minds preoccupied, taking possession of her in their fantasies. Because this creature will not resist them, yet she will be in command.

The girl makes a beeline for the restaurant owner. She slinks past the brick bar counter. She pointedly ignores the other men although she knows their eyes are on her. Her body knows. She whispers something to the owner. He kisses her hand courteously. The girl leaves. Her disappearance plunges the space into drab anxiety at their pointless lives and unpaid bills awaiting them in their mailboxes.

But she comes back.

The restaurant breathes a sigh of relief. The body sweet as honey brushes past them toward the restroom, undulating. Her large eyes register two elderly women sitting at a round table by the window. One of them is ogling her openly and with delight. The other sips her coffee, clutching the pendant round her neck; the chain cuts into the double-chinned dough, disappearing in it. Her eyes skim the women fleetingly, the way a violinist's hand touches a string. A moment of surprise. A second of eternity. Image after image, cut of meat after cut of meat, blink after blink. Taken in by her surprised eyes. A sneer steals into the corner of her mouth, unconscious contempt for these losers, she won't turn into one, she'll make sure her body stays young, beautiful, shimmering. She tucks behind her ears her long tresses parted in the middle, drawing aside theater curtains. Earrings sparkle from her earlobes.

Birgit's eyes catch the glint. The earrings are shaped like miniature bulls inlaid with multicolored pieces of glass, a Gaudí mosaic. A bit of Spain dangling from the ears of a girl, a young lady, a woman.

Why can't you just say, a *person. Because,* Birgit snaps at Diana's voice in her head. Because, Mother.

Not even the bead curtain that wraps itself around her shoulders with dogged admiration can hold back the fair-haired apparition; the curtain follows her out into the street, and flies back with a clatter, frightened. The men start buzzing like a beehive. Even those who kept silent up till now turn to the owner, aquiver, all talking in their mother tongue, haggling like in a marketplace, foisting banknotes on him. Their blood is aboil. The owner collects the money. He is firm and decisive. He is nice and knows what he wants. He no longer bothers to fawn over Birgit and Erika. Not even a generous tip conjures a smile upon his face. His mind is elsewhere.

"Thank you, it was delicious."

Erika tries to appease Birgit but her friend remains silent. Erika stands up. She hobbles over to the owner to ask for the recipe. Birgit hurriedly passes through the bead curtain into the street. The red and orange fringes coil spitefully around her neck. They let her pass, indifferent to *her* body. Birgit scans the street. Her eyes follow the tall, slim blonde cheerfully weaving her way through crowds of bodies. Electrifying her surroundings. A beauty, Birgit thinks. Honeyed beauty. This moment. And she knows it. She knows that her magic works. She knows that it's not something taught at school, she'd never learn anything like this at school. She has a lover, she already has a lover. Beauty must be destroyed every day, shattered into tiny pieces and fortified by being destroyed. So that it can stay alive. And beautiful.

There's a glob in Birgit's belly. As if someone had spat into her. The beads behind her ripple.

"It's the building across the street, he owns it. He's letting the apartments on the first floor and keeps the second floor for his own use. Quite clever."

"I thought you went to ask for the recipe."

"I've got that, too. A good pretext to see the office at the back."

Erika hands Birgit the scribbled recipe. Below it, her gnarled fingers are clutching the restaurant owner's passport.

"That'll make Diana happy."

Birgit slips the passport into her handbag, next to the white-leather case for her reading glasses. Before she closes the handbag, she opens the passport an inch and admires the photo. The man is beautiful. In his prime. The man who served them.

"These are the best years of his life," Birgit says.

"Not the best of the girl's, I suspect."

Who knows, thinks Birgit. Her index finger touches the man's name. Yusuf. A handsome face, powerful jaw. Hawk eyes; chirping quails. All leading their own, independent lives. Perhaps it's because he knows that these are the best years of his life. This is not how he had imagined his life would be.

Birgit clicks the handbag shut and rubs her hands gleefully.

"The kestrel is in the bag."

"So, what do we do now?"

"Let's see what Diana says. She should be home by now."

◇

The Detective stands behind the back of an elderly professor, hovering impatiently. The man with the eyes of a merlin is a medical examiner, most of whose professional life dealt with suicides by hanging. *My hangmen*, he refers to them. The Doctor's back is now bending over photos of the body of a good-looking male of athletic build. His nimble leached fingers shuffle the cards and pick up the largest one. He examines blown-up photos of the neck with two grooves in the skin through a magnifying glass and under the microscope. One of the grooves resembles a thick garden hose, the other remains almost undetectable even after being blown up and placed under the magnifying glass. A thin violin string. The Doctor's back confirms that the straight groove is unusual, indicating the man may have been strangled before being hanged. But he can't say for sure. He rules out the use of brute force, if anything, this suggests a kind of delicate decadence. If it were not a contradiction in terms, he would say what killed the man was great, extravagant love. The fingers shuffle the cards again. The Doctor asks the Detective if there is any evidence of someone having helped the body to hang itself.

The Detective is frank. There is none. It is just his intuition that makes him carry on with this case. He has no hard evidence, *only* a tingling in his guts, but that's not enough. The man's body showed no signs of violence, no signs of resistance, he wasn't attacked. And his beautiful wife is . . .

The Doctor cuts the Detective short. He doesn't want to hear any details of the dead man. That's the kind of mistake he used to make early in his career when examining a body, amassing excessive amounts of detail. Sometimes he felt sorry for the body, sometimes it troubled him that it had brought its end upon itself. He no longer allows emotional garbage to swamp his work. He is interested in the wood, not in the trees and splinters.

The Detective diverts the conversation from the dead man back to himself. "My chief is keen to close the case and file it under suicide, but I'm not convinced. You know what we say in the police, if *only* one tiny candle were lit in graveyards around the world for every murder that remains unsolved, the world's graveyards would flare up in a blaze of fireworks. I need more time. And I will only get it if you endorse my request for a detailed forensic examination of the scene and another autopsy."

All this time, the Detective has been speaking to the Doctor's back bent over the photos. Bending even lower, one hand reaches for the magnifying glass. The eyes focus on a thin strand of hair wound around the neck and going over the Adam's apple.

"I know this is just guesswork, *only* an inkling that this might not be suicide, but then again, perhaps it is, or perhaps . . ."

The bent back doesn't answer. The hand reaches for a form, the pen scrapes across the paper as the nimble, leached fingers neatly fill black columns, finishing off with an illegible, spider-scrawl signature.

The Detective suppresses the urge to hug the Merlin's back.

The Detective walks out into the evening, a nightly pilgrim, Humphrey Bogart in a film noir. The bell of a streetcar tinkles at the traffic island. The door opens and a body rolls out onto the pavement, two guards with armbands give the body a kick and spray a green cross on its back. The streetcar gives another tinkle, the guards leap hastily back into the moving car, chatting to the smiling woman driver. The streetcar drives off. The body with the green cross sprayed on its back is cleared away by the crew of a passing truck. A massive shovel emerges from its rear.

The Detective flees from the streetcar and the truck. The city has banned homeless people from riding in streetcars, buses, trains, taxis, ambulances, and police vehicles, because they smell bad. The city has banned the free movement of migrants and asylum seekers unless they can recite the names of every citizen of the republic since its founding. The Detective has written a letter of protest, saying that, to him, the ones who smell bad are ambitious men in suits and ties who slather themselves with creams and are drowning in cheap aftershave. They are the ones who should be banned from this country. Along with the Blacks and the Jews for good measure, hasn't that worked well in the past?

The Detective has never received a reply. But his chief summoned him for a gentle slap on the wrist, delivered with a dribble of honey. The Detective was reassigned.

The Detective picks up his pace. He lopes along, a mare's smell in his nostrils and her blonde mane in his eyes. He is enjoying the blood pumping through his veins in anticipation of his Lauren Bacall waiting for him in the house in the affluent Prague suburbs. He passes night owls, vagrants, and weirdos. His own neighborhood is not a good one. Although there are no good or bad neighborhoods in this small city. A heaven of metal and industrial beauty. He leans against the wall of his apartment block. Lights a cigarette. A homeless man hobbles out of the shadow of trash cans. The Detective offers him a light. And his jacket. The homeless man puts it on, stuffs his green-cross-marked coat into a trashcan and inches back with a gentle bow.

Back at home the Detective puts on Bob Dylan. The rasping voice of his later recordings reminds him of Tom Waits. The Detective likes Tom Waits. The apartment doesn't seem right for a Detective. It seems more suited to a wild boy, a good guy, or a man who is mystified by this world. Are there any words that define us? What labels do we attach to ourselves and what labels do others attach to us as we go through life? However hard we try to get rid of them, however much we hate them, playing hide and seek, trying in vain to peel them off our skin, they catch up with us with a jeer. The Detective is in the bathroom brushing his teeth. An image multiplied by dozens of oval tears flashes in the mirror, a reflection of golden tresses tied in a bun and a pert little nose. He soaps the ring finger of his left hand, and takes off the engagement ring inherited from his grandfather and, after rinsing it under hot water, stows it in the bathroom cabinet.

Sleep eludes him.

He pours himself a shot of iced vodka. Two shots. Three. He spreads out his notes on the desk. And focuses on the article signed with the harsh-sounding name—Birgit Stadtherr.

◇

Yusuf's passport is passed from hand to hand. They like his dark, gentle eyes. The boyish face. They like his full lips and cropped raven hair.

They piece together a rough outline of the day's mosaic. Insofar as language makes this possible. Language prevents us from articulating the truth, even when it doesn't lie. Words are sufficient up to a point, they serve the intellect. But how do you convey the experience of the moment? When it comes to expressing feelings, glimpses of the unconscious, intuition, body language, words are inadequate, they just grit their teeth impotently. They are inadequate for expressing a flash in the eyes that melds the experience of past centuries with the current, fleeting moment: *only* swallows can do that.

Ribcages and stomachs swell. Shoulders rise. The air rushes forward, a surging torrent drilling a tunnel from shoulders to navel. The diaphragm heaves.

Diana has taught them the ABCs of situations they will encounter in life. Diana doesn't believe in words because they distract from body language, which *never* lies. Language is *only* an instrument of lies.

"What if it turns out that this girl Julia lied? This is something quite different. They seem to go there of their own accord."

"I believe her. Her words don't lie."

"Newspapers lie. And you know full well who controls the media."

"They did quote *her*."

"She's from a different generation; one that I can't protect. This generation has to protect itself. It's under constant assault from aggression in the movies. The internet spews out more aggression, it's freely accessible, every adolescent has access to porn, which peddles the idea that aggressive sex and humiliation are appropriate forms of loving. I don't understand this generation. We've got it all wrong. Maybe they like it. Maybe it's *only* curiosity. And maybe it turns them on. This is not a case for us. Let's call this all off."

"No."

"Let's settle down. By the sea. Up north. On an island."

"No."

"I don't want to teach other people yoga anymore. My own body needs me."

"No."

"Erika, what has you so fixated on this girl, Honey, of all people?"

Erika doesn't reply. She puts on music that merges with the raindrops. "Swallows Soaring" by Norwegian composer Agathe Backer-Grøndahl, a slender work, so brief at twenty bars that this swallow won't make a summer either. Diana's gaze skewers Erika, searing her with the rancid frying oil of her squinting eyes. Erika recoils. She quickly puts on different music, "The Swallows" by Benjamin Godard, a different cup of tea, swallows that are graceful, vigorous, hot-blooded, yay! Drops of water hopping on glass. Music settles on their backs. They groom each other.

Diana glances up at the sky.

At night she tucks in the two sleeping bodies. Gazes at their faces. The past gatecrashes before daybreak. It kicks the door open, flinging off its coat. Under the coat it is naked. The only way of outwitting the morning is by getting up before dawn.

Bodies more fragile than the bodies of birds. More fragile than the fall. Dust in the face.

It is never going to end.

For Birgit is no longer a swallow, Birgit is a kingfisher, *ledňáček* in her native Czech, *Eisvogel* in German, *Alcedo atthis* in Latin, a bird hovering in the wind above the water, all alone and silent, she feels threatened if she encounters another individual of the same species, she wants to muscle out the other one, pecking it until the wounded bird flies off and she keeps chasing after it for a while before coming back.

Diana strokes Birgit. Her fingers trace a cross, a circle, and a diamond across Erika's forehead.

◇

The chief is wrangling with the Detective. The chief is normally reliable: as soon as the going gets tough, he backs down, but he's quick to take the credit when things work out fine. But this time he waves under the Detective's nose sheets of paper stamped with the Merlin's medical authority. This victim was a celebrity. The Detective is wasting the time of the entire police department with this cheap ploy. It disrupts discipline and breaks the professional code of conduct. He doesn't care if the Detective refuses to travel by streetcar, but now he's gone a step too far. The case could have been done and dusted by now, damn it. But now they have to follow procedure. Because it's no longer about "closing a case of suicide" but rather "ruling out murder," so get on with it, will you? That conscientious nutjob, the boss unburdens himself once the Detective is out the door. But how to get rid of him, how to drive him out of here?

◇

Surya namaskar, salutation to the sun, spines ripple. Erika eats a prayer for breakfast.

The summer is visibly coming to an end. Diana walks into the yoga studio.

Three men are waiting in the corridor. They haven't come for yoga. They pass on plastic folders with a jagged wing logo in the corner and marked with some numbers. One of the men hands Diana a specially modified mirror. He turns it in his hands as he explains something. Diana nods. The men leave. Diana slips the hidden-camera mirror into her pocket.

Diana rolls up a garish green yoga mat and a length of white rope. She is on a one-hour break. She walks down the glass-fronted building. Passing closed doors, she listens to singing, the sound of musical instruments, laughter, stamping feet, and words she cannot make out.

In the cafeteria on the first floor she buys a glass of fresh-squeezed orange juice. She picks at slices of tomatoes with mozzarella and basil, drizzled with olive oil.

The class can begin.

◇

The Detective is one of the male bodies that leaps out of a car and barges into the big glass nest on the outskirts of Prague. It has been raining. Summer is nearly over but the gardenwork is not done yet. Heavy shoes sink into the mud, leaving behind small puddles filled with murky water and floors covered in a sticky sludge. Once inside, the men take their shoes off, ashamed of the mess they have made in the hallway. They tread softly in gray woolen socks.

The Detective is surprised by how thrilled his body is to be back at the crime scene. More thrilled than ever. His team scatters throughout the house, bumping into walls and furniture. They spend the longest time in the attic, in this house called the loft. They take fresh fingerprints, sweep for invisible fibers, scrape off specimens. Just as they swept the man's body, prizing fibers from under his nails. In the light, two identical, shell-shaped outlines on two doors: the main entrance and the door to the man's study: the outlines of a human ear that had been pressed to the door for a long time. The same ear pressed twice to the chest of the glass house like a stethoscope.

A silver car pulls up in front of the house. The Widow sees muscular bodies of climbers abseiling down the roof, sweeping the outside of the glass inch by inch. Cracks and outlines emerge and flowers bloom under their hands on the glass among the dried raindrops. The men's bodies dangle in the air, looking for fingerprints as if suspecting the house of some evil deeds. A swallow detaches itself from the flock on the telegraph wires at the back of the garden, flies over their heads and, having described an arc, returns to its friends, tweeting a report. As if by command, tiny black bodies swiftly rearrange themselves on the stave.

The Widow gets out of the silver car. She is dressed in black. The sky above her has cleared after yesterday's showers.

The Detective apologizes. And apologizes again, and again. He apologizes for apologizing. She is pleasant and affable: why, it was she who asked him to come again. She's standing here in her tight black trousers and black, v-neck sweater, wide stance, heels black. The Detective's eyes snag on her sexy pumps. And the ruby red varnish of her long fingernails. The air is filled with flying rubies, drops of blood she's shedding. She has come home *only* because of him, she understands the house has been sealed off, she is staying with a friend, just a friend, not a boyfriend, she stammers. "An old friend of mine, gay, I met him at yoga class, I don't really know him that well, everyone does yoga these days and travels to India, not that it helps much, well, perhaps for a while, it may not even be the yoga, but it's better than nothing, well, so he said I could stay with him, or rather, I could hole up in his place, I didn't want to stay with relatives, they keep talking about what happened, crying and making a big deal out of it, and then all the journalists and my husband's friends, all his ex-wives and children, and their children's children asking when the funeral will be and about the inheritance, I'll leave all that to my lawyer, it's not my fault that he's left everything to me, it really isn't, I'm such a mess."

She is scared and relieved to see me, thinks the Detective. I'm elusive and besides, I'm not jealous, he says, as if it were a contagious disease. A touch of jealousy is essential in love, she says, smiling through her tears.

The Detective takes statements from the hanged man's relatives and friends, reconstructing the final days of a stranger's life. The man kept his life on a tight leash, riding it confidently. Apart from a tiny speck erased by the police: a number of his former assistants had reported him. One had gone to the police years back but the case had fizzled out, swept under the carpet, the man knew people in high places and the woman was intimidated. The case came to court only after the women joined forces.

The same scenario every time. He'd grope them in the office. If they protested, he became violent. He treated them like objects. He demanded sex while away on business trips. If they refused, he threatened them or simply slapped them. He whistled sweet tunes to ensnare his little bird, then clipped her wings. One woman claimed he'd raped her in the office. But this little blemish had been whitewashed, there is no police record.

The Detective is wary of neglecting any clues or ruling out anything. He summons the women. He can't make much sense of the long procession of maidens. The women are clever and they all refuse to break their silence. It only happened because they were young and naïve. Some are in mourning. Some howl in despair, feeling partly responsible for his suicide. Some insist they had loved the man. Others have never had better sex since. Sex is joy, he used to say, and each of the women made a small contribution to *his* joy. He was a stud, chivalrous and permanently horny, one of the women tells the Detective, they don't make men like him anymore.

He can't make sense of this procession of maidens because he has seen the medical records, including photos of black and bluish faces and broken wings.

The Detective doesn't know how to vent his frustration.

He goes back to visit the wise Doctor. The old Merlin lights a pipe and gives a laugh when he hears what the Detective has to say. It is not surprising that the Detective finds present-day women confusing, so does he, and neither age nor experience make things any easier. He understands why the Detective has kept marriage at arm's length. He's never been married. There were two long-term relationships in his life. He did everything he could to please the women. Although that's probably what all partners and husbands say. All partners and husbands who cheat, I mean. On the other hand, the Merlin bends down to the Detective's ear as if sharing the medical secret of a devastating diagnosis, on the other hand, the history of joy knows a greater variety of roles than just that of a faithful loving wife and the mercenary love of a whore. Between the two extremes—the marital heaven of virtuous nuns and the hell of sexual perdition—there lies a vast and as-yet unexplored terrain, a far-reaching sexual realm, of which *only* a minuscule part, known as the demimonde, has been recorded. The Detective ought to acquaint himself with specialist literature on the subject. But most importantly, he should read novels. Alexandre Dumas fils, for example. It's all beautifully laid out in his books.

The demimonde, the Detective repeats, knocking back another shot of home-made slivovitz, a gift to the Merlin from another detective in need of counsel.

Yes, and the demimondaine. A woman who is not a part of a bevy of courtesans. Morally, she is above a prostitute. On the other hand, she is not *only* a virtuous wife. She lives on a slippery slope. A deliberate descent into the underworld, from where she can climb back again. Provided she finds the right man. Or she remains stuck between these two worlds for the rest of her life. In the past, what separated a decent woman from a demimondaine was public scandal, and what separated her from a courtesan was money.

The Detective can't make head or tail of the Doctor's words. He feels patronized by the Merlin's pontificating.

"Surely there isn't as much hypocrisy in present-day society—we don't need to lead a double life, each body in this world enjoys equal rights, each body makes its own free choices. The century of Alexandre Dumas is buried in the trashcan of history."

"Nothing is buried in the trashcan of history," the Doctor's pipe puffs grumpily. "The *only* reason I never married was so that I don't have to get divorced. One of the two loves of my life was an American. In Europe, a divorce is rarely profitable. But we all know that America is the land of limitless opportunity. In America, courts set alimony at a generous enough level to make sure that a divorced woman stays financially independent; divorce doesn't pose as much of a threat to American women as to European ones. Rather, it's a source of income. A woman marries a rich man *only* to divorce him as soon as she can."

"I thought beautiful wives no longer count as evidence of their husbands' talents."

"Whether they do or not, it passes as a career these days. Some women have a special talent for it, a real flair. It's an art on a par with the crafting of filigree glass. Like specializing in diplomacy or depth-psychology. And the ability to act fast, before their bodies begin to show the ravages of time. They have turned marriage into gold mining. They're professional gold and platinum diggers. In the nineteenth century, some liaisons between demimondaines and wealthy men might last for years but nowadays a gold digger gains *social* standing as well. She is accepted into society. And she retains her status even after the divorce, rather like wealthy widows did in the past. And as you well know, even a *widow* can be young, my friend."

The Doctor empties his pipe by knocking it on the windowsill, and after cleaning it, picks up another pipe and fills it nonchalantly. He spends most of his life surrounded by corpses, yet is a model of health and strength. The curve on the other pipe is covered in greasy residue. "As I've said, a widow can be young."

"You said you were not interested in case details," says the Detective, going on the counterattack. He spatters slivovitz all over himself.

"That's right, I'm not interested in the detail. I take pleasure in larger sociological entities. And I take pleasure in the study of the human brain. Because the brain determines the behavior of the whole. Take language, for example. The gift of language is a uniquely human one. And it occupies a *huge* part of the neo-cortex."

"I have no idea what the neo . . . cortex does," says the Detective, offended. Through a fog of fury he sees a body in tight-fitting black pants and a black v-neck sweater, wide stance, black heels.

"It's the youngest part of the brain in developmental terms. Geoffrey Miller believes that the development of the neo-cortex was motivated by the cognitive demands of courtship. Get it? *Court*ship."

"No, I don't, and I have no idea who Miller is."

"Never mind Miller. Basically, the development of the neo-cortex was motivated *only* by the need to be entertaining, sophisticated, witty, clever, quick, ingenious. And that also includes the need to be able to lie and detect lying in others. It's a question of survival. So, let's call a spade a spade. Forget the gold diggers. It's possible that, in women, the neo-cortex isn't yet as important and that intuition plays a more important role. The young widow of your thoroughly and lovingly hanged man will be a smart and hard nut to crack. The sort that breaks the jaws of a nutcracker. I have only your best interests in mind."

With a mischievous wink at the Detective, the Doctor tops up his glass of slivovitz. The Detective watches the Doctor's face and suppresses the urge to knock the pipe out of his smug mug and give his learned ass a kick. But the boy is too young, he's not up to it yet, his neo-cortex is still evolving, it needs *only* hundreds of thousands of years.

Lab reports of fingerprints, footprints, words, smells, syllables, mucous membranes, letters, and lives pile up and sprawl out across the Detective's desk and computer. Fingerprints of the inhabitants of the glass house. Nothing unusual or suspicious there, except for the outline of someone's auricle. It doesn't belong to the victim, his wife, or the little boy. A saintly nuclear family. Nothing unusual or suspicious anywhere: on the body, the white rope, the toppled teak chair, the transparency of the glass.

Except a bundle of papers attached to the most recent lab report. Photos taken through the eye of a microscope.

The Detective rubs his eyes, which take offence and well up with tears. The photos resemble a human embryo in an ultrasound scan. From another angle, they look like a hurricane forecast for the North

Frisian island of Amrum, close to the Danish coast. Like a tangle of conquering sperm wagging their little tails. Like photographs of those parts of outer space we can observe, without knowing its shape, whether it is finite or where the dark energy and black holes grow. He thinks of summoning the head of the lab. And the woman who took the photographs resembling a tectonic map. As well as the man who supplied the detailed notes on what they show. He changes his mind.

Instead, he goes to them.

At the central lab people take turns over the microscope and the ultrasound. A swarm of chemists and biologists, and another swarm of physicists, a swarm of experienced practitioners and young theoreticians. The Detective is confused by what he reads and sees, let alone what he hears. The swarm of people behind him is up in arms since the language of science doesn't seem capable of capturing certain phenomena and even less of articulating them. In natural sciences it happens quite often that intuitive ideas and hypotheses come first, followed only later by evidence, the head of the lab informs him, with a shrug of his shoulders. "What the hell are you saying?" asks the Detective, flying into a rage. His frayed nerves, hangover, and self-pitying fury explode, and he punches the door frame.

"I'm not trying to say anything, see for yourself," the lab boss says, defending his staff. "Whichever way we look at it, we've all reached the same conclusion, I'm afraid. The microscopic particles found under the man's fingernails are *just* letters of the alphabet. I have no idea if it's a code or what language they represent, but it's definitely the Latin alphabet. As if before he died the man had scraped off calcified words or something like that, and as if words had no meaning."

The Detective bursts into hysterical laughter. Quiet and insulted, the swarm of wise lab men and women disperses to their respective labs, back to work.

The Detective now has a rough map of the last days of the man's life, a life that had grown pale and thin. Now I *only* have to capture and describe the final fixed points of that Friday, he thinks, and tells the Widow that he is planning another visit to the glass house. Over the weekend. Yes, over the weekend, why not.

◇

Julia perches on the backrest of a battered bench in a grim playground next to a sandpit. She is writing a text message. A lush park encroaches on the sandpit.

Julia jumps up. She throws up in the grass, cellphone in her left hand. Three elderly ladies pass by. The one with a walking stick hands her a tissue. Julia spits. She dabs the tears from her eyes with the tissue. Then her lips. Her cheap make-up is running. It stings her eyes. She drops the tissue into the wilted grass strewn with beer bottles, ice cream cones, and condom wrappers. Julia glances at her phone. She straightens up.

Three sea-swallows follow her body. The kind of swallows that are long-lived, their leathery eyes gathering wisdom. When they reach Julia's house they go their separate ways.

Diana sits down on a bench next to a broken merry-go-round. Birgit Stadtherr heads for her creative writing class. Erika Eis is headed for the Uxor-Hiom restaurant in pursuit of the honey-colored apparition. There is no one else around. *Only* this autumn evening, drawing down its blinds and spitting into the yellowing grass.

Diana gets up and puts on her glasses. She reads the name plates next to the round bells. She presses one. The buzzer is not working. Diana waits. She hears footsteps clomping noisily down the stairs. Julia opens the door. A jay's eye blinks in the crack. They face each other.

There are bags under Julia's eyes. Swaths of reddened skin make her lips look fuller. She's been removing the fuzz from her upper lip with hot wax. Or else someone covered her mouth with duct tape, then ripped it off. Diana is also sporting huge bags under her eyes.

"What do you want?"

"Hello."

"Hiya."

"Nothing."

"Nothing?"

"I just want to talk to you."

"You're from social services."

"I'm not."

"A Jehovah's Witness."

"No, I'm not."

"The gas bill is overdue again. Talk to my mom."

"It's not about that."

"My mom's upstairs, she'd be mad if she sees me talking to a stranger."

"Your mom isn't home."

"How do you know?"

"Why don't we take a walk?"

Julia, the turtledove compelled to turn into a jay, tries to slam the door in Diana's beak. Diana stops her. Puts her foot into the doorway. The physical strength of the petite, red-haired bird's body surprises Julia. It's a body that flies, has to fly. Before Julia realizes what's going on, Diana grabs her by the elbow and caresses it with her thumb and index finger. Julia is paralyzed.

Diana presses into her hand a scrap of paper with a phone number and a few words scribbled on it, gently pointing to Julia's belly.

"I'm not here about the rape."

"What, then?"

"About humiliation and feelings of guilt."

The girl finally clocks what this is about. She panics. She bites her fingernails with their flaking blue polish.

"Piss off." The door slams shut.

Her phone rings. Julia doesn't pick up. A text beeps. Julia doesn't read it. She stands behind the curtain and weeps, watching the smartly dressed elderly woman in the street.

The woman takes a walk around the block. She comes back and sits down by the tilting merry-go-round that lies on the trampled ground propped up on its elbow.

The phone on the table vibrates again. It spins around like a wounded animal. Who's this witch? The name on the piece of paper is Diana Adler. Followed by the words "movement therapy" and some numbers. Julia is trapped in her own room. Trapped in her own body, which doesn't do what it wants. Trapped by her genes. Scared of the fear that might bury its teeth in the nape of her neck any minute. She is furious with the old biddy down in the street, she wants to be left alone. Who is she? How does she know? She must be one of them.

Flustered, Julia reads the text message. She goes down the hall and looks out the window of the room facing the other way. She sees Honey approaching, phone in hand. A limping pensioner is struggling to keep up with her, then sits down on a bench. Birds flock down as the pensioner tosses crumbs to the pigeons, moving her mouth as if talking to them.

Julia takes a warm hoodie off the hook. She kicks a bucket in the pantry with dirty rags in it and rummages in the vacuum cleaner box. The slot machine gives a familiar tinkle: bingo! Julia fishes out one of her mom's bottles. She takes a big swig.

Diana looks around. She ignores the women chatting and smoking by the playground. She picks up some toys the children have dropped. She wipes their noses. Seeing them sit on the broken-down merry-go-round and try to make it move, Diana takes them gently by the hand and walks with them to a patch of grass, has them form a circle and starts to sing ring-a-ring-a-roses, *kolo kolo rýnské* in Czech and several other languages, inventing new words and encouraging the kids to spin around with her and pretend to fly away. Their little legs stumble, and instead of taking off they roll joyfully around the long-suffering grass, the wreck of a merry-go-round forgotten.

Diana sees the front door open. Julia emerges. The turtledove is approaching. Something about her suggests she's already been through the worst in her life. Without even realizing, the poor thing. She pulls the hood over her head and lights a cigarette. She has plucked up the courage and now is unstoppable. Diana stands up, dusting the grass off her knees.

"I'll call the cops on you."

The moms stop talking. They prick up their ears and summon their children, showering them with endearments: come here, you little stinker.

"Suit yourself."

"And also on that scheming relation of yours."

"I haven't got any."

"The old biddy feeding pigeons behind our building, do you think I'm stupid?"

"Right."

"What do you want? Who's sent you? Must have been him. Or the cops. And now you're going to blackmail me. Forget it, you won't find anyone around here who'll be surprised by what you have to say, or who'll give a damn."

Julia hops around Diana like a squirrel. Diana points to her belly.

"This is my problem. I'll be fine."

"It will give your mom an excuse to throw you out."

"Oh, yeah?"

"Let's go for a walk."

"I'm not going anywhere with you."

Honey is snooping around the block. Julia turns her back on her, defiant. Unexpectedly, she takes Diana's arm.

"All right. Let's go."

Honey, who's been waiting for Julia, is stunned to see her leave with a stranger. She calls out to her. Julia doesn't look back. She calls her name again. No response.

Honey goes back the way she came. The figure feeding pigeons heaves itself off the bench by the disheveled park and leans on a walking stick.

A hobbling shadow and the rustling of wings follows Honey. The pigeons have gone wild.

Diana walks with Julia to the river. Diana is shocked at how willingly the girl follows someone she doesn't know from Adam. *Only* because that someone has shown her some kindness. How eagerly and carelessly her body craves trust and the healing of cracks. It is high time for the turtledove to strangle the jay and the black swan inside her and realize that the best is still ahead of *her.*

Diana keeps close to the river. It is easier to talk by the river, letting the water carry the meanings of words away, words float in a bubbling stream: once uttered, the bubbles no longer hurt. Come, breathe in the last rays of the sun. Diana takes great care to avoid words such as school, girlfriends, first love, everyone knows the sun sets in the west; instead, she speaks of the river, fall, this city, and what it's like to run advanced yoga classes as well as yoga for troubled kids. To stimulate the nervous system with deliberate movements and help it find balance and stay balanced. That's the *only* way to find one's true self. The *only* way to understand one's feelings and have them under control. And to open oneself to new experiences. Like this little girl Diana saw the other day, who bashed her doll against the wall. Or the three little girls back in the grubby Tertiary whom she had taken away from Europe. And whose intuition taught them to seek out new experiences only once physical activity helped them relax. It made Diana so sad to see they retained no warmth for themselves in their empty hearts.

"You talk weird," says Julia. "And your name is weird too."

"It's actually quite simple. I use deliberate movements to help bodies find their balance so that they don't repeat the experiences their minds have suppressed. It would only provoke further violence of the kind they have endured. They would keep absorbing the same unhappiness and attracting the same tragedies. Do you know what really matters, Julia my dear? Let me tell you what really matters: the body doesn't just passively take in every experience, that's not how it works. The body itself can be a mediator of change. This is true for children. And it's true for adults. It's true for you."

"But I'm fine," Julia says. "Besides, I think it's ridiculous to stand on one's head. Or lie on a bed of nails."

"The body must not sit still. It must not *only* sit in a psychotherapist's armchair or lie on an analyst's couch. And *only* talk. The neo-cortex is the youngest part of the brain in terms of development. Talk alone doesn't help, Julia. There's a catch, you see. Well, not a catch but a pretty big hook from which the body is suspended in space. Emotions that are immured in the body. The human body is an organism, as you must be aware, and an organism is something we can influence and change. But *only* and *solely* if we grab a broom and sweep out the old, rusting, cemented feelings. And we can sweep them out *only* in an environment where we feel safe and confident. What I do is show bodies a new direction. Do you get me, at least a little bit?"

"Got any gum?"

They pass a white tree. Diana won't release the eagle before she's spotted the hare in the field. Julia picks a birch leaf. She remains silent, chewing.

Diana won't tell her that in the three cases she's mentioned her technique failed. Ingrid is dead. And she has failed with the other two as well: Birgit and Erika have yet to shed their respective burdens and rip off their blindfolds. They are reluctant, hanging on defiantly and vehemently. Birgit has brought sons into this world and at least has shown interest in their news and in her grandchildren. When they were young, she sought their protection rather than protecting them.

Diana tells Julia things she has repeated and written about many times over, although she can't make all the world's pregnant women listen to what she has to say. Even though none of it is news to the swallows, however banal it may sound. Diana keeps repeating that childhood is crucial for the development of the soul, that childhood is what determines whether we will feel good in our skin as adults. Whether we will crawl under a moldy blanket and hide under a musty eiderdown. Or whether we will walk through life with our head held high. That it determines how we deal with relationships. What matters most is the close bond between two bodies. Diana shudders as she emphasizes, for the umpteenth time, the importance of one's connection to their closest person—one's mom. A mother's job is to make her child feel safe and to banish stress. Stress is the way a child responds to the strange, unknown world. It is possible to rid a child of stress. The blue fingertip on Diana's left index finger proves it. She doesn't mention that there is a kind of touch that is more piercing than a sword. You have to hold up your index finger and believe it can really kill your enemy.

Julia is bored with Diana going on and on about what yoga means to her and what it was like to attend ballet classes when she was a little girl. Julia pricks up her ears *only* when Diana talks about having worked as a fashion model, how she, in turn, used to take photos of others; how careful one has to be when choosing friends, and how she spotted Julia sitting on a park bench. Julia is interesting; a swallow can tell what's happening in another swallow's body, yes, Julia has problems but there is also something special about her. She could take up yoga, she could take up ballet, she could . . .

"You really think so? But whatever. Can't afford it anyway."

Julia tears another leaf off the birch tree and feeds it to the river. The river sticks out its tongue to catch it and flees with its prey. Julia spits out the chewing gum. It glues itself to the surface of the water.

Julia's body is no longer cramped. The girl looks at Diana. Lights another cigarette. Drawing the hoodie tighter round herself. It's cold, the kind of cold that creeps under the blue-painted fingernails. Diana takes Julia to the botanic garden, the pavilion of tropical flowers. It's Julia first visit. She finds the ornamental trees, the Japanese cherries with their purple blossoms boring. Next, Diana drags her to a tall glass skyscraper. Yoga could work for someone Julia's age. Being her age, Julia doesn't believe her.

At that very moment, a few floors higher, Birgit enters a semicircle of seated faces, a slice from which someone has taken a bite.

Birgit is feeling great, having offloaded her anger on Erika. She dances about juggling with words, frolicking between sentences and giving of herself freely. She parses and polishes sentences that excite her as she examines their entrails. Stethoscope in hand, she holds her breath over paragraphs so she can hear the text breathe. She gently directs her voice toward a fluttering goal: respect everyone because everyone has a soul. Today she treads around them carefully, like on eggshells. Everything is easier once you've thought it through properly, the worst thing is indecisiveness. Some of the faces here have unique stories to tell, stories written by their days, their experience, their hearts. Their experience is the truth. The slightest progress of her students makes Birgit happy. They are gifted, yes they are, and Birgit loves them. She gives herself away to them. Unschooled words are not enough. Now she has spotted her, yes, she's got her, caught in Birgit's web of words, one of the faces in the circle: Milena, a fourteen-year-old schoolgirl.

Julia and Diana pass the elevator. They climb the stairs and walk down long, narrow corridors. They whisper as they pass dozens of doors behind which classes are taking place.

Diana knocks gently on one of the doors. She exchanges greetings with a beaming woman in red velvet slacks, white blouse, and a purple turban, stomping around in high heels around a semicircle of silent, baffled faces.

The flamboyant woman in red and white gives the skinny Julia a joyous glance, and an encouraging wave. Julia peers into the classroom over Diana's shoulder. Her eyes meet Milena's. Both stiffen, their pupils widening. Milena lowers her gaze. They pretend not to know each other. Neither Diana nor Birgit notice. Or maybe they *only* pretend not to. I don't know. Why should I know everything *only* because I'm writing this. I find their company stifling.

They have reached their destination. Diana shows the turtledove into a bare room with a trampoline at the back and a bunch of green yoga mats, as thin as filo pastry.

Diana demonstrates a few exercises. Julia forgets about her body. Childlike laughter bubbles up as Diana shows her the importance of breathing and explains that most people don't realize they are not breathing correctly. Diana speaks of hatha yoga and asanas, noting that there are countless offshoots of yoga but the *only* thing that matters in life is maintaining one's inner calm. It's not about making yoga the main focus of one's life, you see, Julia, yoga will send you a signal to let you know when to engage with it and when, in turn, it will engage with you.

Diana does a headstand. Her mouth speaks.

"If you feel depressed or jealous of your boyfriend or . . ."

"Haven't got one."

"Or if you overeat or succumb to the dozens of temptations that lie in wait for us in this world, confusing us and throwing us off balance, or if you pump your lungs full of nicotine or your stomach full of alcohol, it will prevent you from taking the regular, deep, and calm breaths that yoga demands."

"You said by the river that yoga makes no demands."

Julia squats down, lowering herself to the level of the older woman's head. Diana's ginger mane fans out on the green mat, electrified.

"So this is supposed to be good for you?"

"It is. Whenever I do it, I come out feeling cleansed and ready to start from scratch. It helps me rid myself of any tension."

Diana's bare feet land back on the floor. Julia the turtledove smoothes Diana's hair down to stop it fluttering around.

Diana bends her left knee, placing her left foot onto her right thigh with the heel facing upward. Then she bends her right knee and crosses her right ankle over the top of her left shin with the foot facing upward.

"Neat."

"Try it."

"I don't want to."

"It's the lotus flower. Its roots are in the mud, and its neck sticks out of the water until it blossoms into a beautiful flower. The flowers look up to the sky where flocks of birds fly, and the male signals to the female that it is ready to build a nest in the territory it has conquered while warning other males of the same species not to encroach."

"But they're trapped in mud."

"They're looking at the sky."

"Hm."

"There's a lot more yoga can do. Some moves are mightier than the sword. Resolve is mightier than the sword."

Diana disentangles her legs, letting the petals down.

"Give me a hand."

They drag the trampoline into the center of the room. Diana leaps onto it. Bouncing gently, she beckons to Julia to join her.

"I'll get nauseous."

Diana grabs Julia the turtledove by the hand. It's hard to live without confidence. She draws her closer. Julia takes off her hoodie, flinging it behind her. The hoodie sails through the air, landing on the parquet floor, sprawling there like some sleeping creature. They join hands.

"This is embarrassing."

They start to bounce. Gently, together. A shared rhythm. Trust. Safety. They jump higher and higher. They are flying.

"This is why our bodies expel adrenaline, that's why we are able to flex our muscles, quicken our pulse, breathe deeply, or curb our appetite."

Julia's body resists words. But Diana knows when and how to relax the muscles. She knows when to begin dance therapy and when to ramp up the relaxation. But even on perfect nights, when the moon is full, the effect can still not quite fall into place: the heart chakra is the hardest to stimulate.

Julia doesn't smile, she is turning pale. Diana resumes talking as if words could dispel nausea. She talks about the importance of picking the right friends.

"You have a point there."

Julia is about to throw up.

"It's the cheap ciggies," she says, apologizing. She jumps off the trampoline. "Where's the bathroom?"

Julia retches into the toilet bowl. She is shaking, unaware that her breathing is shallow and fast. She wishes she could stop the shaking and the anguish. She suppresses the urge to dig her nails into her wrist and drown her anguish in screams, to silence the anguish, strangle it. To dig her nails into her wrist, sending a signal via the skin: stop it now, stop it please. She breaks down in tears, kneeling on the white tiles, leaning her forehead against the white cold. She drinks some water straight from the faucet, lapping it up like a dog. Water spatters the tiles. She dries her face with a paper towel, scrunching it up into a ball and tossing it on the floor. She comes out into the deserted corridor. She looks around, then goes down one floor. She stops at a door behind which the slim and ridiculously attired red-and-white lady is hopping around like a sparrow and a girl is crouched at a desk: the fucking little bitch Milena, who has been sucking up to Honey.

Julia the turtledove presses an ear to the door. A peal of laughter. Startled, Julia pulls her ear away. She feels uneasy being in the same building as this girl, she barely knows the old biddy up there, but how come the old biddy knows her? Don't trust anyone over twenty, the old biddy is way past her grave time, just like Julia's mom, who is thirty-two. She feels like bolting. But she has left her hoodie there and her mom would kill her if she lost it.

As Julia returns to the exercise room, she sees Diana, motionless, propped up *only* on her hands, her wasp-like butt sticking up in the air, her knees on the elbows of outstretched arms; she is frozen, her eyes are closed. The turtledove changes feathers and without taking her eyes off Diana, she furtively dips her hand into the black leather backpack hanging from a hook by the door next to a coat. She tiptoes to her hoodie, spread out on the floor like a splayed frog, as if not wanting to startle or wake it. Diana soundlessly slides down to the floor.

"That was the crow."

"What?"

Julia grabs her hoodie and pulls it on. The woman is unhinged, a real nutjob. Julia isn't scared of her. Her own body slackens in the woman's presence.

"Kakasana. The crow pose. An exercise to improve physical and mental balance."

Diana helps Julia out of her hoodie. She rolls out another green mat and lays Julia's body on it. She cushions her thin nape with the hoodie. They lie next to one another in silence. Breathing. Julia's body is not capable of exhaling fully. Diana touches Julia's forehead with the tip of her index finger. There is a kind of touch that is mightier than the sword.

"If you decide to go through with it, they will report it and social services will investigate, you know that."

"I gave them a fake date of birth. I know how to play the system, don't you worry."

"Let me show you the best way to relax."

Diana sits down and crosses her legs as if tying a ribbon. She props her hands on the mat and extends her arms. She is a lift truck, her entangled legs rise, ride up in the elevator and freeze, poking up into the air; those who are sick should draw a line on the floor and it will turn into a river.

Diana slowly releases her arms and bends her elbows. Her entangled feet touch the ground.

"Impossible."

Yet again, Julia the turtledove forgets herself, fascinated by the flexibility of this wrinkled, beautiful body. She wants to try it right away. She fails. Diana is pleased. This girl has guts, she's not a deadbeat inside. A lotus flower punctures the surface of the water, aiming at the sky.

"What are you going to do?"

"What do you think. Get rid of it."

"I mean, in life."

"Dunno, I'd like to have a rich husband, a house and kids. But I'm not pretty enough to model."

"You're beautiful."

"Yeah, right."

"Wouldn't you like to travel?"

"Not really."

"And you don't want to study."

"I'm not smart enough, my mom says."

"*Everyone* is smart enough for something."

"Hmmm."

"I can hold this position for as long as I want. The weight of the legs is in the air. It's best in the open. In the grass. With the sky above me. I close my eyes. I'm a bird. I fly away from everything. A swallow against the blue sky."

Diana closes her eyes. She will teach Julia how to fly. The fledgling has been pushed out of the nest before anyone has shown it how the world down below works, before it has been taught to fly.

Only human beings toss their only hope into a trashcan. It's hard to be surrounded by nice and upright people. Upright trees grow in the mountains. She sees the upright trees, she sees Birgit, Erika, Ingrid, young songbirds begging for their parents to feed them. They are gone, those people are gone. That's what Diana has been whispering into the canopies of trees all her life. Let your mind capture only what you want it to capture. This is not about rape. It's about humiliation. A humiliated body will never stand up straight. Don't keep humiliating it, that's what she's been drumming into them ceaselessly. She has been going on about it for centuries, holding their hands and jumping up and down on the trampoline with them. Don't crouch, she breathes into Erika's ear, don't be small, cling to the *heavens*, open your arms to the sky. We do what we can, you're right, Erika, when people kill each other it's not to the heavens' liking. So why is it that the heavens kill people? Don't ask me, Erika, I don't know, I *only* know that the twentieth century has branded me with the mark of knowledge—the illusion that misfortune humanizes people has shattered for good. The twentieth century's problem is the problem of victims.

Diana inhales. If she had a few more years left, she would devote them *solely and exclusively* to male bodies. She would join another flock. Female and male victims react in different ways and becoming a victim doesn't make one more humane. A female victim is crushed, she carries her humiliation through life like a stigma, attracting more male brutality. But a male victim, as swallows have observed, can turn into a killer. Because a body tries to forget pain and humiliation, and a male body wants to forget *in a different way*. A male body thinks it is humiliating to achieve something with someone else's help; if a male-bodied swallow dropped to the ground, it couldn't bear that the *only* way it could soar again is with the help of another. It would never forgive the other swallows. It would destroy the flock. A victim flees and escapes *only* when it kills or humiliates someone weaker, over whom it can prevail. Some victims invariably assert power over a child, and an overwhelming majority assert power over women.

Diana sighs and opens her eyes. Birgit's book on Beneš should focus on the body. She would be surprised what sorts of things were decisive in history. Things such as a glass, a plate, or a bed. What a statesman ate and drank before negotiations. He may have suffered from indigestion or nausea. Or acid reflux. Was there something wrong with his gall bladder? Or was it his glands and hormones? Or was he floating on the wings of love, seeing the world through rose-tinted glasses? Even a monkey's tail seems attractive to someone who is in love, while someone who is not will ignore a yellow tulip in full bloom. Perhaps his mistress had left him. Or was he bearing a grudge? Had he had enough sleep? Did he have a headache? What mood was he in? Was his vanity flattered? Or did he depend *only* on things others have said about him? Was he swayed by his first impression? In terms of bodies, it is not allegiance to political parties that matters—bodies' sympathies and antipathies follow different rules.

Diana doesn't have the time to devote herself *only* to men's bodies. She needs a new life. She is not worried about the aging of her body. She is worried about the aging of her soul.

Four shadows of frightened swallows outside the window rip into the fog of memories, delicate as silk. If you're not honest, not even Diana the eagle, how do you come to terms with others? Swallows know no self-pity. Self-pity is lethal.

"You could give the baby up for adoption."

"I don't want anyone to know. I don't want to walk around this town with a big belly."

"You shouldn't blame *only* yourself. Get rid of it if you think that's the right thing to do. I know someone who was born in these circumstances.

"A girl or a boy?"

"A girl."

"And what happened to her?"

"Hard to tell. She still doesn't know that she's a child of rape. But her body knows it, and sometimes it freaks out."

Diana doesn't force the turtledove to try out the yoga poses. As she rolls up both green mats, she suggests casually that Julia is welcome anytime to observe a class. Free of charge. Or to attend a creative writing class one floor below, run by a friend of Diana's, a great writer, slightly eccentric perhaps but very nice. Julia could build a little nest there and get it all out of her system by writing about it. They saw the teacher in class a little while ago and, again, she's very nice even though she is stubborn and a bit quirky.

"Have you sent anyone to her class before?"

"No, I haven't."

"Honestly?"

"Honestly, that's everyone's private business. I'm *only* telling you that this option is available."

"So what is it you want?"

"I want to help you."

"But why?"

"Because that's what I've been doing all my life. Helping girls like you."

"I don't need help. I can look after myself. I've *only* asked for help once, and this is how it ended."

"How?"

"What do you think?"

"Do you want to talk about it?"

"No way."

"So when are you going?"

"As soon as possible. In four days."

"I'll come with you."

"No need."

"Let me walk you home."

Julia pulls on her hoodie.

"No thanks."

Julia trots down the stairs and out into the fall wind. The clouds have thinned out in the dusk.

"Make sure you take off the nail polish before you go," Diana's brown, velvety voice calls after the shivering hoodie.

◇

In the state-of-the-art house sheltered by a hedge of hornbeam, the Detective is rocking in a black leather chair. He sits alone in the dead man's study, wedged behind the massive semicircular desk. The slender water carafe with the embedded crystal no longer glitters on the dark brown surface. The beveled crystal in the window sparkles. A teardrop flashes blue in the double glazing, its reflection redoubled. The Detective's eyes catch sight of a swallow. Passing through the crystal, its body turns into *four* identical swallows. A *single* body flies out again.

Turning his eyes back to the words on the monitor, he hears the little boy chirruping in the other room. The Widow's head appears in the doorway every now and then. She is now absolutely sure that her husband committed suicide. She treats the Detective with reserve, despite herself. He has turned her personal tragedy into a complicated case and has been picking at it, provoking a rattlesnake with his bare foot. Whereas she would like this miserable time to be over. There are bags under her eyes.

She enters, tray in hand. Strong coffee, crab pâté canapés, apple pie. Water with grated ginger. A white saucer with bright yellow slices of lemon. Honey. Ruby-red fingernails drop a slice into a glass of mineral water for the Detective. The Widow gives her tasty fingers a discreet lick. The Detective watches, wishing he could lick her fingers too.

The Widow stands behind his back. As she gazes at the screen, she unwittingly touches the Detective's shoulder. This bothers him, his groin vibrates. This time it is not intuition about murder or suicide.

The Detective moves the cursor down, unable to figure out what it is he's reading here. Apparently, the dead man was working on the outline of a novel whose main character he envisaged as an extremely smart businessman underrated by everyone else, worn down by having to deal with dumb employees and caring for his insatiable family, selfish parents, rambunctious children, and unmanageable mistresses; weary, sucked dry and half-strangled by his wife's outrageous demands for houses, cars, holidays, and yachts; a lonely and extraordinarily, truly extraordinarily smart and witty lone wolf, misunderstood by everyone, a man seeking advice from spiritual leaders, following them to India, rewarding them generously for every piece of advice, and slapping around his pesky kids after returning home. The Detective's eyes are sore. The text is a tousled nest, glued together week by week while swallows' bodies irreversibly decompose in it. The Detective's bulging eyes stumble over uncouth words. He wishes he could read the words that have been redacted.

The Widow bends down, her soft, warm face, and the peachy down on her ears within the Detective's reach, her breasts spilling out of her low-cut top. The Detective grits his teeth, his fingers grip the mouse tightly. A hand with ruby-red fingernails closes around the back of the Detective's hand. Delicate fingers rest on his bony ones. The warmth of their bodies passes back and forth. "To survive, you've got to forget," says the Widow, closing the file. The mouse, surprised at being grasped by two hands, opens another file.

Now they are looking at the man's private notes. What he drank and when, what he ate and when, the amounts of food and their calorie count, whom he slept with, when, where, and how many times. And things he learned from his spiritual advisers as well as quotes from politicians, statesmen, and popes, mostly picked out of books by Birgit Stadtherr. Purposefully, the Widow moves the Detective's hand, gone limp under hers. The Detective's voice stammers into the silence. "Yes, I think so too . . . if we remembered every one of our failures, each and every disappointment and grievance, it would be hard to find the strength to keep going . . . because this kind of experience might prevail in the final reckoning. . . the capacity to forget is quite similar to the gift of hope and a new beginning . . . there's something utopian about it . . ." The Detective stammers, the mouse roaming across pages as if it lacked the patience to plow through everything the high-performing husband has left behind. A sentence makes him freeze: it sends a clear message to the Detective to close the case, not to screw up. The words can be read as a message from the husband's body, which didn't learn its lesson and succumbed to the pressures of old age. *If this is the life I was meant to live, I might as well give up.*

The Detective takes control of the mouse. The Widow doesn't loosen her grip. She lets herself be led. Their hands skate playfully around the table. The Detective pauses over the novel's sentimental passages, dripping with soured honey: *My life has come to a crossroads. It's turned out there are many roads leading from here. I will pick the one that leads to love.* The Detective senses the feminine warmth. Now her hand takes over and clicks on a list of non-work-related meetings. If the notes don't lie, he had a meeting about his manuscript scheduled for Friday afternoon. One that was not in his diary, crammed full *only* of official meetings. He was meant to visit Ms. Stadtherr in person and proudly noted it down as a one-on-one consultation. The notes in the computer ought to tell the truth, no one could have deleted or altered them, I'm the *only* one who knows the password, the Widow's astonished eyes whisper, the ruby-red fingernails clamping down on the Detective's bony hand, inflicting pain. The letters blur before his eyes. A hiding place, a hiding place. The Widow releases the Detective's fingers, raising her hand and stroking the nape of her neck hungrily. "Why don't you stay for lunch? You've been working too hard."

"No, thanks. I'm not sure. Maybe next time."

◇

A frightened Julia stands outside the clinic stamping her feet, a double billow of steam rising from her. The smoke of warm air wafting from her roll-up notices Diana. The turtledove stubs out the joint.

Julia has removed the blue nail polish. Diana looks at her, trying to gauge how unanchored Julia is. Those who grow up in a happy family and enjoy a contented childhood learn to pick up subtle signals the body uses to assess new situations at the emotional level. Those whose early life was unhappy still pick up these signals, but *only* if the warning they convey is loud and clear; they feel a swallow's feather tickling their belly *only* if it warns them not to go into a dark alley.

Julia does not pick up these signals, or she wouldn't be in such a rush to let strangers into her life.

"You did come! Got the cash?"

"Sure."

"I don't want to go in on my own but I don't want anyone else to know."

Diana makes to hug her. Julia's body recoils, startled. Diana perseveres and plants a kiss on the girl's cheek. Calmly, she takes her by the elbow. Calm flows from Diana's body into Julia's, slithering through it like a bewitched snake.

The waiting room is crammed full of mothers, screaming babies, snotty-nosed kids running around, and irritable pregnant newly-weds. Julia nestles up to Diana.

"I don't want it."

"I know."

"What would I do with it?"

"You should have a word with your mom."

"No way. She'd kick me out."

"No, she wouldn't."

"She'd break every bone in my body."

"She might be happy, you never know. I can talk to her."

"She'd kill me. I don't want it."

"OK."

"You're not trying very hard to talk me into keeping it."

"You wouldn't make a good mom. Not right now."

"So you're going to help me."

"If you help me."

"I should've clocked that it'll cost me. You're blackmailing me."

"No, nothing like that. Just tell me about the father of this child."

"No."

"You don't need to cover for him."

"I don't know who he is."

"You do."

"Promise not to tell anyone?"

"I won't tell anyone, my girl."

"I'm not your girl."

"Sorry. Even if I did tell someone, you'd deny it."

"You think you're so clever."

"You're ashamed."

"How do you know?"

"I know you."

"No, you don't."

"I've known you for a long time."

Julia is stubborn, Julia is obstinate, Julia is unfathomable and determined. Diana hands her a few banknotes.

"This is *only* for you. The hospital bill has been settled."

She knocks on a door and talks to someone. Julia's name is called. Blood is taken from the body. Julia is reprimanded. She hasn't brought a sample of her morning urine. She is handed the cup of humiliation, the winner's cup. She slips away from prying eyes into the bathroom, giving a V sign. Diana waits for her. She smiles at the kids, the long wait has made them crabby and annoying and no one pays them any attention as they toddle up to her and stop by her knees. She plays with their tiny fingers. She strokes their hair. She dandles them in her lap. They jump around the granny from a fairytale they haven't read, gurgling and dancing around the fastidiously dressed lady bedecked with expensive jewelry. They settle down.

Diana accompanies Julia's dissociated body to a ward on the top floor. She hands the paperwork to a nurse and signs on Julia's behalf. The nurse scolds Diana with a contemptuous glance, as if Diana were the irresponsible one who was to blame for what's happened to the turtledove.

Diana hands Julia a bag with slippers and a robe, bought by Erika. Diana promises to come back tomorrow at three in the afternoon. Words would *only* confuse Julia now. She keeps to herself what is on her mind: the tireless battle waged after the war by a swallow named Ingrid to have rape recognized as a war crime of the most severe degree, and the ruthless ridicule she endured. Diana keeps to herself how tirelessly she fought after Ingrid died so that the same recognition was given to women and girls raped in all military conflicts. Because unless their bodies go through therapy, they are prone to reject their own children subconsciously. And once grown up, they will suffer from depression, struggle with weight gain, addictions, heart disease, cancer, diabetes. The trauma of rape shortens the lifespan of a body by as long as twenty years compared to bodies that enjoyed a happy childhood and didn't go through the same experience. Diana doesn't say any of this out loud. Just hands the bag to Julia. And scolds the nurse with a radiant smile.

◇

The Detective asks a fellow policeman to interview Professor Stadtherr. There is nothing he's more scared of than hysterical women intellectuals. Especially elderly women intellectuals. Meeting her would be sheer masochism, shush. He hides behind the excuse that he has to speak to every one of the hanged man's ex-wives.

The first one doesn't tell him anything. They got married as students and she had written his dissertation: "He owes his success to me, and owes his second wife to that success." The second wife looks familiar to the Detective. A confident, resolute businesswoman. She imports meat from Argentina, supplying hotels and high-end restaurants, more recently also to select supermarkets. Her smiling photo graces the wall above overpriced chunks of meat. Ah, that's where he's seen her. He's never bought any of the stuff. It would make him feel like a cannibal: as he looks at her photo he can't rid himself of the idea that he's buying a piece of her body.

Yes, she does have a motive: she hates him from the depth of her being. He was tied to her via their children. Children tied him to all his ex-wives. This was the upbringing he received from his parochial parents. A couple must stay together for the sake of the children. *Only* for the sake of the children, nothing else matters, if you get my drift. What's a guy to do? He cheats in order to get rid of the tension brought on by the birth of children. A guy's got to get rid of the burden of responsibility for his family, which is wearing him out. Which entitles him to sleep around. He can even start an affair with his ex-wife after eleven years if he feels like it, adds the Argentine steak with a scowl. The Detective asks what made her marry him in the first place. To his relief, the woman doesn't notice that his question is not quite appropriate, as it's not likely to move the investigation forward. "Well, how should I put it, he was different. He wasn't boring, seemed to have strong opinions and, first and foremost, he wouldn't tolerate a handbag by his side." The Detective doesn't understand. "He wanted his women to be interesting, you see, he had always been impressed *only* by interesting and smart wives. Except that later it turned out that he wanted them to be interesting *only* up to a point. He pretended to be supportive but didn't really want them to have a career of their own. He thought that being chosen as his wife was an honor in its own right. And his wives were meant to serve him forever, grateful that he stuck with them. But that's not really grounds to kill a man, is it?"

"Did he ever hit you?"

"You mean like he'd do to those minions of his, I mean, his assistants? No, never, I'm a butcher, I would have hit him back. But the thing is, he drew a distinction between his wives and other women.

He looked after his own property in an exemplary way. While plundering the property of others. He feels . . . I mean he felt, entitled.

"As for his current wife, well, he taught her a lesson right at the beginning. She was thinking of leaving him, I understand she was the one who landed the first punch. And that's something he really couldn't stand. If he could have, he would have had her locked up in a convent or slapped a chastity belt on her. To make sure he wasn't supporting someone else's bastards. If anyone were to leave, it had to be him. But again, that's not grounds for her to kill him? Or is it?" Says the Butcher with a sweet smile.

The Detective returns to his office. He is piecing together the portrait of a man who was successful, friendly, and popular with other men. Yet in the company of women he would turn into something different. What an interesting life he had. But instead of writing about his own life, he was concocting some drivel, a would-be novel.

He ought to go and pay the Widow one more visit, but not today. He will send the other detective to speak to her, the one who isn't scared of predators. Who had no trouble dealing with an aged author.

The other policeman summarizes his findings to the Detective. On two occasions, he and a few uniforms went to Professor Stadtherr's temporary abode. They rang the bell.

There was no answer. There was no point asking the neighbors. "She lives in a detached, orange house at the foot of Petřín Hill, which can be accessed *only* from three directions. It has nothing to do with our hanged man. Even though the orange house is quite something. All its residents are foreigners. I discovered that it's changed hands a number of times since 1989, most buyers being wily wheeler-dealers with unpronounceable surnames. The last one to purchase the house was an American, Max Adler, who used to work for an intelligence agency. After he died, his wife Diana Adler, née Bussard, inherited the house. A well-heeled Brit who married an even better-heeled American dude, just imagine. She specializes in body memory and God knows what else. She has inherited Adler's entire fortune, including real estate. The couple had no kids or siblings. She rents out the apartments. A friendly and popular woman, she travels constantly and receives visitors from all over the world, so there is also a guest apartment. Over the past six months, another woman has lived there in addition to the writer: Erika Eis, a documentary filmmaker, of German descent. The first floor serves as an office for an American film-production company, QUAIL, its central and east European branch that is. The usual story—Prague, the heart of Europe, you know what I mean. Phew, I'm glad I don't have to pronounce these tricky names anymore, they just don't roll off my tongue, why can't these people have normal Czech names like everyone here, what a mess, dude, before you get shot in the heart like a stag hunted in magic woods overflowing with honey.

The Detective is floundering, he has to forge ahead on his own, a lonely pilgrim. He's starting to panic, what if his hunch was wrong? What if this is indeed a case of suicide? Even though the man was a healthy and vigorous stud. But who knows what might go through the head of a panicking stud his age, who wants to milk life for all there is, but finds that the milk can is empty. The Detective wonders how much trust he can place in the forensic psychologist's report and analysis. The dead man was a narcissist. The most common disorder these days. Like hysteria in the past century. The single blind spot—his alleged aggressive behavior toward his assistants—seems to suggest other mental issues.

But what kind of issues, damn it?

The police lab results aren't much help either. The head of the lab raises his voice as soon as he hears the Detective's footsteps around the corner:

"What do you want me to do? Yes, the tiny particles with letters from under the man's fingernails could be plaster, though not plaster from the house where the body was found; it might be contaminated with some skin cells. Don't give me that look, this is not a TV crime series, I mean skin cells that were not his own. I'm just trying to help, sometimes even I can't catch my ancient breath in this maze."

The Detective latches on to a safety rope. He goes to see the Merlin, whom he greatly respects. The Merlin is unflappable. He lets himself be persuaded. He accompanies the Detective on a trip to the *alleged* crime scene. The part of the glass house that interests them the most is the attic, which the owners call the loft. And the bedroom, as the man was in his pajamas. The Merlin opens the door slightly, puffing on his pipe. The body of a swallow flies through the ring of smoke as if through a loop. A Japanese cherry blossom falls out of its tiny beak. The startled human body shuts the window.

The Merlin's eyes linger on the Widow's warm body. The Widow's eyes, filled with questions and flickering with tiny flames of reproach, are fixed on the Detective. He *only* shrugs his shoulders. Further question marks flare up in the Widow's pupils as they say their polite goodbyes. The Merlin indicates a courteous kiss of the hand.

They return to the Doctor's study in silence. The Merlin reads through the findings so far. He jots down a few sentences for the Detective, amplifying the interpretation and the yet unsubstantiated hypothesis. The Merlin then presents his theory: if we accept that there was a perpetrator, it had to be someone the victim knew very well, as he was not scared of said person. The man was choked slightly, but I can't tell to what extent and by what means. He enjoyed it, felt as if he were being transported to nirvana. As if the circulation of his blood had slowed and his body had stopped oxygenating of its own accord. The unconscious body was then dragged up to the loft. There the man was compassionately hanged. All this requires considerable physical strength and courage. So, provided we allow for the existence of a perpetrator, it would to have been a person of the male gender, heavily-built, a body pumped full of testosterone, some kind of Arnold S. That is my rather private and somewhat daring hypothesis, says the broad-backed Merlin. That's what I posit although I can't be sure, of course. And to be honest, I'm not particularly interested in the garbage found under his fingernails. Perhaps he tried to hold on to something or someone he'd been kissing. Nowadays people inject or have all kinds of shit sown into or tattooed on their skin."

The Merlin ignores the Detective. His eye finds the Detective and his glass house boring. The Detective gets the message and sighs. He doesn't like to sigh.

The Detective spends the night in his office. The sight of the file, bulging and billowing with statements and stunned testimonies, makes his stomach turn. The sight of perfect photographs makes him sick. The sight of the letters of the alphabet in general makes him nauseous.

He believes in hunches. But he can't mention this to anyone, he'd make himself a laughingstock. He wishes he could tear his chief's conclusions out of the file as they claim that the *young* Widow doesn't seem especially bereft by the passing of her devoted *elderly* husband. That her statements are incoherent and confused: she'd been to the seaside, claims to have returned on Saturday afternoon.

And yet her fellow passengers, the airline, and the stewardesses all testified that she flew back and arrived on Friday, and that she parted ways with everyone else that evening. Confronted with these statements, the Widow's response was that she got the dates mixed up in her head. And that she spent the night with a friend who is gay, allegedly, so that . . . and . . . because . . . since . . . and . . . The chief slaps a bloodied seal on the end of his report, sticking the Widow's pert little nose into the hot wax.

The Widow lived a pampered life and she is their prime suspect. The only thing in her statement that is accurate, says the chief, is that she spent the night in question at a friend's place and that this friend is a faggot, the chief concludes, but who knows, he may well be bisexual, it's all so fluid these days. The Widow has motive. She is the sole heir. Time is of the essence. Neither rain nor the Widow's intent to remarry—there's nothing that can stop it.

The Detective has been caught in a trap. It's a trap he has set himself, poor guy. He needs to speak to Professor Stadtherr and discover why a man of this caliber, a man who had everything—house, money, career, a weekend cottage in the mountains, a beautiful wife, kids, mistresses, fields, trees, sports cars, photos taken with presidents and heads of TV stations, why a man like this felt the compulsion to scribble mendacious drivel about his life, why he so desperately needed a worldly-wise woman who does *nothing but* play with words. The Detective doesn't read. The Detective is naïve. He needs someone who understands people. He believes that writers understand the silence that envelops the soul. He doesn't know that the reason they write is that they don't understand anything.

For several days he tries to get hold of Stadtherr or have someone in the apartment at the foot of Petřín Hill answer his calls, all to no avail. The old biddy has no phone. The old biddy has no email. The other policeman contacts her foreign publishers to find out the name of the town in England where she is currently located. They write the letter together, as the other policeman is the one fluent in English. The Detective writes in Czech, the other man translates it. The Detective is on tenterhooks. No reply.

His nerves snap. He requests permission to enter the apartment by force, to search her apartment in the orange house at the foot of Petřín Hill. Permission is refused. Your request is evidently unjustified, you rookie, says his boss.

◇

Erika is riding the escalator to the top floor of the shopping mall where, at a fast-food counter, Honey is gracing two teenagers with her attention.

Erika watches as Honey ensnares the girls. They suck up to her. They squeal with laughter, grateful for the privilege of being in the company of this hot chick. She has taken them to the mall, promising to pay for anything they like. She buys them dinner and takes them to a bar. They play at being grown-ups. She lights long cigarettes and joints for them. They emulate her supple feline movements. As the afternoon draws to a close, some of the girls disappear into the apartment above the Balkan kabob place, Pakistani skewers, and Greek gyros joints across the street from the Uxor-Hiom restaurant. The girls don't emerge before midnight.

Erika waits until midnight, thinking of the lotus country and the breathing of lotus blossoms.

After some time she begins to attract attention in the glare of the streetlights and the glittering ads. One of the guys snarls at her drunkenly.

"What are you doing here, you old cow?"

"I'm looking for my granddaughter, you moron."

◇

Exhausted, the Detective sits at his computer until the early hours. He browses the internet, goggling at photos of extremely young, extremely attractive, and extremely naked women. Suddenly an idea flashes through his head. He types in the name of the glass Widow. Photos of a black crow at the funeral come up, gorgeous, she is truly gorgeous. He saves some close-ups of her head and arranges them one after the other, the crow nodding wisely and calmly as she receives endless condolences. He wishes he could lift the black tulle obscuring her features. He misses their face-to-face meetings, the tap-tap of little beaks, the subtle changes in facial expression, the body language, and *her* scent. He wishes he could touch her with his temples. The Detective masturbates.

He decides to take a shower. He opens the bathroom cabinet and weighs his grandfather's engagement ring in his hand. He thinks of his restless parents, and his Grandma Josefa and his Grandpa who raised him in the village of Jindice. Remembers the inner turmoil he felt, though his younger brother and sister did not. He would wake up every morning, worrying whether his school satchel, bike, or starched monogrammed handkerchief would be in place. He would wake up every morning with a fright. Often, his satchel wasn't in its place. He had to go out to look for his bike in the fields or the woods, by the pond, or in the village square. He'd find his clean white handkerchief hanging from blackthorn in the garden at midday as the hens clucked, or on briars at the edge of the village. He was scared to blow his nose into it. He would blow his nose into burdock or squeeze one nostril and blow his nose onto the dirt road in the field. He wasn't given any homework, yet felt as if he had worked on it. In his hand a cup of tea brewed from shamrock, elm, or orange marigolds that bloomed in the garden and in the front yard. He would be so absorbed in playing that the world and its immediate reality would dissolve. The world around him forced him to watch out for himself. To observe not only through his own eyes. To play and, at the same time, observe the lone child playing under the walnut tree. He had a head start on the others. He may not have been the fastest, but he did have a head start. He learned to see the world from a bird's-eye view. Like the swallows.

He knows what is on the mind of his cunning boss. He has no interest in the apartment in the house at the foot of Petřín Hill, convinced that he has his perpetrator. His boss is not looking for the truth, he is punishing the Detective. But the Detective will distract him. He will use his own investigative skills. He will gather information on what happened in the past in his own way. He will pick up every bit of information about the past behavior of everyone the dead man ever met. He will run his fingers through the small pile of hay. And then he'll link the dry stalks with what he knows of their current actions.

He's not working this weekend. And he will take an extra day off. He will investigate on his own. And observe himself as he investigates.

FEEDING THE BIRDS

At the crack of dawn on Saturday, the Detective is standing at the foot of Petřín Hill. He has reached a dead end. The orange house with its red pantile roof and white shutters scrutinizes him. It doesn't know what to make of him. They squint at one another.

Gingerly, the Detective slips on a pair of chamois gloves. He picks the lock on the front door. He is breaking into the bowels of the house, breaking the law. He is doing it because he has fallen in love although he doesn't yet know it. It is love that is guiding his steps. It is love that is navigating his body. He opens the door. It submits easily, obediently. The door has been expecting him and now shivers with excitement: come on in. His own body is animated. The door is not scared of him. There are no nameplates or buzzers by the entrance. It is a single trusting space under a single pantile roof. The Detective climbs up a wooden staircase. It gives a sigh.

He passes a large room on the first floor. It is the office of the film production company. The room next door is the house owner's yoga studio. All the corridors and apartments are white, austere, sparsely furnished. Wall-to-wall paintings and sculptures in corners.

The largest apartment on the second floor must be Ms. Stadtherr's. It boasts a huge library, rather monothematic, the books in meticulous order. She is clearly not interested in looking at those she has penned herself: they are *only* in the guest room, displayed on a long shelf for the benefit of dauntless visitors: biographies of rulers, politicians, popes. Ms. Stadtherr has been mapping the exploits of powerful men of the past. The guest room, too, is furnished sparsely, rather like a cheap hotel room. It has its own darkroom; the landlady sometimes develops photographs for fun, in the old-fashioned way.

The guest room is in awe of an aggressively protruding bookshelf that looms above the bed; here Ms. Stadtherr's officers and generals stand guard in rigid array—a philosophy of male dominance and violence that often leads to crime. The author herself is towering above the books, legs akimbo in leather trousers, a riding crop in hand, her head crowned with graying dandelion fluff. Hirohito, Emperor of Japan. The German Emperor Wilhelm II. Biographies of Joseph Stalin and of Alcide de Gasperi, postwar prime minister of Italy. Biographies of Winston Churchill and Konrad Adenauer. And stories of the Medicis and the Indian prince Fuckerjee, rumored to have had sixteen thousand concubines. Dozens, hundreds, thousands of men. The *only* book the Detective has plowed through is the biography of John F. Kennedy, it was his concession to this case, as otherwise he is too busy to read books. This work of hers caused an international scandal, which Stadtherr actually rather relished. In letters engraved in stone, she asserted that, rather than political interests or the military-industrial complex, what was behind the President's assassination was simply the CIA and the FBI, specifically the latter's powerful, prudish, and closeted director, J. Edgar Hoover, striving—quite understandably—to cover up the President's burgeoning obsession with women. Because for Hoover this went beyond the mere release of sexual energy, representing a danger of global proportions. It was not *only* the predictable movie starlets in diaphanous dresses who thronged the President to give an undulating public rendition of *Happy Birthday* and no longer had to steal into the White House via a secret passage: he had started to proactively pursue fresh liaisons, disappearing into the night. He was beyond help as he sought out encounters with unvetted bodies, making it increasingly difficult to keep it all under the bubbling lid. The President's lust posed a danger to the country, especially the American dream of a tight-knit family united by God till death do them part . . . The President's lust was a danger to the country's security and the entire dignified Kennedy clan headed by mamma Rose. And he became a danger to Rose, the twittering little bird made of granite who did not fly away to the happy hunting ground until the age of one hundred and four, having survived a husband, a gaggle of sons, daughters, grandsons, granddaughters, great-grandsons, and great-granddaughters. Mamma Rose, who didn't bat an eyelid when her once wild daughter, Rosemary, was disappeared from public view to prevent her from bringing disgrace upon the family. She agreed to let her own daughter be lobotomized, the epitome of single-minded parental love. A decent girl must not be wayward and follow *only* her own mind, a girl is to obey her father and a wife her husband. Anything that plays havoc with order must be eliminated. Rose didn't bat an eyelid, and the sixties, rolling over her brood with all the drugs and free love, left her feathers unruffled. Rose just looked the other way. How much is hidden in routine and ritual. Stadtherr wrote this book as patiently as if plucking feathers, sniffing out details strenuously concealed by the intelligence agencies. No one knows how she secured these details and although she faced numerous lawsuits, she won them all hands down, as the book cover and afterword to the most recent edition assert. The author dusted herself off and continued to be provocative. She said in her defence that everything is *only* ever a question of perspective and context By 1947, nuclear arms were no longer the greatest threat and Senator McCarthy regarded *sexual liberation* as a weapon in the fight against communism. He was a fanatical, paranoid anti-communist who voted Republican and loved President Dwight D. Eisenhower. History repeats itself, with macho kobolds lurking all around. At a secret meeting with J. Edgar Hoover and the robin-like editor of the *New Republic*, who turned out to be an FBI agent, McCarthy presented his plan of counterattack: if droves of American agents infiltrated the Soviet Union, impregnating Soviet women one by one, the genetic base of communism would be massively weakened. The gene of American democracy would prevail, putting an end to Soviet expansionism. *Although in fact, this has been happening for ages. On both sides*, Stadtherr's afterword states. *The character of James Bond didn't really help either*, she concludes on a characteristically sarcastic note.

The Detective puts the book he has been reading back on the shelf and thinks he has understood, aligning it with the other foot soldiers. On the bedside table are yet more intractable examples of the age-old instruments of psychological torture, brainwashing, and thirst for power: the Bible and the Quran wage war against the military array of books on the oak shelf. Wherever our pilgrim looks, he sees the footprints of dreams left by warriors in a good cause, unexploded shells, and protective overalls.

The Detective tiptoes away from the bookshelf, out of the apartment. The apartment opposite Stadtherr's is exploding with decadent colors and woven throws adorned with ornate knots and fringes. It is crammed full of lexicons, dictionaries, atlases, maps, volumes on art and photography. The walls are adorned with enormous wall hangings. Each sports bright-colored beads. Tiny red beads strung along ropes like giant necklaces stretched from one house to the next by an outsized hand in the sky. A hand that resembles a claw with long, hooked talons painted pink. Red berries glued to dark green leaves of felonious trees. Little red balls gently bouncing off the dimples of faceless children. Flying swallows, solitary hummingbirds, singing chaffinches frozen in the air and swooping eagles clutching red birdseed in their beaks. Even the cream-colored tiles in the bathroom are sprayed with tiny red tears, spat out by someone choking and gagging after being thumped on the back.

The chamois fingers run over the white tiles. They caress the bulging redness of a glass protuberance.

The Detective winces. He feels an itch in his crotch. As if one of the nipples he had imagined under a black polo neck had suddenly sprung out and dropped into his hand.

The Detective walks up to the third floor. The stairs give a soft sigh. The third-floor apartment is clean and uncluttered, minimalist. The Detective takes feather-light, soft, balletic steps. Except for a brass candlestick everything here is gratingly white, the bathroom a paradise of blue. The Detective is walking around a sanitized museum of beautiful objects.

A shadow flits past the window.

The Detective opens the window wide and leans out. In a nest underneath he spots the white bellies of swallows that should no longer be here. They have built a ledge of nests on the outside wall, parallel to the window ledge inside. Boxes at the National Theatre, built of straw, sticks, twigs, cherry blossom, and saliva and packed tightly next to one another. With a view of the main stage—the Prague Castle. A hand in the chamois glove chases the swallows away, off you fly, you country bumpkins, you little bitches, you. Tiny beads in the birds' little heads glimmer red. The Detective slams the window shut and turns the handle before removing his gloves for a moment.

On the white table a framed photograph stands propped up against a brass candlestick. It shows four young women. They look like a family: three teenagers and an older sister or mother. Intensely absent, the three faces look away from the camera, immersed in themselves. They are laughing. They are on a trip to the northern seas; a strong, youthful wind is blowing, blow, you crazy wind, blow, the churning sea is drunken with hope, the wind ruffles their hair, its powerful teeth tearing at their wide skirts. They squint, caught in the clutches of the crushing rays of the sun. The Detective squints, too, suppressing the urge to put on sunglasses. He runs his hand over his face and finds grains of sand stuck to the grooves in the palm of his hand. The Detective quickly wipes his hand on his thigh and puts the gloves back on.

The next photo shows an upright, gaunt child. It is standing there resigned, giving the camera a cold stare, holding its hands open, as if birds have just flown out them. Or as if the hands have just dropped a live grenade. The Detective bends down to the photo for a closer look, but he can't tell if the child is a girl or a boy.

The final, slim photograph shows a violinist in a dress suit. A grubby, emaciated girl with a bandaged leg is clinging desperately to his coattails. The violinist gazes serenely at the camera. One hand is delicately clasping a violin and a bow, the other is poised awkwardly on the girl's shaved head as if his long fingers were clutching a fuzzy ball, or as if he was about to unscrew a jammed lid on a demijohn. The little girl's head is in profile, gazing ecstatically at the man with the violin, entranced, as if seeing the apparition of a saint. The Detective quickly takes snaps of the pictures, saving photographs of photographs.

To his relief, there aren't too many books on the shelves in this apartment. *Only* books written by Diana Adler. The Detective sighs; wading through all the books in this house at the foot of Petřín Hill is a grueling task. There is an unpleasant taste lingering on his tongue, left by the dead man's notes for a novel, suffocatingly mindless and self-centered. This is what it's always like. Victims and murderers are alike, the *only* books they keep on their shelves are the ones they have written themselves.

There are two books whose backs look like a pair of obese, identical twins with a whopping ring of belly fat around the middle: two volumes of an expanded Czech edition of *The Body Remembers.* The text as well as the accompanying photographs of joyously frolicking children are by Diana Adler, *photographer, anthropologist, and ethnologist, who has traveled Western and Eastern Europe and India in the course of her research*, the Detective reads on the flap. *Her writing typically represents a symbiosis of anthropological search for myths and rituals with philosophy and anatomy.* The Detective leafs through the book, slightly puzzled by the title, *The Body Remembers.* The book is narrated by swallows that have been circumnavigating the world since time immemorial. Their beaks don't understand what is happening down below, they see *only* human bodies and they are unaware of borders between countries, nationalities or religions.

We don't have memories. We are *memories. Negative experiences from early childhood are not lost. They harden. They remain imprinted in us as in concrete, often for as long as we live. Time doesn't heal the wounds of the early days, months, and years of one's life. Time preserves wounds; rather than vanish or evaporate, they become an integral part of the body. Implicit memory knows much more than we are conscious of. It knows things that can't be described by words alone. One thing I've learned through years of experimentation, research, and observation, as well as from the experience of swallows that fly above human bodies, is that even if a two-year-old who suffered abuse a year previously may not recognize its tormentor in a photograph, the child's body reacts instantly by becoming intensely stressed. Bad experiences sear and drill especially deep into our emotional memories. Unfortunately. But why is it so? It's in order to warn us of future damage. Young children express feelings by means of their limbs, through every pore in their bodies. At a certain point, however, a new medium—language—suddenly emerges.*

I believe that language inflicts further pain. As time passes, the body might come to terms with a bad experience and cleanse itself, provided it is at one with its feelings. But the minute our consciousness focuses on language, a distance is created between ourselves and our bodies. Language betrays the body. While initially "we are *this feeling," now we suddenly say "we* have *this feeling." Traumatic experience remains trapped in the bones, it seeps into the very marrow. It takes control over our awareness. And it makes traumatized people increasingly dependent on what others say about them and when they say it. Tackling deeply entrenched trauma by means of language, the preferred form of treatment since introduced by Sigmund Freud, with people lying on the proverbial couch, is simply not effective. The* one and only *thing that is effective is working with the body: total relaxation, intense joy and unconditional acceptance of one's own body. The bodies of traumatized people constantly replay every memory their subconscious has retained. Often they spend their whole lives trapped in these reiterations. As a result, they actually lose the gift that life undoubtedly represents. They incite the violence which they have endured, casting themselves in the role of the victim. And they pass the trauma on to subsequent generations.*

Being deprived of physical contact with and feedback from its mother weakens the infant's defense mechanism, leaving it trapped. It doesn't know anyone else in the world. Lack of physical contact can bore a hole in body memories. Physical contact makes the body feel safe, boosts growth hormones, reduces stress hormones, stabilizes the heartbeat, breathing, and blood pressure. Every time someone touches an adult body, the sort of physical contact the person experienced as a child is revived. And bodies that have missed out on being touched lovingly and respectfully as children, or if their mother didn't know how to touch them because she herself could not bear being touched or if she smothered the child with hugs while at other times leaving it unattended in its cot, will repeat this see-saw pattern in the arms of their partners. Revulsion can develop and build up, later presenting, for example, as an eating disorder.

The Detective puts Diana's sentences to one side—here's another predator as wise as an oracle. He prefers Professor Stadtherr's narratives. He puts Part One back on the shelf. For the sake of fairness, he takes down Part Two as well. As he opens the book, the pages flutter and regroup, proffering their own words, or rather, *the swallows'* own words: *The swallows have noticed an epidemic: these days many people are afflicted by a disorder I call alexithymia. Such people are incapable of reading the signals of their own bodies. Unable to decipher the messages sent by their own body, they wonder: am I upset or is this a stomachache? Is this just a sensation, or am I really sick? The area of their brain that reads changes in the body as feelings has been damaged. Often permanently. Such bodies don't respond to emotions. They don't feel sadness, they don't feel joy or anger. People like this are dead inside. It sounds like a dreadful disease, as indeed it is. An awful disease that has germinated in early childhood, a defense mechanism against unendurable fear, anger, or desperate longing.*

Irritated, the Detective puts the book back. Some people concentrate on pseudoproblems, it's a disease of the rich, a cramp in the calf that you get from reading stuff like that. He adjusts the book to align it with its twin. Luckily, there is no other reading matter here, *only* things to listen to: music by the American composer Edward MacDowell, his brief pieces for the piano, the majestic "The Eagle" and his bravura whimsy, "To a Hummingbird." And an impression, known as "The Restlessness of Hummingbirds," by Alberto Williams.

The Detective's cheeks are burning.

The Detective leaves the apartment radiating whiteness.

He picks the lock on the last third-floor door, another place he ought to stay away from. Old trees outside the wide windows are taking on a pastel hue and the grass under the trees is dangling its feet like a bored little girl on a summer's afternoon as vacation comes to an end. This is the only apartment that has a kitchen. It resembles a chemistry lab. It is all white and equipped with built-in ovens, fridges, freezers, a microwave, and even an oven that runs on steam; there are food processors and assorted coffee machines, scales, measuring beakers, intertwined glass tubes and dozens of white pestles and mortars. The Detective opens doors, pulls out drawers, rummages through cabinets. There are no plates or silverware. But there are glasses, excessively large, big enough to pour a whole bottle of champagne in.

A plain wooden crucifix hangs above the bed with a few heron feathers stuck into it. Stretching its arms above its head, the overloaded bed groans under piles upon piles of documentaries on conductors and musicians that alternate with towering mountains of music recordings. There are so many records here they have to struggle to breathe and make a sound. All meticulously labeled and categorized: *Conductors. Violinists. Pianists.* Only a small pile of CDs on a half-empty shelf is able to stretch out and breathe freely under the longest description: *To be filed under what—conductors? composers? violinists? pianists?* The Detective lowers his eyes. Some of the names ring a bell, though they don't mean much to him: Daniel Barenboim, Leonard Bernstein, Pierre Boulez, André Prévin. The same names occur in captions under photographs adorning the walls. Besuited gentlemen with bow ties under their chins. High society.

One is holding a violin. The Detective has seen a younger version of these aquiline features in the photo of the girl with a crippled leg in Mrs. Adler's apartment. The gentleman's name is Yehudi

Menuhin. Next to his photo hangs a single female nude. A treble clef on a naked back. The Detective straightens up. He takes pictures of the photos. He saves the photos of photos as well as the photos of the copies of photos. Monastic austerity and tidiness. A baton frozen in mid-air.

Yehudi Menuhin's recordings usurp the largest amount of space. Erika Eis has come to Prague with her treasure trove of vinyls and CDs. Glenn Gould's piano music takes second place in her collection. Recordings of Arvo Pärt squat in third place. Her Olympic podium.

A record sleeve has been left on the black record player. The chamois gloves carefully pull out the gleaming disc from its sleeve and place it on the turntable. The black magnet in the center catches the gleaming disc and sets it in motion.

The Detective saunters from one door to another on the second and third floor. He takes photographs of everything. It now seems to him that the apartments don't have that much in common. Except for the austerity that robs them of any intimacy, and a sense of intense absence. Music trails him like a faithful dog. The Detective scurries through the bowels of the building; the music catches his scent and scampers after him wherever he goes. It licks his heels, begs and fawns upon him. It runs through the rooms with him. Music permeates the walls, cutting through them. Some notes are mightier than the sword. Determination is mightier than the sword. Lost in thought, the Detective takes pictures of empty wardrobes. He rummages through drawers of emptied desks. There are no personal items here. Where are their clothes?

The Detective returns to the music room. He notes down the title of the piece that is playing. *Für Alina*. He stands still, listening. This is a recording of a two-minute-piece repeated over and over, ad infinitum, recurring with barely perceptible variations, changes of tempo, and length of notes. Like the changing face of a woman whom you might fall in love with. Piano, alternating with violin and cello, then back to piano. Three instruments melding into one. A single, subtle change in nuance is enough to make each repetition completely different. The instruments respond in different ways, no longer ignoring each other. The first swells while the second fades away, the third remaining tactfully silent. The piece has come to an end. Life has come to an end. The Detective brings the music back to life.

He has found nothing. Calmly, he climbs the stairs to the empty attic before heading back to the first floor. It is the weekend; he has all the time in the world and he likes it here. He is not in a rush and won't let anyone get close to him, *only* work.

On the first floor there is an exercise studio: here students of yoga and those interested in body memories tend to flock to meditate in the semidarkness. A cozy fitness studio with thin exercise mats in yellow and orange, but mostly in gaudy green. Blue straps, white ropes, and a trampoline lurk in a corner. Snakes coiled into balls sleep in willow baskets.

The door next to the exercise studio has nothing to do with this case. But the Detective's curiosity is still in full flow, he would feel he had failed in his duty if he didn't search the whole building. He is convinced that courtesy demands that he scour every corner—for some reason, the Detective thinks of the house as a she—or she might take offence. *QUAIL Studios, Inc.*, says the label on the mailbox outside and on this inner door. The only business card this choses to present to the public. The Detective will take a quick look, *only* a fleeting glance. And then . . . Then he will ask the young Widow to take a Saturday walk on Petřín Hill. His heart is brimming over.

Gingerly, the Detective steps into the semidarkness. He squints and blinks. He turns on the light. Purple striplights flicker on the ceiling. The colossal number of film synopses makes his head spin. The place is a maze. A maze without windows, with high ceilings. Lined with shiny metallic structures all the way from the cork floor to the purple ceiling. Lined with state-of-the art, tailor-made shelves and packed with orderly stacks of metal boxes of every hue, red binders and card indexes, interspersed with trestle tables and easy-wipe white plastic chairs and folding deckchairs with checkered throws; complete with new technology, microscopes, and giant flowers of tottering lamps. Narrow aisles among the shelves. Wide enough to let *only* one human body through.

The Detective's broad shoulders snag on metal. The Detective has crawled into a burrow, trekking along interminable paths for minutes, maybe hours, on end. Astonished, he tries to calculate the length and width of this space by counting his steps. The numbers confuse and defy him: leave us alone, you greedy man; leave me alone, you bitches.

He compares the number of steps with the size of the apartments on the upper floors that he has noted down scrupulously. They don't add up. The size of this space doesn't correspond to the floor plan either. It is as if the room on the first floor has burgeoned, biting into the soil and rocks, eating its way into the flaccid hill behind.

The Detective feels he has found himself in an unarchived archive, a spectral insurance company, or inside the mind of Franz Kafka, lately drawing masses of tourists to Prague. The offices of this firm, or whatever this may be, are crammed full with registers, ancient filing systems, yellowed index cards. The walls are lined with floor-to ceiling shelves. Each red binder is marked with a number and a letter, M for meat, a pentagram code, footprints of birds in the snow. The place is like a crematorium with coffins waiting to be incinerated but with no one to mourn the deceased. Like a concentration camp *only* with the barbed wire missing. What the hell is this place?

The Detective's head spins. His hands tremble in their chamois gloves. His skin itches. He loves the feeling of catching the scent of something lurking silently in the semidarkness. He can't resist and lifts some of the lids closest to hand.

He browses through metal boxes and red binders, intrigued by the movie synopses and scripts.

He doesn't feel like plowing through them all; maybe all he will find is some sample footage, various edited copies, trailers. He sits down at one of the computers under a giant lamp. It's like sitting under a hairdryer in a salon. He turns on the computer. The familiar faces of four young women flash up on the screen. They look like a family, three adolescent bodies with an older sister or mother. They are laughing, on a trip to the northern seas, a strong, youthful wind is blowing, blow, you crazy wind, blow, the sea is churning, drunk with hope, the wind ruffles their hair, its powerful teeth tearing at their wide skirts. They squint, caught in the clutches of crushing sun rays. The Detective squints, suppressing the urge to put on sunglasses. He runs his hand over his face and finds grains of sand stuck in the grooves in the palm of his hand. The Detective quickly wipes his hand on his thigh.

The women's faces disappear. The computer is not password protected. It explodes into columns of strangulated numbers and hungry calculations threaded onto red beads of a child's abacus.

The air fills with muted music. Abandoned notes strike a bell. Not a single note is *abused.* Clear, lucid tones. What the Detective finds here is staggeringly simple and ingenious. Like Pärt's music, accessible *only* to certain ears, certain eyes, and certain muscles.

◇

"We can't give up," Ingrid would say to Diana, giving her a shake, "for as long as people scoff at this kind of violence and refuse to consider it violence, we must not give up."

"No one is scoffing at anything."

She had hoped she could placate Ingrid. Open her eyes and make her see *nothing but* the web of the actual state of affairs. And prevent heedless activity which releases disruptive karma. Ingrid's ego retreated, cleansing itself and blossoming into a yellow tulip. Memories laden with meanings that words cannot articulate. Some things that happened in the past may or may not have seemed important at the time, but their memory is charged with significance and makes tears well up for no reason. She used words to retreat from herself. She had nowhere to return. She no longer wanted to participate in any of this. She did not detach herself from life. Life detached itself from her. She didn't want to stand in the way.

She lived at a suicidal pace. She was the first swallow that failed to keep flying, the first swallow to fall, they weren't able to lift her back into the air as she no longer had the strength to raise her head or spread her wings. She got rid of the body that was forcing *only* the past on her.

Ingrid used her adult beak to hack away. She thought they ought to take justice into their own hands, burst the dam where *only* the winners get to write history, but what about the victims, who are neither winners nor losers? Diana tried to calm her down, convince her to finish her studies first, stop this insanity, stop this nonsense and forget. They would fight, feathers would fly. Fixing her eyes on Ingrid's claws, Diana conceded, reluctantly. They would do something.

But what?

The key was to ensure a gradual change in *legislation*.

Ingrid thought it was ridiculous, she didn't believe in utopian projects, she was furious. When Simon Wiesenthal founded his organization and set out to catch Nazi criminals across the world, Ingrid traveled to Vienna to meet him. Mr. Wiesenthal courteously granted her a meeting over coffee and Sachertorte. After comparing the numbers tattooed on their wrists he was prepared to hear Ingrid out, conceding, yes, this is horrible for sure, but worse crimes were committed, so what is it that you want me to do? A wide-eyed young beauty like you should be concentrating on her studies, her life, and future, that will be your best contribution to our cause.

"What do I want you to do?"

"Yes, what do you want me to do? I've told you: what I do is track down criminals."

"So do I."

"Oh, but these are two very different things. There was a war. And part and parcel of war is always extreme behavior of every kind. Including sexual. You should be careful."

"About what?"

"To make sure you don't turn into a suffragette. No one likes those."
The elegant gentleman doesn't realize that Ingrid is a predator.

"What's that got to do with anything?"

"Those women are misguided."

"They are not. They *only* want their femininity to be respected."

"They are misguided."

"They are not. And neither am I. Let's call a spade a spade. I want equal rights for all. Do I hold it against you that you surround yourself *only* with men? Or that all the top Nazis were men and that by hunting *only* men you . . . Life under Nazi occupation was the life of a masculine society, no one cared about what we had to say. Life is masculine in every war, men are not interested in what women think. You're the one who should be careful."

"About what?"

"About me."

Ingrid forgave him. He doesn't have the body of a woman, she told Diana, century-old lies and prejudices about women are etched into his skin. This is a crime that is not considered a crime. A vagina is nothing but a commodity, always at the ready. God dislikes proud women. He has given them a weak body. And has put it on display. The body is to be plundered. The body is a thing. A discarded piece of flesh.

Ingrid took a decision.

Defiantly, she founded her own, secret organization. She would track down the criminals herself. Starting with a man with a riding crop and finishing with Taras. Ingrid was a predator hunting for meat, she would use Max Adler's list of contacts, which Diana managed to get hold of. She would recruit women and men from the ghetto whom she could rely on. Imperious, Ingrid took a decision, stamping her foot and flapping her wings. She would punish crimes that were the same irrespective of country. She would put the raped century to rights.

Ingrid was damaged.

Diana sees a flock of swallows fly past the window.

A stream of damaged women coursed through Europe. They were silent. They have attached themselves to Ingrid. Meanwhile, Diana went looking for her after the Simon Wiesenthal Center alerted Max Adler to Ingrid's activities. As Wiesenthal's work reached more professional levels, he forged links with the intelligence agencies. However, his network was disrupted by Ingrid, and invariably at the least convenient moment. She would surface around individuals who turned out to be former Nazi leaders. She scared one of them off.

But mass panic did not break out until it was discovered that Ingrid had her own network of beautiful women. Working as translators and interpreters, they would pop up in close proximity to political leaders from the Soviet Union, as well as those from the US, Britain, Japan, and Brazil, and so on and so forth.

A conspiracy was suspected. Ingrid was a loose cannon and the vagina was a time bomb.

Simon Wiesenthal disavowed her vehemently.

Looking out of his window, Wiesenthal looked down at the Vienna street, this time taking notice of women. Then he dictated a statement vehemently disavowing the activities of crazy and hysterical females who were discrediting his movement to hunt down war criminals. This group of women was making a mockery of his endeavors and denigrating the suffering of victims by focusing *only* on marginal issues.

Ironically, it was at this point that Wiesenthal enjoyed the greatest support from the highest echelons of power. They were concerned about the women's activities muddying the waters, disrupting public order and pigeonholing winners along with criminals. They closed ranks, fearing that they might also be targeted. This could cause an intolerable mess, which would bring about a new reality and a reclassification of war crimes, taking everything to a new level. Chaos might ensue. Intelligence agencies worldwide, including in Latin America, suddenly took an active interest. Men sought to protect themselves and divert attention from their activities.

"We have a clear definition of war crimes," Wiesenthal told the Austrian Chancellor, "and Nazi criminals must be punished. That will send a clear signal. Crimes and criminals have been defined."

"Absolutely! This is ridiculous! Just because a woman has given someone a blowjob . . . simply ridiculous."

The CIA also entered the fray. The men of the CIA and FBI had their secret plan, their own mindsets, state borders, and political clichés. They believed that women were incapable of solidarity, that they did not help one another, preoccupied as they were with their own bodies. Men, by contrast, hunted in packs. It is a well-known fact, after all, that had the American agents infiltrated Soviet society and impregnated Soviet women, they would have weakened the genetic base of communism and the gene of American democracy would have prevailed, bringing Soviet expansionism to an end. Ingrid posed a threat to this project, quite unawares: just imagine, her women did not distinguish between nationalities, citizenships, or religions: how incredibly naïve!

Diana's husband, Max, finds himself under pressure from his bosses. He puts pressure on Diana.

"You've got to find out what this broad has been up to. I've had it up to here with her."

"But how do I find her?"

"They're about to arrest her. And they're right. She's out of her mind."

"She's hunting war criminals."

"War criminals? She's out of her mind."

"I've started her treatment, I know I can make her better."

This was the first time Diana spoke openly to Max about Ingrid's plan. Ingrid the predator was hunting for meat. Diana was hunting for Max's contacts. She got them, and Max kept helping her until he died.

Ingrid committed suicide. Diana committed herself to work.

◇

Pärt's music repeatedly falls quiet, the note each time breathing its last.

The Detective sits in the silence. He turns off the computer, which emits a beep. The Detective turns off the round lamp as well as the faintly flickering purple striplights. He locks the door. He doesn't want to know.

He returns to the cozy apartment with men's faces on the walls. They wear their success on their lapels, instead of a carnation or a daisy. The piles of records prey on the Detective's imagination: a miniature version of the shiny metal boxes, red box files, and paper files on the first floor.

He wonders what he should do, nervously weighing the cell phone in his hand.

He replaces Pärt's silenced music in its sleeve. He heads for the door.

On reaching the door, he turns on his heels. He returns to the photos on the wall. The end of the day curls up like a charred match.

He flips through the music, trying to find something modern, contemporary, melodious, a tune he is familiar with. He rummages through the piles as if looking for tranquilizers or aspirin. He needs to take something. His forehead is on fire, his temples burning, his hands in the chamois gloves sweating, his body aglow as if he were carrying a heavy edifice of candles, leading a rapturous procession. But this is not the Swedish holy day of Saint Lucy, not a procession led by maidens in white dresses with red headbands and a crown of burning candles on their heads, carrying the light out into the long Northern night, singing. And neither is it a procession going back to pagan fertility rites in celebration of a girl who refused to marry a man chosen for her, defying her father's decision.

The burning body resorts to playing *The Crazy World of Arthur Brown* on his phone, the fingers in the chamois gloves are slippery: *Fire!*

Except that this is not 1968 and this music doesn't suit Petřín Hill. The squirms, its back bristles, the house at the foot of Petřín Hill is independent in a different way, by definition, it needs no nameplates on the front door, it doesn't need anyone to be aware of its independence, has no need to pigeonhole anyone, no need for barricades or chanted slogans, no need of government declarations, resolutions, charters, or petitions, of sporting cockades, long hair, dreadlocks, or uniforms, it needs no political parties, academic degrees, tables in coffeehouses, no careers, genders, expressive gestures, religions, screams, alcohol, drugs, Sunday barbecues, it has no need to join with any other group of those similarly lonely, strong, or elitist; this house is *only* aware of them and awaits them.

The Detective turns the music off, his feelings hurt. A swallow flies by the window without slowing its pace. The hand in a chamois glove chases the swallow away. He points his index finger at the windowpane, pulling an imaginary trigger.

The Detective calms the house down and pacifies the walls, stroking their skin and feathers. He has taken a random pill. He needs music to wash it down. His hand reaches out, picking a random record beginning with the first letter of the Widow's name. The body comes to its senses and reprimands the heart. The chamois glove stops and goes no further. Gidon Kremer comes to the rescue, as he gets his teeth into J. S. Bach's *Chaconne* from his *Partita for solo violin in D minor, BWV 1004.*

The Detective gently closes the apartment doors and goes down to the first floor. His mind resists but his legs take him without the slightest hesitation back to the maze. The violin awakened by Kremer's hand drills into his ears. To the sound of music under the light of wandering lamps, the Detective opens one red box file after another. He is unable to tear himself away.

He forgets about the case of the handsome hanged man. He thought he was addicted to it, now it no longer holds his interest. He is spinning in a whirl of tiny bird footprints in the snow, a whirl of letters and data, incomprehensible names, a flurry of photographs, crushed countries, and hollowed-out villages and cities, flying into infernal whirlwinds, grabbed by the collar by the beaks of swallows that do not befoul their own nest. They drag him through fluffy clouds, soaring higher and higher into the whiteness. Down below, crowds spattered by the sun resemble an icy expanse of white marble with shadows of imaginary giant palms scattered all round. Peaks of high mountains where eagles build their nests pierce the marble. The flock of swallows is now calmer, flying lower.

The Detective is excited, he can't believe his own eyes. It was the man with the noose like a dog collar who has dragged him here, repaying him with doglike loyalty. He has caught a scent and followed it to the orange house at the foot of Petřín Hill, a seemingly unremarkable building that has turned out to be explosive, a minefield full of incendiary devices from cellar to attic. The safety fuses of the entire world seem to converge here in Prague, under the red pantile roof of this house with a chimney. Should it ever explode, the house might make more than just the hill at its back rise into the air.

The Detective's body shivers with bliss.

He isn't going to tell his boss. He isn't going to tell his subordinates. He doesn't trust the man with the noose. The man with the noose has directed him here, it might be a trap. He wants to be alone with the documents. He wants to study them. Never in his life has he read as much as over this astounding weekend. To begin with, he takes dutiful notes in his notepad. Then he photographs the files and saves them. He has found himself in an enchanted cage.

Someone has put a spell on him that holds him captive there. And this is where he wants to be. He gallops through file after file. Forgetting time. Time doesn't forget him; when the hawk can no longer see, the quails in the bushes start to chirp.

The narrow paths of the maze in the orange house at the foot of Petřín Hill are lined with synopses, film treatments, scripts, and films categorized by bird claws; closed cases from criminal and legal practice. Bird codes covering continents of a planet carved up and sold out by humankind, though the swallows don't know that. The swallows fly around the globe, bringing back in their beaks an astute, clearly laid out report, a bird's eye view.

They are not scared of returning. They are not afraid of rebuilding their old nests. Or of the word home. And yet they don't belong to anyone and nothing belongs to them.

The oldest cases hail from Europe. Cases that don't fit the category of crime of passion. For they have been scrupulously, calmly, and clear-headedly documented. The same scenario over and over again. A shadow "trial" planned over an extended period of time and thought through to the tiniest detail. The defendant is not aware of a trial being planned, let alone that it has already started. No one but the swallows have any idea of the kind of iron that is being struck here. Failed executions are documented in purple handwriting.

The Detective is confused by the tangle of bird footprints in the snow.

The endings of completed stories are marked with a cheerful dot, a sarcastic red cherry on a cake with too much sugar in it: a newspaper report about the given person's suicide.

Suicide by hanging.

The Detective is thrilled. His brain, straining at the seams and with sweat trickling down his forehead, tries to delude his intuition and convince it that the room is filled with grotesque film treatments, proposals, made-up horror stories, to be fed to oversaturated audiences. An endless number of ideas that are only just beginning to hatch and ramify. Data and facts patiently gathered into baskets, with costumes, props, and sets. Scriptwriters, officials, and policemen have been bribed. The wine has been bottled, now it has to be drunk.

The Detective can't make sense of some of these stories, they would bomb at the box office, as the plot is *only* gently bubbling behind the set, the auditorium is dark and empty and the spectators' eyes are trained on people who might be suitable characters in a future movie. The red beads of the abacus multiply like swallows on telegraph wires. Beads of red causes and purple effects.

The Detective can't tell from the scripts who is victim, defendant or perpetrator. More recent, computerized files contain *only* endless columns of figures, like pulverized grain. The stories are written down in grubby, azure-colored notebooks.

How do these scripts reach the film crews? The azure notebooks are filed in plastic envelopes. Oh well, at least they are protected from the rain. The parched little rooster craves water: the Detective randomly flips open shiny metal boxes, ripping random azure notebooks out of the red box files. Every now and then he dips into the computer files and copies out the addresses of Swiss banks. His brain is fried, none of the information here has been marked confidential or is password-protected, nothing has been consigned to a safe. The production company and the whole moviemaking process is just a transparent and pathetic ruse.

This is a money-laundering operation.

He ought to warn Professor Adler, she should check out the companies that rent offices in her house, they might compromise her, they have got hold of her brass-framed photograph. The Detective downloads long columns of financial data onto his phone, snakes of figures crawl from one device over to another, while the Detective's body can't wait to encounter the Widow. He is looking forward to it more and more. *Only* the orange house watches him with a sneer, arching over him wisely and bending his ear: we are transformed along with the world, turning into something new, the moon of Saturday night is edging toward Sunday, and Sunday, young man, is covered in blue velvet.

The Detective snaps the paper files shut without looking through all of them. He stands up.

The chamois glove is trapped by bird claws. His sleeve is caught in a maze of grainy metal, sharp feathers, and words written with a goose quill. His eyes are drawn to casting shots taken in exotic locations and to screenings of historic war movies. He is trapped in a past smiling at him from the lips of beautiful, bejeweled, glammed up, made-up women in flowing frocks, their wasp waists imprisoned in corsets and dainty ankles in dancing pumps. Thronged by women wearing military uniforms, old regimentals cut up and patched together, as well as prison garb. Processions of barefoot eyes in tattered rags. Pigtails, chignons, ringlets, fringes, bangs, shaven, onion-shaped skulls. Something seems amiss about these blurry, oppressed bodies of actresses in full make-up. The Detective's body slumps back into the chair's plastic embrace.

None of these women are adults.

Petřín preens itself in ripples of Sunday light. Inside the maze, the blazing purple striplights and lamps are indifferent and immutable. Here the sun doesn't set in the evening and doesn't rise in the morning, here there are no boundaries, here day doesn't turn into night or night into day. From the written storylines bodies emerge, assaulted and touched by other bodies, protected by their status as military heroes who fought on the side of victorious powers, bodies that have never been taken to court and never faced justice since it all happened in wartime, stories forever set in stone by historians who allocated them a plus or a minus sign. One of the wars involved soldiers who served in the Wehrmacht, the Red Army, and the Japanese army, but also included names that look Polish, French, Czech, Slovak, Hungarian, Austrian, Italian, English, American, Spanish, Australian, and so on and on and on. The women have never seen justice. Let alone compensation. Or received an apology. Or understanding. Why would anyone compensate such bodies anyway, bodies subjected to mass rape by men of every country, forever united: forward march, backward never, why should anyone be interested in second-class citizens at a time when we celebrated the victors from every country, unite, unite, backward never. These bodies have been trampled on by the tanks of one vast army, the global army of men, an exhilarated, solid army united by solidarity beyond the grave. The names of heroes.

The Detective runs his chamois thumb over his lip. The thumb runs over the softness of the young Widow's velvet lips.

This is unbearable. Secret internment camps: starting in 1932, the Japanese caught and imprisoned young women in occupied parts of Asia, making their bodies available to the army. The number of "comfort" women was somewhere between one and two hundred thousand, no one ever counted them, except for the swallows. Most of the women were Korean, their bodies raped ten, twenty, thirty times a day, if they tried to escape, they were tortured, suicide offering the *only* escape. They were given Japanese names: Lee Yong Soo was fifteen when she was kidnapped from the street and locked up, the lines of men were longest at weekends, she had to rinse the condoms in a hurry and until her dying day she could not bring herself to take even one sip of milk, so powerful was the association with the water from the rinsed condoms, or bird's milk as they called it. Eighty-four-year-old Lee Yong Soo sits outside the Japanese Embassy in Seoul, she has sat there for a very long time, motionless, a living exhibit, resolute, branded, her body waiting for the return of the life it has lost. She demands compensation, an apology, she wants the Japanese man who ran the house behind the barbed wire to be found and punished, but no one has been arrested, or ever will be, Japanese politicians insist that these women were prostitutes, there of their own free will, the army had nothing to do with it. The word prostitute is a sticky meringue whipped up from egg whites and sugar, it sticks to the enamel of the teeth, abrading and mocking. In the 1990s, during the wars in Yugoslavia, girls and women of a different nationality and faith were locked up right away and impregnated en masse.

These scripts must have been written by psychopaths. The Detective has to go and splash his face with cold water. A carp gasping for air.

The Detective switches off the purple aurora. He locks the door, doesn't look back. He climbs the steps to Ms. Stadtherr's bathroom.

He opens his lips and drinks the cold water straight from the faucet. Lolling out his tongue, he bathes it in the icy waterfall's stream. The water splatters, bouncing off the bulging springboard. He is not hungry or thirsty, he doesn't want to touch anything and yet his throat is parched. His body bends over the basin in the bathroom covered in white tiles with their protruding red nipples. He gasps for water. Gasps for air. Water spatters on his black shirt as well as on his brown leather waistcoat. Silvery water dribbles out of a corner of his mouth. Day is breaking, the house has been transforming him, knowingly. The Detective is being transformed, turning into someone new, unknowingly.

The Detective has now spent two days in this maze, he is spaced out. Every now and then he runs up and down the creaky stairs to feel his body, put different music on, take a drink. He laps up water like a dog to put out the fire in his head. All in vain. He has been drinking gasoline.

The Detective takes pictures of the final recess in the maze. A shelf with old reels of film. Celluloid, flammable strips on reels bearing the QUAIL Studios logo. This section is set apart from the rest. The wall behind it recedes, vanishing into the womb, Mother Earth's vagina. Here the plastic folders are half-empty. The bird markings and numbers are missing. The pages have yellowed, they are school assignments in a child's handwriting. *INGRID*.

Inside the folder is a photograph of a group of young men with runic symbols on the lapels of their long coats and crosses in purple ink hanging above their heads, the largest cross above the head of a man with a riding crop. Strange-looking names coil around some of the crosses, with the name Taras boasting *only* a tentative question mark. The question mark has been crossed out and a purple cross added later by a firm hand. The envelope underneath is stuffed with the typed-up biographies of the men in the photo. The Detective immerses himself in the film script handwritten in purple ink. He jumps over trenches. *TARAS*.

The grandfather was the first to starve to death, the father was next. Both had been sick. Taras, the elder son, had fought his father for a potato. On the trampled floor under the window there lay a pile of nests. Boys would climb trees, take out the eggs and take the nests down, disentangle them and boil the dried sprigs and twigs. Taras collected the nests, piling them up under the window. Sometimes he would bring a withered branch, placing a nest on its top and setting it on the windowsill. It was beautiful, but no one saw the beauty. Mother didn't eat at all. One night she shook Taras awake.

"You've gotta try."

No one had managed to escape. An invisible high wall had been erected around the entire country. The high wall was also inside the heads of the country's population, an ingrained idea that they would never get out. Some were convinced that the whole world was like this; that the whole world was starving. And the invisible wall protected them from the enemy, the enemy that would invade and kill and eat them. The high invisible wall protected their lives.

But something was amiss. The Russians arriving with red stars on their uniforms had round faces. And when their own scrawny faces asked questions, the Russians yelled at them and read out a fresh proclamation, before nailing it onto a wooden gate. One of the proclamations named the culprit.

"The enemies of the Soviet Union, the enemies of freedom and socialism, have used all possible means to destroy and subjugate our fighting spirit. We have shed the yoke of bourgeois reactionism. Our land belongs to all, our factories belong to all."

"And hunger belongs to all," thought the elder son.

War is raging everywhere, people said, there is hunger everywhere, things will get better next year. Ukraine is a country with fertile soil; millions of starving bodies will fatten up the soil again.

"You've gotta try."

She never said why. She didn't tell him that it had started to happen to her, too. That she had snatched a dead mouse from a cat. That she went down on her knees and fought the cat for the mouse. She was about to strangle the cat but thought better of it, the animal belonged to Taras, who was looking after her. But once Taras was gone, there would be something for her and her younger son to eat, they could have the cat for supper. Taras was looking after the cat, it was his only possession and only toy, he'd had it since he was a boy.

Hunger hurts. It clouds the mind of some people. The mother sits in the middle of the room and her younger son, age ten, is no longer. He is dead. She has taken him back into her body. Where he met the cat. She sat at the table for hours waiting for the fly to start buzzing. She watched the fly as it buzzed above the remains of the body, alighted on the table, and rubbed its little feet as if in prayer. Then she pounced and slapped her fist on the rough-hewn table, swatting the fly, licked her hand and swallowed. The mother had lost her mind.

The life of her elder son, Taras, was saved, she had sent him away a long time ago, having managed to bribe the guards. He would return years later only to find his village gone. The locals would tell him what happened to his mother and brother, both buried in the same pit in one body—the mother's.

First, they had come to take the cows away. Then they took the goats and the horses. There was nothing left to catch in the woods or the fields. Even animals sensed that people had started to behave differently. First, they began to resemble animals. They would feed on grass, tree bark, and leaves. Next, they turned against the animals, all of them. They would catch every beetle, fly, mouse, hare, pheasant, partridge, frog. They had caught them all, and the next year there were none left. So they caught all the dogs and cats. They wrote letters that never reached their addressees. The word bread screamed from every page.

One scream with the image of fragrant, crunchy bread slipped through.

Everything was ready the day the International Red Cross was due to arrive. People from a different world were ferried in a week earlier, round and smiling, dressed in local clothes. The starving eyes were chased out of their cottages and loaded onto trucks.

The starving eyes were driven to some unknown place. No one ever learned what happened to them. The driver and the people in uniforms spoke Russian and sported red stars. The pits behind the villages were filling up.

The elder son, Taras, saw all this in a movie theater in a documentary. He saw valiant Ukrainians, total strangers, standing in front of his house and swearing that they would never be subjugated, that they would work the fertile soil, and would win this fight. Fake Ukrainians smiling into the cameras, waving little red books.

They, too, would later be forced onto trucks, driven into the woods, and shot next to a pit they themselves had dug. The village shown in the documentary was deserted, nobody was left behind, the symbol of happy communism fell apart, the wood rotted, the wind blew all traces of it away. No one here was interested in memorial plaques.

The elder son realizes he has nowhere to return. But now he also knows that the whole world is not starving, he knows that hunger was in the heads of his people and that their heads will never rid themselves of this hunger.

"You've gotta try," his mother had told him back then. So he crawls out, like the small animals he catches and eats on his way. He has worked out that he has to imitate their behavior, and his animal of choice is a field mouse. He can't imitate birds, he can't imitate swallows. The only language he hears at the border is Russian. He hears men's voices. One says:

"It's all the Jews' fault anyway."

All night long the elder son digs into the soil, the fertile black soil, loosening it with his filthy hands. He digs a hole, covers it with green turf, and hides inside. He listens in suspense, hearing steps reverberate at regular intervals, he squats in his burrow like a field mouse, all brown, only the whites of his eyes shining while his brain goes dark, but only half-dark, and at night he manages to crawl across the border only because the Soviet army has just started running in the opposite direction, intent on catching more monsters on the far side of the invisible wall of hunger, monsters with emaciated faces and bloated bellies. And while their attention is diverted, Taras, the elder son, disappears. He is cunning and doesn't run, he knows that the sound of his breathing would give him away, so he scurries for a while on all fours, then he lies on the ground to catch his breath, to slow down his pulse and calm his heart, before scurrying ahead again; it's running Ukrainian style.

The only thing he has to offer are his hands. He works, slaving away and gaining strength kilometer by kilometer, never telling those who hire his labor where he comes from, and whenever he senses danger, he runs a little bit farther. He has turned into a small animal, but as this is not the way he was born, he has become a monster.

He is happy when the Soviet Union is invaded, happy that a proper war has begun, that he will be able to feed the monster inside him and silence it. It hurts. He is happy to be able to fight. He is happy. He fights on Hitler's side. The small animal already knows that Stalin has killed his mother.

He does whatever he is told. He does everything because he has already been through everything. He has grown up in it. He is assigned to a unit manned by Latvians and Lithuanians. They travel west to eliminate the main enemy.

"The Judeo-Bolsheviks," says their commander, an Austrian whose uniform bears two SS bolts.

They learn to do as they're told. All they need is the prospect of fresh-smelling bread, some vodka, and cigarettes. They hate Stalin for turning their brains black, every one of them has lost a family member, lost in a way that beggars description. Some stories can't be squeezed into syllables, they resist words. They don't resist yelling. They love the German language but only because they hate Russian. They have suffered atrocities committed by Russians, they've been through the wringer, they themselves are adolescent monsters living life without rules. Hitler holds out the distant prospect of a bundle of hay to his donkeys. He promises Ukraine autonomy under his rule. And also to Lithuania and Latvia.

Stalin has cleansed Ukraine. It had a surplus of bodies. The fertile soil was feeding the wrong ones, he needs its soil for Russia.

Hitler will cleanse Germany of the Jews, their wealth was in the hands of the wrong people, Hitler needs their wealth for Germany.

The unit commanders are Austrians, they are the ones who mostly volunteer as commanders of concentration camps to avoid being sent to the front. Life is easier and one enjoys more power in a camp. "Hitler is Austrian," the commander tells his unit. "We Austrians are artists. We have a well-trained imagination."

A column of trucks reaches the city called Warsaw. The elder son Taras is happy, now he can fill his stomach every day. He is seeing the world, he is traveling, hurrah!

The city is beautiful. He likes cities within cities. How much is hidden in routine and ritual.

His job is not difficult. He has to stuff cattle into trucks.

Taras is 33. He is falling apart. He drinks. He is losing his teeth. Wherever he goes he notices birds' nests. The birds take no notice of him. Whatever else happens, they build their nests to lay their eggs in.

Taras, the collector of birds' nests. He kills birds to have a better look at the nests.

The Detective can't make head or tail of Taras's story. He reaches for some sheets in a child's handwriting The writing balances on the lines like a drunken tightrope walker whose knees are buckling. The letters bounce on telegraph wires drawn along a wooden ruler in a pencil, their tongues sticking out. The Detective immerses himself in the lines headed INGRID. He understands some Polish. A typed transcript is attached to the yellowing pages, translated into English, German, and Czech.

Ingrid is fifteen. Someone has drawn her picture in black chalk. Black hair. Eyes the color of chocolate. She lives in Warsaw and yet not in Warsaw. She and her dad live in one of the guarded neighborhoods forming a city within a city. Ingrid doesn't mind. A boy comes to their tiny apartment. He helps Ingrid's dad copy music. His dad and her dad play the violin. Playing music is still allowed. As long as it's not by Felix Mendelssohn-Bartholdy or Fryderyk Chopin. The girl's dad and the boy sit at the table. Ingrid has crawled under the table. They have only one chair and one stool. She sits on the earthen floor. Cross-legged. She smoothes down the skirt in her lap. Two pairs of knees in shabby trousers are at her eye level. Like two pairs of eyes staring into hers, goggle-eyed. The boy is wearing shoes without socks or laces. Her dad's socks are darned. A big toe is forcing its way out of one sock. The toes stick out of nonexistent shoes. White skin shows between the socks and the pants. Ingrid's dad and the boy are copying music, dropping sheets of paper on the floor. Ingrid picks them up and sorts them. Sometimes she helps them with the copying.

"We are threading beads."

No one replies. Ingrid has no one but her dad. When she was eleven and they were still living in Galicia, she found a dark stain in her panties, brown as the plague. She thought this was the plague the teachers had been telling them about at school. She got changed. She washed her panties. The brown stain reappeared. She broke down in tears. She told her dad she was dying. He didn't say a word, just looked the other way. He kept her out of school that day. He knocked on a neighbor's door. The neighbor wiped her hands in her apron and invited Ingrid to come in. She told her to sit down at the table and went on making lunch, darting around the steaming stove.

"You've got your period. The monthly visit, the crimson wave. Your mom didn't manage to tell you."

Ingrid concentrates on herself, disconnecting from her body. An alienating effect unknown in the world of theater. The body does as it pleases. Breasts suddenly pop out, grass sprouts from the pudendum and from the armpits. Blood pouring from the place where the thighs converge. The body lives a life of its own. Only women can be asked questions about this body. In secret and hushed tones.

Her dad and the boy sit at the table copying music. Pens scraping on paper. Her dad's hand is trembling. Ingrid is late. "Go out there and bring her back." The boy scampers off cheerfully. He sees the usual crowds. He is the same age as Ingrid. He sees dead bodies laid out by the walls, covered with newspapers. Newspapers in desolate corners. A city within a city. It is still possible to go out, and walk around the city beyond the city within the city and return: fifteen gates remain open. For those who have a pass. People with money stand a chance. They take money out of their pockets and hand it to the Germans. They hand some more to the Poles. The Poles and the Germans hold out their hand in the same way, palms up. When it comes to the Jewish question, the Germans and the Poles are of the same mind. The Pope, in his red slippers, is of the same mind, too. The boy does a quick round of people they know. He races back to the apartment consisting of a single room and a kitchen nook. The girl's dad raises his eyes from the sheets of music. Long fingers extend like a frozen fountain across the neck of the violin. The boy is out of breath.

"Has she come back?"

"No."

"We must have missed each other."

The girl's dad breathes shallowly. Fear starts playing the violin. The boy leaves. He runs out into the street, his eyes fixed on the ground, eyes accustomed to searching for things that look like food. Eyes that seek anything edible. He approaches the dining hall where chamber concerts are sometimes allowed to be held. He is not surprised to hear shouting. Two Poles and two Ukrainians stand guard at the door. They are implacable, especially Taras who carries around in his head the imprint of an invisible wall of starvation which none of his loved ones managed to surmount. The streets are teeming with Germans.

They take no notice of the boy.

They barge into houses, pulling out girls by their hair. Only the pretty ones. Did someone say that pretty girls have it easy?

The girls are corralled into the dining hall, joining others already there. They are oblivious of their own fear after years of being steeped in it. As usual, they are told to clean the place up. Then they are ordered to take off their panties. Ordered to wipe the floor with them. Some women hesitate. One plucks up the courage and whispers, in fluent German, that she is on her period. The German nods, the woman is allowed to leave. A few more dare to raise their hands as well. The German is annoyed, this time he shakes his head. Fear is gradually supplanted by shame. The women take off their panties, some have blood streaming down their thighs and calves. They are made to wipe the floor. Wiping what's been wiped already, over and over again. Some, the prettiest ones, are ushered into the room next door, where daily rations are usually handed out to those working in the heart of the city and where concerts of chamber music are held. Now there are two film cameras there, some cranes and spotlights. And some men. One is rubbing his thigh with a riding crop. They order the women to undress. Once again, shame pervades the women's bodies. Shame is worse than fear, for nothing can disguise degradation. They order the women to fondle themselves. To rub their nipples. To lick other women's nipples. The man traces the naked bodies with his riding crop. He orders some of the women to lie on the table. Then he orders each to lay her beautiful legs on another woman's shoulders. Some are told to lie on their stomachs or get down on their knees. Some are made to sit on the frightened faces of others.

"Tongues, I'm not seeing any tongues," the man with the riding crop says calmly, lashing a bare bottom.

The camera whirrs, the men pant. This is a picture with no beginning or end, the bodies linking up with one another. The interlocked image is one of sheer hell, the bodies conjoined, stuck together, and abused. Bodies linked to one another stick together because they don't know whether this is the worst thing that is possible, although they sense that it has to be, that indeed this is the worst thing imaginable, because they wish they could cease to exist, they wish they were dead. The film will be completed. No one will ever talk about it. Or about those who watched it in Berlin, masturbating while they watched, deriving sexual gratification from the sight of bodies that, within months, would come to the end of their journey, the ultimate undressing. This is not the filmmakers' original idea. Scenes like these have already had their premiere, staged by the burghers of Vienna in their cellars as part of the celebrations of the Anschluss. By men and women from good Austrian burgher families. If they could, they would have picked the prettiest Jewesses and locked them in their own cellars.

Ingrid is among them. Ingrid is one of these women, and she is horrified to see some of the bodies glisten and climax, defying the will of their owners as the women are betrayed by their bodies, betrayed by the last thing they have left, their naked selves; some moan, but these are not moans of delight but rather moans of revulsion as their dignity is drained away along with their sweat. This is the end of the line. The women don't look at each other. They avoid eye contact. As soon as they are allowed to uncouple themselves and break up the chain, they hasten to put on their clothes. They slip away.

The filmmakers keep some women in the room. They bring in a few young male bodies.

Ingrid creeps over to the nearest gateway and hides there. Her body slaps itself. She slaps her cheeks. She slaps her belly. Slaps her thighs. Scratches herself. She wants to scrape the skin off her body. She doesn't go any further. Not a step further. Some do go one step further, out of a tall window and onto the paved ground below, or they choose a washing line, or refuse to feed their befouled body. In this weakened state it does not take long for the body to draw its last breath. The next morning the body is dragged out onto the sidewalk, laid by the wall, the face covered with a newspaper.

Some unburden themselves to their loved ones, but the only reaction is silence. Some unburden themselves, but the only reaction is raised eyebrows and a scowl. Some unburden themselves and by doing so, make their bodies available to others. The bodies begin to whore themselves.

Ingrid's dad is practicing the violin. He doesn't ask where she has been. Ingrid does not seek help. Only in secret does she slap her body, the body that keeps her imprisoned and won't let go. The only hope her body can see are the swallows circling freely overhead. Ingrid fixes her eyes on them. She pulls herself up by her own bootstraps. She decides not to give up. She will let other bodies take the brunt. She will distract the predator, shush.

Squirming, the Detective drops the manuscript in which someone has highlighted every occurrence of the word *only*. He replaces it in its dungeon and snaps the lid shut.

No, he is not going to read this.

And here he was, thinking that what he had to plow through on the second and third floors of the orange house at the foot of Petřín Hill was perverted. No, *this* is not something that he is going to read.

The Detective's body gives a shudder and his head bumps into the neck of the metal lamp as he gets up clumsily. The lamp sways, nodding as if lost in thought.

There are more computers in the vaults of the film company but the Detective ignores the information they contain. He's fed up with columns of figures. What is all this anyway? Movies inspired by real life. Biased synopses. Imagination is also real.

The artists' world is a world of psychopaths.

He flees from Europe and invites shelves with Asian and African comedies to dance. A movie from Mali, a random pick. But no, this doesn't look like a straight comedy either. It's something more suitable for a film festival about people in need. The village forces *only* girls to fetch water even though everyone knows that on their way they will be raped by soldiers of *every* warring faction. It also focuses on a single prototypical case of an eleven-year-old body. All the expert and legal opinions as well as lawyers' fees are financed from the bowels of this house at the foot of Petřín Hill.

The Detective stands up. He glances at his watch. He has spent twenty-five hours in this place. It is Sunday. His body is hungry and craves sleep. The house belongs to the well-heeled Mrs. Adler, let this be her problem. Seeing as they use her brass-framed photograph as their desktop image.

It is not the subject matter itself the Detective finds most noxious. It's the childlike handwriting that is the hardest to bear. What the hell is going on here? The music is irksome, the violin's sound grates. He walks up to the third floor and throttles the music.

In the apartment on the second floor, he checks for drops of water that cling to the shiny washbasin: they have dried now. He takes out his monogrammed handkerchief and polishes the surface. The handkerchief also wipes the drops from the white tiles on floor. He locks all the doors. He has never set foot in this place.

He has never been to this twisted home for retired film makers.

He flees from the war years, he has never enjoyed history lessons. He flees from a mighty surge of ancient mysteries. He flees from the irrationality of human life.

He flees into the present. Which is *totally* different, that much he knows.

He hesitates for a moment. Should he put the house under surveillance? Should he have Ms. Adler's bank accounts investigated? He looks at the old Doctor's phone number and hesitates: he'd like to see the smart Merlin saw off the iron ball shackled to his ankle, get rid of it.

Except that, even if he did so, he could not pretend that the weight didn't exist.

A dense, ruffled flock rises up over the house at the foot of Petřín Hill, dispersing across the sky and flying away. Like someone scattering a handful of poppyseeds.

Back at home the Detective takes his time rubbing down his body with yellow soap. He brushes his teeth. He brushes off the dental plaque. He sticks his hot tongue into a stream of water, scraping the top. Drops of water bounce off the pink trampoline. He combs out drops of water from his short black hair. He shaves. The electric razor growls as it mows the stubble.

He fries up some eggs with bacon with a generous seasoning of salt and pepper. He eats ravenously, struggling to swallows huge mouthfuls. Then he wolfs down some leftover cold pizza with cheese and onions, which now sits heavily on his chest.

He puts on some rock music. He smokes and drinks. He feels like a plebeian who has just left the residence of degenerate mutants.

He sings, hoarsely. He pours himself a shot of whiskey. He knocks back another. He turns the music up. Full blast, he tells himself. At full blast, that's the way to live. If he hadn't dragged this case out, he would never have visited the house at the foot of Petřín Hill and never got involved. He downs a third shot of whiskey.

He sends a message to the Widow with the address of a restaurant, asking her out for dinner. If she is not too busy, that is.

He goes online, and to the accompaniment of the reassuring sound of *his* favorite music, he types in QUAIL Studios, Inc. The internet spews out titles of movies directed by Erika Eis, one after the other: documentaries on classical music, featuring debonair musicians in jackets and white tie and tails. The Detective roars with laughter.

After decades of movie making, the extravagant globetrotter retreated into silence. She never dropped anchor anywhere, never letting anyone pinpoint the country on whose behalf she had made a particular documentary or won awards. The list of awards is long. The filmmaker's sponsor was one Diana Adler.

Damn this smiling lady with her awards, what the hell is this, why I am sitting here trying to figure out this damn thing called QUAIL, Inc.?

Fired up, the Detective hunts for interviews but gleans nothing from them. He watches clips from documentaries: melodramatic, righteous, whipped up boredom, seasoned with sedate bliss. The woman sounds cheerful and suspiciously positive in interviews. He finds *only* authorized, formal photos taken at press conferences.

The Detective surfs the waves, hopping from one to the next, alternating names he searches for, millions of pages and meaningless factoids, an avalanche of names merging and colliding, ebbing and flowing, a surge of flocks of birds that distract attention from the pages as they crisscross the screen.

The Detective is riding a surfboard, legs akimbo. As the waves swell, he waits for the right one and tries to keep his balance. He types in the name Max Adler: the charming, lovable scion of a billionaire American family, part of Chicago's Warren clan, for whom money had never been an issue; his self-conscious statements gush with fake modesty; decorations for military merit, an entire professional life working for intelligence. That's the whole story, another one of those who didn't need to work but chose to.

The Detective's weary body is trying to shake off the dark labyrinth of the house at the foot of Petřín Hill, to resist the pull of the dazzling, intertwined lives of these three kindly ladies, these passionate elderly women so close to the grave. Where the hell could the old girls be now, why do they rub him up the wrong way, why can't they stay abroad and leave Prague alone, in this country we like our peace and quiet, *that* world is of no concern to us, why can't they keep all this vermin and smut, their microbes and viruses to themselves, he doesn't need this, he's in his boss's bad books anyway, he *only* wants to do his job, he wants to help others, he'll go crazy if this goes on like this.

He sets the alarm clock left by his grandma. He draws the blinds to keep out the flying little bodies that swish past, keeping watch. He pours himself another whiskey. He resists the temptation to use his service gun to shoot the cheeky swallows through the window.

He lies down, hugging the bottle of amber-colored liquid. He gives the bottle a kiss and flings his body into the arms of sleep, letting them rock him.

There is someone sitting on his crotch, pinning him down. Someone is touching him in the groin, on the balls, the most sensitive place, he is chained. A rooster crows in his head. The Detective swats down the alarm clock. It is Sunday evening. His body is broken and drenched in sweat, a splinter lodged in his head. *All* this was *only* a dream.

The sight of his phone and notebook sprawling on the desk in front on the computer instantly banishes his good cheer. It's all stuffed full of numbers, photos, and scribbles reminding him of the house at the foot of Petřín Hill. The orange house is real.

The Detective rips out the notes from the notebook, flinging the plucked feathers into the trash, next to the empty whiskey bottle. He wipes his phone clean of all the photos he took in the movie company's office.

He takes another hot shower. Emerging from the steam, he rubs his body down with a white towel. He brushes his teeth again. Combs his hair and sprinkles on some cologne. Puts on a clean blue shirt. The Detective feels both repelled and attracted by the house at the foot of Petřín Hill because he doesn't know what to make of it.

The glass-walled house on the outskirts of Prague suddenly seems the only good thing that comes to mind. Yet again, in a short space of time, he is about to break every professional rule. He has asked the Widow out to dinner even though she is the prime murder suspect. And she has accepted. Even though she knows that she is violating the unspoken rules of widowhood: to mourn and turn down invitations from other men. She ought to have been burned on a pyre along with her husband; how much is hidden in routine and ritual.

Both of them have violated the rules and both are beginning to enjoy it. Their bodies need each other. The Detective feels liberated by the orange house at the foot of Petřín Hill, as if it had touched his forehead with the tip of its index finger, setting off an electric spark.

The house *is* its own master.

They sit facing each other in a Thai restaurant. Slender smooth fingers clutch a glass smeared with orange lipstick. A smiling Thai waitress, wrapped and belted in a shimmering brown dress, bows as she places a long-stemmed yellow rose in a vase by the wine cooler. The Detective is distracted, his mind is elsewhere. The Widow took great care over her clothes and hair, still low-key as befits her status. She wants to win the Detective over and dispel his suspicions. She explains, breathlessly and eagerly: "Yes, it's true that I came back from vacation on Friday, I just didn't feel like going home, didn't want to see my husband, things hadn't been working well between us for a while, it was just a small marital tiff but that's quite normal, not grounds for suicide, I just didn't feel like going home, I just wanted to wait until he left for the mountains, so I stayed with a friend who is very discreet and doesn't ask any questions . . . Oh but that doesn't mean anything either, you know that he's . . ." "Yes, I know, he's gay," the Detective beats her to it, "we've checked him out, we're no amateurs, you know." As he says this, the Detective takes a long sip of white wine and tops up his glass from the bedewed bottle. We're no amateurs, believe me. Yeah. Totally professional. Kind of.

"There's no need to be jealous," purrs the Woman.

"I'm never jealous," says the Detective.

"Sorry, I forgot." In silence, she helps herself to some jasmine rice from the bowl.

The Detective is riding a current, trapped in a sequence of actions triggered by past events and engendering new ones. He is entangled in a swallows' web.

They sip their wine. With every sip they swallow their unease. They eat. It's all very easy-going and enjoyable. They play ball with words, catching some and dropping others. The Detective feels that only now is he taking a cleansing shower and washing away this weekend. He is talking to someone who understands him, who is on the same wavelength. Here and now. This is a miracle, a different world. He would like to unburden himself to her about these past hours, but stops himself. He loves this woman. And he wants to protect her. A purple cross will never hang over his head.

Not over his head.

Never.

They stay until the restaurant closes, he's lost all track of time. He is sitting behind the wheel of a racing car, hurtling around bends. And what a ride this is—instead of stepping on the brake, he steps on the gas. He is grateful to her for speaking to him and for letting him love her.

◇

The sun salutation, a set of movements to strengthen the body which will, in turn, strengthen the soul. Spines crack, joints creak, rasping breaths in and out, rusting door hinges, sweating men below deck shoveling fuel into cauldrons to the rhythm of wheels and gears, overexcited sails flapping. A picture of energy, love, and grace, a picture of Diana's beautiful body stubbornly demonstrating exercises. Her body channels energy to those from which it is escaping. Time does not heal wounds. Time *only* preserves them.

A rumble of thunder. Even swallows grow weak in a thunderstorm. Sensing danger, they react by fleeing, by flying away. But sometimes the change is so abrupt that they don't have time to react: in the wet and cold fall of 1957, even those ready to fly away were taken by surprise and fell from the sky, starving and disoriented. The fall of 1957 saw bodies of swallows rain down from the sky. That year saw Ingrid's body rain down from the sky. Swallows are capable of changing and disconnecting.

Erika is no longer a swallow either, she is a chaffinch, a solitary bird that lives on its own, *Fringilla coelebs*: Erika has chosen celibacy.

"You've ripped us out of all relationships, Diana."

"But what you wanted was to be independent and free. Not happy. Which doesn't mean that you are unhappy."

A swallow flaps its wings as it observes countries, houses, men and women from on high. What it sees makes its tail fork. It would like to stay in the human nest. But it has to fly away to gather strength. So that it can return in hopes that *something* has changed in its native land.

In these parts no one can run away from themselves.

Erika is praying. She sees the lanky violinist, she sees his bow sawing the strings. She sees his extended index finger and she sees Diana's hands tugging at the string, the string swells as if being stretched, the hand reaches for a rope, the rope stiffens, changing under the violinist's neck into the body of the violin with a double clef on its round hips.

Birgit calms her breathing, pranayama, breathing practice, speed is shunned in yoga. In her head she hears Diana's scolding, sounding like a steely lecture: "You are different, Birgit. Each hemisphere of the brain plays a different role, and they are not the same in men and women. For *your* organism to be in balance, it must stimulate both hemispheres evenly, ensuring the air flows steadily through both nostrils. Inability to breathe through the nose, or blocked nostrils, is detrimental to the harmonious development of the personality."

She adopts the seated position. Straightening her spine, she closes her eyes, places her hands on her knees, and concentrates on breathing deeply. Surya bhedana, penetration of the sun's rays whose stimulating effect helps to fend off depression, fatigue, and lack of motivation. She keeps breathing in through her right nostril and out through the left. Then she moves on to lighter breathing patterns. By now she ought to feel her body getting warmer.

But thoughts can't be killed. That is why she must watch them and be very careful as to who she allows to get very close to her. Oh, to buy a gun and fire at the thoughts in the head, wouldn't that be something.

Birgit gets up and picks up a notebook headed *March Drowning in Blackness*. She sets it alight over the toilet bowl. The flame swallows words, choking on them; it doesn't like the taste of what's written there and spits out the syllables.

The *only* sheets she hands Diana are those covered in a girl's handwriting.

"Milena, the schoolgirl from my creative writing course."

"She's written it all down?"

"Yes, she has. What about the lawyer in your class?"

"You mean the lynx-like woman who does yoga with me? Ambitious, organized, unflappable."

"You will prize it out of her."

"She's not too complicated."

"How much time do you need?"

"Well, she's not exactly an open kind of person."

"She must have an Achilles heel."

"She does. Her family."

"We are a family and we are falling apart."

"There is something that can weld us together."

"Honey."

They get changed and go to the park. Swallows fly low, it is about to rain. They walk along the river in the fall air, past birches and crouching willows with eyes lurking behind their long hair. Leaves on the hawthorn are still a rich green but the poplars have already started to shed theirs. Not yet frenziedly. Once the trees are completely bare, fall will be over. Ducks swim in the river. Two green collared ducks leave the group and plunge down, headfirst, bodies flipping over and legs flying up; imitating the willows, they dive *only* up to their necks. When both dive at the same time, they resemble synchronized swimmers.

A continuation of the yoga class. Synchronized swimming.

Diana is holding a green Louis Vuitton bag in her hand. Birgit is carrying a small case with plastic folders. They have checked out of the boarding house shaped like a white goose neck, passing a trashcan full of barely used clothes and used newspapers. They hail a cab. They are moving to a rented apartment. Diana sits in the passenger seat next to the driver and without turning her head, she talks to the other two women in broken Czech. She declares that the Job they have come here for should Get Done now, it should get done as soon as possible. After that, she will clear out the orange house at the foot of Petřín Hill, hand it over to hummingbirds, and will settle down in the north, by the water, on the island of Usedom or perhaps Amrum. There she can look out at a sea that is too cold to swim in and yet teeming with creatures that emanate strength. She wishes to have *only* her body and the sea wind for company; she will never think of other bodies again.

But her priority for now is *to get this job done.*

THE INDEPENDENCE OF THE SWALLOWS

The Detective has checked and rechecked every droplet of circumstantial evidence to do with the Widow and its every conceivable implication. Her alibi is rock solid, the Detective informs his boss, humble contrition personified as he apologizes in a husky voice for having reopened the case, causing unnecessary delay. He is ready to close the case now and confine it to oblivion. That's out of the question now, the chief sneers grimly from his high horse.

The Detective fills his days with other cases. He wills himself to forget the orange house at the foot of Petřín Hill. He locks the case in a safe inside his head, fleeing from it. It was *only* a suicide.

And whichever way you look at it, it will remain a suicide, chirrups a voice in his head, dripping with schadenfreude. The name of that voice is conscience. Conscience has a sense of humor. The chirruping proves impossible to shake off. If he points his boss in the direction of the orange house, his attention will be deflected from the Widow and turn to Stadtherr, which would be perfect. Except that his boss would laugh it off, he would split his sides laughing, and that would be the end of the story. The chief needs a straightforward and neatly ironed story. A story starring the Widow is straightforward and neatly ironed. Whereas that broad, Stadtherr, what possible motive could she have?

A motive! Ha ha!, laughs his colleague. Apparently, the Detective hadn't redacted some highlighted passages in his scribbled notes as instructed.

The other policeman had tried to gain entry into the orange house at the foot of Petřín Hill before him, after his letter to Professor Stadtherr failed to elicit a reply. He ended up emailing the head of an international college in England where the professor was currently running a master class. The head printed out the email and passed it on to her.

"I called him a couple of times to make sure she got my letter," says the Detective's reliable partner. "And?" the Detective whispers with a sinking heart. There is a lump in his throat, a funnel gasping for air.

"Well, the call went on and on, he made me listen to an endless stream of drivel and baloney. The letter was apparently instead collected by Ms. Adler, who said she would deal with the matter. The two women are guest lecturers at the college, based in an imposing brand-new building: glass-fronted, eighteen stories high. It offers a huge selection of language courses—pick any language under the sun and they will ram it down your throat; English for foreigners and Chinese being the most popular, but there are also acting workshops and dance classes, art, meditation, tai chi and kung fu, martial arts, yoga, creative writing. All the classes run from September. The head couldn't wait to meet Ms. Adler, with whom he had been corresponding since March. He sounds like a nice guy, quite efficient, very chatty, he said they scheduled a special intensive master class in yoga aimed primarily at specific people on a list Ms. Adler had sent him from Prague in advance.

"I had to cut his monologue short and remind him that I was interested *only* in Professor Stadtherr. 'Ah yes, the creative writing class, right. We are so proud to have her teach here. It makes us proud that these two women have chosen us and our storied town. I guess they needed a change, somewhere off the beaten track, far from more glamorous cities, and although our town may not be, how should I put it, your typical bucolic spa resort with a promenade and swimming pools, we do enjoy a high quality of life. We don't normally offer creative writing courses to local schools as that would use up our funding from the local authority, but this time we had to advertise it to a number of specific schools that Professor Stadtherr had requested. Ms. Adler sent us her list, but we couldn't justify such a narrowly defined target group, so we offered her course to the general public, we are here for everyone after all, that is a key principle of our outreach. The course sold out within hours even though it's the most expensive we've ever run, so most of our grant was spent on Ms. Stadtherr. Their mail comes to the college address, of course, sure, no need to thank me, I'm happy I could provide information on these esteemed ladies, I'm glad you are keeping an eye on them, thanks to them our college has been the center of attention, and not just at the local level, I'm honored that they've chosen me, I mean us, and come to our town. What else can I tell you? The first meeting with them was unforgettable, Ms. Adler glanced at the list and nodded her approval, put it in her bag, and said thank you. When I gave Ms. Stadtherr the list of people signed up for her creative writing class, complete with ages, addresses, work or school affiliation, she passed it under her steely X-ray eyes, shook her bouffant head and said, with a disappointed glance at Ms. Adler, *only one*, then hastily folded the list and stuck it into the pocket of her bright-red pants. And that was it. I was taken aback, or rather, hurt—all the participants had been asked to write an assignment in advance, she said she wanted to take a look at them before the class started, so we had them all printed out, a whole wheelie bag full, we had to borrow the bag from our acting class, the printing kept two of my assistants busy for a week. I was as helpful as I could be to both ladies, I really did my best. Of these two, the kind Ms. Adler is the one who commands respect. Her name is a brand. They signed a contract for a rather limited number of hours. Ms. Adler wasted no time and started on the first afternoon as agreed. Everyone loves her, adults, children, therapists, and teachers alike, we are in regular, close contact, very close indeed. Ms. Stadtherr, on the other hand, started much later and has already managed to, how should I put it, alienate several students, they were petrified, right now I'm dealing with the first complaint from a local artist, she is the mayor's ex-wife, a talented lady with a serious foot issue, no, it's not a fallen arch, anyway, when I first met Ms. Stadtherr, she didn't say a word, she just shook my hand like a man, grabbed the bag and left, making the wheels rattle even on the polished floors, with her purple caftan trailing after her, and the next time we met, she again didn't say a word and later sent me a brief note suggesting I use our local government grant to pay for a self-awareness class for the mayor's ex-wife, even though we don't have this class scheduled this year, but don't get me wrong, I'm not suggesting anything, God forbid, I'm, I mean we're happy to have these two distinguished professors with us . . .'"

The Detective wishes he could get his partner to shut up, if only he could block his ears, tingling with anxiety. He doesn't want to hear any of this, and it annoys him that his colleague is aware of the *existence* of the orange house. His partner repeats what he learned from the college head: the women are staying in a boarding house, a second-rate establishment, its shape meant to resemble a goose neck, the Indian owner is one of Ms. Adler's yoga students. That's the way it is, well-heeled pensioners having their cake and eating it, they make a few cents on the side while traveling so they can spend some time someplace *just* hanging around, strolling around town and along the river. What's formidable about Ms. Adler is not her person, but her power.

Each species and subspecies on this planet uses signals to communicate, to follow the scent, signals barely discernible to others. The Detective's colleague hands him the reply. It is handwritten.

The Detective recognizes the handwriting.

"Would you believe it," his partner brays, "this Stadtherr broad writes by hand, she uses a pen and purple ink, I bet she has an inkwell and a goose quill, who does that these days, she doesn't even have an email address even though she's gone off to some godforsaken place for a semester to teach."

The letter conveys her deepest condolences and her astonishment at the news of the unexpected demise of her former student. The deceased had no literary talent whatsoever and as an artist he was totally impotent, neither had he much empathy or respect for others, and yet this eunuch felt the urge to write, yes, he wasn't short on appetite, he virtually oozed it, he was hard work, to tell the truth. If someone has nothing to say, it is extremely difficult to teach them *how* to say it. They were supposed to meet on the Friday in question but unfortunately, he didn't show up, he sent his apologies, said he would be out of Prague that weekend, was going away with friends, not with his young wife and son, if she remembers right, to the mountains, presumably, he liked high altitudes and avoided valleys. It's quite common for people to develop anxieties and get depressed as they age and then decide to write their memoirs for their grandchildren who couldn't care less anyway, they only do it to introduce some order and meaning to their failed lives with a hint of a story, I've seen this hundreds of times, she added, but it wasn't like that in his case. I am very sorry, but I can't be of any further help, I didn't know him well and don't regret that in the least, best regards, good luck, and keep up the good work, boys. And please don't bother me with any more trivial matters like this.

The Detective's colleague cobbles together a reply and prints it out. The Detective's boss denies his request to seek a meeting in person, calling it unwarranted. The Detective agrees, her outrageous reply will have to do.

◇

Having a tooth pulled would have shaken her more. Julia is chirruping in the whitewashed corridor. She is happy to have gotten it over with. Problem solved, she thinks naively.

"The nurse was really horrible, she was, like, made of stone. She made us all stay in bed, to get some rest, she said, before we were checked and discharged. And the other women, they were all old, like, over thirty. You wouldn't believe the old women's bullshit they went on about, it made me wanna gag." They don't know the first thing about life. They know a lot about sex though. I hate the way they talk about men, like they're losers. All my besties at school are boys, girls are all back-stabbing rats."

Julia takes a drag on her cigarette.

"So, it's all over now. I need a drink."

Diana snatches the cigarette from her mouth. She stubs it out on a fingernail. She remains silent, breathing heavily. She pulls Julia away. She emanates a force the turtledove doesn't dare resist. A gentle touch makes trust blossom, makes it open like a calyx, like a yellow tulip. Diana needs her trust, she needs to discover *as soon as possible* what is going on behind the closed doors of Yusuf's apartment across the street from his restaurant.

Diana hauls the girl into a maisonette with a small front yard. A cozy little apartment. On the table there's a gift-wrapped packet tied with stiff green ribbon that resembles Diana's crossed legs. Diana makes Julia lie down.

"If you want to deceive yourself, be my guest. But you can't deceive your body. Your body has been through a shock. It will come to terms with it, but that has to happen in a mindful way, you have to love your body, be aware of its feelings and nurse them."

She takes a blender jar out of the fridge. It's filled with a greenish liquid. She makes Julia drink the lumpy cocktail. She stands over her until she has swallowed the last drop. She tells Julia to lie down on the lurid green mat. Julia doesn't resist. Diana massages Julia's body, her fingers knead her tension and cramps away. Julia breaks down in tears.

Julia's body sobs as it succumbs to purifying sleep. The first purifying sleep of her life. She doesn't yet know what species she belongs to: short-winged, long-winged, or wader. The lost youth of this world. She doesn't yet know what impact this experience will have on her proud and exuberant soul, but the fact that she denies having been a victim of abuse, the perpetrators of which should be locked up, demonstrates the extent of the damage. She is lying to her own body, which is confused, forever doomed to think of revenge, as long as the man she would like to kill remains alive. It is disgusting how easily the kestrel Yusuf shrugged it off.

Diana bites her tongue. She keeps guard over the gutted Julia.

Her eyes feast on the curves of the turtledove's body. There is a discrepancy between its mental and actual age. The child is intellectually above average. No delayed development there. A silk moth dwells within. Diana passes a verdict that is neither just nor unjust; it is a verdict known as the revenge of the swallows.

Diana adopts a yoga pose, keeping her eyes on a green bag. But this is not yoga. Every cell of her body is filled with her breath, nourished by her mind and the unhealed scars in her infertile womb. Her strength coils into a knot of snakes, their venom mingling with Diana's blood. A taste of this mixed blood is what she will offer on Judgment Day.

Diana's body practices martial holds, making her energy mingle with that of all the other bodies she has touched or held in her life. A single, calm, concentrated touch of the tip of her index finger on the core of her adversary's body is enough to transmit the venom. Determination is the *only* force that cannot be overcome; Diana is freeing herself of *human* failures. Of behavior entrenched in defensive rituals that serve *only* as embellishments for the body, empty mannerisms. Diana finishes the exercise. She no longer needs her breath. Determination is a word containing a multitude of other words. A person without determination is unsteady. Their will, their inner strength, and character are unsteady. When you hold a sword, the Shaolin monks say, you must believe that you really are going to kill your adversary.

Diana unzips the green bag. Its bowels hold a man's tie, the one Max Adler wore when they were leaving postwar Europe. Diana sniffs it. She undoes the knot on the tie and makes a fresh knot.

A snapped string from Menuhin's violin, his gift to the spellbound Erika. It reminds Diana of little Erika with a body bathed in music and a mind that was a void. Diana runs the tip of her left index finger along the string.

A length of cattle rope turned gray with age, which she cut down in her attic after Ingrid died. The rope was the last thing to feel the warmth of Ingrid's living body. Diana strokes the rope and kisses it.

A bunch of letters tied with a green ribbon. Posted after the war by Birgit from an immured Prague, an enchanted forest of unsmiling people. Some words have been circled in red ink, some so covered by the red they're lost forever. The stained paper is strewn with red circles of censorship. These are words written by a young girl lacking a gift for organized life, whose life was nevertheless whole, determined, and firm. For she doesn't belong to anyone. Because she *only* is. When she breathes, her nostrils flare.

The index finger of her left hand traces the lines written in a little girl's hummingbird script.

By the time Julia opens her still drowsy eyes, the green bag is cowering in the dark wardrobe. All the bones in the turtledove's squashed little body ache, her eyes are puffed up from crying, her face crumpled. Diana sits by the window, reading glasses on her nose and a cup of tea now cold on the windowsill. Julia prepares to say something; her scared voice comes out in a whimper.

The dozing Diana stirs. She moves Julia's sweaty hair off her brow. She runs a lavender bath for her. Passes her a clean white towel the size of a tablecloth.

Julia emerges from the bathroom languid and warmed through and through. She finds the music that is playing disagreeable, it annoys her. Her body squirms. Fortunately, the sound of the violin doesn't last too long.

"Vivaldi."

"Whatever."

"The largo from *The Four Seasons, Spring.*"

"But it's fall now."

"Spring is when the swallows return."

"Oh yeah?"

Diana pushes a gift toward the little voice. Julia unties the stiff green ribbon. Inside is a shiny metal box containing several smaller packets. Julia crows with delight at the tablet. She doesn't know what to make of the two volumes of a book, *The Body Remembers.*

"You wrote this?"

"I did."

"Hm. I'm not really into reading."

"Neither am I."

"Really?"

"There are too many books and authors who have damaged humankind."

The packet also includes a film documentary about some scrawny violinist. And a tiny box wrapped in silken paper: a gold chain with a cross adorned with a ruby. Children who have grown up without a father are more likely to prioritize material values, it comes from lack of trust, Erika likes to say. Inside a tiny shimmering purse of gold cluster four miniature bottles of nail polish: blue, peach, yellow, and ruby. Julia greedily reaches for the cheapest bottle. Diana looks on as Julia coats her chewed nails with yellow polish.

"Blue is no longer in?"

"Nah."

Julia shakes the yellow bottle. She pushes the cross to one side.

"I'm not . . . religious."

"That's no problem."

"It isn't?"

"Religions are wars of the future."

"Is this real gold?"

"Yes, it is."

"Can I sell it?"

"Do whatever you like with it. But you should think of it as symbolic protection. A friend of mine says that she doesn't mind gods and faith, but what she has an issue with is churches, institutions, and any other ideology like that. She grew up in an atheist country, you can't imagine what that does to people who live there. Perhaps you are like that, too."

"I gotta go."

"All right."

"I'll keep my part of the deal . . . but some other time, OK?"

"No, that's not OK."

"It's not?"

"No. Now."

"I see. A deal's a deal."

"This is not a deal."

"All right, I'll tell you about the . . . its . . . father, when and where he pumped it into me. Can I have another glass of that poison? Why is it so green?!

"There's some . . . spinach in it."

Diana tops up the green cocktail. Julia is finally breathing out fully through her mouth and breathing in through flared nostrils; indications of trust. Julia is a bag of sawdust. She allows Diana to cut a slit through the bag. Sawdust comes pouring out. Diana is not listening. She is trying to calm down but the egg has been hatched, the die has been cast.

As she sits there watching Julia, Diana is happy and feels grateful, not just for her own passionate, wild, and mature life and for all the joy it has given her, but also for having found the strength to escape her golden cradle and golden cage and empathize with the little gray sparrows in the dust of the road as well as the swallows and swifts in the barns, and to help them fly back onto their branches. A life split into two halves. She is like a swallow's tail.

In her mind's eye, Diana sees a gallery of her feathery photographs. Her camera has captured a fascinating montage of bodies frozen in positions that even yogis dare not dream of, as a stream of bodies that were barely alive promenaded before her. They included girls who had stopped menstruating, had lost their hair, breasts, and teeth, and yet would brazenly and matter-of-factly offer to soldiers the last scraps of flesh still clinging to their bodies. Her camera has recorded the faces of women and girls who had been snatched and left at the mercy of anyone who wanted to touch them. Faces ignored by the eyes of historians. Faces that had bodies but no names.

Julia has finished telling her story. Dumbfounded, she looks at Diana, whose mind is elsewhere.

"Miss . . ."

"It's nothing, Julia, I *just* . . ."

"What?"

"It's just that I don't believe in words, I don't believe in cultural considerations. The path I must follow is buried in my mouth. What I believe in is the language of the body, which is the same all over the world."

"You're weird. But the stuff I just told you, I'll never say again to any cop or court. I've been burned once. You don't know how they treated me. The way they looked at me. And nobody gives a shit. All I get is: forget it, it's *only* this and *only* that."

Without a word, Diana empties her black leather backpack, letting paper tissues, a green wallet with Hittite script on it, and a hand-mirror tumble onto the table. She stows Julia's gifts in the empty backpack. She knows she will never see the black leather backpack again and that Julia the turtledove will pretend they have never met. Diana doesn't say she saw Julia steal some cash from her black backpack last time.

Years later, Julia's body will remember her. Tooth and nail, it will cling to the memory. Diana gives Julia a hug.

"I'll walk you home."

Diana doesn't bend down to pick up leaves from the ground. She looks up at the sky. A flock of birds flies overhead. Swifts maybe, or swallows, her favorite birds with their forked tail, perhaps yes and perhaps no, it's hard to decide, it's all bubbling in the same kettle. The sacred tea kettle simmers gently.

The swallows. One particular variety is her favorite. The kind that lives *only* in flight. The three of them are also like that. These swallows are alive *only* in flight, they even sleep in flight, it took scientists a long time to figure out how they do it. Eventually they discovered that when one falls asleep the others flying on her side stay awake, connected by invisible threads of energy, perhaps intuition. If one swallow falls, if it drops out of formation and struggles to take off, unable to manage on its own, it needs another to help. At least to get up to a tree from where it can try to take flight again. It never grows tired, never ever, never ever, it even mates in flight. It can live no other way.

◇

The Detective is trying to swat away flies but the question marks around the three ladies won't stop buzzing.

At home he sits at his computer. Investigates their background. He pounces on the lives of the inhabitants of the orange house like a raven. In Prague, they maintain *only* work-related contacts. Diana Adler sees her yoga students. Birgit Stadtherr has taught *only* one creative writing course in Prague for the past twenty years, although she regularly teaches abroad. She never meets her students outside class. Erika Eis goes to concerts, her *only* acquaintances are conductors and violinists, none of them Czech. The women spend most of the year flying around the world. What has attracted them to Prague is clearly the orange house at the foot of Petřín Hill, purchased by Max Adler twenty years ago. Prague is convenient, Prague is at the center of Europe, Prague has no heart; Stadtherr was born here. She is the *only* one who has had children, her sons live quiet lives, nothing suspicious there.

The Detective forces himself to look again at the books written by Stadtherr. He has read only one, flicked through the others, and struggled through a few written in English. He looks up reviews of Eis's films, superfluous paragraphs put him to sleep. He watches a popular 1980s series of yoga videos with exercises demonstrated by Adler. He can't make head or tail of any of it. Sparkling, civilized ladies. Instead of lipstick, they carry success in their handbags.

The Detective is dazzled by how much they have achieved. They could also have their photos framed and mounted side by side, sliding them along the wall as required. What amazes the Detective is that, apparently, these women use their dazzling beauty *only* to distract attention from the real purpose of their house. The orange house at the foot of Petřín Hill.

So much energy. So much energy.

The three ladies hailing from the previous century humiliate him by the ease with which they operate across languages. They have known each other since 1945. They persevere. The Detective, by contrast, is alone, has nothing and no one and he is beginning to weary of life. He's going soft. He is weaker than he thought.

I have to put a stop to this, thinks the Detective, filled with self-hatred. I will leave them alone. But more importantly, I wish these cavorting hags would leave me alone.

While brushing his teeth, he touches the roots of the hair on his scalp. Tiny flakes of blue enamel paint shake loose instead of skin.

The Detective hurries to the new house on the outskirts of Prague. He wants to see the Widow, wants to hear her. He doesn't dare touch her.

They cook dinner together. Hash browns are part and parcel of the season. They have grown up with this tradition. They peel yellow potatoes into a deep white bowl and grate them on a box grater.

He grates his coarse, she hers fine. They make dough out of their respective piles and fry them, standing side by side at the stove, then dry the greasy patties on kitchen towels. They happen to touch each other inadvertently. She pulls the back of the Detective's black shirt out of his blue jeans, planting a kiss on his skin just above the belt. The Detective pretends not to notice.

The little boy judges the contest, declaring his mom's hash browns with a topping of sour cream the winner. Imprinting is very important for fledglings: they hear their parent's voice even before hatching from the egg. But the boy also takes another helping of the Detective's creations, which have tiny pieces of chopped bacon mixed into the dough. The Detective puts what's left of the dough into a small pan and bakes it as a meatloaf, the way his grandma Josefa used to do it. He slices the baked dough, fanning it out on a platter. The Widow piles the dirty dishes in the dishwasher. The boy is playing on the floor and refuses to take his bath. The Detective gets down on the carpet beside him. Lying on their bellies, they play with toy cars. They load the toy cars with plastic, warriors with automatic guns, soft toys, mice, donkeys, and puppies. No soft birds. They attach tiny carriages to the engine. The little train sets off. A bowl of jelly bears lies on the floor, within the boy's reach. The Detective reaches for the candy but instead grabs a soft toy and is about to stuff it into his mouth as if by mistake. The boy's body bursts out laughing, rolls onto its back, roaring with laughter. Both bodies roar with laughter.

The Widow watches them. She asks the Detective to entice the boy into the bathroom. The Detective gets down on all fours. The boy leaps onto his back and grabs hold of his neck, spurring his horse. The Widow gently lifts the boy out of the saddle. She undresses him and dips him into the bubble bath. The Detective, suddenly awkward, goes back to the kitchen. He tidies up the toys. The Widow puts the boy to bed.

The Detective looks out at the fall garden. They're out there, tucking their heads under their wings. The forked tails help them keep their balance. The light fades as he waits.

The Widow sits down by his side. "I need to believe that the world can also have a different face," says the Detective. "What kind of face do you mean?" the Widow asks. "This one," replies the Detective. He looks deep into her eyes, which grow wide. "Wouldn't it be nice to just sit here, chatting. It's unprofessional, I know, but the case will soon be closed. I'd like to keep seeing you. And I wouldn't ever want to hurt you in any way." "Why would you want to hurt me?" asks the Widow, genuinely puzzled.

They both get up at the same time. The Widow brews some coffee. Suddenly she stops, feeling a presence behind her back. She turns around and looks him in the eye. The Detective's mood lifts like a fog. She has never looked into anyone's eyes for this long, it shows courage and devotion. She kisses him.

"You love me."

"Madly."

"You love me."

"Infinitely."

The Detective and the Woman kiss. Their bodies overflow with joy and grow languorous, shedding tension. This is the most straightforward, but also most difficult, kind of yoga, as bodies can rid themselves of tension *only* if they feel safe and trusting, not just desire. If their souls feel safe and trusting. If their hearts feel safe and trusting. They have come to rest in deserted places and this is their contribution to the history of joy. And they respect one another's otherness. The wind whistles. "You're the only one. I wish I could look at you as I lie dying." This kind of yoga works *only* if one soul respects the other. If they look into each other's eyes. The man's lips roam the woman's neck. Their little beaks taste each other's skin. The man's lips slowly move up to the peaks of her nipples, then down again. His hands assist, careful not to interfere with this moment, they discard obstacles, throwing off shirt, trousers, blouse and bra, panties and boxers. The woman's lips lock on to the scent they desire, the bodies change positions like a pendulum, now her mouth leads. They move to the bedroom and make love, touching each other where words cannot reach, making love unhurriedly, without rushing to climax; they make love, astonished by the force of their desire, they want *only* the other one to come, they hold each other, their existence justified by this closeness, this is the first time in her life that she doesn't close her eyes but looks into the man's, relaxed, every muscle supple and yielding; he enters her from the front and from behind and it feels natural, so natural, music without instruments, music that *only* the two of them can hear. He wants to protect her and she wants to yield to him. She wants to protect him and he wants to yield to her. This *is* love. He needs her because he loves her. For the first time. He has grown up. Up to this moment he had been screaming silently: I don't want to be alone, I need you and that's why I love you. Hope and hopelessness erupt in a mystic orgasm, he sobs himself back to the roots of his boyhood. They rest in silence. Though she is thinking of something that is too distant for him to see.

"This is all about sex, that's why you're here."

"I'm here because I love you. And because I don't know any other woman who goes parachute jumping. And you—you don't mind that I'm broke?"

"Who knows, we might win the lottery."

"I don't think so."

"Why not?"

"We didn't buy a ticket."

◇

The receptionist has laid out a pile of mail on the coffee table in the morning, sorted according to the individual attorneys.

The Lynx opens a letter written in purple ink. The envelope has no postmark. The letter was dropped directly into the office mailbox and gives off a strange scent. Her pinky slides into the slit and tugs it open. One Ingrid Wiesenthal urgently seeks her advice. She suggests they meet. Giving a time and a date: one P.M., today.

It's nine A.M. There is no return address, no phone number. The impudence.

The Lynx is taken aback by the fancy envelope and hand-made paper stamped with the monogram IW. She's about to throw the letter into the trash. She sniffs it again and her vision blurs.

She doesn't throw the letter out. When she tells her husband about it later that night and he asks why she didn't throw it out, she says, "I don't know, I don't know how to put it, there was some strange and classy urgency to the handwriting, the hummingbird letters so tiny yet self-assured, they've seared themselves into my mind. Into the middle of my forehead, right here."

Her husband rolls his eyes.

The Lynx changes tack. "Tell me now, who writes letters by hand these days? Plus, it was a welcome change in the routine of an attorney's office. Oh, I don't know, quit asking."

Ingrid Wiesenthal doesn't show up at the agreed time. Diana Adler is waiting in reception instead. Her honey-colored hair has a ginger tint. The scarf under her neck matches her shoes and a new leather backpack. The outstretched arm is covered in liver spots and expensive cream. A circle of white gold gapes from the ring finger.

Arriving at one o'clock on the dot, she offers to pay in advance and in cash. "To catch at least one chicken, you need at least two grains of rice," she says to the receptionist, who doesn't understand what Diana wants to pay for. Diana turns down a glass of water. She turns down the offer of a cup of coffee. She refuses to provide any information.

The Lynx opens the door of her study and instantly mellows, recognizing her yoga teacher. The Lynx apologizes, she is very busy. Her diary fills up weeks in advance. And in addition, there's this mysterious woman demanding to see her all of a sudden.

"In fact, that's why I'm here," Diana says. "Ingrid sends her apologies. Unfortunately, she can't come and sent me in her stead." The Lynx's curiosity is piqued. She wonders why Diana didn't arrange the meeting herself. Their conversation takes exactly seven minutes. Caught off guard, the Lynx manages only a few sentences. She doesn't discover who Ingrid is. She is disconcerted but doesn't let on. The Lynx is a pro. Diana is a pro.

In this morning's yoga class Diana explained to her students that nothing would throw them as long as they hold on to their breathing as if it were a railing. It works as a lightning conductor as well as a weapon.

Diana has a favor to ask. Since Ingrid's request has also disrupted her long-planned schedule, she wonders if they could continue this meeting outside the office. On the Lynx's lunch break. A quick lunch. She'll meet her in reception. The Lynx agrees, not daring to say no. She doesn't even try to look for an excuse. Diana leans close to the Lynx's ear. She whispers something in it. The Lynx shrugs her shoulders; she is really not sure if she will be able to find the required information so quickly.

Diana is sitting demurely in a shell armchair in front of the silent fortifications of the reception desk, facing the main entrance, the breeze created by the revolving door ruffling her ginger hair. The Lynx roots around her office, ransacking her computer. The assistant frantically prints out the documents she emails her.

The Lynx bursts out of her office, heels clacking, arms pulling a dark, army-like coat onto her body, eyes running over the printed lines. "Back in thirty minutes," she says buttoning up her coat and making a dash for the door. A radiant Diana rises from the shell chair. The two women step into the revolving mill that grinds them up and spits them out into the din of the street. The Lynx takes out her car keys, the pile of papers squeezed under her arm like a bagpipe. It won't play her tune.

It's just around the corner, says Diana, touching the piper's arm.

The Lynx gets into her car, feeling stressed. She opens the passenger door. Diana hesitates before the opened wing. She gets in. The car folds its wings and sets off.

◇

The house at the foot of Petřín Hill attracts the Detective's body like a magnet. It has drilled under his skin. Its flaking plaster sticks to his forehead. It matures in his mind, sprawling about his head, frittering his time away. Idea is action. Every Saturday and Sunday morning, the Detective's legs set out for the house as if going to a public library.

He sees the apartments with different eyes now. The eyes of the women whose temporary abode it is.

The Detective rifles through individual files. He looks for photos, emptying envelopes and frenziedly scouring their contents and . . .

It is there, every time.

The purple cross. Hanging over someone's head. The Detective finds it hard to breathe. The air is getting thicker, turning into magma. The residents of the medieval house at the foot of Petřín Hill, these practitioners of the dark arts, who have dedicated their lives to the pursuit of something illegal and twisted, all for the sake of justice, are not alone. They have spread their web and built nests for fallen fledglings all around the world, teaching them to fly under the rafters of barns and stables, in flocks that don't recognize carved-out countries and profess a different set of values, with their own headquarters in country after country, each like a miniature folding version of the original orange house.

Whenever the time comes for a purple cross to come swooping down and be suspended over someone's head, the worldwide web of folding houses is rent apart. They go into hiding, learning how to fly below the chirruping surface of the information noise. The Detective is torn. He has turned into an invisible ally of the orange house without putting up any resistance. The chamois-clad index finger staggers around the boxes of cold metal and red ring binders as it follows the trail of nests from Albania to Zimbabwe and back again; in India he is captivated by a photo of a nice-looking guy in uniform and a pair of seventeen-year-old eyes that committed suicide when the police failed to help after she was gang-raped. The local investigating officer, the nice guy, did not even record the case, let alone launch an investigation. In fact, he doggedly tried to persuade the girl not to report the thugs, to come to an agreement and marry one of them, any one of them. A sarcastic comment has been scribbled in hummingbird handwriting on the margin of a blue schoolbook inside a plastic folder: *Come on, my little quail, why are you making things so hard for them?*

The Detective recognizes the hummingbird handwriting. The letters assemble into syllables and sentences, the sentences assemble into information, a silk moth doesn't know what makes an eagle happy, but that doesn't stop it from enjoying life. Surprisingly, the information accumulated in the sentences does not concern the rapists, but the nice police officer. It is *his* uniform that sports a purple smudge, a purple cross rising to heaven from the uniform's pocket like smoke, floating above his head; a discharge of an elitist ribbon, a presidential medal, an order of the Legion of Honor.

The Detective's head is abuzz, a smoke bomb has been set off in the basement, there is a reproach floating over *his* head, too, the future is no longer what it used to be. He is sucked in and crushed by a whirlwind. The Detective's eyes decipher hastily scribbled pages. They scrutinize and appraise a photo of a crowd on vacation in the Punjab, and discover under a magnifying glass a tiny head marked with a red pin. A woman's head. With a purple cross fluttering above it. The wind has ripped a tulle scarf off her neck, sending it flying over other people's heads.

The Detective's eyes skim the pages of the azure-blue notebook. He leaves it open. A cluster of moths fluttering their wings and rearranging themselves. He weighs down the open pages with a lamp. He walks over to the computer. Compares the data and the figures in the bank accounts. It's now dawning on him, he is beginning to find his bearings amid the smoke and mirrors, the flare of a shooting star. A flash of lightning pierces the darkness. The house at the foot of Prague's Petřín Hill was not directly involved in this case, it *only* gave an indifferent yawn and sent money instead.

Some of the money was used to bribe local officials.

The money has been flowing every which way, but it is not money that is at stake in this game.

They abseil into nests on extended nets and tangled spiders' threads. The Detective sketches out a map in his long-suffering notebook, like an airline with lines connecting Prague to every corner of the world. The first three threads lead to the male kingfishers at the banks in Zurich. The spiders' web is thickening. Long rays radiate from the Petřín sun. Long fingers scrabbling around, reaching every continent. Sums of money recorded in long columns slide along the rays like a cableway, money from foundations run by Mr. Max Adler and Mrs. Diana Adler, née Bussard. The money is slipped into open beaks. The Detective is confused by the bird vernacular, finds the language inarticulate, little mice in nests don't squeak when they see young sparrows, shush.

The nice Indian policeman is dismissed from his precinct. *Someone* higher up reported the case. *Only* two rapists were arrested; a woman assisting them was tracked down. The purple crosses are fading.

Swallows and quails speak of peace and harmony.

Which will come once they have eradicated the evil.

The Detective gets up. He goes to the second floor, takes off his gloves, and splashes cold water over his face. Is he overwrought? Come on, young man, courage and perseverance!

◇

Two women are waiting for them in the Chinese restaurant. Lovely, civilized, polished, overbred and neatly dressed middle-aged ladies. They look like faded movies stars. Diana and the Lynx join their table. They compliment the Lynx on her plum-colored suit. They keep her for seven minutes, thirty minutes, forty minutes, an hour. She learns nothing about them. They are interested in a long-forgotten case from last May. Julia, a fifteen-year-old girl, an unfledged young jay, evidently drunk, barged into an Uxor-Hiom restaurant and smashed the bar counter, no big deal.

Utterances are mysterious balloons. They float around the Chinese restaurant, crashing into windowpanes, cracking their skulls. Every now and then Diana raises her eyes to the sky, sees the swallows, it's time for them to leave. I will fall into line again, I will, I promise.

Madam Stadtherr speaks. Then Madam Eis.

Diana seems to have used up her allocation of words.

The Lynx can no longer tell which of the ladies is speaking, it is music from a single throat; a duet, a higher and a lower note, a difference of twenty years between the pink and the purple. The Lynx feels as if she were facing a self-appointed tribunal, she won't receive her bowl of plain rice until she speaks, and when she does, they try to make her feel guilty, she has no idea why. She'll go crazy if it goes on like this. Her eyes hold fast to Diana's silence. Diana encourages the Lynx with a kindly smile, like a tight-lipped, untouchable, and unbiased defense counsel; good people can be easily deceived, shush.

The Chinese waitress cheerfully places bowls and plates on the table. Home-made noodles, sliced duck, sweet-and-sour chicken, bowls of rice, a tray of flatbreads and moo shu pork, stir-fried daylily blossoms, scrambled eggs, wood-ear mushrooms, and pork tenderloin. A small pudgy hand tops up the pot with jasmine tea. Erica gives the sugar bowl back to the waitress.

"In China, tea is never served with milk, lemon, sugar, or honey."

The Lynx orders some soup, Diana plain rice and chrysanthemum tea. The ladies wield their chopsticks skillfully and wipe the corners of their mouths with yellow cloth napkins like children expecting Diana's praise. Casually, between bird-like mouthfuls, they throw in squawks of questions. The Lynx answers. She addresses her answers to the face of the sphinx, who inspires respect in her and whose mysterious smile buoys her like a gulp of jasmine tea. The face concentrates on chewing plain grains of rice.

"Why are you so interested in this? I don't get it. I've told Ms. Adler I would try to find out as much as I can. And what I found out is that she got off."

"Got off?"

"Got off with a warning."

"Actually, we're more interested in her police testimony."

"You must know that unless you are immediate family . . ."

"What exactly did Julia say?"

"She claimed that she was controlled by a gang of guys."

"What did she mean by being controlled?"

"Ehm, she said she'd been raped more than once."

"But that was never investigated."

"It was. But the case was deferred. Because she actually looked and behaved like a criminal. Her language . . ."

"Language?"

"She called the cop a motherfucker and sonofabitch."

"Her language."

"She should have been glad to have gotten off with a warning."

"You didn't believe her."

"She wasn't trustworthy. She came from a socially deprived background. She drinks and probably does drugs too. She has a record of truancy."

"If your boss had a fourteen-year-old daughter and if she reported a rape, would you also just shrug it off?"

"Excuse me—"

"You must try the duck."

"No, thanks."

"It's delicious. Cured for just the right length of time over the right kind of wood. Not fatty at all."

"If we pay you, and we will pay as much as you ask, will you try to persuade your superiors to reopen the case?"

"But there's nothing to reopen."

"You are smart and competent. The best in town. Ingrid knows that."

"You mean the lady who has sent you, Ingrid Wiesenthal?"

"She wasn't able to come. We are *only* here on her behalf."

"There wasn't enough evidence. Except . . . they found traces of DNA in her underwear that belonged to the man she referred to as the boss. The owner of the Uxor-Hiom restaurant. But later she withdrew her testimony. She said he was her boyfriend."

"But he's over forty."

"What if she went with him voluntarily?"

"And what if she didn't? You can't squeeze blood from a stone. You must try these wood-ear mushrooms."

"Thanks, but I really can't. That's not enough evidence."

"We will find the evidence."

"Are you related to her family?"

Now, for the first time, Diana speaks up, softly. She strokes the Lynx's face. Her thumb goes over her cheekbone, tracing a line modeled on the war path of native Indian women and wood bees.

"We're all family, my dear."

◇

Each of their nests follows the same rule: cuckoos are let in to sit on the eggs. Branches of QUAIL Studios maintain close ties with the SWALLOW Media Group, which is headed by neither men nor women. Cuckoos don't live in couples and are known as nest parasites and for the ravenous hunger of their chicks. These isolated individuals are detached and dispassionate and cannot allow themselves to be infested with the dandelion fluff of prejudice, they must not go native and adapt to the local culture—what's there to admire in the darkness anyway. The next purple cross caught in the net of Birgit's words rings a bell with the Detective. It sent crowds out into the streets, a wave of protests coursed through the land, even gods and geniuses lose their sword one day, shush.

As they fly, the swallows see such joys playing out daily across the world. A twenty-three-year-old student was the victim of a brutal gang rape. She suffered brain damage as well as abdominal and lung infections. She didn't survive her injuries.

The Detective's hand reaches for another azure-blue notebook, his eyes gliding over the hummingbird handwriting. The student had been to see the old British movie, *Close Encounter*, with her boyfriend. It had gotten late and there were no rickshaws to take them home. A private bus pulled up and offered them a ride. The windows on the bus were blacked out. She was assaulted on the bus. Her boyfriend was struck by a metal rod. She tried to call the police. The men took her cell phone and dumped their bodies on the road. Not a single car driving past stopped. They would slow down, glance at the naked bodies, and drive on. Police arrived after several very long, oh so charmingly long minutes. As they stood over the warm bodies, they argued as to whose jurisdiction they came under.

The police drove to the nearest hotel to borrow some torn sheets to cover the naked bodies. The girl was bleeding heavily.

The Detective dashes to the computer, the abacus in his head buzzing, sending red beads flying, he shuffles them back and forth, the records in the ledger coalesce; the sums in the columns on the screen tally with the numbers jotted down in the margin of the azure notebook. What a splendid, crazy child's game, better than Monopoly. The money travels to filmmakers and predatory attorneys. And first and foremost, to the media.

The Petřín sun keeps a particularly close watch over the media response. The media stir up the neighborhood where the cuckoos' nests are located; as soon as the eggs hatch, they make orchestras roar under the powerful baton of an eagle's wing. Professionally, deliberately, calmly, the conductors make use of advertising agencies and counseling services. First the case is dramatically blown up by comments on the internet, on a global scale, fly, swallow, fly. The Detective finds TV reports on the case. They don't frighten him.

What frightens him more are the cackling and warbling voices echoing through this maze of orange and dark yellow. What frightens him is the link between the long-forgotten colors of the Austro-Hungarian empire and the goings-on in a flock of wild geese.

The dependably calm and detached way the world once spoke to him used to serve as a protective glass wall behind which the Detective used to live. That wall has been shattered by words. The tangle of information and the online noise used not to seem real; it might have been, but equally it might not have. His body, though, *is* real.

The Detective's body itches, truth is like scabies. He is standing by the roadside, holding a grubby hotel sheet with yellow stains. He is linked to the body of the Indian policeman standing by a flashing rectangle. He doesn't want to be linked to him. But they are glued to each other by swallows' saliva. Swallows with sugar candy in their beaks glue the whole world together.

The dead girl's father goes on television and delivers an emotional speech. His face turned to stone, his words like the lashes of a riding crop, all the kind words of this world stand to attention—in action, not in books; the press conference has been co-organized by SWALLOW, a local film and media agency that helped prep the girl's father for his appearance. A trembling hand holds a photo of the girl, even though Indian legislation prohibits making public the identity of a rape victim. The father yells that he has agreed to speak on television to make sure that other victims are not afraid to report rape to the police and so that the perpetrators are caught.

His final sentences visibly don't roll off his tongue, they struggle to pass his lips, they haven't originated in his own head, his subconscious is trying to stop him from uttering them, it feels like a betrayal of his beloved clan, there is astonishment in his eyes—if you engage in combat, why should you mind touching another, inferior body, a lower-caste body, he has done it, too, the *only* thing one should avoid is to cause death. After all, isn't a bus with blacked-out windows a well-known and tolerated trap for women? Self-service on wheels?

Surely they have buses like that in other countries?

The illiterate father of the raped Indian girl breaks down in tears. He wrings his hands; the six assailants deserve to be hanged. Especially the one who was a minor at the time, who raped the student after she lost consciousness. He was the one who suggested they throw her out of the moving bus. Now he is the one playing the part of a victim, claiming that it was an organized, brave, proud, and unflinching political protest, the girl had been to see a *British* film, all things British still have to be boycotted because the Brits had made India stew in a pot for so long, in the late nineteenth century they intentionally let millions of Indians die of starvation, this kind of fascism mustn't be forgotten, and those in power know that what works best is to point a finger at an enemy group, someone who is not one of us, kicking them down the ladder to humiliate it.

But a daughter's body is not a battlefield. Or is it?

The girl's father makes a public appeal in support of legislative changes. He has thought it through, he wants the amendment to be read out and tells everyone not to be afraid, to add their signature and their support, this is the email address to write to . . .

On the desk before the Detective lies the jumble of the father's utterances, his polished speech and the draft amendment. Each and every word has been drafted in the hummingbird handwriting. He replays the recording, double-checks what was said, an obsessive interpreter, obsessive translator. The first draft is in Czech. More brushed up versions are in languages he doesn't understand, those are not in the hummingbird handwriting: Hindi and Urdu, Bengali, Nepalese, Romani. But here again, a fountain pen could not resist a squeak, a sarcastic purple smudge: *A bunch of Indo-European languages, the gentlemen pretend to be unable to communicate with one another and turn up their noses at the swallows.*

A blast of cold air. Fall is turning to winter, looking for a way out. Like that swallow below the rafters of the family home on the outskirts of Prague that flew around in circles in search of the dormer window. How many ideas will be sown and set off by purple Japanese cherry blossoms, a silk moth, and the sighing of the fall wind.

◇

Diana has finished her chrysanthemum tea. A clump of white blossoms is left at the bottom of the kettle, having turned gray and yellow at their center. Birgit sips purple plum wine from a small cup. The Lynx orders a bottle of Tsingtao beer and some mineral water. Erika asks for a café au lait. The Chinese waitress gives her a meaningful smile. And serves the coffee black. No sugar, no milk.

"I love it," says Erika, looking the waitress in the eye, in a language the Chinese woman doesn't understand. "This is not about food. It's about philosophy. Achieving perfect harmony through the unity of opposites, yin and yang."

"I've got to go. I have to get back to work." The Lynx takes a sip of mineral water.

"Yin and yang exist not only in the spiritual sphere. Yin is soft, cold, dark, and feminine. Yang is strong, warm, light and masculine.

My cooking is different. There is a unity to it, to me cooking is not a unity of opposites, it's *only* unity."

Birgit's eyes glance at the Chinese waitress padding around. "They are capable of killing a daughter soon after she's born because she is worth less than a son." Birgit's eyes smile. The Chinese woman smiles back.

The Lynx doesn't understand Birgit's clacking words.

"Excuse me, what language was that?"

"Czech."

"Chechen?"

"No, Czech."

"I really gotta go."

Small talk bounces around the table—weather, kids, family, politics. Birgit lays it on thick, to put the Lynx at ease: she, too is a mother of three, one of her sons, a doctor, lives in Zurich and two are lawyers working for a law firm they took over from Max Adler; she has a granddaughter, as well as a grandson who is a gynecologist, and there is also a great-grandson whom she has yet to meet; when she is not so busy, she'll have him over for a vacation for a week, maybe, hmmm.

Birgit is about to add something when Diana's cup of chrysanthemum tea lands abruptly on the saucer with a clink. Birgit withdraws into her shell, then leans closer to the Lynx's ear.

"Break words with a pickaxe like frozen soil. Hack at them like there's no tomorrow. To make them hatch and fly off, nimble and truthful. Quickly, before the world tames them and teaches them to lie. Words communicate with one another, absorbing stories, adapting, conforming. Their ego grows weaker. But it's still in there, chirruping softly," Birgit's lips whisper into the curve of the Lynx's ear. "I am a sociable person. For the sake of men, for the sake of the more gutless part of my ego. I used to be sociable for the sake of children, to show that it's good for them to stay in lively and cheerful contact with others. It's what's called being in touch with the world."

The Lynx is unnerved. The cup of chrysanthemum tea clinks resolutely on the saucer for the second time, and breaks.

They leave the Chinese restaurant. The untouched bottle of Tsingtao beer is left behind on the table, the Chinese waitress by its side. Her smile evaporates.

Outside it is overcast, the wind chasing gray, frightened shreds of cloud. Diana's mind flies to the Fresian island of Amrum, close to the Danish coast, its broad beach with sand as fine as dust and a sky that is free. Dunes like humps of resting camels, birches like brooms turned upside down, sweeping the sky clean of clouds and lynxes. When it rains, the clouds shoot gray arrows.

The Lynx heads for her car. Diana beckons to her as if she'd forgotten something. The Lynx cuts the engine. She winds down the window, her expression noncommittal, the face of a clerk at a railway station giving information on the arrival and departure of trains that don't stop there. Diana is the one who provides the information.

"This is not about the rape."

"What, then?"

"It is about humiliation. A body remembers being humiliated and unless it gets justice, its behavior remains affected for the rest of its life. It demands more humiliation."

◇

The Detective pieces together little fragments, gluing them into a swallow mosaic. He weeds out daisies, free spirits growing beside flowerbeds. Why can't a daisy be Pope?

The Detective is at his computer, from breakfast until bedtime. He investigates, waging his own, highly-strung, private battle. He thought he was living in the heart of a city, a country, a nation, and a continent where he was safe and *outside.* Outside of events, photos, and news breaking predictably behind the backs of beautiful, smartly dressed, smiling women and men in fancy TV studios.

He is not safe. Why should I, of all people, be dragged into something that I'm not up to, something hanging in the global atmosphere, and what's this fucking global atmosphere anyway, why do I have to get involved in something that police and intelligence agencies in other countries should deal with, why do I have to be involved in something that's been distilled, that will suck me in and destroy me. Old Europe's cycle of civilization is nearing its end.

Which country's police force is in charge, what kind of supranational force is this, and what the hell is this whole thing about? They control one another but is anyone in control of them? All this could be just a clever game. Bored elderly ladies in a house at the foot of Petřín Hill playing dominoes. With swallows as invisible assistants in a computer game.

They are playing with technology that is not of their era.

It is the dead man from the glass house on the outskirts of Prague who mocks him, dragging him into the eye of the storm. A stray swallow has led him to a cunning flock. An individual case that forms part of a whole, with the context changing constantly: what started out as the central case has turned into a minor detail, a discarded dot on the canvas of an impressionist. What kind of a vicious game is this?

Not even a flash of lightning is straightforward. The Detective takes his cell phone and goes online. While a superior may start a fire, others are not allowed to even light a candle. He punches in the word

SWALLOW. Bodies of various species of swallow come up. Startlingly long wings and short bills, courage, perseverance, and more courage, three claws in the front, one at the back; the courage of angels, reams of articles and comments. Outstanding flyers, swallows are found in every corner of the world. They feed on insects, which they hunt on the wing; they have a highly developed capacity for communicating and signaling, they communicate visually as well as by the way they fly. A barn swallow sports black feathers, a red patch under the beak, and has a yellow and white rump and breast; it builds cup nests inside houses. The common house martin is also black, with white tail streamers, a white rump and a slightly forked tail; it builds closed nests with a round entrance on walls. Bank swallows are gray-brown and nest in burrows at the ends of tunnels bored into sand or gravel.

The Detective adds a forked tail to flesh and feathers, typing in *film distribution.* An international express rolls up on his phone: lists of foreign branches, sister and daughter companies. SWALLOW, Inc. was founded after the war by someone by the name of Ingrid Kafka, who died by her own hand in 1957: she hanged herself, and her final wish was that her gravestone be inscribed with the name Ingrid Wiesenthal. SWALLOW, Inc. buys up exclusive movie rights to synopses and scripts for feature films and documentaries, co-organizes film festivals and retrospectives, sets up and co-finances national film archives. Over the past ten years it has collaborated with Ted Turner and Sheikh Hamad bin Khalifa al Thani, reaching 360 million households across multiple countries and regions. The networks overlap, the networks don't tear, mingling and consolidating instead. But ideas can't be translated into wealth without social contacts; even in the era of the World Wide Web it is not enough to have access *only* to an electromagnetic frequency; a high-speed internet connection is not sufficient to establish a new network, it says on SWALLOW.COM The final destinations of the rays of sun emanating from the orange house multiply in the Detective's notebook, filling a heavy sack; addresses carried in beaks of swallows.

It is a straightforward, direct flight.

A flight of swallows no one is aware of, as they are simply here, and if they're not, they will come back. They know when the time has come for them to leave their native nest and when the time has come to return to it. They are not afraid to return despite knowing what they know.

It is simple, straightforward, and ever so neat, not a complex espionage thriller, trees don't move without a breeze, you *only* need to know your way around this tangle, comb through the roots, the fixed points and links to intelligence services around the world, CIA, NSA, MI6, and GCHQ, nests within nests, a kingdom of European and non-European cities, you *only* need to set up a wiretap, steal some passwords, and know the sound the silk moth makes, measure the length of wings and the sharpness of beaks. All the three sun ladies do is set out for a little trip every now and then, as if there was nothing happening.

Money travels from the orange house at the foot of Petřín Hill on swallows' wings. The house spits and breathes a sigh of relief, stretching its back until its bones crack. Finally, someone has cracked it. The case of the rattling bus, perfectly pieced together.

A considerable sum of money also found its way into the pocket of the raped girl's father, that was the *only* reason he agreed to name his daughter publicly. Words and banknotes stream out of the house at the foot of Petřín Hill to ensure that the bus with the blacked-out windows doesn't get buried in the anonymous traffic of global public transit, to make sure it is aired in public. The public is a Golem, it needs a *shem*, the magic word to be placed in a hollow in its forehead so that it can decipher and properly interpret what it has seen and heard. The rest of the world remains unreadable.

The Detective's body has grown heavy, he can't breathe in this maze.

Arrogantly, the house at the foot of Petřín Hill teaches the police a lesson. Its message is that this is not *only* about rape.

It proclaims that rape *is* a crime.

He can no long bear to see the word, hear it, feel it, or taste it. It makes him nauseous. The word is stuck to his forehead as well as below it. His skull is crushed by falling leaves. The house at the foot of Petřín Hill can rejoice; it has a gotten a hold on the Detective. The Detective feels he is being watched by the eyes of a stranger. Eavesdropped on by the ears of a stranger. He feels like he is being recorded and documented by a hidden camera, actually, two cameras, no, three.

He is not surprised to spot purple crosses hanging above the names of all the policemen who had bickered over the naked bodies by the roadside.

The Detective's phone beeps.

He doesn't reply to the old Doctor's merlin call. The Detective opens his eyes, his eyelashes scorched by fire.

Some children are so traumatized by what they saw that they don't speak for years.

The Widow is playing with her child, aware of the Detective's unshaven cheeks. She is aware of the stubble on his face and the bags under his eyes. She is in love, and she is scared of being in love. She doesn't expect her feelings to be reciprocated.

She is afraid, believing that at this stage of widowhood and orphanhood she is not allowed to be in love. It would be unseemly.

Instead, she is supposed to embalm herself in grief, grief is to be her *only* perfume. She should be left alone. In order to gain perspective. All mothers claim that when God closes the door, he opens a window, but which one and when, I'd like to know. She can't help it, he has taken hold of her, yes that's right, a bird is able to fly again and it doesn't find it surprising.

The woman lulls her child to sleep, pressing her forehead to his warm face.

The Detective is weary. He has dozed off on the sofa. He wakes up, standing up shakily. His bulging eyes are bloodshot. He is about to say something. She stops him.

"I don't want to know what you're up to when you're not here with me. I want to trust you, I don't want to be afraid and insecure."

She leans her head on his chest, unbuttons his shirt, buries her nose in the dark growth and inhales. He strokes her fair hair, caressing the smooth surface, a ginger streak sparkles in it, a ginger spot under his beak. He strokes her back, tracing two large, rounded clefs along her spine.

The Widow peels herself off. She brings glasses and a bottle of chilled white wine, Pinot Grigio from Cantina Tramin. The Detective takes the bottle from her and opens it. They kiss and he pushes her before him like a bulldozer, heading for the bedroom. The Widow moves backward.

They make love. For her, sexual passion is a value added. For him, sexual passion is salvation. A safety net that lets him forget the world of swallows, that lets him forget himself.

The Widow leans her head on his shoulder. The Detective gets up. He needs a cigarette. He puts on his black boxers. As he stands half-naked on the glass-fronted terrace, in view of the whole world from the level of wings, he feels lost. The glass is fragile. The Widow puts on a silk robe with Chinese characters. She brings the glasses with wine. The Detective raises a toast to her but he is not really here. "Hello. I'm here," she says, "and I love you."

He shoots her a surprised look. Gives her hug. His memories are enmeshed in meanings that words cannot convey. Something that happened in the past may or may not have seemed important at the time. But memory imbues it with gravity, making tears roll down his cheek for no apparent reason; he would like to unburden himself, teeters on the edge, the glass shatters but this is not a breakdown. Outside the air is teeming with tiny white bellies and yellow-and-white chests with ginger spots under their beaks. The Detective rests his hand on the glass; a white belly on the other side rubs past him in flight.

The Widow is on her fourth glass. The Detective has started his eighth. The wine comes from the hanged man's special deliveries from France and Italy. His favorite dish was coq au vin: "That's the kind of wine I like, the rest is just plonk," he used to rail.

I don't want to know this, thinks the Detective, I really don't. He downs a shot of whiskey between the glasses of wine.

A voice inside the Detective mutters that it's all pointless, his work as well as his life are pointless. He directs the glassy-eyed tension at the Widow, accosting the silk robe, aiming lozenge-shaped shards at her. She is a great lay. The Detective demands that she lists every single man she's ever fondled, ever kissed, ever necked, ever made out with, and ever slept with; his faltering voice on the attack, he insists that she lists their names and addresses, discloses who and where and when taught her body to make love so passionately, trained her mouth to give such perfect blow jobs, come on, say the word, say it, say fuck, spit it out, don't run away, don't try to weasel out of it, stay here, damn you.

The Detective flies off the handle, his voice savage, his finger on the trigger. The despair raging inside him slyly eggs on the rattled voice. Who knows if the respectable Widow isn't *only* pretending to be in love with him, the accomplished gold digger, the accomplished platinum digger that she is. It's his turn now. She's lost no time twisting him around her little finger, surely he is *only* one part of her clever scheme to sweep every trace under the carpet, having been the prime suspect all along, she's so cunning, so crafty, so wily, like the swallows flitting around as if nothing happened, taking off with their white chests whenever and wherever they feel like it. They just whiz past, simplifying everything and there's no way to make them testify.

The tortured voice soars to the virtuoso high-note of a bird of prey, a note of evil the Detective never knew he'd been stifling inside. As the highest note screams out and the glass on the terrace shatters, he sees reflected in the Widow's blurred face a confusing mix of painful memories, faces of all the girls and women who have ever betrayed him, deceived him, cheated on him, or abandoned him. You are incapable of love, you *only* love yourself and your child. And as if that wasn't enough, I now have to deal with those crazy, unhinged females who have gotten hold of a house at the foot of Petřín Hill, that hovel that has robbed me of sleep, with cats caterwauling all around and that scrawny black dog that's always there, sitting on the cobblestones outside.

"We're either going to kill each other or we'll stay together until the day we die," the Detective's voice barks before breaking off.

So both options are still on the table.

Furtively, the Widow removes the amber bottles from the Detective's reach. She tries to lighten his mood. She gazes at the drunken man with sober eyes; she won't drink any more. She tries to bottle up his anxiety with black humor, her gentle touch, a smile. She tries to make his bad temper fade away. In vain.

The Widow recoils. She resumes drinking. She hits the bottle. Her gestures, pumped up by alcohol, grow coarser. Her voice, now brazen, snaps at the Detective.

Yes, she *is* independent. And she won't have anyone order her around anymore. What is it that the Detective really wants to hear?

"What I want? I wanna know about your best friend!"

"My best friend?"

"Yes, your best friend. You have this friend who reminds me of Stadtherr."

But what does he want to know?

"Everything."

"All right, let me tell you everything about her. Admittedly, she behaves like a man, she doesn't take men seriously, but she does take sex seriously. And that takes guts! For men sex is a feather in their cap, but you know that, don't you? For a woman, it's a way of making the relationship more intimate, but that's presumably news to you! And each gets what they want. Their intentions are different, hm, one or the other ends up being deceived, hm. Yes, she is just as promiscuous as heterosexual men. She may even be more promiscuous than homosexual men.

"There is *only* one thing she's after, just like men. She collects these feathers for her cap. Sex is joy. It's her contribution to the history of joy. No one has ever been able to control her, to understand her fully or to put up with her. What surprises me is that you should find this surprising. When men have a choice between their sixty-year-old wife and a mistress who is twenty or thirty years younger, bodies of older men know which one to choose to revive them. Older men can't just forgive or forget. They get more excited about men with whom they work and with whom they conquer the world than by women they sleep with.

"My friend simply doesn't understand the word adultery. She was astonished when her husband was furious *only* because she did the same thing he did: took control of her orgasms. She has never been unfaithful. She has never promised to be faithful. She doesn't understand what faithfulness means, it has vanished from her flock of words. She has never asked men for anything. She has given birth to children. While her heart took a nap, she snuck out on it. Her mind and body disconnected. She has never been with a man more than once and in parting she has never said, see you again. She offered men a refuge. A nest from the outside world. But they felt weakened and baffled by this, a femininity that didn't levy a tax in the form of jealousy. Men's superficial understanding of women gave her an advantage. It's known as polyandry. She behaved like an ordinary, confident male."

"Has that cunt told you any details?"

"Details?"

"Yeah, details."

"There are bodies that are *old* and vain and care *only* about themselves, about endurance and big challenges, a surfeit of broad-mindedness that masks pride. There are bodies that are *young* and vain and that care *only* about themselves, about endurance and big challenges, a surfeit of broad-mindedness that masks pride. She didn't cheat. She would let them bite off a little piece of gingerbread and help them calm down. She offered them a non-threatening nest. She saw *only* the best in them, fanning sparks of forgotten dreams. She tried to persuade them not to give up if they grew weary in their twenties, thirties, forties, or fifties, in their sixties or even seventies. She told them not to leave their wives and partners. To spend time with their children. Right from the get-go, she made it clear that she wasn't expecting a relationship or emotions, that this was *only* about sex. Initially, they breathed a sigh of relief. Oh, what a marvelous woman! Oh, the heavenly music of candid words! She validated their own image of themselves. They needed an opinionated woman, one who was clever, lively, and independent, while at the same time totally and unconditionally devoted to them. The minute they started demanding a more intimate and possessive relationship, the minute they tried to break through to her *ego* and tried to control, transform, and enfeeble it, she pointed them toward other women and pushed them away. She felt safe in this male club *only* as a part of the whole, that way she wasn't at the mercy of any single tree-creeper or raven, waxwing or self-heal. They used to come and drink from her as from a fresh spring. It felt natural and wonderful. Each and every one of them she gave *only* the part of herself they could reach and they were aware of, that was the *only* way they wouldn't be frightened by her intensity. She never wanted anything from them. She never wants anything from them."

"You will dump this friend!"

"She's the *only* friend I'll keep."

The voices jangle and scream, wreaking havoc in the room.

"Let me tell you one more thing about her."

"No, I don't want to hear another word about that woman!"

"Why do we have to talk *only* about you all the time, I want you to listen to me, for a change! She would break up with them without any regrets, always calm and matter-of-fact. They used her as their Christmas tree, on which to hang their hope that *she* would change *their* lives radically. They wanted her to be a driver of change, but only for them. They never spared a thought for her life. Instead, she was to be there for their bodies, their souls, their dreams, and their new beginnings, and new offspring would fit neatly into the picture.

They didn't bother asking her. They never wondered whether she wanted to change her life. Men who *only* wanted their bit of fun. Men are clever, they know how to wriggle out of things and distract attention from their amoral actions, just like women. They would hurl insults at her, reminding her that twenty or thirty years from now she wouldn't escape menopause. At the same time, they longed to erase the trench of age between their bodies. As if menopause were not a part of the body, but the socially recognized brand of inferiority, a brand on vulnerable, cast-off bodies. As if she ought to jump for joy just because they took notice of her. Instead of thanking her for the time *she'd* given them. She told me that she was looking forward to striding through life gracefully after menopause."

"She's pathetic," yells the Detective.

"Why? Is it her fault that the world is infested with seventy- and eighty-year-old fathers?"

"How old is she?"

"She lies to them about her age. She knows that the brain is sensitive to numerals. She offers her body *only* to men who don't whine. She enjoys a life that is easy to grab by the scruff of the neck, because this mendacious world we live in is a dream, not a world. The bitterness of men who've been cheated on *for the first* time while they've been cheating on their wives all their lives is insidious and it will die with them. She has sprinkled a little water of life on them and sent them back refreshed, to the wives they were ready to ditch without a second thought. To her this degree of cowardice is offensive. They stay with their wives although they don't want to be with them. With wives who humiliate them, going through their email and phones, the pockets of their jackets and pants. Wives to whom they have to report every hour. Wives who are nevertheless cheated on all their lives and don't have the faintest notion of the illegitimate children their husbands have fathered."

"How do you know all this?"

"She's told me everything, I'm the only one who knows. They don't have the courage to leave with grace and pride and live on their own, in a one-room apartment if need be, they are too chicken-livered to give up their creature comforts, cooked lunches, hot dinners, and tedious sex, and to wait instead until they meet someone *for whom* they might leave home; they wait for some incentive but once that is gone, they crawl back into their shells. She would send them back onto the beaten track and they could no longer pretend that the track didn't exist. They were furious, she had trodden on their toes. They were used to being the ones who did the dumping. It made them furious that she humiliated their manhood, their erect mast, pumped up and stimulated by pills. She wasn't searching for young flesh. She was looking for a body not hardened under a crust of consummately concocted lies, shod in tailor-made footwear and expensive jackets. They thought they had failed as lovers, that was their sensitive spot, they aspired to be the world's greatest lovers, and the cleverest ones too, they boasted they had figured out how to achieve a four-hour erection and were ecstatic about still being up to it. They wouldn't have been half so furious had she been less successful, less authentic, less strong, if she had faked her orgasms, or if they had been the ones saying the things she said. That's not what you call love, honey, a great fuck is all it was, honey, let's call a spade a spade."

"And you?"

"What about me?"

"What did you say?"

"I pointed out to her that narcissism is equally enabled and nourished by wives who dominate their husbands, while silently ironing their synthetic pants and jeans, who fuss about their husbands and serve them in fear of younger women, and seeing as the flocks of younger women grow with every passing year, they build a wall of apartments and houses with gardens, of vacations in Thailand and Brazil; cycling holidays in the Dolomites, and skiing in the Alps with their elite friends, a wall of weekend cottages where every object has its immutable place, opening them in the spring and closing them for the winter. Year after year, decade after decade. Places where they've parked the joy of their bodies. Where they've parked the truth."

"I don't wanna listen to that."

"But I love her."

"I hate her."

"She is not afraid of being alone. She behaves like a man, but without being possessive. She doesn't demand blind loyalty. She wants freedom and she gives freedom. She is not possessive of anyone, doesn't have the slightest understanding of such a notion. What she fails to realize is that she is hated by both men and women. She doesn't realize that she disrupts the peace because the petit-bourgeois don't want to see their lives for what they are. What she does understand is that those who just go along for the ride are the worst. Worse than the Nazis or the Communists, worse than murderers. They never take any real risks and never really help anyone."

"You're going to dump that friend."

"She's the *only friend* I'll keep."

The voices have been enlisted to serve as recce and attack units for the bodies. The voices hurt each other, brandishing words preemptively to avoid hurting the bodies, the nesting places of souls. To prevent the hearts from bleeding, hmmm. The voices ooze uncertainty as to whether the other really means it—and how far. The bodies are scared, choked with old and profound experiences of relationships in which one always gives while the other always takes. The bodies know that this is the *only* moment when the roles diverge.

The Widow gets up. She staggers into the bedroom with her glass. Her body in the shimmering robe sprawls provocatively across the entire bed. Leaving no room for another body. She falls asleep instantly.

The Detective puts on his shirt and pants, tightens his belt. Once dressed, he sits on an armchair. He pushes the armchair closer to the bed. He watches her.

He reads the Chinese characters on her shiny robe. No, I'm not letting myself go into this. We'll end up killing one another.

He gets up. Goes out into the street.

He drops by a Vietnamese convenience store for booze, stowing it in a paper bag as a night streetcar, this time without any homeless people, rattles past. His body is a vagrant looking for shelter. He finds it in the orange house at the foot of Petřín Hill. The foot gives the scrawny black dog a kick. The dog doesn't even give a whine.

The Detective collapses onto the white bed in the guest room. He stares at the ceiling. Stares at the matching spines of Birgit Stadtherr's books. Lovemaking is connected to love, fucking to rage. He sticks his tongue out at the spines of the books and takes sips from the brown bag. Life, wonderful, glorious life.

A few hours later he receives a call from the Widow. The Detective sticks his tongue out at the sobbing phone. His hand picks up.

His voice is slick with drink like the wings of birds smothered in an oil spill.

"It's all because of my fucking character. I'm an asshole. I want *only* the best for others and to give them *only* the best, and then I end up beating myself up for being a kind-hearted idiot and hurting myself."

The Widow's voice sobers up: "But how do you know what's best for others? You've got to protect your boundaries. *I* will help you protect them."

She asks cautiously: "Surely you don't feel like that about me? You don't regret wanting *only* the best for me?"

"But I do," he snaps.

Anxiety stifles the Widow, she is on the verge of tears, but she continues to nag him, she wants to hear what he has to say while fearing what she might hear. She's about to lose her mind. Drunken speech fills her ears.

"You'll be back on top again, as soon as you've found the right man, you demimondaine, you won't have to worry about causing a scandal anymore. His death will soon be yesterday's news. And the scandal hasn't made you any different from clean-living women, but your money sets you apart from sluts. Your cunt is a time bomb. It's not that complicated. Just see what happens when the woman in you finally wakes up. I've seen your fuck-me eyes. *A single cunt against the stream can pull up to four boats against the current*, I'm quoting Stadtherr here, why aren't you laughing? There are all kinds of little things about you I find annoying. I bet you feel the same about me. It's in our nature, that's what emotions are about."

"What kinds of little things?"

"Investigating, are we, Miss Marple? I can't tell you just like that, without context, I'd have to explain it in the context of my life. It's quite banal, really. I'm like this cop I work with. He's got two young kids and as he gets older, all he wants is to move to his weekend cottage and live there on his own because his wife *only* takes and takes, and doesn't give him anything."

"But what is it you can't stand about me?"

The drunken voice falls silent, trees don't move without a breeze, the drunken voice rouses the body and sends it out into the streets for another brown paper bag. He doesn't know how much torment he's causing her. He doesn't realize that he is losing her. She has offered all of herself to him. Dejected, she pulls away, feeling beaten up like the scrawny stray dog. She knows there is no point trying to explain, she has to wait for the body to sober up; he doesn't have an issue with her, he *only* has an issue with himself. And he doesn't realize it.

Early in the morning, after a sleepless night, she sends him a text message.

If you want to lose me, you're doing pretty well.

Welcome to relationships, my little partridge. Relationships are painful, says a signal sent by her body.

The man wakes up in the orange house. He replies right away. *I love you. I'm sorry, I'm the problem, I keep wanting to help others, I want the best for everyone, and my mood fluctuates, I feel depressed, destructive, you name it. It's all because of my fucking character, I'm difficult, I'll try to explain in person.*

The woman kisses the phone. Grateful that he's not lying to her. Even though he is taking a big risk.

No need to apologize, we'll work it out, I have your back, the main thing is to talk about it, I'm so glad you replied, you can't imagine how glad I am, I felt awful, all broken, there's still stuff I don't understand but I want to, I love you, kisses all over. I can smell you on the pillow where your head was.

The voices soften and begin to retreat from the battlefield, lugging the armor of embarrassing words and leaving their tormented bodies behind.

As a new day dawns, the man barges into the glass house. He is repentant, ashamed. Words are inadequate. Words can cause a lot of damage but they can't make amends. Doubts and fear speak from both of them. What if they hurt each other. What if the other has been taking the history of joy for a ride.

But no, neither of them has. Heavy breathing sends a signal from both bodies. Closeness, distance, and isolation. Nothing less is at stake here, this is the *only* thing that is at stake here. Flaring nostrils, signaling safety and trust. They have survived this wild ride along hairpin bends. Swallows on telegraph wires don't bother rearranging themselves, they have watched boring scenes like this played out by humans all over the world for centuries, they are not surprised.

The house retches.

The Detective will collect everything he's seen so far, leach it, and pluck it out like the stone of a purple plum. He'll start from scratch. He'll distill the plum brandy and then distill what's been distilled once again.

The *only* cases that have been firmly closed are the faded ones dating back to the war—1945 in particular has been pampered, ironed, vetted, weighed, measured, photographed, shaved, soaped and a neat bow has been tied around it. The backs of the musty photographs bear the blurry official stamp of an intelligence agency, a date, and the name of a young photographer, Diana Bussard. The rugged years 1933 through to 1946 have been retrospectively combed through and weeded. The fifties and sixties not quite so thoroughly. The records have been kept by a firm hand. Some are in the childlike hummingbird handwriting, tottering on the lines of bent telegraph wires that belong to someone else; swallows flock together, not surprised by evildoers. Instead of the letter M written on the lids of current boxes, the old ones are branded with the cleavage of a letter V: a split swallow's tail.

A V like a pair of spread legs. A V like a slice of bread that's been bitten into. A V like a segment cut out of a round cookie. V like violence, V like all those vanished, vilified, blotted out crimes that no one in a position of power had seriously pursued or regarded as war crimes in their own right. V like victims who knew there was no point fighting for justice denied, victims who knew that their call for justice would fall on deaf ears and who were treated by the authorities in a perfunctory way, as in the case of the gentle seventeen-year-old Indian girl. None of them had been taken seriously, their cases never logged, no investigation ever launched. Forgetting has been armed and decanted into bottles, the corkscrew nowhere to be seen.

Hand-picked cases relating to the fateful 1930s and '40s had been pursued doggedly and meticulously. Driven by a determination to find the lecherous villain, to vanquish him, make him vanish and to vindicate the victim, who has no idea that someone has taken up her case. Particular care has been lavished on adolescent girls, spatial orientation being another remarkable feature swallows are endowed with.

Reams of dredged-up cases dating back to World War II leap out at the Detective. Lists of names marked with a faded purple cross and the letter w tattooed on the wrist. War criminals. It is obvious what offence the terrified criminals are guilty of. Rape.

Purification. Deep cleansing. Once the decade has been scrubbed clean, a precarious split can be observed among the flock of swallows.

In the decades that follow, it is impossible to trace a single deep and continuous subterranean river. This is a time of tiresome, proliferating small rivulets and capillaries, of bodies under surveillance across the world. The flock disperses and the chief swallow, dressed in eagle's feathers, begins to run out of breath. It is not until the end of the fickle 1980s that a quail helps her find a new direction.

She devises a new strategy.

She no longer struggles to pick up every fallen body. She no longer tries to settle personal accounts. Her strength is redirected at gently protecting the whole flock. At transforming the unresponsive system. She picks out *only* one fledgling from the flock at a time, a fallen nestling, nailing down a representative case, pinning it to the banner, and generalizing from it. A swallow can estimate the general direction of flight, her sense of navigation allows her to adjust the flight path continuously and orient herself visually, guided by the sun and the stars. The swallow learns from seagulls, which use magnetic fields for orientation. She focuses her strength on changing the *legislation* of a given country. A swallow's kindness carries more weight than rulers' laws.

The Detective needs a drink.

This minute.

The Detective is in the Doctor's study.

"I haven't seen you for a while, my friend."

"I've been rather . . . rather . . . busy," says the Detective.

"Maybe I can help."

"I don't think so."

"I hear that the hanged man's case is about to be closed."

"Mmm."

"So another imaginary memorial candle in a Prague graveyard . . . I no longer care about guilt or innocence. In the context of our irrational lives, innocence could be guilt and vice versa. My *only* regret is that we'll never find out what all that trash under that man's manicured nails was about."

The Doctor pours his merlin whiskey, drops a few ice cubes into his glass, and gives it a stir. He hands the Detective a glass filled with some undiluted, amber-colored drink. The Doctor pushes his pipe to one side and offers the Detective a cigar. Turning around, he reaches over to the windowsill for an enormous glass ashtray.

"So what is she actually like?" his back asks after a while.

"Amazing," says the Detective, "just amazing."

"Mmm."

"And smart, she's got two degrees."

"Mmm."

"She quit work after she married him and became a housewife, a washerwoman, a cook, the model spouse. She also looks after her son, like a proper mom. We share the same sense of humor. And she's the best lay I've ever had."

"Well, well, well, I see you're smitten. Sounds too good to be true," the Doctor laughs through his cigar. The Detective takes a sip. A heavy silence descends.

"I don't care what you think, I don't care if you suspect I'm covering for her, I know she didn't kill him. It was suicide."

The Doctor smacks his lips. He balances his cigar on the rim of the ashtray. A passionate smoker, he holds the smoking pipe in his right hand and the glowing cigar in his left. He weighs up his options. First he puffs on the pipe. Then he draws on the cigar.

"I envy you. I myself have gone all stale and given up. My last girlfriend talked of love, then dragged me off to a swingers' party. I felt like a tired emperor at the fall of the Roman Empire, with her in the role of a drunken empress or Messalina, who frequented brothels and had sex with strangers. I bombed completely. I mean, in terms of group sex. Modern women scare me. They seem to know too much about us. And that does no one any good."

The Doctor puffs on his pipe. He puts the erect cigar to one side. Stretches out. "Why don't you come angling with me sometime? We could go to Norway and catch some cod. The North Sea will make you better. We could cure some cod roe while we're there. You seem tired. Your face is going blue. *Only* men have fishing rods there. You need a shave, by the way."

◇

Honey sashays confidently through the red and orange beaded curtain. She picks up some cash from the restaurant owner. He gives her a fleeting, friendly peck on both cheeks. She reports the number of fledglings recruited for the evening. Honey is highly disciplined. In daytime she sticks to her old routine; the day is not aware of her other life.

She goes to her music lessons and tickles the ivories. She studies languages.

She takes ballet.

Honey goes shopping with her mom. They take their time, have fun. Honey is picky.

Erika watches them through the windows of designer shops as they leave with their haul. Their car emerges from the underground parking lot. Erika doesn't take a taxi to follow them. She knows that the car will pull up in front of the family home. She knows they will cook dinner together, try out new recipes, assisted by Honey's dad. They will sit at the table. A holy, nuclear family. Honey has no siblings. After dinner, Honey practices the piano. Her parents withdraw to their respective studies to work. Honey gives them a kiss.

She holes up in her room. Does her homework and goes to bed. Her dad brings her a goodnight drink: a glass of hot milk with honey. She has to go to bed early because she is frail, she had a breakdown two years ago, went mute and didn't go out for two months. It was brought on by stress, she had pushed herself too hard, she is too strict with herself. After she got back on her feet, they didn't insist that she move on to a private middle school, she now does *only* the extracurricular activities she feels like doing. That's why her parents don't disturb her at night, she needs her rest and immutable order. The doctors have assured them that she'll be fine, it's not a mental disorder, although for a while, for some mysterious reason, she couldn't bear the sight of any males around the house. Even the man fixing their washing machine was allowed to come *only* when she wasn't home.

After nightfall, Honey leaves the house by the back door, her uncoupled body tarted up, glittering like a sheet of glass, with fuck-me eyes.

Erika is usually there, waiting for her.

Erika walks into the Uxor-Hiom restaurant. Yusuf shows her to a table by the window. Two older men smoking cigarettes and tapping their feet to the music give her an indifferent glance.

Erika orders a flaky pastry dripping with honey and a glass of strong tea. She makes notes in tiny handwriting. She keeps watch until nightfall. The restaurant fills up, swelling with blackcaps, wagtails, shrikes, and flycatchers. They sit around staring at the TV screen or their phones, the place is getting noisy. Three young men go over to the counter and borrow some eau de toilette; it is passed from hand to hand, cheeks are patted. Uxor-Hiomian music plays, the room fills with rhythm and fragrance. The two older men chain-smoke.

Erika goes to the restroom and looks around. A poster is pinned to the wall. An advert for Wonderbra. Erika scans the room. Frame by frame. A blink of the eye after blink of the eye. The window watches Honey as she walks through the castrated night, disappearing into the house across the street; corvids are the best songbirds that exhibit advanced patterns of behavior, they are omnivorous and can be found all over the world. Honey is walking arm in arm with two little budgerigars. The restaurant owner silences the long-drawn bedouin wailing: this is the sign the young men were waiting for. A parade of flycatchers, hunting for insects on short forays from their observation post, start to move forward. Collective thrashing of unripe grain. The night is abuzz.

Erika follows them into the street. She leans against the brick wall by the restaurant and scans the windows on the upper floor.

A new girl darts out into the night, a scraggy little budgie. A furious Honey storms out after her, there is stamping of studs and mares, shouting; they yell and fight. A man gets out of a car. He stops the shrieking leaky faucet. The budgie slips away and vanishes. Budgies have the avian world's most developed cerebrum. Erika can't keep up with her.

"You've got to track that girl down," says Diana. "She's new. She'll talk."

"But she . . ."

"Enough." Diana is not interested in details, that was the mistake she made at the start when she used to scrutinize every inch of a body, absorbing too much unnecessary minutiae. Sometimes she felt sorry for the body and gave in to indignation. Now she won't let her work be clogged up by emotional garbage. She is interested in the forest, not in the trees.

The budgie never again shows up in the neighborhood.

"She's from another school," notes Erika. "The birder is widening his hunting ground."

◇

Old cases pop up from oblivion before the Detective's eyes, no longer playing blind man's bluff. They crawl out, clamber into the light, the spores forming a chain. The Detective is at the computer, keeps rummaging online through messages from swallows even during office hours. His ears are buzzing. He can't sleep. Little red lights blink from long-forgotten times, flickering all over the world, blinding him. Lights come on in towns and villages, in country after country, flames blazing; there is no end to the sparks that have turned purple.

The orange house at the foot of Prague's Petřín Hill dabbles in everything. The vulture is a scavenger. It ladles broth into soup bowls. With a pair of tweezers, it picks up a purple cross and pins it down.

The Detective feels sorry for the man from the glass house on the outskirts of Prague, he had a donkey who served him well but wanted the animal to manage without hay, the man from the glass house on the outskirts of Prague has his own file here, in one of the shiny metal boxes, inside a plastic folder. The writer and her hummingbird hand found him boring, she took *only* a brief look at him, out of habit. No sign of the sharpness of vision, energy, and passion the hummingbird handwriting had expended on cases of girls and young women from wartime and the years that followed. This case represents for the hummingbird handwriting *only* a boring repeat offender, a moron, a deadbeat.

The Detective recognizes the photo of the man at a chessboard with the president, both men smiling. Rather than being displayed on the wall, the photograph is crumpled up.

The Detective is baffled by his own behavior. He doesn't know why he has kept this discovery to himself or why he is protecting the orange house and some old biddies he has never even met. He is not sure if he can trust his own shaken senses.

He is captivated by the files he's found in the ghost house, he cuts a solitary figure standing in the village square during a fête. He is the only one who feels guilty. For having broken into the house. He pulls himself together, he's got to get through the last remaining file. He tries to reassure himself that maybe he doesn't have all the facts yet: perhaps it will turn out that these are *only* film scripts.

He is lying to himself. He reads in a fog, so confused he can no longer tell victim from perpetrator. The alleged perpetrator *is* the victim.

The Detective wants to find evidence.

The closer he gets to the present day, the more the fog thickens. Cases break up like dry bread, crumbling in his hands, ready to be tossed to pigeons and swans. Also mentioned in the file on the man from the glass house on the outskirts of Prague is the president, who abused his wife and both sons; the file includes photos of the president's wife who used to hide her coal-black eyes under sunglasses in the 1980s but never said a word, and watched her voracious husband bring home young men, mostly lawyers. She covered for him. *A woman of granite*, a scribble on the photograph in purple handwriting comments sarcastically. *A woman of granite*—he has seen these words in the book by Birgit Stadtherr, the Detective recalls. That's how she referred to Rose Kennedy.

Why would someone collect and hoard this kind of stuff? What kind of depraved pleasure could someone be getting out of this?

He remains glued to the spot. Curiosity being a powerful mistress, he immerses himself in his reading. This is no longer *only* about cases of rape.

More V's come hurtling out of the red folders; bodies held in pincers, V as in violence and murder. The swallows pick the case of two murdered Kurdish girls for an investigation. The house at the foot of Petřín Hill sticks under the Detective's nose the realization that there are communities from which women have no way of escaping, no matter their location, that there are communities in which their fathers and brothers act like soldiers of an army, and even if they fail in everything else, there is one area over which they wield unlimited *power* of a kind one can only dream of; in this they never fail and that is why they will always resist change, always; this will always remain the *only* area that nourishes the exceptionality of their gender and religion, their confidence, strength, and vanity, and they carry their dominance with them wherever they go, no matter which corner of the world their family migrates to or gains political asylum in, because their daughters won't gain asylum *anywhere*. This is where they rule as kings and sovereigns, presiding over life and death. The bodies of their daughters, wives, and sisters are their dominions. And they can't understand why anyone should take them to task for exercising their power. It is what they were raised for.

There is the case of a brother who executes his own sister by firing two bullets at her at a bus stop. In another, a brother shoots dead his eighteen-year-old sister because she was dating a European man. That is, someone inferior, not chosen. The final solution. Five out of her eight siblings are indicted for helping to plan the retribution. After his daughter's murder, the father rewards his eldest son with a gold watch. The file contains a photo of the father sitting in a half empty courtroom, a purple cross hovering over his head. He was not found guilty even though he was the head of the family, even though in broken families servants usually betray their master. He was not found guilty although he could have stopped the murder. The father was not taken to court for being complicit in the murder, even though he was the one pulling the strings.

The father was later found dead.

He hanged himself in the attic of the Berlin tenement where he lived.

◇

They love each other and it's so straightforward.

She believes in him like in the holy scriptures. He believes in her like in the gospel.

At home the Detective revels in the sound of her name. He speaks it into the silence. "Aw, you."

At home the Widow revels in the sound of his name. She speaks it into the silence. "Aw, you."

On Saturday afternoon the Detective arrives at the glass house on the outskirts of Prague. Two female friends of the Widow are there, visiting with their kids. They are having a good time. The friends are taken aback, their eyes appraising the Detective's body. The Detective arouses their curiosity. The Widow proudly puts her arm around him. It is a gesture of trust.

Before long, the women go back to chatting. They revel in the torrent of words. The Detective finds their openness suspicious. They don't self-censor. One of the women picks up the thread of the conversation. She pings words to the Widow.

"So, imagine, we're sitting there, me, my husband, and some friends of ours."

A pair of orange lips turns to the Detective. "Just so you understand, one of our friends has left her husband because he treated her appallingly."

The orange lips continue. "So, we're sitting there and it never occurs to anyone to ask: why, what made her leave him. Instead, they're all panicking because a woman, a mother of four at that, has got herself an eighteen-year-old lover. Everyone is shocked. They've never been so upset about any other breakup. Not even about your husband's death, isn't that right?"

"It is."

"So now the men in the room are panicking, they've recently hit forty and started to form rock bands and that kind of stuff. And all of a sudden, she's a slut."

"I don't understand it," the other woman tells the orange lips, upset.

"Well, they see it as a direct assault, you see, on . . . how should I put it politely, you know, their . . ."

"But *why all that* panic?"

"Maybe they're scared that it's contagious and might spread. Imagine: high schools besieged by horny housewives."

They have a laugh. The Widow turns around sheepishly but the Detective is laughing along. The Widow is happy that he understands. Her two friends say goodbye. They offer to drop off the Widow's son at her parents', it's on their way.

The Detective is dog-tired. He's turned into a floppy rag doll that would fit into the Widow's handbag. He doesn't want to lie to the Widow. He isn't lying, but he isn't telling the truth, either, and this weighs heavily on his body. The Widow stretches her legs across his thighs. The Detective massages the soles of her bare feet in gentle circles.

"There's this house at the foot of Petřín Hill, with a kind of . . . special archive and library."

The Widow leans toward him and looks into his brown eyes. How about they go to her weekend house tomorrow, she'd like to show it to him. Her little boy will be at his grandparents'.

A clear message. A clear invitation. In the language of an untamed body. Sorry, he can't, he's got to go back to the house at the foot of Petřín Hill.

"So that's what's been ruling your schedule," says the Widow, dispirited.

"Perhaps even my whole life," sighs the Detective. "But eventually, these unsteady days and rickety hours will be over," he adds hastily, his voice hollow. "I've still got a long way to go and there are no shortcuts," the Detective says and kisses the soles of both feet, placing the suntanned legs onto the tracks woven into the rug. He adds, vaguely, that someone at work, someone from a different department, has mentioned a pretty weird case.

"I've been playing blind man's bluff," he says and offers a few more crumbs of information to pique the Widow's interest in the house at the foot of Petřín Hill. He wonders what she makes of it all.

"Those women are obviously psychopaths," says the Widow without a moment's hesitation once he's finished.

She gives him a kiss, her eyes like full moons and her hand moving from the plush sofa to his crotch.

The Detective gently pushes the passionate Widow away. He won't back down. Words come pouring out. Cowardly, feeble, shouty, lazy, degenerate words that can *only* blink their eyes in ennui, sprawl around and distract attention. Words are incapable of carrying the weight of what the Detective has been through over these unsteady days and rickety hours. The Widow does her best to connect, to read his mind.

She doesn't understand the blood-stained fairytale of the three murderous Fates, the women in Bluebeard's wardrobe are beyond her.

"I have to go back, and I'd love it if you came along," the Detective implores.

The Widow doesn't want to go. But she nods calmly, *only* for his sake, and embraces him again.

They drive in darkness. Bodies of swallows don't rule the skies, they don't herald dry storms. And why should they, the storms will evaporate before they reach the ground.

First they stop by the Detective's apartment. The Detective lends the Widow a pair of chamois gloves. His excitement grows in anticipation of her take on things, he hopes to justify what he's been up to. He has prized out the innards of the orange house and then covered them up. She is excited about the adventure that lies ahead, breaking into someone else's house with the man she loves.

"You're not scared you'll be caught red-handed?" she asks the Detective.

"Not at all," the Detective answers.

He takes her to the maze. An unexplored box file in metallic yellow juts out from a shelf. The Detective pulls out the yellow box and lifts the lid. Inside, the box lid is marked with the letter F. F like flesh. F like Fuck-Me Honey.

"I know exactly where they are. And I think I know what they're up to there. They'll be back soon. But not today, don't worry."

The Detective shows the Widow around the pristine apartments and the cubbyhole for guests, like a chatelain proudly showing a cherished visitor around the castle. He pauses in each apartment to introduce the inhabitant of the upright walls. The Widow doesn't listen, her attention caught by expensive brands of perfumes, nail polish, and rejuvenating creams and serums.

The kitchen resembles a chemistry lab. All white and perfectly fitted out, with built-in ovens, refrigerators and freezers, a microwave, even a steam-powered oven. There are a few discarded food processors, strange-looking coffee machines, kitchen scales, and spotlessly clean retorts and tangles of glass pipes. The woman lingers over them for a long time. Assorted mixtures sit in small mortars labeled *Hildegard von Bingen's Formulas*. Unripe dried pods of *Vanilla planifolia*, a Mexican orchid. Honey, wax, and royal jelly from the Western honeybee. The Chinese five-spice is the *only* spice the Widow can identify with certainty, the only one she also uses: szechuan pepper, cardamom, cloves, coriander, star anise. They exchange a kiss and the Detective announces that the best spice for any dish is love. Don't be silly, the Widow replies.

The Detective lingers by a bookcase, picking out books by Ms. Stadtherr and showing them to the Widow. She takes off her gloves *only* to browse the scant collection of CDs in the drawer of the bedside table, ignoring the books she had seen in her late husband's study and didn't much care for. There's Joni Mitchell, Joan Baez, Billie Holiday, Nina Simone, Edith Piaf, and the Carolina Chocolate Drops. The Detective gently takes the silver discs out of her hand. Wipes off her fingerprints. Kisses the tip of her fingers. Hides them in the chamois gloves.

The Detective slips out for a moment.

When he returns from Erika Eis's apartment, the house fills with music, with the violin launching its tirade, Mendelssohn Bartholdy's *Violin Concerto in E minor, Op. 64*, "Allegro molto appassionato," a concerto by the charismatic humanist who believed in the good. The chamois gloves grasp each other, the bodies are perfectly in tune, they make love wildly under the bookcase on which an army is arrayed for battle. The bodies make love and the house and all of Petřín Hill shake to their foundations.

Holding hands, they descend into the maze. It is an oppressive and dull office underworld. "So 1980s," remarks the Widow to pluck up her courage. Chamois gloves separate, they proceed in single file.

The Detective points to the right and left. They reach the end.

The Detective measures the space. It has grown longer by several inches since he last measured it. The house is eating into Petřín Hill. The Detective shows the Widow the oldest files. "This looks like the Tertiary," says the Widow, glancing at the pages taken out of metal boxes, some covered in a child's handwriting and others boasting hummingbird handwriting.

"May I?"

The Detective nods and plants a kiss on her neck. He is not alone anymore. He won't lose his mind.

With a blissful smile the Widow opens a file marked with the letter V and the name *BIRGIT*. It contains several versions of the same text with different dates but the same title. The Widow's body is reading Birgit Stadtherr's memoir, recorded in several versions in purple hummingbird handwriting.

A March submerged in blackness.

A bunker, a safe place for a body. A bunker means punishment, isolation, a bogeyman for those who misbehave, solitary confinement. An experimental laboratory. Most people lose their mind here, sooner or later. A prison within a prison. Rules have to be followed on prison grounds and inside the barracks, the system and anonymity of the crowd demands that. There is no pretense here. It's a face against a face. A body against a body. Idea against idea. The master wields unlimited power. The prisoner is a piece of trash, a toy. This is a two-sided laboratory. The guards don't see the prisoners. The prisoners don't see the guards. It's just face against face. No witnesses. No one can escape from oneself here. This who I am. It's up to me how I will behave. Whether I will raise my hand against another person. And how.

She paces three meters in one direction. Leans her right hand on the wall. Groping around, her right hand finds an obstacle. A crumbling wall. She presses her forehead against it. The bunker is her salvation. She will pick herself up here. Away from the others. Toward the light. Light is darkness with a blurred halo. A few rays force their way through a hole in the metal door, piercing a patch of perforated metal. She paces three meters in the opposite direction. Rests her left hand against the wall. Her right hand gropes around and finds an obstacle. The crumbling wall. She presses her forehead against it.

It is the 14th of March. Her only clothes are the four walls. A square, three meters by three. She walks only along one side. By the opposite wall is a bucket. A part of her body. The body rids itself of unclean garbage. But the head can't. Meter by meter, she sorts through everything stuck inside her head. Rearranging the knowledge on the shelves. Ignoring memories, expunging past experience from her awareness. She stacks the shelves with information which won't weaken her. Information that is redundant. Names of writers and the plots of books they've written. Multiplication tables. Math formulae. Names of gods on Mount Olympus. Greek myths. Characters in plays. Movies, their directors and stars. Plant names. Bird species. Sentences in Czech as well as the English ones she has learned from Diana, German ones from Erika and Polish ones from Ingrid. Poetry. Diana's name. Whenever memories of the tangible world force their way into her consciousness, she chases them away by savagely pinching the flesh on her thigh or face, she feels her body and gives it a slap. The body is the only reliable link with the present. Her feet are freezing. Her toes peek out of nonexistent shoes.

The only way to keep warm is to pace up and down the concrete floor. The bunker is a burrow dug out from the ground. She recalls the names of animals that live underground, too, burrowing through the soil. She plucks words out of the darkness. She won't be able to burrow her way out through concrete. A plank bed faces the reinforced iron entrance. After four days they brought a blanket. She paces three meters. She creates fantasy worlds that are stable and new; their spines formed by facts she arranges in her head into folders, stacking them neatly on the shelves.

Twice a day visitors come. In the morning, daylight blinds her. Instinctively, she covers her breasts and sex. She sees the outlines of two figures. An emaciated inmate who timidly sets a metal cup of prison coffee on the floor, placing a piece of bread on top before backing out. A nervous young guard who accompanies the inmate. The inmate doesn't look at her. He dishes out her daily portion of food and averts his eyes. The guard waits. He takes a good look at the chilled animal in the lair, blinded by the light. They face each other. Venus and her pimp. The guard lets out a shriek and the animal in the cage has to stand to attention, peel her hands from her breasts and lower her arms, reporting her name and number. She is standing here uncovered. Waiting. She never looks at her own body; she is scared of seeing it in the light. The body is her weakest link. It is her mind that keeps her alive. The body has latched on to the mind and the mind drags the hysterical body forward, toward life. When the metal door slams shut, light follows like a train. It has peered in to take a look at her.

She closes her eyes. Then opens them again, slowly. To accustom them to the dark again. She rests her left hand against the wall. She does not pace three meters. She drags the soles of her feet along the concrete gingerly, centimeter by centimeter. Until her big toe collides with the cup. Carefully, she lowers herself onto all fours. Tiny fragments of rock press into her knees. Her fingers find the bread. She feels it, then sticks all of it into her mouth and as she chews and swallows, imagines loaves of bread on shelves, endless shelves laden with loaves of still warm bread that you can break into two, bury your face and warm your cheeks in, loaves of bread like a mother's womb one can crawl into to find safety and warmth. She embraces the cup with both hands. Presses her fingers into the metal. The prison slop is lukewarm, a gift. She drinks greedily. Warmth and pleasure course through the body. She keeps on drinking long after the cup is empty. Then she runs the still warm cup along her whole body, from the toes chilled to the bone all the way up to her face, she runs the cup up and down her whole body like a hot iron. She stands up, her mind nursing the image of a warm loaf of bread and a red hot iron, and paces three meters in shaky steps. Holding the metal cup by its handle, she strikes the wall. Tapping out and answering messages.

The visitors return in the evening. The light doesn't blind her, it is astonishingly pink; the sun is setting outside. The sunset mercifully covers what the eyes are searching for. The elderly inmate sets a metal cup with the prison coffee on the floor, lowers his head further as if something on the clay had caught his attention, and tops the cup with a piece of bread. He hides his chin on his chest like a funeral guest. The funeral puppet tosses an empty bucket over to the wall. Loud metallic clatter; a temple ringing to the sound of an organ. Then he reaches for the empty metal cup and the half-filled bucket. The chubby guard, so beautiful, is waiting. He addresses the breasts in a gentle voice. The body stretches to attention. A layer of dirt protects it from the guard's touch.

Darkness swallows the iron door. The soles of the feet move gingerly along the concrete, centimeter by centimeter. Until the big toe collides with the cup. She kneels down carefully. Tiny fragments of rock press into her knees. She feels for the bread. She touches it. A bite has been taken out of her slice. Shocked fingers travel around the semicircle, all that's left is a grimace. She sticks the crust with its soft lining into her mouth. Seasons it with her tears. She knows how to scream: the bastards! But she doesn't. She cries instead. The body is surprised, paralyzed with astonishment, it doesn't call attention to itself. The body remains silent and gains the upper hand, it had been warning the mind all along: you show-off, this will prove too much for you. An inmate taking a bite of her bread is enough to break her. She has no water. She rubs her body on the wall as if to make it peel and flake off. She rolls her body along the wall, giving a faint groan.

The mind, onto which her body has latched like a hook, is betraying her. The mind starts to allow memories to seep through. She tries to plug the holes and patch them up with sheets of perforated metal. She focuses her mind on a list of Latin words. A list of English towns. She lies on the plank bed wrapped in the blanket, shivering. The worst thing happens. Sleeplessness. The mind is scared of falling asleep. And so is the body. The body depends on the mind. The mind whispers something but the body resists, lacking motivation, still curious. She lacks the strength to kill herself. She lacks the strength to resist her body, which weakens her mind by blaming it for the hunger and the cold.

In the middle of the night the body is relocated to a normal penal cell. Behind the HQ.

This room has a lightbulb. It flickers neurotically on the ceiling. As if someone were trying to blind the lightbulb with a powerful light.

The guard clambers out of the hole, leaving the bunker and the mess in it behind. Seen from above, the bunker looks like a grass-covered clump. Having scrambled to the top, he exhales and pulls his coat back down over his knees as the stiff material has rolled up above the leather belt. Properly girded now, he doesn't notice a mottled shape caught in the barbed wire. It is evening as he walks through the camp headed for the HQ. *A cow has bedded down on the camp fence. White streaks of snow and dark patches of black earth. The sun is shining and spring confuses the senses, carrying a promise and inspiring a melancholy longing. It will get warmer. The swallows will return.*

The bunker won't get warmer. And the guard is fed up with carrying the grub all the way to the bunker. He can handle anything, but this is too much. He knows his inmates, he knows which one is a murderer, a thief, or a well-heeled bigshot; who is a German, a Jew, or a Gypsy, a political prisoner, blinkered member of a political party fallen out of favor, a saboteur or diversionist, a kulak or deserter, industrialist or a Holy Joe, or someone who had stuffed his head with too much knowledge or had done too much thinking for his own good and couldn't keep it to himself, or who showed off because he was blessed with good looks. What matters is whether the guard takes a liking to an inmate and whether the inmate knows how to respect his master. Then the labels become unimportant. But he is stumped by that cocoon in the bunker.

No one has provided him with clear instructions. The commander maintains a meaningful silence, this is a matter of greatest importance, the highest degree of confidentiality, and the most generous bonuses, no one is allowed to raise a hand against this inmate, the spawn of some big shot, a movie maker and theater director who made films under the Nazis and will keep making films. They apprehended a boy. And he turned out to be a girl.

The guard is furious. He knows how intoxicating it is to give someone a proper thrashing, back in his days in the rough Žižkov neighborhood he boxed, you bash someone up, give them a good beating, and it calms you down while at the same time pumping you up. When it's over, you want more. To be on the winning side. Things used to be so straightforward. Until this beast of God's landed up in the bunker.

He will find a chink, he'll figure out how to defy orders. He will show her who is in charge here.

"Only you and one other guard will be on duty here, taking turns. No one else is allowed in there, so that no one can know," the camp commander had said.

Lately, he hasn't even been allowed to take an inmate along. He is supposed to schlep the coffee and bread and buckets of shit himself. The young guard does as he's told, but only because he's an eager idiot who follows orders and thinks that the war isn't over, that another war, a cold one, is looming just around the corner. He doesn't know that he has to be smart about looking out for number one. He doesn't realize that a guard schlepping a bucket of piss loses authority. He will never regain it with the inmates who have been stuck here for years. Courage, my boy, hit them in the solar plexus, and make sure you take an inmate along. The guard breaks the rules.

A stumbling inmate follows the guard. He is just a young boy who tried to cross the border, just like the cocoon in the bunker, he'll be easy to shut up. The guard figures out a trick he can justify even to the Red Cross who are supposed to come for an inspection. He will do a good deed. He will drag the cocoon out into human society. And the boys in the cells will thank him for a bit of human warmth. They'll be in his debt.

"Not a squeak about this, boy. Or you'll end up in the bunker, too. Go ahead, help yourself to a bite, you thieving bastard."

The inmate swallows. The bread, softened by saliva, turns sweet. Like biting into a cake.

The Widow's body squirms. Her breathing is shallow. The Widow doesn't want to read further. She rests her brow on a table. The light comes streaming onto her hair as she gasps for air.

The Detective won't find out that the Widow's body has connected to the other bodies even if it cannot express this connection, it is a new, unknown sensation, these doubts about the world she inhabits, identical to the doubts burgeoning in the bodies of the four women who have dissolved and vanished in the maze on the first floor of the house at the foot of Petřín Hill, doubts burgeoning in living flesh because for the body, memories are different from selective memory and tend to mingle with imagination.

Memories of a thousand-year-old body don't lie. The body instantly reverberates with another language, its own, for having been abused once, a body feels solidarity with every other abused body anywhere in the world, and it wants to ease its pain to get rid of those memories. And that is impossible as long as the same thing is happening anywhere under the sun and the moon.

The swallows nod their heads cheerfully.

The woman flicks through the photos in the file. She saw some of them in the morning light upstairs in the room with the brass candlestick. They look different under the cone of light from the sober lamp. They resemble a family, three adolescent girls and an older sister. They are laughing, vacationing on the coast of a northern sea, a powerful, youthful wind is blowing, blow, you crazy wind, blow, the sea churns, drunken with hope, the wind is fluttering in their hair, its powerful teeth tearing at their wide skirts; they squint, held in the grip of the rays of the sun.

The Widow narrows her eyes, resisting the urge to put on her sunglasses. She runs her hand over her face, a few grains of sand caught in the grooves of her palm. The Widow quickly wipes her hand on her thigh. This is a posed photo, not a snapshot. An eagle seems to have thrust its talons into the shoulders of the three children; the eagle's claws, sickle-arched, belong to the resourceful Diana.

A scrawny child faces the camera, its palms open as if it has just released some birds. Or as if it had just dropped some grenades with their detonators triggered. It is impossible to tell if it is a girl or a boy. A skinny little thing, barefoot and with a bandaged leg, holds the hand of a violinist in a dress suit. Two little girls, a dapper American female G.I. in military uniform and cap towering behind them, gripping their bony little shoulders. She looks like an actress from a prewar movie. The girls are holding hands so hard that they might snap. Their eyes filled with fear, they look up toward the military cap and the powerful, curved beak.

The Widow shuffles old press cuttings from her country's newspapers. Reports of people who had crossed the state border illegally; Birgit's name, listed among the traitors, is underlined.

The Widow stands up. She slides over to the Detective, whose back is immersed in the story of another body.

The woman embraces him from behind and kisses the crown of his head.

The Widow retraces her steps down the narrow gorge, as if condemned to finish reading the manuscript sent into exile and discover what it brings to light. Instead of reading, she skips over lines. Her body breaks out in a sweat. Her hands join over her pudendum. Her vagina contracts. Sentences whirl in her head, words unable to find their place. She catches them and commits them to memory, firing shots into the air, and missing. The flock scatters. The sentences depart like scraps of paper blown away by the wind.

Her trial won't be open to the public. Why?

She refuses to speak Czech. She insists on testifying in English. The language of the enemy.

She must be disposed of.

◇

They nibble hummus in the Uxor-Hiom restaurant. Erika launches into an endless lecture on how she prepares hummus, on the right proportion of tahini and the type of chickpeas she has bought and from where.

Diana has dolled herself up. A hand mirror is passed from hand to hand. A hand releases the shutter. Yusuf serves a special treat, on the house.

"*Only* for my old and loyal friends."

"We're definitely old. And loyal too," Birgit can't stop herself from quipping. "So how long have you had this restaurant?"

"Ten years. I opened it with my brother."

"Is your brother here?"

"He went back to the old country last month. To find himself a wife."

"He doesn't like the local women?"

"He wants to start a family so he needs a strong and upright wife, a virgin."

"And he doesn't like the local girls."

"You know what young people here are like."

"No, I don't."

"They don't know what's right and proper."

"They sure don't."

"All that depravity. No respect. Can I get you anything else?"

"No thanks, we're fine."

Yusuf, the nice young man, gives the three faded Graces a wink. He joins his pals at the bar. They switch to their mother tongue.

Diana watches him. Diana whispers, three feathery heads nod in agreement, their beaks full of hummus.

Erika and Birgit head for the school. Diana gets the check, inadvertently brushing Yusuf's hand.

◇

The Detective sits at a desk. He has stopped rifling through documents. He wishes that the door would open and the three Graces would walk in.

He confides to the Widow that he feels the ground slipping from under his feet. One day he will have to explain why he put off exposing the orange house and arresting the old ladies.

"Perhaps they have filled the gap left by your grandma Josefa," says the Widow.

"That may well be. Perhaps that's how I imagined her to be in her dotage. A lady. I feel like I should protect them."

"To reach such an age and remain sane and retain one's wit, humor and charm is the most wonderful thing one could wish for from life," says the Widow dreamily.

"They seem so youthful. My favorite surrogate grandma is Diana. A born leader, the passionate kind, but without any lust for power."

The Widow takes the Detective by one chamois hand and leads him over to her lamp. She shows him Diana in a G.I. uniform, a military cap on her head. The Detective explains that Diana is the widow of an American magnate and intelligence officer who recorded the war in photographs. Diana is a photographer, too, an American anthropologist and ethnologist who has made several study trips to both Western and Eastern Europe, as well as India, she practices yoga, has studied in India with a guru named Iyengar, the same guru who looked after the bodies of violinist Yehudi Menuhin and Belgium's Queen Elisabeth. An old photo online shows Diana doing a headstand, with the caption *A Great Lady*.

"They remind me of a fairytale queen who no longer cares about Snow White," the woman says with a smile. "I like Diana best, too. And look, here's Birgit Stadtherr as a little girl, or Buch, as she was then."

"I'm sorry that I have to report them," says the Detective.

"You don't have to."

"But I do."

"Don't forget what they've done for me."

"What have they done for you?"

"They've liberated me," says the woman earnestly. "If it weren't for them, I wouldn't have met you. Look at this file from India you've been reading. A woman is raped every twenty minutes."

"Concealing a crime makes me complicit," say the Detective.

"But no one knows about this house. Just you and me, my love."

Just then the house at the foot of Petřín Hill steps between them. The Widow is clear-eyed and hears the signals the body sends. The Detective, on the other hand, still feels that the house is booby-trapped, that it has turned Prague into the capital of the world, the house rules the world, invisible threads tangled and massed to prevent strangers' eyes from seeing through the thickets, the threads freshly woven into a rope that threatens to strangle him too this time, they are already preparing the noose for him, though he isn't sure where. He needs a drink but perhaps he should think twice, a Russian muzhik can't control himself once he starts drinking, hmm.

Sentences emerge from the mist and surface from the water, written in invisible ink. A blind man has taught himself Braille, he can finally read the story he suspected was there: a kind of a war is being waged and it is being waged on a daily basis.

The Widow from the glass house had also waged her private war.

The details of which the Detective will never learn.

The Detective and the Widow are back in the glass house on the outskirts of Prague. The sliding door to the glass terrace is open. They are leaning against the door frame, smoking cigarettes. Two small stalks with tiny leaves have pushed through the cracks between the terrace tiles. Cigarette butts, not stubbed out, are flicked into the night. Little bodies swish past, their beaks catching the tiny glowing lights. They are still here, the swallows. No one feeds them. But down below there are insects: predators and victims—a food chain that in this instance makes sense.

Sitting on a Japanese rug inside the glass terrace they browse photos of parents, grandparents, and themselves as children. "One day I'll show you the video of the garden by the house where I grew up with my brother and sister, planted mostly with cherry trees, so no meal would be complete without stewed cherries. My grandma Josefa wanted a record of the garden in each season. After Grandpa died, the house was sold, her eyesight was going by then. But Grandma herself makes *only* three, very brief appearances in the video. She looked like a bouquet of wildflowers, a precious dandelion, a Japanese cherry blossom. Whenever I see her, I tear up."

"Don't show it to me then," says the Widow.

"But I like a good cry," says the Detective.

They gaze into the night, sharing a cigarette.

"Please don't touch me."

"What's the matter?"

"Not now."

Love needs no words. In love, it's bodies that speak. And bodies don't lie.

"If I'd been afraid of you, I wouldn't have gotten involved with you. And being involved with you, I'm not afraid," the Detective says.

"Had I been afraid of you, I wouldn't have gotten involved with you either."

They discuss everything freely. The Widow shows him her wedding photograph and tells him how her parents had kept her at home by force, how every girl worries she may end up without a husband, just like farmers used to worry about a bad harvest. She tells him about her love life with her late husband. They didn't understand each other but his sexual appetite was boundless. He had to take medication because he seemed to have a permanent hard-on. I've landed my own private Disneyland, she thought back then, young and stupid that she was. She saw in him what she wanted to see. Strength and safety, kindness and support. He saw in her what he needed to see. She didn't know that he was one of those men who derive their confidence *only* from sex, the quality of love making. He would have been mortally offended if she had taken a lover. He would have killed her. He even trolled his ex-wives, sending them crass emails if he discovered they were living with someone. He would never have understood what she had now with the Detective. He didn't understand that sexual violence has nothing to do with love and everything to do with power and humiliation. He didn't understand that the women who worked for him were not his playthings, that the war was long over, that he wouldn't get away with it.

He would never have understood that a woman could fall in love without having slept with a man first. That real love and joy was selfless and that it wasn't the same as lust. Or that she and the Detective take a long time making love rather than racing to orgasm, that it's about making a connection. It's about gazing into each other's eyes and caressing each other. Her husband would fall in love after having slept with a woman. During lovemaking he would watch himself contentedly. When he felt like sex, she had to reorganize her day. He would order her to a hotel room, like a hearty breakfast or an afternoon snack. He would assail her in the morning if he had some spare time and she had to set her work aside, as *only* his work was important. He would strip naked and stand before her wordlessly, penis erect. After carefully folding his trousers and shirt. Before she got pregnant, he had not taken her to a single exhibition, walk, concert, or a day trip, they never saw a play at the theater. She married young and from day one regarded it as her priority to make a home for him. And he was evidently happy to let her do that.

More recently he would show off with quotes from books by Birgit Stadtherr, née Buch. He would parrot things Voltaire had said about women being weaker than men simply by virtue of physiology. Regular bleeding exhausts them, he would say. The long pregnancy and breastfeeding did exhaust her. All this *only* went to show that she was not made for work or any activity that required strength and stamina. He would parrot Rousseau, quoting from *Emile, or On Education*. Women are infantile and incapable of rational thought. If she contradicted him, he yelled at her, quoting Professor Stadtherr who likewise thought so, and Stadtherr was a worldwide authority. He had fallen under her spell. Completely.

They are chatting without lying to one another; the Detective had a home without a lady of the house, the woman had a body without a master.

In her husband's study, which no one has bothered to dust, they browse Birgit's books to understand the context in which she used those quotes and read her scathing commentaries. She must be really smart, but as cold as steel. I'm scared of her. But I'm not scared of Ms. Adler.

They open a bottle of wine. They snuggle down on the sofa. The Detective takes some papers out of his briefcase, copies of copies, Birgit never gave interviews, she would *only* say a few words at book launches or fulminate at readings. Erika Eis has given a few interviews, her answers brief and to the point, driving journalists to despair. These women have mastered the art of talking without giving anything away. The Detective reads from an interview:

Erika: At some point I became an observer of situations. Not a participant.

Question: Is that why you became a film director?

Answer: I had no other reason.

Question: You've been accused of being cynical and uncommercial.

Answer: There's something to it.

Question: Were you surprised to hear that your film has been chosen for the Cannes Festival?

Answer: No, I wasn't. Were you?

Question: To tell the truth, there was an element of surprise in it.

Answer: An element of surprise is a part of life. Anything else?

Question: We've barely started.

Answer: I no longer feel like starting.

Question: Last question then. What do you regard as the greatest danger in the present-day world?

Answer: Infantilization.

Question: What do you mean?

Answer: Rampant consumerism combined with the media and the internet have turned people, and not only in Europe and North

America, into kids in constant pursuit of novelty. Until they reach some extreme point where they won't be able to tell the boundary between game and reality.

Question: My question was actually about —

Answer: What is dangerous about the way people behave is not so much the trend to hostile behavior, but rather the fact that it is infantile.

Question: Our readers won't understand this. Let's go back to movies—

Answer: Ever heard of Karl May?

Question: No I haven't. I—

Answer: What about Adolf Hitler, that name must ring a bell?

Question: Sure.

Answer: Infantilism is unpredictable. Hitler was afflicted by an infantile and passionate love for Karl May's novels.

Question: That's not what this interview is about.

Answer: Unlike everyone else, Hitler wasn't a voracious reader while a child, but he was between the ages of twenty and thirty. If you'd read Karl May, you'd know the kind of stuff his hero Winnetou dreamed of. Hitler was a narcissist. For the narcissist, fantasies are more real than tangible reality.

Question: Can we go back to your first film about the violinist, Menuhin?

Answer: Are you familiar with the music of Benjamin Godard? You're not? Well, you should be.

The Detective pushes another text in front of the Widow, something written by Birgit Stadtherr and published a long time ago. He passes it to her like a love letter, in constant readiness to accept that the other person is different from the way we read them while they're in our presence or in our thoughts. We should bear in mind that the other person is almost certainly different, perhaps completely different, from the way we read them.

The Widow is tired, she has stopped listening, she *only* nods and revels *only* in the Detective's ardor and *only* drinks him in with her eyes; she feels his face and circles his lips with her eyes, she has pins and needles between her legs and desire prevents her from taking in the words, she loves him so much it makes her bones ache.

Perhaps it is possible, the woman thinks. To speak and behave with integrity. The *only* way to speak to men is with openness and integrity, and without making any concessions or having any regrets; *only* that way can we all be liberated and enjoy relationships on a new, equal footing. Down with relationships based on dominance/subservience! Thinks the Widow.

She glances at the Detective and says it out loud.

"The *only* way to speak to men is with openness and integrity, without making any concessions or having any regrets; *only* that way can we all be liberated and enjoy relationships on a new, equal footing. Down with relationships based on dominance or subservience!"

"Right," nods the Detective. "Quite right."

"I don't want to know what you're doing when you're not with me. Leave the three ladies alone now, my love."

"I'm obsessed with them. I can't let go."

"So go ahead and join them."

◇

She strolls around, pointing them out with one finger. She is not lazy, she is methodical. They cling to her, purring with delight. To be friends with Honey is a distinct honor; they walk with their heads held high. Honey is the chosen one, they all jostle to get closer to this cool chick, it's a badge of honor to walk side by side with this slender beauty, their guide, the one who is wild, tough, and oh so cool.

The one who guides them from childhood to adulthood across a bridge that leads nowhere and ends in the midst of a carnivorous ocean.

The one who ignores boys her age, damn it, dude, hey asshole, look at that piece of meat, see those tits, dude, what's your thing, you into tits or cunts? Moths around the flame, they are irresistibly attracted, all these well-mannered Hansels and Gretels who hold hands and can't wait to taste the gingerbread of adulthood, to taste its promise. A bit of necking and sucking. They will end up in the oven.

Honey teaches her flock of downy, confused fledglings to fly. The chirruping is stuck in their throats. She kisses their little beaks. She pecks out their eyes and clips their little wings. Honey hands out free dope. Honey knows an apartment on the main drag. Honey has money. Honey is a luscious receptionist, waving the key to the sanctuary before their eyes, twisting it between the vaginal lips of virgins and making juices flow, this turns her on. Their minds make love to Honey while their bodies are being plundered.

She is a vulture, thinks Erika.

But no, vultures are so hideous that everyone turns away from them with a snort. This girl is a rare and charming cuckoo, a co-creator. She has surrounded herself with chirping, twittering, chittering, warbling, and preening budgies and turtledoves, wagtails and goldcrests, wrens and robins, bluetits and pipits, redpolls and starlings, doves and prattling baby blackcaps.

Honey has class. She turns all of them into goggle-eyed owls, shush.

Erika is spying on Honey. Honey is a mystery. She has money. She comes from a happy family. She excels in school. Young boys drool over her; old men snoop around the nymphet that dances a salutation to the moon in a tutu, wagging her fingers. Perhaps it is possible, Erika thinks, that she just can't tell good from evil. She is bored. She is simple. She doesn't know the meaning of empathy or compassion. It's all a game to her.

If I were fourteen, I would let myself be ensnared, too, I would also snuggle up to her honeyed wing, so thrillingly hot and dangerous, I would happily hole up there, Erika realizes. I would fall for the honey trap and let her beauty initiate me.

A new little bird has attached herself to Honey. Honey has lured her into the cage with the promise of better food and bright feathers. Carefully, she carries the cage all the way to the birdcatcher's home. Want some crack but have no money? There's still enough flesh left on your bones.

Only the most beautiful birds end up locked in cages. Their soft bodies are gently taken out, the skin barely covered in down is fondled. The swallows' hair or rather, plumage, is fondled. Before it is constricted.

Every night, Honey delivers food to the birdcatcher's nest. Every night, she brings a fresh supply of tender white meat with braces on their teeth. She is not Honey, she is the Honey Demon. No one mentions this in the daylight. No one ever talks about it. The abused fledglings don't warn the others.

Erika tears off a leaf of basil solemnly laying it on her tongue. She swallows it like it's the Eucharist. She needs to find an elm tree.

◇

He makes love to her and doesn't want to let go. They keep their eyes open. Their eyes latch on to each other. You're incredible, he whispers. You are fluid, impossible to grasp, stubborn, willful, unbearable, and yet you are a wonderful mother, you're my goddess, I worship you. They whisper to each other. How do you like it, he asks. How do you like it, she asks. I love it when you first enter me and bend down over me, I love holding you in my mouth and I love being on top of you, I love it when you lick me, when you lick your fingers and gently massage my clit, the king of pleasure, but you know all that. I love tasting you, I love you being on top of me and I love being inside your tight ass, I love it when you blow me, I love your hot little cunt, and I love your hard cock. As they speak, the words in their soft embrace turn also soft, there are no crass words in this world, words mean nothing.

There is *only* the language of bodies and a vacuum. A free bond. One that is rare and highly appreciated.

They tell each other about their first time. She tells him what it was like losing her virginity. He is pleased to hear how curious she was and how very much in love. Without grubby clichés, without a rollicking party, without being drunk or more or less raped by adolescent friends aping the porn they saw online, the harder the better. It didn't happen on her parents' sofa. She wasn't pressured by an older boy. It happened at university, she was nineteen and already knew a thing or two about her body, she had seen and heard and sensed what was happening to it. Her body knew what it didn't want. Lots of boys want to hold the girl's head during oral sex. She was able to say that she didn't want that. The worst thing was the peer pressure, her schoolfriends who boasted of having done it at the age of twelve. She now knows they were lying. How strange: in the previous century *only* virgins were desirable, but these days it's the virgins that no one wants.

He tells her what it was like for him losing his virginity. The ballet dancer he fell madly in love with, how he pursued her, how he moved in with her, without realizing she was a nymphomaniac, how they had sex several times a day and she would freak out if three days went by without him making love to her, and berating him for not loving her enough. He went to work during the day and studied at night but she would wake him up at four in the morning for another hour of languorous sex, and pounce on him the minute he came through the door after an exhausting day. Sounds like big love, comments the Widow. "No, it wasn't," says the Detective, "we had nothing else in common, it was *only* the sex, I was young and had a permanent hard-on. It's not normal, it wasn't normal. And I watched myself screwing her. But then she just went and cheated on me, so I did too, out of spite, with all her girlfriends, and then I just screwed around, the ultimate Lothario, she really hurt me, it was painful, but we stayed together. But then I buried myself in work and decided to put an end to it once and for all, refused ever to commit again and told myself I'd had it with women. I loved my new job, I thought the world would make me better and I would make the world a better place. And provided I worked hard enough, stood my ground, and treated others decently and openly, then everything was bound to work out, that would be my contribution to the history of joy."

"And now?"

"Now I'm in love. I thought I wasn't the jealous type, but I am jealous, for the first time in my life. I'm nearly forty and still discovering the world."

He makes love to her. Her face relaxes. She is warm, emanating that warmth like a stove, her whole body relaxing in pleasure. He tastes and sniffs her. He wants to drink her up. She wants to suck him. They want to get to know every pore of each other's skin.

As they lie side by side, they drown in each other's eyes. A sharp arrow suddenly pierces the Detective's mind. A drop of honey hangs from its tip. Retrospective jealousy. She doesn't mind anal sex. Many consider it sick. She has made love to other bodies. How many and what were their names.

"How many? I want to know their names!"

She nips his jealousy in the bud by ignoring it. She stops the words forcing their way up his esophagus. He kisses her passionately.

Swallows fly past the glass wall and don't pull a face.

The Detective is alone in the orange house. Dawn ruffles its feathers in front of Diana's window. Swallows slip through the dawn as if giving the Detective a wink with their white chests, raising their tails *only* so that he can see the V for victory.

The Widow doesn't want to return to the orange house. She is terrified of words forged by swallows in the air and hidden in the maze. They haunt her. Her eyes have swallowed too many words, it has upset her stomach.

The Detective is thorough. He makes himself read every single word, leaf through every page—to get to know the master you have to watch his servants first. The documents relate to Egypt, Syria, Algeria, Tunisia, Nigeria, the US, Spain, Mali, and-so-on-and-so-on, country chasing country, each trying to get ahead, but no amount of effort manages to change the legal position of women based *solely* on the reading of the Quran, Sharia law in Yemen, United Arab Emirates, Saudi Arabia, Bahrain, photographs of Afghan women who tried to escape from forced marriages and had their noses cut off, photos of schoolgirls who disappeared into the Nigerian bush, their bodies transformed into a flock of birds; the purple hummingbird handwriting appraising individual bodies. And over this multitude of bodies, purple crosses rise up like a spear, crosses with no one crucified.

The austere handwriting does not write, it sends telegrams. Where from, when, and how the violence is organized. In what way and to what extent sexual violence is tolerated, by both tyrants and the abused bodies.

Birgit's hummingbird handwriting is losing its luster. He tackles another metal box, one with letters staggering across the lid, things that the rich can achieve by monetary means the poor can achieve *only* by using force; many a swallow has paid for this with her life, unable to return home; they described the events seen through two separate eyes: the right one sees something different from the left, but the flight path is always straight ahead. They describe things that happen in the spring, year after year . . .

The Detective puts on some music. It flutters through the house conducted by the sweeping gestures of a man who is not scared. Menuhin. A town square. A protest rally. A naked young woman lies on the ground, the police walk past, ignoring her. Men in the crowd take the woman aside and drag her to a dark corner or a tent. When they're done with her, they take a knife and inflict injuries to her vagina. The hummingbird handwriting does not enjoy tapping out words to the rhythm of wings. But the austere eagle handwriting is not losing its luster: women played an important role in every human revolution. And now, too, they are being intimidated. To make them disappear from the public arena.

The time has come for a revolution of bodies. A war of the sexes has never taken place. A war of the sexes is now inevitable. A new civil war. The North against the South. The South against the North.

A red folder includes the exact wording of a speech, not just a media advisory but statutes of a new non-profit under the auspices of QUAIL Studios, an organization women can turn to.

The Detective feels no tiredness, his head moves to the rhythm of the violin. The orange house is a nest where he now goes to recover. Where he can disconnect from the home where he lives and does his futile work.

He understands the three swallows. Work is not supposed to be futile and life is supposed to have a meaning.

The Detective remembers his grandma Josefa after she had lost most of her eyesight. When they discharged her after two weeks in the hospital, she cleaned the whole house and distributed her possessions among her relatives. A nest of certainty, strength, clarity; don't forget to add some dried coconut to the cake topping; it's hard to live if you have no confidence, she said as she caressed him. She gave him a painting: two young women weaving, and the Grim Reaper standing by the loom. Death brings peace and joy, she said. She gifted him a cuckoo clock, an alarm clock, and a pile of white handkerchiefs with a monogram embroidered in the corner. She gave him his grandfather's ring. His grandfather had never worn it; it used to be engraved but the pattern was no longer visible. Grandma's ring, which she had never taken off, was all worn and faded. The Detective put on his grandpa's ring, trying it on his middle finger. His grandma used to make *bird's milk*, she had brought the recipe from Slovakia, poor people's food, floating islands, white flour whisked into hot milk.

His other grandfather outlived his wife by seven years. For seven years he suffered, longing to follow his wife to the grave, for seven years all he did was wait to die, life for him turned into shallow water. But he didn't speed it up. Those seven years of life were futile, filled *only* with regret and memories of his beloved wife; remorse and guilty conscience are bad counselors. Back then the Detective thought that this kind of life was futile. He wouldn't eat when he visited Grandpa, even though he had made roast tenderloin with dumplings, and different kinds of sauces specially for his grandson on his rare visits.

He used to stuff his mouth full and then spit it all out in the toilet.

◇

Moon salutation. They ladle imaginary water with the palms of their hands. They fill a yellow chalice with water to wash off the dirt and scum of the day.

Swallows fly by, the word *only* dropping from their beaks.

Diana travels with Max, officially as his assistant. Unofficially, as his lover. She is issued a uniform with a smart tie. A military cap for her reddish blonde hair. A helmet.

The *only* thing reflected in the eyes of swallows after the war is an intense void, they are absorbed in themselves. They are not aware of having their photo taken. They look like still lifes in nineteenth-century houses, like the girl in paintings by the Danish artist Vilhelm Hammershøi. Diana's father had owned a portrait of the artist's sister, painted in 1885. It hung in his study and if Diana stared at it long enough, the girl would turn into a swallow with one wing outstretched, as if she was there and not there at the same time. The painter captured her in an unguarded moment, brooding over something, troubled by something, something within, not of this world. The picture looked less like a painting and more like a photograph taken by a swallow.

Erika stands against a wall, poking the damp soil with a stick. She waves her arms, conducting flocks of birds. Her index finger and thumb meet, forming a circle. She looks through it. Her eyes move, capturing clouds. The clouds escape from the circle. The clouds crumble. The sky has psoriasis.

This is how Diana's camera captures her for the first time.

Diana doesn't let the taciturn Erika out of her camera's eye. Erika is standing alone, to one side, watching other children play. The kids impale a white butterfly on a stick. They enjoy looking at it as it flutters before it dies and disintegrates. They pick up an earthworm, pull at its ends and tear it in half. The cheekiest kids beg for food. They lie about not being given their ration.

The violinist Yehudi Menuhin visits the camp. Erika attends a brief concert at the field hospital. She is gripped by fever. Diana captures the fever for eternity. Erika gazes at the slender violinist. Erika is twelve. This is the first time she has seen fingers tap dancing on strings.

She jumped out of the window on her family's farm. She hurt her leg. She trudged several miles on the injured leg.

The soldiers in the hallway spoke Russian. The soldiers in the field speak German. Erika doesn't tell them her name. Her mother has pushed her ahead of herself and offered her to the Russians in the hope of salvaging their house. The barns. The last cow.

Erika jumps out of the window. The cow has been saved, the family shot dead, the soldiers pull her brother's and father's boots over their swollen calves.

Diana flies into a rage when she hears the word *only*. She demands that Erika's case be investigated.

They roll their eyes. She has no documents. No one cares about such trifles.

She was ONLY raped.

That intense void in their eyes as they don't look at the camera.

Just then Diana raises her eyes skyward and sees the swallows. She sees their formations, the ballet they perform in the sky and their astonishment at human history. They fly around the whole world but it is *only* among people that they see mass murderers. Human beings are the only creatures that have not adjusted to their own society.

Diana reads the messages etched into the sky.

It feels as if it had happened to her own body. Reach into yourself and beg forgiveness. If this is the world one is meant to accept, I want nothing to do with it. Filing a criminal complaint won't solve anything. Max is angry. She doesn't care what nationality the perpetrators are. She doesn't care what nationality the victims are.

She has stumbled upon a battleground that knows no time of peace. There is a tacit agreement and a territory that has not yet been liberated and never will be, one that anyone may conquer, where everyone is allowed to do whatever they please. A plowed field. A vast field of black, fertile soil. Its name is the body of the one who is weaker. The body as battleground. Filing a criminal charge against the conqueror is absurd.

◇

Diana is sitting at a coffee table in the Lynx's office. She spreads a fan of crisp new banknotes on the table. The Lynx counts the money, twice she loses count, starts from scratch. No one pays cash these days, *only* rich Russians. The Lynx makes a feeble attempt to resist.

"The evidence is flimsy."

"My body never lies."

The Lynx won't let herself be drawn into the trap. Why does Diana have to bring yoga into this? Yoga is *only* a pastime, a hobby, a bit of fun, there is so much one can fit into human lives on the banks of a raging river, *only* shallow water divides death from life. New documents are handed over. Those Diana has brought include a sheet of paper covered in handwriting that is still somewhat childish, the paper has been folded into the shape of a swallow.

"Here's Milena's testimony."

"How long have you three ladies been traveling around like this?"

"We've been friends on and off since the end of the war."

"And you've always lived together?"

"We've lived together ever since our friend Ingrid left us and Birgit's sons grew up. And the reason I stay with them is that Birgit's and Erika's bodies needed a long time to rid themselves of the twentieth century."

"And how did you get over it?"

"We'd laugh together. We still make jokes about it. Sometimes. And I showed their bodies the power of self-cleansing. Detach yourself from the past, don't look back, that's what I tell them. We practice yoga together."

"Have you ever got really close?"

"What do you mean?"

"I mean, have you ever been intimate?

"You mean, slept together?"

"I'd never dare to imply that."

"No. We *only* hug. We love men's bodies. We are a *family*, but a different kind of family. The smell of walnuts. The world as our home."

The Lynx is lost and stops asking questions. She hurries things up. A big mistake, she has missed a once-in-a-lifetime chance: Diana was prepared to tell all.

"As you know, I have asked for a retrial on the basis of new information received and examined. Many thanks for the background material. But they are not willing to testify."

Diana doesn't reply. They won't testify. They feel complicit. Their bodies get in the way Their bodies have betrayed them. The bodies have had an orgasm.

"You know, Ms. Adler, I think you're making a mountain out of a mole hill. I live in a different world from the one you describe.

I follow the rules. Without histrionics and historical sentiment. I need words that are clear-cut and firm. I need witnesses, I need evidence. You can't play games with the law. This is all very vague and wishy-washy. I have already apologized for having jumped to conclusions when we first investigated this."

"Jumped to conclusions?"

"Let's say we made a mistake. Would that satisfy you?"

"You made the victims feel even more intimidated."

"Yes, I realize that now."

"How about you come and visit us one day?"

"But where is . . . that home of yours?"

Diana thinks of the orange house at the foot of Petřín Hill.

"I no longer have a nest and don't intend to build one. But spring can be full of hope and beautiful in Prague. See you in court."

"Let me make one thing clear, Ms. Adler. The girl, Julia, is an unreliable witness. Her school attendance is patchy. She lives with her mother. The mother keeps changing partners. She works at a supermarket checkout. She was only seventeen when she had Julia. She trained as a seamstress, like most women around here. The textile plant is the local safety net. She's had more than one abortion. Julia goes to school *only* occasionally. She pretends she has gone but stays home, texting. Instead, she hangs out at the shopping mall with her friends. Shoplifting clothes and make-up. She comes home only once her mother has left for her afternoon or night shift."

Diana looks at the window. A protective foil. She feels she's been locked into a can. Diana is uncompromising.

"They chased down one of my swallows today. Six men."

"Sorry?"

"My swallow. A photojournalist in India. As long as these things keep happening, I won't give up. I won't surrender to an army of men.

Or to women who belittle these things. They are scared of youth and competition so they lend their support to men. Silly me, I believed that dog won't eat dog. But women put up with so much from other women. I'm up against everyone all by myself *only* because I know what a victim goes through."

"What are you talking about?"

"The monolithic army. The cowards. They rape *in packs*, you see. Just like during the war. Not face to face. They hunt in packs. They hunt for flesh. They hunt for bodies they consider *only* pieces of flesh. And they enjoy it. Rape as a weapon of mass destruction."

Diana stands up. She bends down to the Lynx.

"You are no longer welcome in my yoga class."

"Excuse me?"

"You are in cahoots with them, that gang."

"What?"

"You and all your investigators. You could have routed this gang years ago."

"We followed the rules."

"They got them blind drunk, raped them, and forced them to have sex with others. Twenty guys in one case."

"But the evidence . . ."

"Evidence, evidence. This is organized crime, don't you get it? What would you do if this happened to your daughter?"

The Lynx stands up abruptly. Their foreheads almost touch.

"Such a thing could never happen to my daughter. She has been well brought up."

"That's what all those girls' mothers said."

"Don't you ever mention my daughter in the same breath with them."

"Or what?"

The Lynx is taken aback. She knows full well that Diana is not afraid of anything. She has touched a nerve. That was a mistake. Never underestimate the maternal instinct.

"Is Diana even your real name?"

"Does it matter?"

They part without shaking hands.

A shadow flits by outside. It is not a bird. It is a leaf that the wind has thrust against the window.

They cram all their stuff into huge, blue plastic bags that they throw into trash cans. Migratory birds. Snow falls on the city and white swallows fly about the sky, but no one notices them until they drop to the ground and until the puddles left by the recent rain are colored purple by letters of the alphabet.

It is and isn't the same thing. Everything has been here before and yet there are things that haven't yet happened.

Erika escapes into her language. She puts on Brahms's *Ein deutsches Requiem*. Birgit rolls her eyes. Erika moves her lips, mouthing *Selig sind, die da Leid tragen*, all the way to *Selig sind die Toten, die in dem Herrn sterben*. She keeps moving her lips even after the music has stopped. As if trying to articulate silence. Her arms flail, feeding imaginary pigeons.

SWOOPING FOR PREY

The Detective is desperate for a drink.

So am I. It's blustery outside. The fall wind is on its last legs. There's nothing left for it to do in this town.

The Detective and the Doctor are getting drunk at Bar and Books. A nocturno. The Merlin is smoking a Cuban cigar. The mere sight of all the books around makes the Detective nauseous. The Merlin talks about fresh cases of rotting bodies. The Detective listens respectfully, trying to wash down his yearning to tell the Merlin about the orange house at the foot of Petřín Hill. A big tree attracts the wind and the amber liquid coursing its way down his throat forces the secret out into the open. The alcohol level in his blood rises, taking over his body and letting the secret bob up to the surface like a cork. It sits on his tongue, waiting to be spat out.

"Maybe it's time for me to . . . to . . . look for another job."

"Hear, hear! Burnout, young man? That's quite normal. Come angling with me, that'll do you good."

They watch women entering the dark room, the reflection of the candles shimmering on their bodies. Male eyes are glued to a smooth back and its tanned skin, the cool, glittering blue fabric with a long, plunging slit that exposes the vertebrae as they snake down toward the alluring groove beneath the hem of lace panties. The Detective keeps blabbing, just to prevent the secret from slipping onto his tongue. Is this what you call a demimondaine? Or is this a feminist?

The old Doctor can't tear his eyes from the snake, he's been bitten. "Search me. I've never understood the type. The *only* things I value in women are the art of flirting, making the house cozy, and keeping it spick and span. And cooking, of course. I've been in love twice and twice it ended in disaster. *Only* those who are not in love are in control of the strategy of romance. But what is it *they* want?"

The Detective's bloodshot eyes sweep the sumptuous oak shelves laden with hefty tomes while ladies of the night cling to the walls of the bar, other exquisite props packed tight at the round tables. The Detective is on stage, subjected to the intent, mocking gaze of books, a fickle audience. The Merlin sips his drink.

"Take Truman Capote and his story, 'Mojave.' Have you read it? You haven't, I see. I get it, you don't want to read another book ever again. Anyway, the gentleman whose books you haven't read and will never read, says that women are like flies, attracted to sugar or manure.

"Ms. Stadtherr, the writer I've *had to* read for this case, she . . ."

"Ah, your happily hanged suicide case."

"Anyway, she . . . she would say that it's not Capote who says that but his character."

"OK, it wasn't Capote then, but his character was right."

"Capote was a . . . fag."

The Doctor bursts out laughing and inhales a cloud of smoke.

"He loved demimondaines just like I do. But what is it *these* females want to achieve? What have they achieved by means of all that?"

"Perhaps . . . perhaps . . . compared to men, they have a more limited repertoire of classic roles available."

"But what do they want?"

"What they want . . . well . . . how about equal pay for equal work?" offers the Detective.

"Don't be silly, when a big bird decides to build a nest in the forest, the smaller ones have to stop twittering, that's how it is, men are simply more committed to their work."

"Do you really believe that?"

"I do, and so does Capote, and his character," says the Doctor with a smile. "I've never worked with a female who was my equal. And I don't want any more women doctors on the team. The *only* females I want are a secretary and a cleaner who comes regularly to sweep up the ashes from my Cuban cigars and my pipe on the windowsill."

The Detective orders another scotch and the Doctor offers him a fat Cuban cigar.

"I like reading Stadtherr," the Detective says, "she's not a feminist. She tells it as it is. And she understands men. She doesn't need a sex toy in her handbag. The *only* thing I can't stand is her theorizing and waffling about belles lettres while she writes historical works about strong men."

"You've lost me . . . again."

"What I'm saying is that *only* literature cuts right to the bone. Because it explores every possible hypothesis, character type, state of mind and situation, and because it shows, without prejudice, what is possible and what is not. Because it is able to capture the zeitgeist."

The Detective squirms in his chair.

"So what's your problem?" the Doctor retorts. "I agree with that. History shouldn't be depicted in purple and white, people shouldn't be divided into guilty and innocent, executioner and victim, that sort of simplification doesn't work, just as an eagle doesn't eat from its own nest."

The Detective struggles for air, defiantly and ravenously spitting out thoughts that have been going round and round his head, worried that he might miss the turn-off, ignore a no-entry sign, and fail to apply the handbrake before it's too late.

"But didn't you just say that you no longer read anything, my friend?"

"I don't, really, but I keep my eyes open," says the Detective." If I kept them closed I would never catch anything, not even a sparrow."

"All right . . . I've come across a few competent nurses and perhaps one competent woman writer. But have women actually achieved anything in any other field?"

"Let's leave it there."

"Leave it there?"

"Hmm. So, who's your favorite writer?" asks the Detective.

"Louis-Ferdinand Céline. He understands women, he knows that they are by definition bitches or maidservants or, best-case scenario, witches and fairies. And please note that this is not something said by a character of his. It's he who says that. Or rather, they both say that."

"Céline was . . . an antisemite."

The Doctor bursts out laughing. He enjoys the Detective's griping.

"His alleged antisemitism has nothing to do with this. The worst person he knows is himself, that's something he shares with Stadtherr. I wish that wacky lady were younger. I would have liked to meet her forty or fifty years ago. I'd have hit on her right away and had some fun with her, she must have been a great lay."

The Detective takes the fat cigar from the corner of his mouth to have a drink. It goes down the wrong way.

"I don't mean to be nasty," the Doctor explains. "But a beautiful woman wearing red lipstick is the root of all evil. They can do whatever they like. But they shouldn't kick up a fuss about it. I've seen murders committed by women and let me tell you, those murders were pretty sadistic. Ninety-nine out of a hundred women are jealous. All those headstrong mothers of devoted and polite sons whose confidence they've sucked out and whom they keep stifling. Because mothers have to look after themselves as they get older and their sons will do everything for them. I'm not saying they don't care about their sons—they do: you know the type that makes sure her little boy—never mind that he's forty or fifty—has had a decent meal and hasn't caught a cold in winter. And you know those mothers-in-law who can't stand young women. The *only* thing a headstrong woman is afraid of is a good thrashing. Patriarchy is society's only salvation, it's not an option, it's salvation. Just like democracy. No one has so far come up with a better idea."

They both fall silent. Each in his way.

Their eyes linger on the young women's beautiful bodies.

"A beautiful woman shouldn't be too bright."

"No."

"You know why I never married?"

"No, I don't."

"Because I spent too much time analyzing the world around me and that's not healthy. And because I enjoy sociology, in addition to hangmen."

"Yes, I know."

"Norms are something that groups of individuals agree on, based on their culture—norms are not given by nature, they're just cultural patterns no one can escape. The Kamasutra spells it out clearly. When starting a relationship with a woman, a man may touch her *only* in four ways. The universe of Indian eroticism distinguishes four kinds of embrace, like the four seasons. My friends all married dutifully. Things progressed quickly from there. I saw the screws being tightened. It was getting to me. They began to complain about stuff beyond their control. They developed stomach disorders, I know all about it because they came to me for treatment. Some were on their best behavior, but however impeccable it was, they would be constantly upbraided and nagged by their wives until one day they snapped and gave them an almighty thrashing. And next day everything was fine. These women have a kind of slave-like attitude toward men, you see, yoke and plow. If you love me, you have to keep me on a tight leash. But now that my friends are getting older and weaker, their wives are gaining strength. They will look after them. They have some kind of engine that powers their renewal, a backup generator. Whereas I . . . have been turning into a misogynist."

"Perhaps it's *just* a generational problem."

"Perhaps. I've *only* ever enjoyed the first phase of love. The boundless and crystal clear devotion, a kind of unique servitude."

Oh, go on, keep prattling on, sip your drink, snort your coke, or whatever is your poison, thinks the Detective, contemplating his glass of velvety honeydew, picturing the Widow's face. To make just one small concession is the right thing to do. Speak and behave with integrity. The *only* way to treat women is to be radical, without making any concessions or having any regrets: that is the *only* way both sides can be free and enjoy a new kind of relationship, one that is equal. Down with relationships based on dominance and subservience. Friendship requires two people: man and woman are one.

He doesn't understand why he does not say this out loud.

"Can you hear the baby swallows?"

"You've had one too many, young man. Let me call you a cab."

Out in the street, as he gets into the cab, the Detective turns around and gives the Doctor's body a firm hug.

"I do like you."

"There, there, this isn't the last time we're seeing each other."

The Detective gets into a yellow cab. Loud and clear, he gives the address of the glass house on the outskirts of Prague. His voice has never before sounded so firm and decisive. He has grown wings, and there is no room for them in the cab.

◇

Erika is feeding pigeons' beaks.

Honey emerges from the school building, ensconced in a gaggle of little girls. As she points her finger, *only* two girls peel away from the gaggle; the others retreat, disappointed. Erika tosses her last crumbs to the beaks.

Erika follows Honey. She is no longer hiding her body.

Their bodies are aware of each other, their eyes have felt each other up. Honey takes the girls to the mall. She lets them pick lace underwear. They rifle through brassieres, panties, bustiers, and giggle at garter belts. Erika's hand clutches a diamond-encrusted cross.

"Can I have a word with you? Just a quick one."

"Why? Can I help you with anything?"

"Yes, you can."

Honey puts down the tangas and turns to the two redbreasts.

"A word with you *only*."

Abandoned by Honey and disappointed, the girls drop armfuls of underwear they didn't manage to try on. Their stuffed wallet is leaving them.

Erika sets to work, flinging Honey right into the midst of a whirlpool. She introduces herself as a filmmaker about to shoot a documentary about young people across the world, this is her first time here, she doesn't know the city; the script is ready, it will feature local teenagers.

The words "documentary," "part in a film," and "script," fail to light any sparks in Honey's eyes. The *only* thing she agrees to is being interviewed. Erika suggests they go to a nearby Uxor-Hiom restaurant where they can chat undisturbed. Honey refuses. They will stay at the mall.

The escalators take them upstairs. They find seats in an area pretending to be a café.

Ruffling her feathers, Erika gets ready to run and leaps across a moat. She is ready to storm the ramparts without needing a drawbridge being lowered. In a firm voice she states that she has come across a case in this city that she finds interesting although it goes back some months; she has already spoken to Julia, surely you know Julia, the skinny brunette with buttons for breasts, she's at the same school as Honey. It was Julia who told her that she, Honey, is the top dog among the local youths, the *only* one who can shed light on anything. Erika prepares herself, then goes for the jugular.

"You knew what was going on. You, too, were raped and blackmailed."

Honey doesn't bat an eyelid. Doesn't avert her gaze. Her pulse remains steady.

"Except I enjoyed it. The missionary position, the butterfly, the spoon. You're too old to remember any of that."

Erika has tumbled into a moat of her own digging. Frightened, the waters close above her head.

Honey gives a smile. She gets up and leaves Erika, who has turned to stone. One day the world will calm down and we will feel it but it will take some time for our senses to get there. The two happy redbreasts join Honey, as if tied to her by an invisible thread. The three girls take the escalator down.

On the lower floor Honey bumps into a red-haired woman who grabs her by the elbow. Honey is paralyzed by the pressure, shivers run down her spine, her stomach heaves. Diana's clutch is firm and Honey, hooked, can do nothing but follow the wizened redhead to the bathroom. This is the first time Honey is scared. The redhead gently taps the middle of Honey's brow with the tip of her left index finger. Her beauty is stifled. She instructs the redbreasts to wait outside.

"Put a stop to it. If you stop what you're doing and help me release them from the cage, you won't come to any harm."

"Who are you to order me about?"

"I know what they did to you years ago."

"I've no idea what you're talking about."

"They hurt you."

"I've no idea what you're talking about."

"What you're doing is a crime. You've crossed all the red lines. And for what? For money."

"That's not what it's about."

"I see, it makes you feel special. It is gratification. A reward."

"Of course."

"Reward for what?"

"Never mind."

"What for?"

"For being the best."

"Who says so? Is it Yusuf?"

"I'm simply the best. You need a gun license for that cunt of yours. That's what he said."

"If you don't stop . . ."

"Then what?"

"I'll speak to your parents."

"They'll never believe you."

"These girls will speak out one day."

"No they won't."

"*Only* because they're scared of you."

"Of me?"

"I know what you've been doing to have them over a barrel. I know what online bullying can do. Stop laughing."

Birgit is waiting for a journalist. She has promised the head of the college to give an interview; Diana has already given one to the local rag, on yoga and birds.

Erika is not here; Birgit calmly goes over her own music collection. She puts on the Carolina Chocolate Drops, "No Man's Momma." The bell rings. Birgit muffles the music.

The journalist is not the youngest, a man with a soft, milky complexion and square glasses. He is nervous: he is not interested in literature and now he's been sent to interview a writer. Birgit is a pro. She makes coffee and proffers a pyramid of chocolate pralines and melon slices while announcing that she has *only* thirty minutes to spare, so let's get on with it, what would you like to know. As she prattles on, the dictaphone greedily devours Birgit's sentences as well as the journalist's voice, which sounds confident despite a slight speech impediment, and why shouldn't it, the first president of Birgit's country after the Velvet Revolution was unable to roll his *r*s either and look how far he got, the journalist was devastated when he passed away. Birgit realizes the *only* reason the journalist revered the Czech politician was that they shared this impediment. "Hm," she muses, "the *only* thing that matters is to live one's life in dignity, ripping off the labels, skin and all if need be, while the system has to be ignored, there is no other way, religious faith and political persuasion are private matters, like the color of one's socks. Gender also has to be a private matter."

The journalist has prepared for the interview like a model first grader. The same template all over the world, hmmm.

Birgit is holding her own against the speech impediment. Her eyes wander over to the receding hairline where a red spot is poking its head out of the black stubble. Next her eyes fly to the building across the road. The journalist promised she could talk about any subject she liked. Is there anything you'd like to tell our readers? Birgit speaks again about the world being a complex place, one that is hard to read for everyone, women as well as men, she doesn't distinguish between women's and men's topics, she wants to talk about politics, work, and literature, including that written by local authors. The journalist nods. A gong sounds. The thirty minutes are over.

Birgit turns the tables. Russian roulette.

"How about you?"

"What about me?"

"Do you remember the first case of alleged rape?"

"What case?"

"I mean the one in this town."

"In this town?"

"Yes, in this town."

"No, I don't."

"Hmmm."

Birgit turns off his dictaphone flirtatiously. She twitters casually about what she's heard. Things that had apparently been whispered about only to be hushed up. The whole affair has been hushed up, the Lynx was involved. It's been swept under the carpet, perhaps the journalist might like to take a peek under that carpet. Seeing as he is so perceptive, so smart. He will take a look, won't he? Surely he will. And he'll have some whiskey, won't he? Surely he will.

Birgit pours a stream of the amber-colored liquid onto the remaining drop of water at the bottom of the glass. Her hand brushes his. Inadvertently, matter-of-factly. She crosses her legs. The tip of her tongue licks the drop of amber off the bulbous glass.

"You should write about the clitoris."

"Excuse me?"

"Although . . ."

"I really must go now."

The journalist's bare butt is perched on a hot tin roof; a red patch appears on his cheekbone, coursing down the delicate white face, the eczema spreading. He needs her to authorize the interview as soon as possible, the deadline is tonight.

"You'll have to come back in person. I have no cellphone or email."

Diana walks into the restaurant. Her eyes appraise Yusuf's body. The body of the father of Julia's unborn child. A holy trinity: dad, mom, and baby, wherever you look. She didn't manage to stop Erika feeding pigeons; a feeble smokescreen for watching holy nuclear families around sandpits, parks, swimming pools, and wading pools. What Erika finds least exhausting is watching maternal love. As long as the bodies listen to one another. For Diana, the world of humans and birds is interchangeable, she sees *only* accomplished buildings, nests glued together with the saliva of swallows.

There are some islands in the Indian Ocean where a species of swallow builds its nests out of saliva that has turned solid, produced by its body *only* during the nesting season. For some people these nests are a delicacy.

Swallows are obsessed with being faithful, as well as with nests that they would never build were they not to live as couples. The male flies hither and yon, collecting mud and twigs. The female builds the walls of the nest . They waste no time, spring after spring. Storks return to their old nests instead of building new ones.

The female swallow lays eggs in her newly built home, hatching them with the warmth of her body; she doesn't move, all she does is sit around. The male feeds her lovingly and protects the nest. I need you because I love you.

Once the fledglings have hatched, both the male and female hunt for food from dawn to dusk, giving warning signals by tweeting. The chaffinch likes order and this is order. How much is hidden in routine and ritual. The chaffinch is not interested in exceptions harshly and comprehensively reeled off by the kingfisher.

Diana slips through the drape of red and orange beads. The beads coolly stroke her neck.

Yusuf watches the neck being licked by the orange and red runners. Yusuf can't help it, Diana thinks. He has been brought up, and lives, in a different tradition, he has been programmed, his body has been programmed, except that his program doesn't work in this part of the world. He fails to understand that he is unable to develop a new, less conspicuous program, to settle for a compromise. Yusuf is not burdened by thinking. The program collapses, attacked by a virus. He panics. He doesn't want to end up a cuckold. He doesn't want to provide for and raise children conceived by someone else. He is scared, just like generations of others have been for centuries. The social and religious customs, virgin marriage and the *droit de seigneur*, locked chastity belts, or purdah, the separation of some Hindu and Muslim women from all males apart from their husbands—none of this has helped.

Diana looks at him wondering about *her* droit de seigneur.

What kind of games do blue men and yellow women play these days? Why have relationships become so ruinously liberal? Do men pursue the sole goal of having as many sexual partners as possible? Is the *only* goal women pursue finding a suitable partner who will provide for them and their offspring? Or do they *only* look for a donor who will pass the best possible genes onto their nestlings? Or is none of this true any longer? What form does a family take? Will polygamy become acceptable? Will incest be no longer a punishable offence? Will a family consist of twos, threes, fours, and so forth, regardless of gender? Will friends live together? Are biological fathers becoming less relevant? Are individuals who are not related to a child but provide it with proper care becoming more important? Does this pose a threat to the child? Do men pretend they wish to remain faithful even if they have no intention of doing so? Do women want to expose their deception? All legal systems that called for punishment for male and female adultery have failed. Legal systems don't take love into consideration.

Honey pops in, as is her wont. Honey loves Yusuf and Yusuf loves Honey. Diana can tell. Honey becomes entangled in the bead curtain. She casually passes the redheaded eagle. She bends down to Yusuf, her fragrant breath hastily whispering into his hairy ear; a pair of surprised good-natured eyes turn to face Diana. Warning shivers lick Diana's back. Diana leaves a few coins on the table to pay for the glass of tap water she's had. She will find another restaurant. As she leaves, Yusuf runs out into the street after her. Diana steps out of the dusk. She strokes Yusuf's stubble.

Erika emerges from the church where she hid after her encounter at the mall. She can't stop thinking of Honey and how she has suppressed the fact that she was raped. She has been protecting her own body by luring other bodies into the dragon's den. Like a cruel brothel madam who had once been a prostitute herself. She has won the rat race and treats women no better than male pimps do. She employs mental instead of physical violence. Men tend to be masters of blue, physical violence. Women excel in yellow, mental violence. The end result is a victim who is excommunicated, goes insane, or commits suicide. This is what male and female slave masters have in common. Female solidarity is *only* an illusion. The more one group subjugates the other, the fiercer the competition among members of the lower ranks: women who share the same perch set upon each other first. It dawns on Erika what it is Diana has been fighting for all her life. She has tried a new model. One where women support other women. Bodies supporting and protecting other bodies. A swallow is not scared of another swallow.

Erika raises her head as gray clouds grow heavy in the sky. Someone up there is frowning. Dear gods, please be so kind as to explain what strange unease has been driving me. An unease that constantly insinuates I'm not good enough, constantly mobilizing doubts about myself, putting me down. Theology has a word for this: sinful. The entire Middle Ages were scared of women's bodies. Your wife's body may have been used behind your back but it may not kill the adulterous fetus. A woman's body is the devil's vessel. And the devil can be driven out by giving birth nonstop, to the point of exhaustion. By physical work, to the point of exhaustion. And if that is not enough, the body must be killed. It is a miracle that the nun Hildegard von Bingen wasn't burned at the stake for describing human sexuality and libido not as the devil's subterfuge but as a function of the human body. She explored genitals, which cause the bodies of girls as young as twelve to flow with juices, and the bodies of boys to spurt semen, oh those beautiful nocturnal emissions, beautiful onanisms, and masturbations.

My body is sinful because it is a female body. Dear gods, Birgit is right, the question needs to be rephrased: I love myself without having to achieve something or making sacrifices. I can accept and trust myself the way I am and *only* the way I am. But is this even possible, what with centuries of layers under my skin that put words into my head about playing second fiddle, words chipped from someone else's rib? Sinking deeper and deeper through centuries. Right to the very core of my being.

A sudden shower of nasty hail. Erika doesn't open her umbrella.

She's headed for a meeting with Birgit and Diana in a Chinese restaurant.

Erika is mystified that Birgit should have so much love for men, all men.

Birgit is reading. The journalist stands in the doorway, legs spread, passing her printed sheets of paper, holding them by their coattails between his two fingers. Birgit finishes the final page. She is fuming.

"If you talk the talk, you've got to walk the walk. You can't criticize the system and then help enforce it by censoring me and picking out *only* the most banal, casual, and stale remarks about child-rearing, fashion, men, and marriage. I'm not interested in discussing the height of heels. And marriage is a discipline I'm absolutely no good at."

"Our target group is . . . mostly women readers."

"Exactly. Are they brainless?"

"Well . . . Erm . . ."

"Don't impose stupid roles on them then. If you must cover women's topics, do it differently, write about their bodies differently, cover something that really matters. Where is your dictaphone?"

"I've really gotta go."

Red patches appear on his forehead and the nape of his neck, red clouds wandering around a windswept sky. Birgit snatches the dictaphone from his pocket and switches it on, her honeyed voice whispers into the secret transmitter. The journalist scurries behind her to try and get hold of the dictaphone. Birgit has him on the leash of her words.

"Clitoris, the king of pleasure and joy. Clitoris is my kind of penis. Even though I have always been told that the be all and end all of heterosexual sex is coitus resulting in the man's satisfaction. If my orgasm has ever been mentioned, it was *only* in the form of vaginal orgasm. Why don't you come back when you're less busy, come back, step over the threshold, and I'll give you a juicy interview about the clitoris, what it does for me, when and how. For centuries, men have grumpily pretended that it doesn't exist, so please don't confuse it with the vagina or the vulva."

"I'm not confusing anything . . ."

"You have to slash words with a whip. To make them precise and sharp." The journalist prizes the dictaphone from the orange fingernails.

It is not just his hands that are sweating. Birgit smiles, lifts her index finger and points it at the middle of the journalist's brow. The journalist's body backs away. Birgit curls her index finger and attacks. She presses a button on the dictaphone, erasing the recorded words.

"You don't have my permission to publish this interview."

The sweating journalist pleads: "But it will be great publicity for you."

"I don't need any publicity."

Birgit never discusses the subject of women's bodies or the subject of rape. Especially not in women's magazines. They are the best servants of the slave masters, the best at humiliating the victims.

She tells the journalist to go and interview the head of the college, he'll meet his deadline for sure. Then she heads for the Chinese restaurant to meet Erika. It is cloudy outside, it is pouring with rain. It is outrageous how women's bodies and women's orgasms are ignored. How the clitoris is ignored. It wasn't until 2005 that she read a detailed medical study that said that there are eight thousand nerves in the clitoris. Birgit joyfully fishes out an umbrella whose handle is inlaid with mother-of-pearl, given to her by Max Adler, her secret lover. Don't you think, Max, that embryology actually mocks the myth of Adam and Eve? Phallic bodies, the king's erect scepter, oh my, what if it's less potent than the other sex. Panic ensues. Women achieve pleasure by a different route, she used to tell Max, mere penetration is like the penetration of someone who is blind and scrambling down a dark tunnel in search of coal and misses the diamond. You know what, she used to tell Max, the embryo takes time to develop and decide what gender it will be. There is *only* a being, which might mean that the lord of creation is *only* one version of the female principle. Why not, what difference does it make, don't give me Adam's rib, why are you so scared, why do you stare at with me with such despair, why don't you say something, Max? Come on, talk to me, talk to me, what are you scared of, Max, don't go, don't run away.

She has never talked about these things to Erika because her friend is opposed to such a crude form of femininity and believes that *only* the spiritual path offers a freeway leading to a just world. Erika can't understand Birgit's independence. Birgit tells her about men's futile attempts to teach her to lie. "Some were obsessed with aggressive sexuality, which leaves no room for love. No man was able to put up with *my* independence. And what's worse, none would let me be independent." Birgit tells Erika about Marcel Reich-Ranicki, the illustrious literary critic who, in his dotage, would walk around Frankfurt with his wife of decades, pointing out the buildings, floors, and windows behind which he had enjoyed his trysts. "Can you imagine me doing such a thing? Can you imagine that? Me walking around town with my former husband and pointing out all those windows? Why do you stare at me with such despair, why aren't you saying anything, talk to me, talk to me please, I beg you, what are you so scared of, Erika, don't go, don't run away."

Diana is the last to reach the Chinese restaurant. Without a word she sits down to munch spring rolls and prawn dumplings. A large

Mongolian kettle is bubbling away in the middle of the table. Birgit replaces her reading glasses in their white case.

Erika dips thin slices of lamb, colorful vegetables, and glass noodles into the bubbling water and then into the hot sauces, some bitter, some sweet. The food of nomadic Mongols, the food of northern China: they never stayed in the same place for long and had to devise a simple and easily transportable way of preparing food. Erika forces down a tangle of hot soft noodles. She stops in her tracks when she notices that Diana is stiff and silent, she was supposed to reel off a summary of the latest news. Diana is the boss here; it's always been like that and always will be.

"They won't testify."

"None of them?" Erika asks, nearly choking on her food.

"Not one."

"Not even Julia?"

"Not even Julia."

"What about the skinny girl from the creative writing class, Milena?"

"Not her, either."

"And Honey?"

"Nope."

"They're all scared of being hounded on social media. They don't stand a chance with that sort of hounding, the woods are thick, webs interwoven, their endless paths treacherous. This sort of 'documentation' can't be wiped and destroyed *just* like that, once it's been shared far and wide. It's as if it has always been there. And they don't yet know that the *only* thing that is true is experience, *their* experience. Not what others say about them."

"So it's down to us again."

Diana orders ginger tea with honey.

"It'll be down to me again."

They order a small bottle of champagne. They bend in the wind like stalks of grass, leaning toward the earth spasmodically, like in a tattered silent movie. They yield, hoping in vain for someone to finally come and trample them down. A single momentary mistake means lifelong regret and lifelong regret is the kind of saliva swallows have no use for in building their nests.

"And what about the Lynx?"

"She keeps treading stagnant water and spouting tedious clichés. She is smart but pretends to be stupid. She says the girls were asking for it. But since she pretends to be an adult, I explained to her that adults must behave in an adult way, meaning they are supposed to protect confused bodies. An adult body mustn't abuse an adolescent body, it's as simple as that. An adolescent body is programmed to be attractive. Young girls try on femininity, which has taken them by surprise. They have just started learning to be women. Young boys play robbers with guns. But that's not a reason for me to get a gun license and mow them down with live bullets."

"I have prayed for these swallows so many times. To help them find inner peace."

"Let's draw a thick line under this whole business."

Diana is speechless. Birgit, staring into the empty crystal bowl, repeats that the root cause of the problem is human nature, no political system or religion can do anything about it, the *only* one that can do something is a mother who bends over her newborn lovingly, without expecting anything in return . . .

"Tell me, Blessed Erika, do you have any idea why Diana was so vehemently opposed to us taking up this case?"

Birgit grabs hold of Diana's hand. Diana doesn't try to pull it away.

"Because it's not the turtledoves she's trying to save, not even that mixed up girl, Honey."

Erika doesn't understand. She gulps down Diana's champagne.

"You really don't know, Erika?"

"I don't."

"It's all written here."

Birgit abruptly turns Diana's hand over to kiss her palm, spilling hot tea. Erika reaches for Birgit's untouched, frothing champagne that chokes on its own bubbles.

"Why doesn't she tell you herself? Tell Erika what dear Ingrid did to save her own neck."

"I can't."

"She ended up procuring young girls in the ghetto. You never told us."

"She confided *only* in me."

"She confided on paper. She, too, was a Honey Demon."

"From now on, I want to talk *only* about love and *only* about hope."

Erika sighs: "Why can't a daisy be Pope? Or a marigold, or a swallow?"

Diana gets up and stands behind them; she knows the quail will chirrup. She has been hiding from the hawk all day long. The quail, too, preys on insects. And the insects prey on creatures that are even smaller than them.

"There is so much that is beyond us, all the things we love and won't give up, so many things God likes," says Diana, to placate them.

"Would those things not exist otherwise?"

"They would not."

The three women leave the table. Once outside the restaurant they fly off.

It takes them a few hours to regroup, accompanied by a flock of incorruptible swallows.

In the midst of a snowstorm, Diana books flights and brings her intensive yoga master class to an end. The snowflakes falling are extraordinarily large. A flock of birds flies by the window, passing another flock in close formation.

Memories drift through Diana's mind: Diana as a student at the piano, Diana tickling the ivories and dreaming of becoming a photographer. Diana, supported by her loving family and discussing everything with her father—they would read newspapers together and sometimes she would go to meet him on his way back from the university, taking him by the arm and walking with him along the arcades. Diana on foreign trips with her mother, most recently to Copenhagen, her mother being Danish. Diana's father, who teaches anthropology at Oxford, focusing on indigenous tribes and their rituals, is forced out in the mid-career by another professor, a German Jew. Her father can't help it, these are the words he uses, a German Jew, yes, that's exactly what he says. His own words horrify him. The century-old hatred is ingrained in him, lodged deep within, a prejudice that even the noblest of values can't erase. Prejudice is steeped in emotions relayed by bodies as an unconscious and blazing torch; culturally ingrained prejudice includes preconceived notions of what the male and female body is for, which parents pass on to their children, it is never *only* about specific men and women, it is always about masculinity and femininity writ large. You can pull out the roots, but how deep do they reach? When the mind is under stress, the body is quick to flush out the hormone of prejudice, forcing dregs up to the surface, the rational mind struggling in vain as it tries to keep calm while also being convinced that it is racially tolerant and free of prejudice.

Her father's pride has been wounded twice over. First, by losing his job. The second time, by his own reaction to the loss. He packs his bags and leaves for India, his daughter scurrying along by his side. She believes she is holding his hand but in fact it is he who is holding hers, without realizing that the reason he has chosen this destination is that he is an Englishman and that deep down under his white skin he relishes the respect with which he is being treated in India. Here he can regain his battered confidence and retrieve his lost aristocratic honor, here he is king and they are his subjects, the mere fact that he was born a rich, smart white man in England lets his body thrive. The rich man is revered. He travels to India and introduces Diana to a young teacher, a former student of his, who has given up anthropology and taken up yoga. He gives Diana's body a thorough kneading, dissolving tension and teaching her hatha yoga and asanas. He puts her to sleep and Diana awakens from her first cleansing sleep into a dream.

Diana watches flocks of birds as their little bodies draw shifting pictures in the sky and move around changing shapes and copying the patterns of clouds. Diana watches flocks of birds and sees the hand of a painter, working on a large portrait of her mother. Bodies moving through the sky, resounding with Mozart's serenades and divertimenti.

Diana rolls up her green mat like a university diploma and inserts it into a tube. She winds a long white rope around her sharp elbow into a ball and pushes the ball into the tube, after the mat. She tears up her list of yoga class participants and throws it into the trash. She wipes down the floor. Wipes the door and the window handles with a small rag. Turns off the light. She stuffs the white-gold ring into a chamois glove.

She peers through the keyhole into Birgit's classroom to check if her friend has said her goodbyes.

The body in a green jacket and red tights is still leaping about. She will miss them as she does all her students. They will stay in her mind for months, she has given herself to them and it will take her a year to replenish the energy she has spent. Their writing has stifled her own sentences and made her curse them, but she does love them. Because Birgit doesn't wear a mask, she never has and never will. Birgit nurses a deep wound that Diana has never managed to overcome and never will. Birgit will take all her students back with her, buried under her skin. She hands out their marked assignments, framed with ironic comments in purple hummingbird handwriting, highlighting each student's greatest strength. She hands out farewell gifts. Diana listens out for Milena's voice amid the gales of laughter, but it is missing from the flock. Birgit hugs one body after another. They stand there, holding long straws which they press to her body and heart and suck, even though she used to scream at them, "You're not here to conform to anyone's goddamn ideas, why don't you tell the truth, why don't you admit that you're not comfortable with the life you're leading? That you wear your life like a coat that's too tight or much too heavy, that it's oppressing you and you're unable to take it off?"

Even after they have pressed their straws to her body and sucked her dry of energy, the kingfisher will miss them, these human beings; if they forget about themselves, they will be destroyed by heaven and earth, Birgit knows what human beings are like and how much they must endure before they lose everything. Birgit, so full of cheer and so sparkling today because it's over and done with, done and dusted. She concludes with words that Diana knows only too well: standing there with her ear pressed to the door, she is hearing her own words. Through the keyhole she hears Birgit quoting Diana: every being silently screams to be read differently, so teach yourself to read and begin right now, not through words but through gestures.

◇

The orange house at the foot of Petřín Hill has brought the Detective and the Widow together. It has liberated them. They no longer care what other people think, they don't care about what is expected of them by those around in this skewed, liquid age. They know that nothing can defeat the irrational nature of human life, that the *only thing* that exists are their tangible bodies and that they were meant to be together, and they were meant to be together at this time. The Detective is in the glass house on the outskirts of Prague, it's freezing outside but the glass doesn't crack. The Detective is looking forward to Advent. He watches flocks of birds he doesn't recognize. The flock shatters over his head into a pool of little bodies that won't give up. The Widow has made a pumpkin quiche. They are drinking strong coffee laced with rum. The Detective sees exhausted swallows sitting on the telegraph wires and a solitary swallow flying close to the ground, a Japanese cherry blossom in its beak, its strength waning. The Detective understands the music they make.

He tells the Widow that he would like to marry her. The mouth stuffed with pumpkin quiche gives a surprised laugh.

"Right now, or can I finish my coffee first?"

"I'll adopt your son and we'll have more children," says the Detective. "Just one, a girl," says the Widow. "And we'll invite the ladies from the orange house to our wedding." "Oh no, we won't," the Detective says. They would pontificate about Chinese swallows, they'd blabber and chirrup about the hard work the noble swallows have to do, they would go on about fledglings in the nest with their eyes glued to the darkening sky, and inform us that as recently as the 1920s married women didn't have a name, that the bridegroom had to pay the bride's parents for her and would lead her away like a sheep, and put her to work in a brothel until she earned the amount she had cost him; and how old women used to be banished from the village to snuff it in the fields like wild animals. The Widow gives the Detective a look and says she married young to please her parents, but now that she is a widow, she will marry to please *only* herself. And that women in Switzerland didn't have the right to vote until 1971, but so what, she doesn't want to talk about that now. Instead, she wants to know when they will be back. The Detective gets up and gives her a hug.

"Who do you mean, our *Old Ladies?*"

"Yes."

"Soon."

"I can't come to terms with it."

"With what?"

"That it was you who discovered the house at the foot of Petřín Hill. That they will be convicted based on *your* investigation and *your* incriminating evidence."

"He was your husband."

"If they had hanged him for something he hadn't done I would have been the first to report them."

"You mustn't think that way."

"I just can't come to terms with it."

They make love. The Detective falls asleep. He holds her body, holds it tight. Her body is his anchor in his restless dreams. He dreams of the three old ladies turning up at his wedding wearing birds' feathers in their hair. He walks them to a raft, grabs a long pole, and pushes them off the shore right into an eddy in the wild river. The three women stand on the raft, which begins to spin as the current carries them away. He clears out the orange house and, once gutted, sets it alight, the house is on fire and so are all the papers, registers, folders, computers, photographs, reels of celluloid film. Blackness devouring orange. As he sets the orange house ablaze, bodies of women and girls come winging out the window, squealing with laughter and soaring toward the sun like witches on invisible brooms, smart bodies that had to burn only because they refused to cook and do the laundry. A diamond-shaped sky towering above the scene begins to open like a vagina into which the bodies of girls and women disappear. The Detective is horny, while at the same time wondering why the swallows had to kick up such a fuss about something that was nothing but a black hole, a black void, a depth that was drawing him in, dark energy expanding across the universe. The vagina is Nothing. Nothing cannot threaten anyone or anything, why are so many people riled up by Nothing, why does it incite so much hatred and arouse the desire to assault and torment and abuse, where does the fear that thrusts a knife between the legs come from? The knife slips from the Detective's fingers. Everything is hanging by a thread.

He wakes up and gently pushes the Widow's body aside, freeing himself from her embrace. He goes to the freezer for some chilled vodka. He pours himself a first icy shot. Then another. And a third. He fires up the dead man's computer, quietly, so as not to wake up the Widow or the child, and goes online. As always, he types in the names of the three women, a compulsive daily ritual; he types in the name of the city where the toxic witches have been staying, searching for news, *honey bunny*. He skims through articles in the local press, including an unauthorized interview with Ms. Stadtherr, the questions trembling like jelly. The Detective has been keeping an eye on local events, on everything to do with the Honey Demon case. A turbulent trial is underway, brimming over with lovers' resentments and convoluted political polemics that are impossible to follow—people showing solidarity with Yusuf, the man who has worked so hard and paid his taxes; it's not easy to make it in a new country and it's disgusting and unacceptable to attack someone who has made this country his home, to bring up his mother tongue, religion, and nationality like this. He clicks on photos taken in the courtroom. He zooms in and focuses on the last row of seats. Next to Adler, who is asleep, and Eis, a smiling mimosa, Stadtherr's face, invisible, hovers over a sheet of paper, an inkwell and a Montblanc fountain pen in her hand. The Detective feels nauseous, his face turns pale and he stifles the computer.

HALF-NESTS

Swallows congregate above the city with bags under their eyes, their departure for warmer climes long overdue. They won't fly away until they can be sure that they will be able to return safely to their nests under the eaves.

The court hearing is open to the public. They sit in the last row.

Diana is looking into her pocket mirror, hands concealed by chamois gloves. She greets the public prosecutor with a nod of the head. The Lynx doesn't smile, turning her back on her instead.

The three women remain silent throughout. *Only* Birgit scribbles something every now and then into a blue exercise book with a sharpened white pencil. On all the notes written by the studious schoolgirl's right hand, Birgit's left hand comments with a purple fountain pen. How labored her breathing is.

The counsel for the men's defense claims the girls were *only* prostitutes and no one had forced them into it. The defense shore up their argument with a confident quote from Yusuf's pre-trial testimony. A kestrel aspiring to be a merlin, a cigar and whiskey in hand.

"It was their job to entertain us, after all. What else are they good for?"

The Lynx squirms, the white blouse under her black jacket buttoned right up to the chin; the glance of one of the defense counsel team has inadvertently slipped into the cream lace that sits around her neck like a displaced feather boa.

"In that case, they have come up with an ingenious new model of prostitution: the girls have never seen a single penny from the men. If someone did pay, it was the men paying Mr. Yusuf and his accomplices who were in charge of the gang."

Witnesses are called. Barrel organs on a conveyor belt. The warblers and nightingales are called. They chirrup sentences describing sexual practices unheard of before the war, but which don't make anyone bat an eyelid nowadays—after all, it's just another way of bringing together two people who've been through a lot in their lives, big deal.

A regular visitor to Yusuf's apartment says that what he'd done can't possibly be regarded as rape as he *ONLY* stuck his fingers into their vaginas.

This sends Diana's blood racing in her temples and makes her hands sweat in their chamois sanctuary. She takes the two other bodies by the hand, shush. The white pencil flies into the air and rolls under the benches. The die is cast. Diana is waiting for the sign, hoping against hope that it won't come, that the pernicious little word *only* won't reach its destination. How much is hidden in routine and ritual. They've never set foot in this place, never breathed the local air, shush.

Birgit bends down wearily to pick up the pencil from the ground. Blood rushes to her head. Don't you ever forget, you kingfisher, that in prison you must never bend down to pick anything up from the floor. The pen comments in purple on the goings-on in the courtroom. Her body fears that the tables will be turned with the girls ending up behind bars. Her body is scared, and instead of purple ink it lets red beads spill from their string and tumble to the ground: the beads rain down from the torn necklace, scattering around the courtroom filled with sawdust and letters of the alphabet that no one wants. She doesn't want to look at them either, having had to look at them all her life and watch them roll about walls and spin around ceilings, crawling like spiders or drops of mercury, abjectly flowing down thighs like drops of blood. Skinny and horny dogs are grateful for any fresh piece of flesh.

Erika is directing a documentary in her head. She will film on two cameras. No, four. A restaurant and a large apartment with Persian rugs. The flaccid face of Julia's mother in the audience; fear in her eyes: she doesn't understand what her daughter has gotten mixed up in. She is shocked and furious at her daughter and tells anyone in the audience who is willing to listen: can't you see she's just a child? Then she throws the switch and says, I can't believe the lies that brat has been spouting, no such thing could happen in my house or in this town, we're a respectable family, a few slaps across the face and everything will be fine. Julia's mother's eyes betray the fear that she might be called as a witness herself. Erika observes the mother's lips, hearing in her head the third movement of Brahms's *Violin Concerto in D major, Op. 77,* allegro giocoso ma non troppo, the hand holding the bow is Menuhin's, the violinist's coat and tails are her mantra.

Hands clenched into fists rise. Piles of trash keep growing. Hands toss more trash onto the feathers of budgies and redbreasts, wagtails and goldcrests, cuckoos and robins, bluetits and pipits, redpolls and starlings, turtledoves and doves. The hands would cast stones if they could. The time for casting stones has come. Trash and rocks are aggressive words, a cesspool of aggressive words and sentences. Words and sentences barked at the victims, insisting that the violent men meant well, that they *only* gave what the fledglings' bodies wanted. And over their morning newspapers, bald-headed burghers, men and women alike, comment: surely this sort of thing can't be happening in our town, as their daughters sit at the table and blink obediently like dolls, demurely nodding and lifting their breakfast to their mouths. Erika would alternate this footage with shots from the courtroom, she would also shoot in the corridor and in the large space outside the courthouse. She would film the courtroom where the case is being tried and the town squares with their screaming slogans. And over the shots she would let joyful music play, *Swallows* by Benjamin Godard.

Groups of young bodies gather outside the courtroom at dawn. Banners are carried by a crowd of protesters in hobnail boots, with triangles for mouths, the scarf ends dangling from their chins. They are calling for a clean planet. They demand safety for their children. Once the scarves are gone, they reveal open mouths. The protesters believe that these men used white girls in revenge for being treated as second-class citizens in this country. They *only* did the same as white men in the colonies who used to take *their* girls with impunity and still do so wherever they can. Starving young girls in Africa are still taken in this way, as are girls in Thailand and Cuba, except, esteemed ladies and gentlemen, over there it's called sex tourism nowadays.

Women's bodies. They are dangerous when they are free. In the old days England had subjugated its colonies. Now *they* have subjugated England through the bodies of these girls.

A dictatorship of violence.

Diana is unnerved by the crowd that has gathered in the square as it *only* distracts from the truth with its pointless labeling and pigeonholing. This is what she has been fighting against all her life—labels should be ignored, the focus should be *only* on bodies—but they have come back with a vengeance. A hot flush. The politicized crowd is manipulated by the Lynx, who has used the internet to divert attention from herself. The young people are here to support her. This is not what Diana wants, it is not what she has ever wanted. Labels such as Right and Left have lost their meaning. Fall is on its way out. Spring is a long way off.

The fledglings are called to testify. The girls are in the witness stand, looking fresh though they are tired, and there is an intense vacancy in their eyes.

Milena is among them, as is Julia. Honey is not here, her dad kicked up a fuss and used the ruckus to take his daughter home, having silenced everyone with his nightingale's song: Honey had no idea about of any of this, we're not that sort of a family, we're not like those junkie sluts and their families, poverty or affluence cannot be hidden.

Erika is not surprised: having followed her golden trail, she knows the Honey Demon like a pair of uncomfortable shoes. The girl is a hard nut to crack. Honey is not stupid, Honey is on her guard, Yusuf has warned her that a limping lady was loitering, claiming to be looking for her granddaughter and making a documentary. Honey goes to school, to her piano classes, she enjoys the support of her loving family. She talks to her dad and sometimes goes to meet him on his way home from the bank. She takes foreign trips with her mom, most recently to Copenhagen, her mom is from Denmark. She's a hard nut. She will be difficult to crack.

The defendants are seated on a bench right behind the nestlings. The nestlings can feel their breath on their necks. The nestlings are frightened. They testify. They testify that *these* men are, in fact, their friends, their boyfriends. Yes, quite a bit older, but why not, love can be surprising, invincible, pernicious, love creeps up and assails the heart from the most unexpected direction at the most unexpected moment, love and death have a great deal in common.

"Are you trying to say that you shared your boyfriend with thirty others and were OK with that?"

"Why shouldn't I, they're my girlfriends and Honey is my best friend, the best ever."

"What about being faithful, does that mean nothing to you?"

The nestlings cheep in tiny voices. Some are anxious and stutter, others stick their tongue out at their fear, are cheeky and seemingly confident, while others, the most naïve and fragile ones, are happy to be at the center of attention for the first time, it's nice to be photographed in daylight for a change and it's not painful, aww, what a joy to exist in real time rather than being in limbo. Erika clutches her diamond cross pendant. Every now and then she speaks to it quietly, oh so quietly, negotiating with God although she has no idea which one, but she knows God understands her, she is praying to her God, her God takes the form of a swallow and a dandelion. Finally.

Birgit teases her, God makes plans and God is laughing, but Erika contradicts her in her mind, arguing that what is happening around them contains *no* words, *only* a telling silence and a thunderous stillness.

The prosecutor points out that the gang was headed by the owner of the Uxor-Hiom restaurant, a man called Yusuf.

Not one of the nestlings testifies against him.

Songbirds caught in a net, crammed into a single cage. They won't open their little beaks, they won't sing. Julia doesn't cheep either. Diana looks at Julia, who has been brutally raped as many times as Diana has played her fledglings *Swallows Soaring* by Agathe Backer-Grøndahl. She played it to them instead of a lullaby.

Finally, it is Yusuf's turn to testify. Beauty has to be destroyed and smashed to smithereens on a daily basis, while at the same time feeding it by making it destroy others. To stay alive. In the azure-blue air, Birgit catches a sentence that keeps being repeated in the courtroom like a chorus.

I tried to get out but it was impossible.

They don't open their little beaks. And the text written by Milena, who sits in front of the Lynx, scribbled on a sheet of paper folded into the shape of a swallow, cannot be used as evidence, it can *only* be thrown out of the window.

Chandra Namaskar, the moon salutation. This is nothing like Honey's birthday party, where our classmates swarmed around her parents' house, sipping drinks and strutting around screaming and shouting and dancing to booming music that made the walls shake.

No noise passes through the walls here, only silence. Cigarette smoke and still-glowing embers in overflowing ashtrays swallow up every trace of noise. The windows aren't blacked out. At the door to the apartment, a boy takes away my phone. I don't like that. I've been saving up for it for a long time. This is a compulsory admission ritual. It's for your own good, the boy says, to make sure you don't lose it, I'm kind of like a hotel safe here, he says with a reassuring wink. We have both been chosen.

I tread across the thick pile of the Persian carpet. There are carpets everywhere. They spill across thresholds continually like a dense lawn, sticking their tongues out under my steps. I look forward to having my pictures taken by a professional photographer. That's what Honey promised me.

The boy ushers me into a smoke-filled living room. A man is kissing a girl on a sofa. They're like a classical statue emerging from the mist. The girl might be about thirteen. As they peel off from each other, tiny stones in the girl's braces sparkle like diamonds in her mouth. The man seems old. They glance at me. He looks me up and down, from head to toe. The girl's eyes connect with mine, her stare is swept clean and empty, I can read nothing from it, then the two latch onto each other again. Two glass bowls filled with white powder sit on the coffee table before them. The smoke and nicotine mist make me nauseous but I don't let on, I want to belong, I do belong, I've made it. After weeks of soundings and failed attempts I've finally done it. Curiosity is making my head spin. Honey is making my head spin. Here she comes. She gives me a welcoming hug. I giggle to boost my courage and shed my fear. Honey hugs me and flatters me, says I look lovely, but all I manage in my excitement is a stutter. She hands me a bottle of chilled vodka. We drink it straight from the bottle here. She puts her arm around me and summons the boy who collects and stores the phones by the door. She is bossy with him, it's obvious who's in charge here. That'll be all for today, she tells him. I can't tell if she's talking about girls or phones. The boy rolls me a joint. I take a puff and shake my head. I give him the spliff back. The boy passes the joint to Honey, who sticks it in the hand of the man glued to the lips of the girl with diamonds in her mouth.

The boy lights a cigarette and forces me to take it. But he treats me with respect, I'm glad he gets it. I'm here with her. I'm proud to belong to her, the rich and beautiful one, the coolest girl in our school, the mysterious Honey. She has chosen ME. Now the boy puts on some music, not too loud. Plaintive music. Honey begins to dance, her arms raised above her head. Her lips are the color of raspberries, covered in a thick layer of lipstick. She lets her hair down. She electrifies the whole room. Other girls join in. She dances in their midst. Everything happens in near-silence, yet it's so deafening, so intense, so beautiful. Honey puts her hair up again. From the adjoining rooms, as if on cue, dark clouds begin to sweep in. They are not boys as Honey promised. And there's not going to be a fashion show like she promised, and I won't get the make-up either. The photoshoot for a modeling agency she promised isn't going to happen either.

The ants come swarming in and traipse around the dancing girls, who are tipsy and stoned, joining and swaying along with them. I feel someone's shoulder touching me. I don't like it. I take a step back. The man prizes the unsmoked cigarette from my fingers, the snake of ash falls off, the man catches it in the palm of his hand. He closes his fist, puts what's left of the cigarette to his lips, draws deeply. I look him in the eye. I think of the glowing ashes in his hand. He has beautiful eyes. Black. A serpent of smoke slinks out of his lips. He steps aside and has a word with Honey. He comes back and wordlessly places his hands on my hips, I'm worried he'll notice how bony they are. He makes me sway and slides his hand inside my panties as we dance, squeezes my butt, it gives me goosebumps, I don't like it but I can't scream in this place, it would make me a laughingstock and Honey would never invite me back, and it would ruin my chance at a different life. He keeps sliding his finger between my butt cheeks, a stick moving upward. I don't want this, I yank myself free, I want to leave. The guy laughs, steps back and says something to another guy in a V-neck T-shirt with a picture of Arnold Schwarzenegger on it, not sure from which movie, the guy in the T-shirt is old. Everyone around here is old, they're all over twenty, some much older. The guy in the T-shirt isn't laughing, now he whispers something to Honey while laying a white line on the table. Honey's face turns serious. This is a different Honey, not the one I know. They are playing Telephone.

Honey is no longer smiling at me, she comes up to me, she is pissed and tells me to relax, not to be a softie, unless I want to blow the chance of a lifetime. She guides me to a table where the guy in the T-shirt has readied the line of cocaine. Have some, Honey says, it goes with photo shoots and filming, it'll help you relax, you'll come to like it here, you want your phone back don't you, but you gotta earn it first, don't be silly, all this is fucking free, tell me where else you'd get all this stuff for free. She forces another gulp of vodka on me. Or do you want something different? One more gulp. Its heat sears my insides, I'm aglow, I'm a torch and I'm slowly starting to like it here, I feel the warmth spread inside me, it makes me sway and everything around is swaying, Honey removes my shoes, I walk barefoot on the soft carpet, from time to time someone lifts me up and I send the chandelier above rocking, the carpet tickles my feet, it feels funny, grass is growing all the way up to the ceiling, and so is my hair, it's turning into snakes, I'm in the bathroom, grab a pair of scissors and cut the snakes, snip their little heads like my grandma used to cut slugs on her vegetable patch, she'd snip each one in two so that she wouldn't have to touch them as she used to before, when she picked them up and tossed them into salted water, I turn on the faucet and let water run through my hands. Honey smells of the expensive perfume that she'll lend me one day, we're already wearing the same nail polish, she's let me borrow that too, and I'm wearing the T*-shirt she's bought me, she's my best friend, I hug her, she hugs me, we dance together, I want the other girls to see who I am, she drags me to the back of the room, I stagger, she keeps pouring something down my throat along the way. My head is on fire, my head droops, I have the body of a rag doll, I'm a rag doll and I am as beautiful as Honey, we have a laugh, surrounded by subdued faces and subdued sounds and subdued light, which is really darkness. Honey takes me to another room, some figures are lurking there in the semi-darkness. She slams the door shut on me, I start pumping the door handle but I feel hands around my waist and tentacles around my breasts and between my legs, an octopus teasing and tickling me, I laugh, the octopus clings to me even more tightly, I start screaming, I don't want this, please stop, who are you, I shout, but it's all so senseless and pointless, I'm reduced to screaming in the chaos and fear without beginning or end, because right at that moment the fear has taken residence and settled inside my body, from now on my body will be its home, it will disturb the delicate mechanism of my soul, it will taint my trust in everyone and everything and it will strengthen the part of me that's never really been me and that I hate, but I need it now,* *otherwise I'll fall apart. One of them holds me down and the others take turns. It's as if my body was being pummeled and hammered inside some diabolical machine to a rhythm that makes me choke and dribble, then my mouth goes dry and I feel paralyzed and benumbed as if pumped full of Novocaine but then the pain comes back and eventually silences me, the pain is a gag in my mouth, time has dissolved.*

When I come to, Honey is standing above me. She pretends that nothing has happened. Call the police. This is what I want to say but words won't make it past my lips, my lips hurt, everything hurts, I'm shredded like an animal. The memory of an article flashes through my mind, we discussed it at school, I thought it was boring, it was about this student who was raped somewhere in India or some other shithole, over there they lure them into fake buses before tearing their bodies into pieces just like they did mine. I'm also riding a bus but this one won't stop, it keeps accelerating and it doesn't even have blacked out windows, I'm still in the same city and the same country, I live in a civilized country, this is Europe, what do I have in common with filthy India, I know nothing about India and don't want to know anything, I'm better, I'm chosen, India used to be a colony, India used to belong to us, that's all I know.

The transformed Honey lights a cigarette. She no longer behaves like a friend, she no longer behaves like a mom to whom I've gotten attached. Blandly, she states that nothing has happened. I'm not going to breathe a word about this. And if I'm smart, I could earn good money. You're Milena now, isn't that cool?

I stare at Honey open-mouthed and my ears can't believe what she's saying. The thought crosses my mind that she's gone mental, that I'm only dreaming. No, I'm not dreaming, my body reminds me of that. As do my wide-open eyes. They're about to pop out of their sockets. There's an empty pain between my thighs, the pain has teeth that bite me and the vodka is gnawing at my insides again, there's something cool on my neck, I feel a draft coming from somewhere, something's panting on my neck, a sour breath, I want to throw off the heavy sack of cement, I want to run away, whatever it is sticks its tongue down my throat, I thrash about but it thrusts its full weight on top of me, I can't move my legs, I'm a flattened frog, I get pins and needles and my thighs go numb, more teeth glittering and ambushing me, what are they waiting for, I resist, now some fingers squeeze my neck, I'm gripped by tentacles and can't move, I can't breathe, the pain bites me and won't let go. I open my mouth to scream, and I see Honey-fairy hovering above me, she places a finger across my mouth and forces another gulp of chilled vodka dusted with the white powder between my lips, her sweet face comes closer, whispering into mine, this is just a test, sweetheart, an initiation rite, I'll reward you if you pass. The vodka trickles down my throat, this time it cools my body, I scream and shout, white teeth flash as my face is slapped, I stop screaming and start counting in my head, I hang on to numbers, it's got to stop sometime, no idea how long I have to count, three-digit figures and salvation, the pincers loosen their grip, the sack of cement slides off, as if on cue the bodies surge out and start to dance.

I no longer have a body. I don't want this body, this body is theirs, I feel like throwing up, I thrash about, the sack of cement is gone, there's nobody here I could pummel, only this body, I pull on my pants and T-shirt, shove my panties into a pocket, I don't wear a bra, what would I put in it anyway, my shoes are in the other room, somewhere in the thick growth of carpet where people are dancing, I see three guys dragging Julia, a girl I know from school, I pretend not to see her, I pretend I don't recognize her, one of them twists her arms behind her back and I hear Honey's voice behind me, look, this is what'll happen to you if you dare to tell, this one's been ratting to the police, and now they're not so nice to her anymore but they were nice to you, quite gentle actually, you'll come to like it eventually, once they've all fondled you, you'll be ours forever, we'll look after you, or else everybody will make fun of you, all of them, me, the whole city, the whole world, it's up to you, but you're really good, so welcome to the club, and if you bring us another kid like you, I'll pay, you'll make good money.

I am a member of the club, one of the cool crew that the whole school has been whispering about, one day maybe I'll find out why this is supposed to be a liberation, why this is meant to be heaven, why the girls around me act so different and distant, why they have this unnatural, loud laugh and why they talk like this and are so fucking happy just because someone's decided that this is what joy is, why didn't anyone warn me, I'll never set foot in this place again, ever.

So you won't, huh? Honey turns serious. You disappoint me. She waves a phone in my face and plays some footage, I've seen this girl before, she's all blurry, naked, totally naked, you almost can't make her out, there's a guy sprawled on top of her skinny body. You behave yourself, or this goes online, no one will believe this wasn't what you wanted, no one. Then she hugs me. You've finally started to live your life to the fullest, something's happening at last now, and I love you, you know that, don't you. My body recoils from her, pricked by tiny needles. Honey gives me her sweatshirt, here, borrow that. She props me up. She's being nice. We go down the stairs and out into the street where a guy in a car is waiting to give me a lift home. Honey is being nice. I won't get in. The guy starts the engine and drives off.

I'm standing inside an unfamiliar body in a familiar street.

Honey is now turning to another girl and nobody seems to be surprised by anything, I'm out in the street, it's night and I'm barefoot and I toss my panties into a trashcan, I throw up on top of them, I don't know what to do, I think of Julia who is being battered up there, Honey said nobody believed her at the police station and everybody now thinks she's a total loser. Two people pass by, an elderly couple out walking their dog, they recoil from me in disgust. Please, I want to say, please help me. I say nothing. They are followed by a couple of staggering drunks, look at that cute little cunt, isn't she a hot little cunt, that's what I hear in their laughter and I start to weep. Please someone, help me, I want to say. Chandra Namaskar, the moon salutation.

I slip through the door at home, everyone is asleep, I load my body into the bathtub and scrub it down with Mom's soap, I don't want this body anymore, I want another one, but this is the only one I have, I have to stay in it, there's no way out, I'll be stuck in this body for the rest of my life, the horror of it dawns on me. But maybe there is a way out, perhaps I can write myself out of it, I will sign up for the class this woman is going to run next year, it's been touted at school. My body is lying, it's lying on the ground, it doesn't want to get into bed because it's like roadkill, a stray dog who has no one, only Honey, only Honey is nice to the bodies.

In the morning, Dad peers through the door, what's going on, time to get up, Mom peers in too, we both have bags under our eyes but she has hers for a different reason, Dad no longer sleeps with her, he sleeps with other women, but she won't divorce him, she couldn't afford the rent without him. And so they both go staggering around in their respective dependencies, unnecessarily singed by them, they've been fighting ever since I can remember. They complain about being alone. Even though they have me and my brother and my sister. I have bags under my eyes because I've lost my virginity. Someone is bound to come and help me, surely. First, I'll get rid of this body. I cut myself. I don't feel anything. My body doesn't belong to me. It mocks me. It is disgusted with me. It has betrayed me. They have betrayed me. She has betrayed me. Fear loves me. But if I go through the same thing again, and don't let it happen this time, show that I can defend myself, if I pull this off without giving a shit, I'll be back in my body. My memory will be erased. Please help me, swallow.

My body is crying. Because it wanted to fall in love, but it had no idea how to move in this hostile territory.

The first days of the court hearing are drawing to a close.

Diana, Birgit, and Erika are exercising in a swimming pool. Their bodies walk, rather than swim, through the water. Thighs moving in slow motion, they are washing off the dirt of the courtroom. They massage each other's backs. They hold their breaths, dive, and fly close to the surface. Swishing through water, they spread their wings. A terrified pool attendant jumps into water after them, and a lady in a gaudy golden swimsuit gives him a reassuring caress.

They go to a Japanese tea house. The front yard is modeled on a Japanese garden, complete with rocks, moss, and a little stream. The entrance is low. The interior is unadorned, except for an alcove with some calligraphy, a photo of Japanese cherry blossom, and a vase with a simple arrangement of flowers. A slender, unpainted column in the middle of the room. Dimmed lights. A gently bubbling sacred iron kettle. An echo of the wind's voice in pine treetops. Greetings limited to bows, the guests are quiet, no one speaks.

A Japanese man stirs strong green tea into boiling water, slowly and solemnly. He proffers one small bowl after another. A shared experience, a melding of the "I" with earth, water, fire, and wind. The deep-felt harmony among the three friends has been renewed, a communality at the time of death; the human heart controls the state of all things.

They take a look at Honey's house through ornithologists' binoculars; she is in the garden helping the gardener and her father sweep up the fallen leaves. As if nothing were happening. Work ennobles us and her dad has found a new school to enroll her in, the experiment with a democratic upbringing has failed, he wanted his daughter to meet children from a variety of social classes. But cultural and social differences really exist and are insurmountable, Honey will now go to an expensive private boarding school surrounded by a wall, she will be given a warm welcome by the head who knows about the ordeal the family has been through and the bullying Honey has suffered. Diana folds the binoculars into their shell case; come the night, Honey will give them the slip anyway, how much is hidden in routine and ritual; the women sit cross-legged talking to Ingrid, who is not here. My old friend is my new friend; I am the same and do the same as I used to before.

The women don't discuss the trial. They open their folders, spreading out photos and rummaging through faces acquired with the help of pocket mirrors. A card game with photographs. At the end of the game two cards are left on the table. The contaminated Honey and Yusuf. They argue, then proceed to a silent vote. Erika's fingers are an owl hooting, she tries to protect Honey's face.

Birgit draws purple crosses over the two winning heads. Erika is upset.

"Men do whatever they like."

"Would you like to be born as a man in your next life?"

"I want to be born a free human being."

Defiantly, Erika puts on Mozart's motet, *Ave verum corpus*. They are clearing out the apartment. They stuff their clothes into blue plastic sacks, tie them with a cord, and carry them to trash cans outside. Diana is wearing her old uniform with the garrison cap, she sits on the floor, her eyes closed, legs firmly crossed Turkish style. Can you die for something you no longer believe in? This is how she felt as she lay in her room as a young girl, promising herself and the night to grow into a decent, kind, and beautiful human being and achieve great things in life. Erika and Birgit burn papers in the washbasin and flush them down the toilet. They strip the beds, throwing the bedding into a trash can which they take to the dumpsters outside the neighboring block. They wipe off the fine dusting of ash covering the kitchen surfaces. Erika prepares a thick, milky cocktail and decants it into a thermos flask. She places it by the green bag, which they have never opened. Diana is the *only* one who opens it. They leave Diana alone and go for a walk. Detachment. A much appreciated attitude.

Bodies of serpents intertwine inside Diana, decisiveness is key; Diana is not going to give in because *only* feathers change with the seasons, everything else stays the same. The war for water supplies is the war of the future. Young women tread through a minefield, through enemy territory carrying water, they are punished for allowing themselves to be raped by being locked into shacks and left to die of thirst, or they are burned as witches without further ado. This kind of behavior boosts egos, making societies stronger, this is how those in power behave, yes, we want all the details, bring them on. Lately, male prisoners of war have been raped too, there is a growing groundswell of protest, retaliation, and outrage, how dare they do that to men's bodies, oh no, spare us the details please, in Srebrenica men were forced to blow each other at gun point, the body betrays them, the body sides with the conquerors, but what kind of conquerors are these, the body ejaculates, oh no, spare us the details, please.

The restaurant on the main drag seethes with indignant words, screams of outrage at the insults endured. Diana walks into the Uxor-Horn restaurant which no girl or woman dares to enter nowadays, police stand guard there though they don't guard it properly: at dawn they have to scrape off with their own hands what's been daubed on the windows. Groups of supporters and opponents huddle outside the restaurant, barking pariah slurs at each other. Before passing through the curtain of orange and red beads Diana smiles at two men. They are plainclothes cops. She touches their chests.

She touches the chest of the restaurant owner, poor Yusuf has shouldered the burden of the sins of this world without realizing it. No one will know, and even should someone find out, one of these days, Diana no longer cares.

Diana thanks him. She thanks him for the delicious food and says: isn't it terrible what's going on today, don't let the gossip get you down, it will melt away with time, it's a shame I have to leave town, you should let your staff look after the restaurant, you shouldn't be working and serving guests today, with all these people gawping and shouting abuse at you, they're all nasty racists and Nazis, you should take a rest, I run yoga classes downtown and could teach you some relaxation techniques and meditation poses, I could teach Honey too, let me just pop over and get three mats.

Yusuf is so dazed that he joins her at the table and agrees. He is a nervous wreck, he's not mad, he just doesn't understand what the problem is, why he can't leave the country, plus he can't find his passport, he doesn't get it, why is he being hounded and chased like some animal, he's a good man, a good Muslim and a good person, he's been sending money to his parents, this country is crazy, he should never have come here, those girls should be happy that he noticed them, they could *just* have had a good time, they're *just* girls, lying bitches, you know the kind, and poor Honey, did you hear the terrible lies they told about her, she is *just* a child from a good and affluent family, Yusuf is traumatized, he'll sue for damages, he'll ask for lots of money because this threatens his livelihood and his honest business, he doesn't care for this kind of publicity, although, on the other hand, you can see how crowded the place is, all the men in this town love his restaurant, they're all regulars here.

"So you feel traumatized, do you?"

Diana touches his forehead with the tip of her forefinger. Heads or tails.

"I could help both you and Honey."

Yusuf's body grows slack. Diana's lips whisper into his languorous ear the mantra of the night they will spend together.

◇

He sits in the kitchen nursing a fourth vodka. Why does it have to be me, he thinks, why me of all people, a person can bear *only* so much. The Detective pours himself a fifth vodka. He must pretend he doesn't know anything.

Once again, our pilgrim is staring out into the night, with pins and needles in his thighs, unease and stress, he can't make up his mind, and so he gazes at the moon, wishing he could be as good and as wise again as he used to be as a boy, but he doesn't say so out loud now, it would sound ridiculous, even the half-empty bottle laughs at this naiveté. But somewhere deep inside his child's voice speaks up and the grown Detective hears it, he can still hear it. No, they won't live in this glass castle, the Detective's body decides. They will get married and make their own way in their own world, accompanied by swallows. The Doctor will be his best man, the Merlin can be a real pain but he has courage. They will move to another town, another country. He already knows which one.

But there's one thing he has to figure out first and he will figure it out.

He phones his sleepy partner, the one who has tracked down Stadtherr before. He asks him to check passenger lists at all airports and railway stations and find all connections to Prague from a certain European city.

◇

Birgit, Erika, and Diana are in the Chinese restaurant, they have brought the green bag and the rolled up green yoga mats. They have ordered prawns and pork dim sum, deep fried spring rolls and miniature pork ribs. Erika doesn't eat, she is praying cheerfully, bindweed and yellow tulip, those won't be my friends either, the blackmailers. The two women are waiting for darkness to descend, then hand the green bag and mats to Diana.

As she prays, Erika sees herself as a child sitting at the table on their family farm humming a tune while her mother prepares to feed the pigs. Her dad has come back from the pigsty and her brothers from the stables where swallows have built nests under the eaves. They warm their cracked hands over the stove. Erika forms circles with her thumbs and index fingers and looks at her family through them; the warm, sweetish stench of the stables mingles with the sharp whiff of the boots they have taken off their swollen feet. Her dad stokes the fire. He feeds it with a log before sitting down to his dinner under the kerosene lamp. He is praying to the light of the lamp. She jumps off her chair, too high for her, and serves dinner. She carries white bowls of hot soup with circles of grease in it, proud that she hasn't spilled a single drop on the floor.

The aged Erika is praying cheerfully, the prayer numbs the mind. It's an anesthetic, Birgit used to mock her. A love of life and the world is quite different from religious faith. Faith is scared, hateful, and divisive. Faith can be *only* destructive, you see. Decades ago Erika used to beat herself up for lacking contrition for her sins.

"Erika, you are contrite about your lack of contrition for your sins."

"Hmmm."

"That's enough. You have my absolution."

Birgit and Erika get up, give Diana a hug, and go to the movies. They make a show of a huge argument while buying tickets to make sure the young ticket seller notices them.

They always go to the movies as the skies start turning purple.

With the green bag in one hand and green yoga mats under her arm, Diana presses her ear to the door of the house across the street from the Uxor-Hiom restaurant. Diana is not afraid that someone might see her body. The bodies of women her age are invisible. She presses the buzzer and chirrups into the speaker. The buzzer sounds, the door clicks. Diana enters. She walks up the stairs. She avoids the elevator.

She presses her ear to the apartment door.

Honey is in tears. Let's run away together, she whimpers and whines, she'll wear a burqa, she's all packed, she loves Yusuf, she loves him so much. The kestrel's flat voice pushes her away wearily, he can't marry her, she is not a virgin.

"It's to you that I gave my virginity."

"You are not a virgin," repeats the voice, pushing her away and reassuring her at the same time. Ms. Diana is going to help us, Ms. Diana is on her way, just pull yourself together.

A beeswax meditation candle is lit in the window of the upper floor apartment. Three hours later, the candle in the window goes out. Diana leaves, carrying the green bag and the green yoga mats.

She gets into a cab with its radio blaring, joining Birgit and Erika in the back seat. She takes off the chamois gloves.

"Would you please turn the radio off," Diana tells the taxi driver, touching the hand he has on the gearstick.

A solo for a thundering silence.

◇

The Detective looks up the latest international news, shouting in a bird dialect, the court hearing continues, fear among the bodies of the girls grows, it is becoming increasingly obvious that there will be no convictions; Yusuf has been summoned to testify again but Yusuf is nowhere to be found.

His body is found hanged in the attic of the house where he lived, among pigeon droppings and a flutter of swallow feathers. He has committed suicide, the budgies and turtledoves, wagtails and goldcrests, cuckoos and robins, bluetits and pipits, redpolls and starlings, doves and baby blackcaps learn from the newspaper.

The Lynx is among the first to hear the news. But that's impossible, he has been under police surveillance.

Some ways of touching are mightier than the sword. Determination is stronger than a sword, as Diana would tell the Lynx, caressing her with the tip of her now-fatigued index finger.

He committed suicide, the men in Yusuf's life learn; suicide is a sin, Yusuf lodges in their bodies in the form of awe and fear.

He committed suicide together with Honey, theirs was a platonic, passionate, and fateful love, what would be the best comparison, oh yes: Romeo and Juliet, or rather, Heinrich von Kleist, the noble spirit who killed himself with Henriette Vogel on the shore of Lake Wannsee in Berlin, on almost the same day in November, *only* over two hundred years ago. Thus the journalists wax lyrical and the whole world parrots their hollow words in a show of universal stupidity; the quails are doing a great job of distracting.

The Detective looks at the photo of two pairs of trusting eyes, honey brown and black. He feels as if a stalk of chaff were lodged under his eyelid.

◇

At the airport they indulge in some duty-free shopping. Their necks try on Hermes scarves, their lips put on dark Yves Saint Laurent lipstick, and their skins sample Guerlain creams. Pursing their lips in front of the mirror, they scrub off the lipstick with paper tissue. Birgit chooses perfumes *solely* on the basis of their name.

It is the feathers that decide.

They mist some fragrance on their wrists, putting a drop on the sensitive area behind their ears as they wave and sniff the scented strips of paper. They are growing younger.

Onboard the plane they order a bottle of champagne. They browse the tabloid journals they bought in the departure lounge. They point to the bodies of men they fancy.

We're going to have a visitor in Prague, make sure you're looking your best, ladies. On the way from the airport they buy some flowers and have them made into a bouquet. Unseasonal young green leaves tumble out, sparkling in the sun. The skulls of flying birds have a particular structure, with a long septum, while the penis of the males is underdeveloped, and the eggs and the young are looked after by both sexes, or just the females. Most of the species have been around since the early Tertiary period.

THE BODY AS BATTLEGROUND

The long-awaited D-Day has arrived; the select crew is coming ashore today. The Detective is seated in an armchair in Diana's minimalist apartment. He is at the helm on the captain's bridge. In front of the window, swallows, chilled to the bone, congregate amid the snowflakes, their paths crisscrossing as if they were darning the outside of the house with invisible thread.

Very soon he will, for the first time, set eyes on the *Grand Old Ladies*, soon he'll learn if they really exist, or whether all this has been just a figment of his crazed imagination. The Detective has been sitting here for hours while the web of birds' bodies outside the windows has grown denser and the peak of the hill behind the house has become more pointed.

His partner keeps him posted on the women's movements. They've landed in Prague. They have *only* hand luggage. They've hailed a yellow cab. On the way, they stopped at a hairdresser's and for a spot of shopping. Clothes, spices, herbs, flowers.

The Detective is as taut as a string. He is not sure which finger to use or how to begin.

Steps are approaching, making a noise like a herd of horses returning from mountain pastures. Their steps disperse around the house.

The apartment door opens, the steps patter into the bathroom, hands fill a vase with water.

Diana enters carrying bunches of yellow tulips as if spring had never ended. The sight of a man's body in her white armchair surprises her, but *only* to a degree. She is certainly not frightened. Or disconcerted. She doesn't ask who he is or how he got in. She sets the glass vase of yellow tulips on the windowsill. Outside the window, small black bodies fly toward the tulips as if the swallows wanted to peck on the flowers or sip from their calyxes. Their little beaks tap out a coded message in morse code, making the windowpanes rattle.

The body of the Detective stands up and introduces itself. No need for introductions, says Diana, tapping her answer out on the window with the blue nail of a swollen index finger. The swallows have told me.

The Detective looks at the index finger, the bruised and inflamed fingernail.

The hand opens the window.

The Detective feels as if he was the one under investigation by this kindly woman with the bruised finger. His body has become immersed in this house.

The body of the Detective is lying. It says that he has come *only* to collect some additional testimonies for his boss, he must have a word with Ms. Stadtherr in connection with the hanged man's case. He let himself in at night after receiving a report that suspicious muffled noises had been heard coming from the bowels of the house. The Detective spouts meaningless words.

The house reverberates with music.

He should have reported her. He doesn't know why he didn't. His body knows why, it knows that speaking out invariably involves betrayal.

Diana is standing at the window of the orange house at the foot of Petřín Hill. She watches couples in love as they climb along snow-covered paths, clambering up the hill. No longer holding hands, they scramble on all fours, scaling a perpendicular wall of snow-covered grass. They are blinded by the brilliant crystals of snow. The hill at Advent time is steep, steeper than it used to be. It becomes more and more pointed as it tapers. It is no longer a rounded hill. Clouds are impaled on it; a pensioner, impaling old streetcar tickets and crumpled up bits of discarded paper onto the tip of a long umbrella. Flocks of birds circle the erect spike, little bodies performing bravura sharp turns.

The Detective's stifled cough summons Diana back.

The observation tower on top of Petřín Hill sways. The hill casts its shadow over the orange house, making it rise. The hill takes a deep breath, puffs out its chest, the deep roots of the house holding it firmly down.

Diana is standing in the chilly semi-darkness. Piano music streams in from the window.

"*Inquiétude des colibris*," Diana says, as if addressing an imaginary crowd on the swelling hill. "The Argentine composer and pianist Alberto Williams dedicated this piece to Arthur Rubinstein in 1922. Williams didn't ask the hummingbirds' permission to imitate their rhythm. The copyright belongs to the hummingbirds. It is their disquiet and that disquiet is growing. Their time has come."

Petřín Hill is shaking from the echo of the black and white keys. The silence that follows surprises itself. The silence is relieved to be broken by the Detective's deep voice.

"You're not surprised to see me here?"

"You're feeding on the grains left over from the harvest."

"You're not interested in how I got in?"

"What about you, aren't you afraid of being in the same room as me?"

The Detective clears his throat.

"I've seen photos from the court hearing."

"So have millions of others. It's about giving young people hope. Hope is what this is about."

"I know everything."

"Do you?"

"And . . ."

"And . . . ?"

"I haven't told anyone yet. Because if I do—"

"What if you do?"

"You're finished."

"Are we going to be lynched?"

"That's not what I meant."

"The end began the moment we set out on this path."

"I know everything."

"I know you know. But do you know what it is that you know?"

"You've been hunting them. You've been hunting rapists."

"To be aware of others is a gift. And we have pursued this gift to our hearts' content, young man."

Diana closes a window.

Fresh flocks of tiny birds, screaming wildly, write messages onto the faded sky. It is snowing, but the sun in the window shines as it were spring, springtime in December has nestled in the air. Diana slams another window shut. The glass keeps out the chilly world, the bare trees, and the frostbitten hands of couples in love. The polished window is not covered by a curtain. Another overexcited, starving, and emaciated black dog stops on the cobblestones. It stares at the house, able to see through the walls. The identical-looking girl dolls, and a boy doll, performing identical movements have been designed and fashioned using the same template. Each has a pair of eyes, ears, legs, and arms, and a single mouth, head, and trunk, all of them walking on their hind legs. Dusk squeaks at the gate. The dog sits down. The orange walls part before him, the streetlights come on. The dog sees a puppet theater, a doll's house for four girl dolls and one boy doll. The black dog stays put, shivering in the cold, its tongue lolling out as it swallows snowflakes. It doesn't bark or bite. The dog is time. Diana doesn't toss it a gnawed bone.

Diana picks up the photo of the four women propped up against a brass candlestick. She touches the faces with her blue index finger. She touches the wind, which is moderate at the island of Usedom but ferocious on the island of Amrum, where it turns into a hurricane. The leaves floating in the air are not leaves but sleeves, pants, trash cans, and cars, everything sails through the air and disappears into the sea, *only* the four women's bodies stand their ground, whichever shore they're on.

"Birgit calls this photo the wuthering harlots."

Diana kisses the photo and puts it back next to the brass candlestick. The Detective holds his breath.

"So you don't deny that . . ."

"Women sought us out."

"You're like the *Black Hand*, the organization that helped old Nazis wipe the slate clean. Their flocks dispersed across Brazil, Chile, and Argentina. They took their name from a secret nationalist society in nineteenth-century Serbia."

"Oh no, you've got us completely wrong. We are Simon Wiesenthal in skirts. Or at least that was the original plan. Only it's gotten slightly out of hand."

"This is not an interrogation."

"They failed her."

"What do you mean?"

"No one would help Ingrid. She was misunderstood. To others, these were *only* women's bodies. Bodies of women who survived, so what's the big deal? The others were not interested in what she had to say, they didn't care about what any woman, let alone a young woman or a child, might have to say. A masculine society. Nazism was a purely masculine society, too. They had no idea . . . Sometimes you've got to take justice into your own hands. There is a species of swallow, which, if it falls to the ground, is unable to take flight without someone helping it."

"*No one* has the right to take justice into their own hands."

"But it was all right for Wiesenthal to do so?"

"He tracked down Nazis and handed them to the courts!"

"We have saved so many lives. It was *taking action* that saved them. Women helped other women and by doing so they saved themselves. It restored their self-respect. Their confidence. Their dignity. Am I confusing you?"

"You are."

"You're succumbing to panic in the bowels of this house."

"No, I'm not."

"Your body is panicking. Because it lacks an umbrella term for us. If this was about communists or mass murderers, your body would understand. If we were fighting terrorism, it would understand. You lack an umbrella term, a label that would bring you relief. It would be easier if we were associated with some political faction. But we are *only* and *exclusively* on the side of the victims. And the victims are the raped bodies. We pick up swallows that fell to the ground and help them fly again. We give them back their forgotten purpose in life. That's what we decided from the start, right after the war."

Diana's blue index finger points to the faces of the three children and young woman in the photograph propped against the brass candlestick. Ingrid, Erika, Birgit, Diana. Blow, wind, blow.

"Call it a struggle against global terrorism. Call it humanitarian assistance. Call it invoking the word humanism. Call it a slapstick comedy. Call it whatever you like. I empathize with those who have been most badly hurt. Usually it's children."

"But what you are doing is *murder*."

"It is justice."

"It is not."

"Retribution."

"No. It's a crime."

"We are all shaped by our experiences. You too have been shaped and defined by your experiences. And your experiences and mine don't intersect. Your experiences will never intersect with mine. My experiences are my truth."

"Isn't the war over?"

"Am I asking too much by expecting those without shared experiences to understand each other's feelings? I draw certainty from blind chance. That's when I can drop my guard."

"You shouldn't have gone there."

"If we hadn't gone, we would have left them locked in an iron cage. They would have taken it as perfectly normal and civilized behavior to be snatched by birdcatchers and butchered. Their daughters and granddaughters would also end up raised in this way. It's like the plague. If we hadn't gone, the birdcatchers would keep gobbling up little songbirds, roasting them on the spit and skewering them, a steady supply of lumps of fresh flesh. Everyone agrees that pedophilia is a crime. But that's just empty talk. And in real life? The war is being waged every single day, and within that war there rages another war."

"You see only one side of the coin, for you it's either heads or tails. You are frozen in the moment the war ended, but we are living in a different world now. You've been meting out death, for goodness' sake!"

"We did it out of love."

"Love of what? Truth? Justice?"

"Love of Ingrid."

"I see."

"The swallows have seen all those false promises of spring and the sham exhortations of liberty, equality and fraternity. But even the most liberally inclined didn't really want to liberate women, that's not what they bargained for, women were not supposed to be out in the streets protesting. They were meant to keep the kitchen and the bedroom clean, to slave over a hot stove."

"You are out of your mind."

"Yes, I am."

"I *only* meant to say that . . . this is . . . absurd."

"The world I live in is absurd. Isn't the one you live in as well?"

"I—"

"That's why we didn't want anyone to know about it. People are moved by the suffering of millions. But not by the suffering of individual bodies."

"Let's say that to a certain degree, but *only* a degree, I can understand . . . those cases right at the end of the war . . . but the rest . . ."

"It is an everyday war. A war against everyday fascists. I disrupt the system. I don't squander my compassion on those who have no time for self-reflection or doubt. Who are trapped in the vacuum of power. Dependence on power is incurable. These are the people I . . ."

Diana leans back against the windowsill. Even though it's daytime, the *only* thing the Detective can see in the window is darkness.

"They are all my daughters."

"And Ms. Stadtherr . . ."

"What about her?"

"How does she fit into all this? She was born in this country, she is Czech."

"I don't care where a body comes from."

"Ms. Stadtherr wasn't . . . raped."

"That's correct."

"Well?"

"Birgit is a child of rape. She doesn't know it. But her body does."

Diana turns her back on the Detective. The Detective's mouth has gone dry, Diana's silhouette is transforming, the eagle shape in the window-frame swells, growing massive, shush. With difficulty, the swallows rise from their nests under the eaves of the building, some of them falling to the ground. The black dog runs around the orange house and feasts. The finger of Petřín Hill, unrecognizable, looms over the thinned-out flock of swallows. Diana addresses the swallows outside the window.

"I did it out of sheer love of them. A profound love. Death will not sunder our love, which is an act of rebellion by human existence against the way this world functions. You may sneer at me if you wish, but this love has always been mightier than death, not some infantile, narrow-minded, utopian illusion."

Diana turns around, and her trembling hand adjusts the yellowing photograph of the four women's bodies resting against the brass candlestick. The Detective is perplexed. The old biddy is getting mixed up, but he is fond of her, despite himself, fond of this old lady made of granite, a label that would suit the adult face in the brass photograph. *A woman made of granite*, it says in Birgit's book, her scathing attack on the good-natured Rose Kennedy.

"You have . . . accomplices."

"If I revealed their names, it wouldn't be of much use to you. No one would believe you."

"I know everything."

"How about some coffee?

"No, thanks."

"I also have green tea. Dragon's Spring."

"No, thanks, I'd really like to have a word *just* with Ms. Stadtherr, if I may."

It seems absurd to be asking this woman's permission in a strangulated voice.

"Sure, young man. You're free."

The Detective leaves the room. Diana opens the window again. They haven't flown away yet. They are arranging themselves in a thinned-out formation. At last.

The Detective knocks on a door on the second floor. Birgit replaces the receiver of the intercom phone. She walks over to her desk. She returns carrying a tray with a bottle of Becherovka and two white cups, a white jug of mineral water and two glasses. She ushers the body of the Detective to an armchair facing a wall covered by a painting. It shows a hand holding a string of red beads. The hand reaches across a city with a stone bridge and a castle on a hill above the river: the city is Prague, the beads wind their way around the statues on the stone bridge as if trying to wrap themselves all around them. Out of some beads that have burst, been trampled on, or disintegrated in the air, letters of the alphabet come tumbling out.

"I'd be happy to gift it to you, but that's unfortunately not possible."

"Why not?"

"No one can take it off the wall. Not even you."

Birgit pours some yellowish Becherovka. The Detective gets up. Walking over to the painting, he scratches it with a fingernail. It is painted directly onto the wall. The edge of the mural is worn, a predator's talons tried to scratch the plaster off and carry it away.

"Cheers!"

They clink glasses. Birgit smacks her lips as she swallows the yellow liquid. The Detective doesn't touch his glass. Birgit brings an azure-colored journal over from her desk.

"But I can give you this. You can finish the story." Birgit tops up her glass.

She walks over to the mural.

"And in case you need inspiration—"

She taps a bead on the wall with her fingernail. Sawdust comes pouring out of the bead. Miniature versions of characters in Roman and other alphabets.

"I just want to ask . . . a few personal questions."

"I know. The Becherovka is not properly chilled. It's a women's drink. But I also have whiskey or vodka. I know you like those."

"It seems you were one of the last people to speak to the man we found hanged in the attic; the gentleman had taken your creative writing class and—"

"Yes, he came to see me."

"But in your letter you said that you didn't meet."

"The letter was addressed to a colleague of yours. Diana wants me to be truthful with *you*."

"What time was it when he arrived?"

"He came in the afternoon. We went over his manuscript. Then I went to the movies with Erika."

"Why did he come to see you?"

"He was planning to go to the mountains, but I told him to throw his scribbles into the trashcan. And to write the truth and compensate his former assistants that he abused. Even though he claimed that God would absolve him and he would do it again. He came barreling in, he was a hot-tempered man, and so influential. And so religious."

"How did he react?"

"He was furious. He asked for his money back for the entire creative writing course. He didn't even want to listen to the music Erika put on specially for him out of the kindness of her heart. I don't like it when people insult Erika. She is fragile and vulnerable."

"What time was it when he left?"

"Diana gave him a lift. Diana is an expert in body language. She knows some calming exercises. She can hypnotize bodies and put them to sleep."

Birgit finishes her second glass. The Detective can't resist and takes a sip of Becherovka, then gulps down a full glass of water.

"I had an inkling that this wasn't . . . suicide."

"You're a real wisenheimer. Isn't that a nice word?"

"Hmm."

"There are other words I like. Make love. Lay, hump, screw, fuck, bang, shaft, hand job, blow job. Languages protect themselves by being misleading, oh so misleading—to *bang someone,* doesn't that sound horrible?"

"But I . . ."

"A rapist won't commit suicide. It's the victims who do. The body is a bastard, it betrays the victim. There are things the body likes even when it's butchered. The body has a good time."

"From a certain perspective you . . . might be . . . I . . . forgive me, I'm exhausted."

"We didn't want anyone to be aware of our good deeds. I've done it all out love for them. Diana *is* a humanist."

". . . and a murderer . . ."

"She values the individual first and foremost. She respects each individual because everyone has a soul. This is what I call explosive individualism. A moral yardstick."

"I really don't think this house is the right place for discussing moral issues."

"In fairytales you have to root out evil to give the good folk a chance. Hansel and Gretel have to shove the witch into the oven."

"You can't root out evil with evil."

"You can root out evil by being uncompromising. That, too, is a human rights issue. There is one group of people that is disadvantaged. If women went around raping and enslaving men, we would come to the men's defense. I like men very much. I enjoy sex with men. It is my greatest joy. But the way to gain power is not by challenging the establishment to a duel. You need to carve out some space within the establishment and then you can trick it. You must forge as many connections as possible. This is not about brutal bosses and meek sparrows. It is about dozens of tragedies and perversions. In its entire history, humankind has not seen a genuine sexual revolution, never, not even in the 1960s, and not until this day. The time to cast stones has come."

"But that's ridiculous. Can I ask . . ."

"You can ask me anything you like, young man."

"What's the point of keeping a paper trail?"

"Paper burns well."

Music rings out in the room. *Für Alina,* Pärt's two-minute piece. On this recording it is repeated several times, in barely perceptible variations: slight changes of tempo, each individual note a slightly different length. Like the changing face of a woman whom one could fall in love with. A piano, but also a violin, a cello, and then the violin again. The three instruments mingling and intertwining.

Though each repetition is enriched with *only* one tiny nuance, it makes everything change. The instruments respond to each other differently, no longer ignoring each other. One intensifies while the other fades away, and the third remains tactfully silent. The piece has come to an end. Life has come to an end.

"This is *Für Alina.*"

"We call it *Für Ingrid.* You're in love."

"Excuse me? Oh, I see. Yes, I am. Madly in love." Birgit caresses him.

"There were moments when we wanted to end all this, but it wasn't possible, you see."

"I see."

"To attach oneself to another person, *just* snuggle up with them, that is the greatest joy there is. Do you believe that one can reclaim the age of innocence and, like the child one was once, find somewhere deep down the hope that people might be good?"

"I do."

"But this is refuted by reality."

"*Only* by one part of reality."

"Reality, real life, all that has something to do with the condition of humankind."

"There is no such thing as unnecessary violence."

"But violence does exist. That's the reality."

"I'm not frightened of reality. What frightens me is *your* understanding of reality."

"All the paintings in this house are murals. And underneath there are letters of the alphabet. This was Diana's idea. We have turned individual chapters of my principal work into paintings. You should read that book. After we're gone. How much is hidden in routine and ritual, my dear."

Birgit gives the Detective a hug and plants a kiss on his lips.

The Detective staggers out, the azure journal in his hand. As soon as he is out of the room, another hand grabs hold of him. And offers him a glass filled with a thick, milky, lumpy cocktail. The Detective turns it down.

"You're going to need it."

The Detective shakes his head and says no, thank you.

"As you wish."

"I'm sure Ms. Adler called you while I was on my way to see you."

"She has."

"This house makes me . . . I feel . . . guilty . . ."

"Why?"

"Because I am a man."

"But we have nothing against men. *Only* against crimes. And just so you know, there is a man I've loved all my life."

"Gould? Pärt? Menuhin?"

"Them too, actually."

The Detective is suddenly at a loss for words. He is really exhausted. Erika hands him her cocktail.

"And thank you, young man."

"For what?"

"For what you're not going to do."

"How do you know what I'm not going to do?"

Although all three wear birds' feathers, they in fact resemble sea turtles. They walk the dry land, know the mysterious depths of the seas and oceans, and live for a long time.

He has to hurry matters along.

He looks at Diana's earlobes, whose imprint is captured in photographs in his study.

"I will have to . . . report you, Ms. Adler. I can't pretend I don't know anything. I can't take this any longer."

"Yes, you can. It's called solidarity."

"No, it's called complicity."

"Allow us one more short trip."

"How much time do you need?"

"Three weeks."

"I don't know, that . . ."

"A week."

"All right."

"Our lives are unresolvable in a way. Why didn't you report us or have us arrested right away?"

"I wish I knew. And I'm still not sure what I'm going to do."

The Detective totters out of the orange house at the foot of Petřín Hill, babbling as he backs out that he has understood, and the case of the hanged man has been closed, deemed a suicide.

Birgit sits down at her desk but doesn't draw a purple cross on a photo of the Detective.

Erika puts on a Yehudi Menuhin violin concerto.

Diana stands by the window looking at the brass-propped photograph and Petřín Hill. The lookout tower on top of the hill is on the verge of collapsing.

She will set them free, she will finally set them free, rid them of their bodies to allow them to be born again, reborn into a world that is kind and benign, into a wonderful life, new and pure, they will be able to start again, they will be reborn and their bodies will draw breath freely, fresh and informed.

It will envelop their calm, restored souls.

We will be free, and words such as "kobolds" and "patriarchy" will become obsolete, and all that will be left is love. Independence means not depending on anyone else. Or else it is not independence.

The three ladies are in Erika's apartment, sipping meadowsweet cocktails, listening to music, thinking of hummingbirds. Erika, who rarely pipes up otherwise, looks at Diana and Birgit and speaks.

"This is a recording with Wilhelm Furtwängler conducting. It felt weird to make a documentary about him. He told me that music was a river that the conductor had to follow, carefully guiding it through its meanders, weirs, and undercurrents. He didn't give a damn about sticking to the rules or the metronome, he couldn't give a damn about technique. There was a disquiet, a sensitivity and sensuousness to his conducting. And a modesty rooted in uncertainty. He was my favorite conductor because he had retained the naiveté of a child. An emotionality. That is the greatest gift, greater than talent. I was there when this concert was recorded. There was a telepathic connection between the orchestra and Furtwängler. But Arturo Toscanini just laughed at me when he heard the word telepathy."

Birgit doesn't point out what she would normally blurt out right away, that as far as she is concerned the old Nazi Furtwängler should have been behind bars. Diana glances at Birgit and Erika. She doesn't point out that they should have stopped all this soon after the war. They shouldn't have poked their noses into a world that was not theirs.

They have lost their feeling for the dislocated arms of justice. They have cleaned up their world, the world they understood, they have settled old, personal accounts with the time to which the bodies belonged in an adult way. They are not of this time.

They return to their respective apartments and prepare to fly to distant shores. Music reverberates through the house.

The Detective is at the wheel. His name is Adam. His face is blue. The Widow's name is Eve. Her face is yellow. She has let down her golden hair with a ginger streak. The boy is humming to himself on the back seat, throwing a red toy car and a stuffed animal up and down to the rhythm of his tune. The woman pulls sheets of paper out of their plastic folders and looks through them again. They are contracts. One sheet, issued by SWALLOW, *Inc., is adorned with the drawing of a swallow. The other, from* QUAIL, *Inc., of a quail. The woman tears up the contracts and tosses them out the window.*

The man steps on the gas. He is leaving the city behind.

A hill used to tower over the center of the city. It was known as Petřín. All couples would make a pilgrimage there to validate their love and never return once they obtained the requisite stamp and certificate, then they would breathe a sigh of relief, free to meet wherever they liked from then on. As they descended, the couples would pass an orange house. It once stood at the foot of Petřín Hill.

Today couples have gathered there with mouths agape and hacking coughs. The orange house is belching out thick, purple smoke as flocks of hummingbirds fly out of the chimney through the acrid fumes, their feathered heads crowned with contraptions in which matchstick-thin candles are burning. Instead of a Japanese cherry blossom, the last swallow carries the fuse in its beak.

The house explodes.

They follow one another. And yet each of them lives its own, independent life.

Nature doesn't know paradoxes. Our brains do know what a paradox is.

The swallows are flying away at last: "Your way of seeing the world differs from ours. Which doesn't mean that the way you see the world is the right way."

Birgit is done with writing. She has carried those words inside her. But she no longer wanted to share them with anyone. The minute she shared her words, they would become unfaithful. She would flirt with others. But the words she told others were not the ones she had heard and they did not convey what she expected of words. Spring is still a long way away. But if spring does return, she will see it again and will have to survive again, somehow. Until clusters of blooms appear on the lazy poplars in a town in England. Until the sky turns black.

But do swallows need courage? They are a law unto themselves, that's the only way they can live. And yet they are so fragile. All drivel and murderous games. She *has* to dance to the inaudible rhythm of her own indomitable heart. Like the swallows that are not in the least fragile and are flying away. The deed is done, they will leave empty-handed.

EPILOGUE

Surya namaskar, the sun salutation. Behind the glass wall of the hotel suite the sun surfaces from the cold Baltic Sea. Warms its bones after a chilly night. Wrenches itself free of the water's embrace, a shiny sheet of metal. Makes a supreme effort to emerge. Stretches its limbs, indecently naked. Everything around it blushes with shame. It emerges from the east. And flees to the west.

Backs of hands bedecked with liver spots. Fingernails painted red. Crow's feet, little fans of laughing wrinkles. Breasts that sag like empty pouches instead of jutting out. Three naked bodies. Unafraid of exposing themselves to the sun that gazes at them through the window. No men lie curled in their laps, rubbing their eyes on the curves of their elbows or breasts, ensconced in soft tenderness.

Three bodies, each moving in a different way, yet to the same rhythm. Perpetually rising. The bodies shimmer. Drops of water from the hotel's swimming pool cling to them. Hands clasped in the familiar Indian salutation, a symbol of unity: palms of the hands together, a gesture of peace and respect. They are paying homage not to the light outside the window, but to the light they carry within. A respectful bow, a tribute to life on earth. They gather strength. They lie on the floor, their fingers and the toes of their bare feet pressed firmly into the mats. Creatures with silvery, scaly skins stretching their limbs and spines.

Bones crack. Imperceptibly, the shimmering skin is peeled off by the warm air and kissed away by the sun that has forced its way in through the wide-open window. Second by second. Seconds of eternity. Deep yet inaudible breaths in and out through the nose. The room is a fish tank with bodies swimming excitedly around. These bodies are different from the ones that have left Prague. One of the bodies, the limping one, concludes the mime show by getting down on her right knee. Her head bowed, she closes her eyes. Clasps her hands together. The bony fingers lock in a cramp, fingernails dig into the skin. The body is scared. A whisper intrudes into the silence . . . *in heaven, hallowed be Thy name* . . . The other two bodies ignore the frightened whispering. Nimbly they rise and straighten up. Start to get dressed. Behind the tightly shut eyelids of the kneeling woman a procession is taking place. A labored haste. Folk of a feather don't flock together. Erika's life is anchored in a homeless, zen way. A thundering silence. She reads *only* Japanese poets. They are fond of cherry blossoms. And of the silk moth.

"Come and listen to the sound it makes, Birgit."

"It's not funny."

"The funny thing is that the silk moth doesn't make any sound. It hatches from its small cocoon, soundlessly."

They don't skip breakfast at the Hotel Ahlbecker Hof. How much is hidden in routine and ritual, my dear. Diana points to a bottle of kombucha in an ice bucket next to the champagne. Erika nods. The waitress fills a couple of glasses.

"This is no longer our world."

"We owe it to Ingrid."

"We don't owe anything to anyone."

"Oh yes, we do."

Diana calmly adjusts the white cloth napkin in her lap. Erika squirms, scared, distraught. She doesn't want them to call it a day in a country where a fire is burning, with the same body burned at the stake every night. She reminds them of all the information they have accumulated and left behind in bulging files in the house in Prague: surely they could still step into the same river a few more times. Erika raises her voice, it is still happening to children who have no idea what is being done to them, who don't know how to fight back because the adults tell them they're doing it out of love and that they will come to like it; someone has to put an end to this, someone has to force every country on the planet to amend its legislation. The majority of people need laws, a whip over them, or they will take it out on someone who trusts them and who won't fight back. She doesn't want to read any more testimonies of choir-masters who say they were provoked by nymphets with the voices of nightingales and . . .

Diana and Birgit calmly eat their breakfast. They ignore Erika's chattering.

"Let's do it."

Diana takes a sip of her fresh carrot and pineapple juice.

"Let's finally draw a line under all of this."

Erika goes into a sulk and conjures on her plate a pattern made of miniature rolls filled with salmon and herring, silver spoons topped with grains of caviar, green and black olives and a small mound of fried eggs with melting white butter and chives in the middle. The knife carves grooves in the butter. The egg mound is bright yellow, like the sun before them. The sun pesters them, scratching the windowpane and a rose in a vase—a famished dog demanding attention. Erika takes a nibble from the sunflower on her plate. The waitress scurries to the table with a platter of cheese and fruit. She returns to the buffet to put glasses of champagne and blinis with sour cream and salmon on the tray. Another busy little bee deposits a newspaper by Birgit's elbow.

Rummaging in her handbag with one hand without looking, Birgit fishes out a white leather case. She extracts her reading glasses and can't tear her semi-shielded eyes away from the newspaper. The writing on the page mesmerizes her, but she remains silent. All two hundred seventy-six defendants have been acquitted due to lack of evidence. The plaintiffs insisted that all the girls be summoned to court. Everyone is puzzled by the procession of innocents. The children are beautiful, and they all remain stubbornly silent. They were young and foolish, allegedly. Some are in mourning for Yusuf and all are in mourning for Honey, whom they proclaim a saint. Some bawl desperately, they feel they too share responsibility for both suicides. Some insist that they were in love with the men. Everyone is puzzled by the parade of maidens, having seen the photos in the medical records, with their faces and their arms black and blue. Two hundred seventy-six men were acquitted for lack of evidence and have now flipped roles, turning into victims: no one is interested in what you do these days, people look *only* at the color of your skin, *only* at your ethnic origin, *only* at your citizenship, *only* at your religion, *only* at your professional status, and *only* at your family background and wealth, that is how leading politicians around the world and all the lobbyists, priests, and all men everywhere comment on the case, all desperate to be politically and linguistically correct, political correctness above all, we mustn't persecute and bully people because of the color of their skin, there will be an election soon, our countries are democratic and everyone enjoys the same rights, we mustn't permit the resurgence of old ideologies of white gloves and Stalinist thinking, we've all read the well-informed and most definitely politically-correct books by Birgit Stadtherr.

Birgit folds the newspaper and lets it drop on the floor. She sees eyes rolling and lips mouthing, off camera, what a load of balderdash, a hand job here and there, what's the big deal. And meanwhile they ask for hand-picked schoolgirls to be brought to their secret bedrooms.

Diana finishes her fruit juice and ladles up some honey for her tea. It melts from the wooden honey spoon in the hot steam above the teapot, the thin golden trickle flowing into the simmering depths and drowning there. Then it picks up pace, spinning and swirling with delight. Birgit raises her eyes. Not her head. She watches the movement of the honey.

Diana's hand freezes. Time is arrested. The thread of honey vanishes abruptly, growing thinner, disappearing into the chubby white teapot.

Diana sets time free.

Resolutely, she drops the lid down on the teapot. The honey sheds tears. The last teardrop falls on the lid. Diana puts the wooden spoon back in the honeypot. She once again lifts the teapot lid.

She licks off the teardrop of honey.

In the autumn of 2011, three women spend a week on the German island of Usedom on the Baltic Sea. They pick the best five-star hotel, Hotel Ahlbecker Hof, room 323, foolishly insisting on that particular room. They have chosen it because they had all been here once before, soon after the war, and they were happy here. Back then they stood on the seashore holding hands, the wind blowing through their hair and up their skirts. Oh wind, strong and youthful, blow, you crazy wind, the churning sea was drunken with hope, the wind ruffled their hair, its strong teeth tearing at their wide skirts; their bodies, then still so young, squinted, caught in the claws of the sun's rays. The wind on Usedom is not ferocious, it was *only* on the Frisian island of Amrum close to the coast of Denmark, where they used to visit over the past few decades, that hurricane-strength winds would toss around the dumpsters, uproot pine trees, and overturn cars.

This hotel is not a man, it is a sophisticated lady. A lady full of life, a lady who takes young lovers and is keen to explore, a lady who studies new languages, tries on new shades of lipstick and designer clothes, and who treats others kindly.

The women, too, are full of life. Made for the air. Swallows. Made for flying. They have chosen this hotel for their last gathering. They hug and thank each other for this life, love and empathy, they love each other in the minutes that dissolve the greasy sediments on their wings, in the minutes capable of killing. It is *only* in these moments that *every* malicious thought can be killed.

The hotel staff love them, as they are kind and not patronizing, they are smart, witty, and generous with their tips. One of the women asks a young receptionist to post a large parcel to a publishing house across the Pond. On the dispatch note it says *The Games That Men Play*. The time has come to tidy up the desk and wipe the mud of her little beak on her sleeve, she tells the young receptionist.

The oldest of the three ladies speaks *only* to the sea, telling it that there are no borders. There are no states or nationalities, there are no religions and no superior sexes.

There are *only* people, swallows and air. There are no languages.

Only the language of bodies.

Every day this December feels like spring, or an Indian summer the likes of which no one can recall. They head for the beach, and in the evenings, they go to concerts held as part of a local music festival. The sea is guarded by a fortification of clouds. The clouds are reflected in the water. The sea glistens like a delicate ribbon tied around the island. The sand copies the outline of the ribbon in the water, wrapping itself around it as the water turns into a coat of thin ice. The two ribbons keep the whole island warm in the palms of their hands.

In the middle of the island there is a deserted bench where I sit, spooling up the ribbons with my eyes, which absorb the silhouettes of three women in the distance.

Life begins from scratch. They can no longer tread along the same tracks they have walked for decades, these have come to an end. At least, I think they have. Like northern seas with their Seebrücken, safe havens for ships. Like the old bridge on Usedom Island, opposite the Hotel Ahlbecker Hof, where they are staying. Bridges typically lead from some place to another. This one just juts out, on piles. It leads from somewhere to nowhere. It leads into nothingness. It ends in the middle of the sea, in a vacuum.

The hotel manager is blissfully happy. Until one morning when a young chambermaid enters the room to clean it and sees tears in the eyes of the fish. She finds the room just as tidy in the evening when she comes to draw the drapes and place a square of chocolate with the message *Gute Nacht* on the snow-white pillow. The next day she informs the hotel manager that the chocolate squares are still on the pillows, untouched. The wardrobes have been emptied of clothes, the personal documents stowed in two handbags and a red leather backpack, a green travel bag containing some violin strings, a piece of rope gray with age, a bundle of yellowing letters, a rolled-up man's tie. The manager reports that three guests are missing.

The last time they were seen was last night. A man who goes jogging on the beach every day at sunset says he saw four female figures holding hands as they made their way through the water. Though the water here is too cold to swim in even in summer, let alone in

December, he spotted them just below the surface, statuesque shadows flickering and dark bullets flying. Swallows flying underwater.

The women looked as if they were walking in the shallows as the full moon wove a lunar path before them, like a long plait of hair as they stepped across a lunar footbridge. In one hopeful blink of a bird's eye they took off, before the wind pierced them through.

"I know it sounds weird," says the man, squirming.

"Four? But only three women are missing," says the hotel manager.

"No, I'm sure there were four of them. They were fully dressed, held their skirts hitched up above their knees, and all four gazed at the water as if looking for something. Then they let their skirts down, firmly linking arms. After that they looked *only* ahead."

The last trace. A mirage. Fly, swallow, fly, before they catch you, my dear.

An athletic male body is running along the beach. How much is hidden in routine and ritual, my dear.

Candles are lit in graveyards around the world, momentarily lighting up the cemeteries like dazzling fireworks. Fall deepens, ignoring the seasons; a toast to the past of a new life.

◇ ◇ ◇ ◇

Usedom, Hotel Ahlbecker Hof, September 2011 — Amrum, Kiwitt house, April 2014. A swallow's flight.

AUTHOR'S NOTE

A complete list of records owned by Erika Eis is not available. Based on the Detective's testimony, the following recordings were found in Diana Adler's apartment:

– Louis-Claude Daquin: *Le coucou (The Cuckoo)*
– Benjamin Godard: "Les hirondelles" ("Swallows")
– Leoš Janáček: *Štěbetání vlaštovek (They Chattered Like Swallows,* from *An Overgrown Path)*
– Edward MacDowell: "The Eagle"
– Edward MacDowell: "To a Hummingbird"
– Bedřich Smetana: *Slepička (The Hen)*
– Arthur Willner: *Vogelsang (Birdsong)*
– Walter Niemann: "Chinesische Nachtigall" ("Chinese Nightingale")
– Klement Slavický: *Opuštěné ptáče (The Abandoned Fledgling)*
– Mikhail Glinka: *Solovey (The Nightingale)*
– Joonas Kokkonen: *Lintujen Tuonela, Laulusarja (The Hades of the Birds)*
– Olivier Messiaen: "La grive-musicienne" ("The Song Thrush")
– Olivier Messiaen: "La colombe" ("The Dove")
– Cyril Scott: "Paradise Birds"
– Mikalojus Konstantinas Čiurlionis: *Lakštingala (The Nightingale)*
– Robert Schumann: "Kuckuck im Versteck" ("The Cuckoo in Hiding")

– Adolf von Henselt: "*Si oiseau j'étais*" ("If I Were a Bird")
– Jean-Philippe Rameau: *Le rappel des oiseaux (The Call of the Birds)*
– Maxime Jacob: "Un Oiseau dans le bois" ("A Bird in the Wood")
– Alberto Williams: "Inquietud de los colibrìes" ("The Restlessness of the Hummingbirds")
– Agathe Baker-Grøndahl: "Svalernes flugt" ("Swallows Soaring")

According to the Widow's testimony, music found in Birgit Stadtherr's apartment included records by Joni Mitchell, Joan Baez, Billie Holiday, Nina Simone, Edith Piaf, and the Carolina Chocolate Drops.

Rights to films by Erika Eis are owned by QUAIL, Inc. and swallow, Inc., the film, distribution, and media production companies whose written archives were destroyed in a fire in Prague in 2011.

In the evenings, Birgit read out excerpts from her notes, which kept growing until they flowed like a mighty stream. The *only* people she read them to were Diana Adler and Erika Eis. The book *The Games That Men Play,* about Edvard Beneš, has never been published as it offered too much of a glimpse into the private life of an asexual man, and also since the author could not be traced and no one was able to answer the alarmed publisher's questions.

THE GAMES THAT MEN PLAY:

NOTES FOR A BOOK BY BIRGIT STADTHERR

Passages Birgit Stadtherr read *only* to Diana and Erika

The day of their meeting is drawing close.

Meetings between Thomas Garrigue Masaryk and Edvard Beneš usually took place in the lecture halls of universities or at health resorts, to the sound of violins and the smell of strong black coffee. How much is hidden in routine and ritual, my dear.

Meetings between Joseph Stalin and Edvard Beneš are like encounters between two animals that must follow their instincts, as the adversary is impossible to read. Like encounters of two kind-hearted men who want only the best for everyone and for this world, which has so many different faces. They have one thing in common: they both think *only* of themselves. They pick up their fountain pens of purple ink and sign a treaty of friendship, mutual assistance, and postwar collaboration.

Stalin is the lord and master of mankind, there is no room in his head for hesitation or doubt. His nostrils are sensitive to the unmistakable odor of his adversary's fear. For him fear is intoxicating, it is the perfume he loves, the overproduction of fear, he has turned his entire country into a fear factory, which he exports to the rest of the world. He is unpredictable and therefore powerful.

He is good at taking quick decisions because the *only* thing that matters to him is power. And expanding his dominion.

Beneš is not good at taking quick decisions because what matters to him is having his peace and quiet. Decisiveness is not conducive to peace and quiet. Beneš is smart and well educated.

Czechoslovakia is a tenderized cutlet. He has sliced off a chunk to feed the Reich and soon is about to slice off another chunk to feed the Russian beast.

There will be peace.

He knows he can count on support from England and France.

But in this encounter, Beneš will need more than sharp wit and irony. Stalin knows no irony.

Beneš's table manners are exemplary, but his refined gestures, impeccable taste, and good education drawn from his European roots are no use to him now. If Stalin can't impale a piece of meat on his fork, he just grabs it with his fingers, licks them, and wipes his hand on the tablecloth, since he has dropped his napkin under the table.

This gesture truly sends shivers down Beneš's spine.

This gesture is crucial. Beneš is frightened because this man doesn't use a napkin or mince his words, the man facing him across the table is capable of anything and, most importantly, doesn't care what anyone thinks of him.

What matters most to Beneš is what people think of him.

Beneš is no fool; he may be a coward but he's no fool. He has figured out that Stalin is not waging this war to save the world from Hitler. Rather, Stalin realizes that opposing Hitler will make it easier for him to achieve his goals. It will make it easier to distract attention from his own atrocities: the man who saves the world from Hitler won't be blamed for, or denied, anything. The people in the West have experienced the danger at first hand, the danger is imminent, and charity begins at home. *Only* people with first-hand experience of Stalin defect to Hitler, under the delusion that they are enjoying the protection of the kinder of the two men.

Swallows chirrup, their bodies on the telegraph wires regroup. The world has gone crazy, though in a sort of voluntary way; it is tying a noose around its own neck and placing a chair underneath.

Stalin's great advantage is that he doesn't care about anyone, to him people are just objects to use for fueling the fire and the front; human lives mean nothing to him. Stalin is incapable of putting himself into anyone else's shoes though he can put on a perfect show of empathy. He learns by imitation, the way animals do. He is convinced that he can do whatever he likes, that he is far above everyone else. He is capable of compassion only for himself, having mastered self-pity to perfection. If he catches a cold he is reduced to tears. He is moved to tears by his own self-sacrifice when he gets out of bed to sign two documents, and his own kindness reduces him to tears when he spares the life of the puppy of his guard dog that keeps the moles away from his dacha.

Hitler and Stalin pick talented folk as their assistants and both make the people closest to them feel obliged to ensure they carry out their boss's every idea, eagerly perfecting it; these people are the real villains and without them the two men would be *only* laughable eccentrics with psychopathic tendencies.

Stalin did admire Hitler for a while, and that makes him angry now. When he signed the non-aggression pact with Hitler he believed that they could form a fraternal union. Hitler can hear *only* his own yelling. In the absence of an ally, Stalin has at least found a worthy opponent. Stalin loves this. He sacrifices everything because he is not losing and has no conception of doubt. They could have joined forces.

But Hitler cheated.

The game Stalin plays is more monstrous because his hatred is premeditated and spares no one.

Hitler targets the Jews.

Stalin targets everyone, and the *only* thing that matters is how he feels when he wakes, it is what determines which group will be made to pay for his body's mood: will it be the turn of the Mensheviks, Bolsheviks, doctors, aristocrats, the intelligentsia, the Tsarist army, the Jews, or his own associates.

He sits on his throne feeding his subjects as if they were lions in a cage. He flings them chunks of fear.

Hitler sits on a throne, feeding his subjects as if they were lions in a cage, promising they will soon be set free. He feeds them words such as Übermensch, Reich, force, power, the German character, blood, soil, future, joy. These words give even the doubters wings and they don them with enthusiasm, they start running with their heads in the clouds: this is their contribution to the history of joy.

Hitler exhorts others to turn their eyes heavenward, while he himself gazes upward like a deranged saint.

Stalin pushes others to the ground, face down, stamping his boot on their skulls, forcing them to their knees, and making them plow the earth with their faces.

Hitler is the leader of a big sect united by the idea of the German character, Aryan blood and wings.

Stalin is a pagan. Hitler is a pope.

Hitler has learned his lesson. Sometimes he shows a friendly face to the great unwashed, a kindly daddy-o in his eagle's nest, it is those around him who are the villains, he himself doesn't know a thing, he means everyone well. And the party, whether it's called national socialist or communist, is their mother and she is never wrong, she will press you to her sturdy chest.

Has she broken your ribs? Serves you right.

Beneš is a coward, but he's no fool. And he takes decisions by himself, which is a mistake. He won't take advice from anyone because that would give them insight into his personal fears, including the fear he has brought back from Russia as a non-returnable souvenir.

Beneš is losing ground under his feet. He lacks decisiveness. He wants his peace and quiet. Decisiveness is a word that contains many other words. Those who lack decisiveness become rickety. Their will, their inner strength, their integrity wobbles. If you wield a sword you must be ready to really kill your adversary, the Shaolin monks say.

Stalin and Hitler have perfected the art of disengaging from reality, but the heavier side of the scales is the one filled with despotism. Instead of becoming new gods, they have become Stalin and Hitler. They set out to mold reality according to the rules of their crazed minds, stunning everyone with their ability to see beneath the surface of things, lives, and societies. Entire nations have allowed themselves to be harnessed like donkeys by the prospect of a distant bundle of straw. The prospect of a just society, an eternal Reich, or eternal communism.

How come it's so easy, dear Lord? How little time it takes.

You *only* need to sow fear. Sow handfuls of fear and terror.

And you mustn't have any doubts. Pretend that it is *only* for the other person's good.

The *only* thing resulting from the experience of the body of mankind and the splinters wedged in the body of the masses is democracy with a tendency to hard-bitten individualism.

Why not toward individual critical thinking?

Swallows fly about, chirruping. They watch infected, nationally frustrated humankind be adorned with fake feathers. Swallows fly about, chirruping, most of their species have been around since the early Tertiary period.

The century of hysterical men was followed by a century of narcissists. Heralded by men in white suits. The body's memory does not lie. It's just a different game in the sandpit, boys.

How much is hidden in routine and ritual, my dear. Oh, the sweet month of June.

It is June 1938, harvest time. Edvard Beneš accepts one honorary doctorate after another. One, on June 21, is from the Mining Academy in Příbram. The solemn graduation ceremony for the freshly minted Doctor of Mining Engineering is held at Prague Castle.

On June 30, he receives the honorary degree of Doctor of Business Affairs from the Czech Technical University. He promises to put his skills and experience to use *for the benefit of the general public, and to work toward enhancing and broadening the peaceful cooperation of mankind.* The academic gown and cap are his favorite attire.

The war started a long time ago, waged by individuals. The war is being waged over the kitchen table, in the fields, on school benches, at the local post office. Fanatic against fanatic. Take the small town of Chřibská, for example. A schoolteacher, Mr. Švehla, married, childless, has lived in Chřibská all his life, as has his wife. He is an educated man, his hobby is entomology. He is also a social democrat, it's his most hallowed religion. Over the past five years, the circle around him has thinned out as his fellow citizens moved away. Even those who share his views have lent their tacit support to the majority, just to be assured of peace and quiet. They exhale and smile at the followers of the Sudeten German leader Konrad Henlein.

Mr. Švehla also believes he can now finally enjoy his peace and quiet. But the kids chirrup at home. They have learned to snoop, pick up signals between the lines, and catch treasonous words. They have learned how to gain advantage.

They observe their parents and learn quickly. They practice making deals and politicking. This is how a duplicitous generation is forged and formed, a generation that will determine the global postwar order. The kids talk at the dinner table. With an innocent blink of the eye and pursing their lips innocently. To distract from smashed windows, ripped pants, bad grades, brawls, and petty larceny. Their parents sit there, mouths agape, swallowing and gulping down words. Some lay their spoons on the table. Others slam them down.

The dads talk at the pub, the moms talk at the hairdressers' and in the grocery store. They unite, having finally found an outlet for the tension that has been building for years. In a meeting with the teachers at the PTA, the parents decide that this Mr. Švehla should no longer teach their kids. He is suspended and disciplinary proceedings are brought against him. But higher authorities intercede on the teacher's behalf. He is to be reinstated. All this happens in the month of June 1938.

Mr. Švehla walks into the classroom, his briefcase laden with books. As soon as he sits down, all the kids rise. They leave the classroom. As instructed. He sits all alone in front of the blackboard and keeps looking at the watch in his waistcoat pocket. He spends several days like this, his hands on the desk, fingers interlaced, classroom empty. He is praying without being aware of it.

The school head calls another meeting, which is attended by all the parents and teachers. Mr. Švehla is not invited. To this day, no one knows exactly what happened at that meeting, and no one ever will. What is clear is that the day after the meeting, not a single child goes to school. The teachers turn up regularly though, to make sure Mr. Švehla is prevented from entering the building and driven away. The town of Chřibská splits into two camps. Mr. Švehla vs the people. Mr. Švehla writes to Minister Jan Masaryk, he doesn't know what else to do, he just follows his intuition. Jan Masaryk's name is the first that occurs to him.

"Why don't you write to the President?"

"I don't know," Švehla tells his wife, truthfully.

The district governor arrives, as does the school inspector. A solution is found: Mr. Švehla should undergo a medical examination. He obliges, and is found healthy and fit to teach.

Thanks to the scheming by Henlein's party, the protest grows into a full-fledged school strike. Josef Rösler, a social democratic lawmaker from the neighboring town of Varnsdorf, personally requests an explanation from the school head. Mr. Švehla stands firm. His doggedness is regarded as particularly provocative: everything would be easier if he bowed to the majority.

"Why won't you make even a small concession?"

He replies to his wife, truthfully: "I don't know."

Mr. Švehla is a German teacher who opposes Hitler. He draws attention to the fact that someone has shoved the portraits of two former presidents of Czechoslovakia behind a vaulting box, but no attempt is made to find the culprits. Švehla writes a pseudonymous letter to a newspaper. *The democratically minded public, Czech and German alike, is outraged by the lack of action on the part of the district authorities, who have failed to protect a democratic German teacher who has committed no crime apart from refusing to turn a blind eye to provocations within the remit of the school head, who is supposed to guarantee order in the institution he runs.*

On the day the scandal is reported in the papers, President Edvard Beneš is receiving his honorary doctorate from the Mining Academy. He browses the newspapers; the ceremony has been duly noted, as has the President's grandiose avowal that *the miners' living standards must improve.* Good luck with that! A line catches his attention: his portrait has ended up behind a vaulting box in a sweaty provincial gymnasium. The matter was not investigated. It hurts his feelings. It's something he will never forget. Then he goes back to the Castle for a meeting with the Education Secretary, Dr. Frank, the deputy president of the Mining University, Dr. Stočes, the university's president, Ing. Dr. Parma, and PhD supervisor, Ing. Dr. Jičínský. They dine on trout in aspic, roast capon with salad and rice, buttered asparagus, strawberries with cream, cheese sticks, and juicy cherries. Oh June, the sweet month of June.

Beneš peels off the areas of conflict. As if the Czech Lands were an onion. Discard the outer layer, the troublesome volcanic rocks. So that he can enjoy his peace and quiet. Push aside all that is disagreeable and shutter himself in calm, in a country that is easy to oversee. Get rid of the Slovak National Party, which demands autonomy for Slovakia. Get rid of those who shove his portrait behind vaulting boxes. Restore clarity and order in the world. Return pictures to their rightful place. Avert chaos.

How much is hidden in routine and ritual, my dear.

He knows exactly what the man he shares the table with is thinking. He will exploit every chink. The *only* thing he wants is to stay in power. Tsarist autocracy. He loves himself. He is President.

He has a suit tailor-made, a white one this time. As the tailor takes his measurements, he wears a strip of material stuffed with cotton wool wrapped around his wrist in which to stick the pins. He looks like a gladiator. A pin sticks out of the corner of his mouth. The President is pleasant enough, but he gazes into the distance. He can't bear the sight of the pin inserted between the tailor's teeth. He can't stand the idea that the same pin will be inserted into the pristine white material. When the finished suit is delivered, the President has it thoroughly cleaned. The thought of the pin drenched in saliva makes him queasy.

Along with the suit, the tailor supplies a handkerchief for the breast pocket and a tie of the same color, both wrapped in tissue paper. He presses a fresh shirt and makes arrangements with a shoemaker, the leading worker at the Baťa factory. The President has his mustache trimmed and his hair done. He is pleasant enough to the barber, but gazes into the middle distance. The barber takes a close look at his neck, blowing on it gently as if about to kiss the skin. A whiff of warm breath on the back of the neck, the little hairs fly off, the neck tenses in disgust, the body stands up abruptly. He is President.

He hasn't always been President.

From the Diaries of Edvard Beneš's Interpreter

I can't argue with him. It's impossible to have an argument with Edvard. He refuses to discuss any personal matters and withdraws immediately. It is impossible to say a critical word about him, or he will turn on you. In a civilized manner. My language skills will be of no use here. I have lost track of how many languages I speak. People call me a polyglot. It started back in Switzerland, my home country: as a little girl, I learned German, soon adding French, Italian, and Romansh; in high school I studied English, Latin, and Greek. Aged fourteen, I was meant to go to Portugal on vacation, but traveled to Turkey instead and picked up a few words. Turkish has remained my favorite language to this day, it works like math, with no exceptions. Learning languages gets easier with each new one. I studied Turkish linguistics at Geneva University, but I can't stand the word "neutrality," neither in personal life nor in politics. I went to London to offer my skills to the intelligence agencies. I've lost count of how many languages I speak, it must be well over thirty, including Swahili, Azeri, and, most recently, Czech. I have been hired to interpret for the President's wife. I have gained her trust and become her confidante.

My confidant is Edvard. Compared with Turkish, Czech is a language full of exceptions. So is Edvard. He believes himself to be compassionate, open, and kind. He abhors conflict. He prefers compromise.

"If there is something I'm not lacking in, it's empathy," he says.

If there is something he is lacking in, it's empathy, I think, but keep quiet.

I know he's going to change the subject now. He feels he has to hint that he has the upper hand. He is a cold pragmatist, and he is bound to come up with something. He stares at me while I just sit there helplessly, eating. Swallowing my humiliation with every mouthful. He gives a small smile. And before carving the lamb, he says softly: "May I tell you something?"

"Of course."

My eagerness is wrapped in these eight letters. He is going to apologize to me, right now. We will speak openly, right now. He will tell me how much I mean to him, right now.

"I don't want to lecture you, but you're holding the fork the wrong way. That is how people who have no table manners and the bourgeois parvenus eat. You must hold the fork with the prongs pointing downward."

I won't pick up my fork. I could not lift a bite to my mouth anyway. Regardless of whether I hold it like a well-mannered harpoon or a ship with its sails up and its prow pointing ahead. Once again, he has shown he has the upper hand. I visualize parts of his body I would stick the fork into. Guth-Jarkovský's *Social Catechism* is of no use to me now. In my imagination, I get it off my chest in every language I know. There is no justice for women in this world. At night I stroll around the ivy-covered house. I'm supposed to keep watch over Edvard. And I know that his wife keeps watch over me.

He is a little boy, permanently amazed. Eyebrows raised. He is fond of boys who don't threaten him. He is small and puny, a gnome made of granite. He is no Napoleon, alas. He is a good boy.

Occasionally, he goes out with Jan Masaryk.

Beneš won't try the cocaine. Or the dancers.

Edvard is fretting. He sits around, that is *all* he does all day. Edvard doesn't know what to do with himself. There are some 35,000 volumes in his library. But *only* one contains what he needs. A small revolver. Edvard's wife Hana finds her husband sitting in the library, his fingers tracing the tree rings on the mahogany desk. He is seated in a black leather armchair whose upholstered fringes are decorated with metal studs and beads on a string. He runs his index finger over them. Mrs. Beneš knows. She has witnessed a similar moment before. Edvard's nerves are delicate like barely visible spider's silk, a web that sometimes gets tangled. Hana Beneš is a kind woman, though deep down she believes that everything is *only* a question of will and self-control. A person, especially a politician, ought to practice the art of keeping his weaknesses under control. Hana Beneš knows how to handle the situation. She reaches for the revolver.

"I'd better look after this for you."

"You don't need to worry about me."

"This is not about you. It's about me. No one would believe me. If you shot yourself, they might come and arrest me. You can be very selfish sometimes, Edvard."

Mrs. Beneš inserts the revolver into one of the books packing the shelves and gathering dust there.

"I prefer music or paintings anyway," says Hana Beneš. She prefers human company to sharing her solitude with a book that blackmails her. At concerts and in galleries she is among people, she sees them and is seen, an agreeable picture herself.

They have to clear out their house and pack in haste, so Hana Beneš asks some students to give her a hand. She shows them a list of books Mr. President wants to take. She praises them with a smile and thanks them. The young men wander along the tall, book-lined shelves, scurrying up and down ladders like insects. As a student picks up a book on the top shelf, an object falls out. It lands on the wooden floor with a clatter.

Hana Beneš quickly picks up the weapon.

"Because of burglars," she says. With a smile. How much is hidden in routine and ritual, my dear.

Beneš goes to the US and returns to England much calmer. He is a changed man. But the latest news increases the disquiet of the body. He can't get out of his mind the image of the short, stocky man licking his greasy fingers and wiping his mouth on the white tablecloth, grabbing it by a corner and drawing it to his face, thus toppling a glass, the whiteness of the cloth absorbing the crimson wine.

When he is alone, Beneš tries to lick his fingers the way Stalin did. He feels queasy and has to throw up into the ceramic toilet bowl with a golden flush handle.

He would be happy if he could stay in England. But can a president emigrate? If he resigned during the war he would be considered a traitor. And would no longer be president. Being president has a number of advantages.

In the evening, after Mrs. Beneš has tucked him into bed and sung him a lullaby, he confides his nightmares.

"Oh, but that's *only* idle talk, my dear. People say all kinds of things about Russia, but remember that H. G. Wells visited the country and was impressed, Julius Fučík has been there and came back equally impressed, and said that Russia is a country where tomorrow means yesterday."

"But I live today, dear. The reports from Soviet Russia never sounded too good."

"But the war can't be won without Russia, you said so yourself."

"That's it. And that's what makes it so dreadful."

During a game of croquet, Beneš suggests again that he and Hana ought to think about their lives after the war.

"When the war is over, we shall live at Prague Castle and the summer residence at Lány."

"No one knows what will happen when the war is over. Just take a look at Stalin, my dear."

"Everything will be just as it used to be."

"Nothing will be as it used to be."

Hana walks Beneš to his study and points to the map of the world.

"This is Soviet Russia. And this is the rest of the world. Communism doesn't stand a chance. America won't let it happen."

"But he licked his fingers," says Beneš, and breaks down in tears.

He doesn't say out loud that he doesn't want to go back to Czechoslovakia. That he would prefer to stay here and enjoy the tranquility and the clear rules of England, a country that is so close to his heart because everything is protected by rituals that make the days and the nights bearable, rituals that blindfold aggressive problems, leaving them groping in the dark, unseen. How much is hidden in routine and ritual, my dear. He loves the Royal family, the industrialists and aristocratic families, he enjoys the colonial atmosphere. Oh, to be a viceroy, to be a big shot, disconnected from the people down below. White gloves.

Power is his ambition. Who doesn't love power. Only those who have yet to taste it, I tell myself as I interpret the ideas of others. I can't wait for the day when someone writes down my thoughts.

Politicians are human beings. I peel off their labels of nationality, education, and profession. The only thing left is the core. Often empty without a label. Like a tennis ball. I peel off the wrapping and find a void. Or I peel off the wrapping and a rich, unexpected universe emerges, lashing out wildly. Profound and subtle. Watching human situations. Watching human beings without the wrappings. Degrees, jobs, careers, mother tongues, nationalities—they are all just varieties of wrapping paper. Exposing what has been wrapped in them. Under the wrapping there is a void. Or a fullness. He was born on April 28, 1884, my man of April. In the Kingdom of Bohemia, the village of Kožlany. Religion: Roman Catholic. He went to school under Austro-Hungary. Girls were not allowed to study at universities back then. The country's education system had a reputation to maintain.

The Czechoslovak Business Academy in Prague. He was a substitute teacher there from 1909 to 1913, and later assistant teacher, teaching French.

He served as Foreign Minister and was elected to the National Assembly. As a member of parliament he can travel by land and on water free of charge.

My head is reeling: honorary positions in the League of Nations; in 1934 he established diplomatic relations with the Soviet Union, signing a Czechoslovak-Soviet treaty of mutual assistance a year later. On December 18 of the same year he was elected President of Czechoslovakia. On December 5, 1938, following the Munich Agreement, he resigned the post of President. In March 1939 he started mobilizing Czechoslovak resistance abroad, drawing on his experience of the secret resistance movement known as "the Mafia," which he had organized in exile during World War I, serving as the Secretary of the Czechoslovak National Council in Paris and, from 1918 to 1935, as Minister of Foreign Affairs. In October 1939, he forms the Czechoslovak National Committee in Paris, organizing troops in the West. In London in July 1940, he forms the government in exile, serving again as President. This is where our paths first cross. In 1943 he travels to Moscow to sign the treaty of friendship, mutual support, and postwar cooperation. I am his interpreter during talks on the future shape of the republic with the Moscow-based leadership of the Communist Party of Czechoslovakia. In spring 1945, we are back in Moscow, discussing the formation of a government of the National Front and its program, later known as the Košice Program. He believes he has outsmarted everyone and looks forward to being president again, and is duly elected in June 1946, oh June, that sweet month of June. But not before signing, right after the liberation, a number of revolutionary decrees, his eyes widening in horror over the decree on nationalization. Mrs. Beneš tried to push me away from him, saw me as a threat, and so I returned to London. Then I went to Geneva. To be closer to him in February 1948, when he accepted the resignation of his government, stepping down as President of the Republic on June 7, 1948. Oh June, that sweet month of June.

The assassination of Reichsprotektor Reinhard Heydrich, code-named operation *Anthropoid,* proves a political success despite the terror it unleashes. Vaněk, a local leader of the resistance, tries to calm the hotheads who treat resistance as a game. He respects every human life and is a staunch realist.

He feels there is something deeply wrong about this plan. His group, *the Eagle,* is asked to give shelter to the two assassins, the parachutists Kubiš and Gabčík. He feels something is not right, contacts the leaders in exile, and manages to reach the prime minister. He would have preferred to speak to Jan Masaryk, but that proved impossible. He doesn't get to speak to President Beneš, who is not informed, it is best not to fill him in, he is a coward who prefers diplomatic solutions, they mutter in secret.

Vaněk finds someone who can speak to Beneš on his behalf but by the time his proxy reaches the President, it is too late. Vaněk's proxy is plain-speaking as always, but Beneš draws strength from conversation, verbal clashes make him stronger, he is a master of the verbal skirmish, whereas in physical combat he hides behind a tree. He convinces Vaněk's proxy of the need to sign the treaty of friendship and mutual assistance and postwar cooperation. Who does this Ladislav Vaněk think he is anyway, to take such tone with him? A moment of high drama ensues, but although the body of Edvard Beneš is at its center, it is not under any immediate threat. He intends to return to his country a winner, the Liberator President. Vaněk's proxy begs him to halt the operation.

"I cannot. It is our sacred duty to stand up to the enemy."

"There are other forms of fighting. The Nazi retribution will cost thousands more lives."

Beneš remains intransigent.

"We have to demonstrate that we are a fighting nation."

"But this operation is pointless, it will result in nothing but terror. Assassinating Heydrich won't achieve anything."

"You're scared. That is understandable."

"If this operation goes ahead, I'm sure it'll make Hitler shake in his boots," the irate Vaněk says to his wife.

He is scared. Nothing wrong with that.

Beneš feels like a commander again, like in the time of the Great War when he was at the helm of the Mafia. He gives the operation his blessing. And Heydrich's assassination will earn the exile leadership credit for being a "fighting" government representing a "fighting" nation. Beneš doesn't explain to Vaněk's proxy that the assassination, a gesture planned by a headstrong elite, is a mere show meant not for Hitler's eyes, but for the eyes of the Soviets who have been pressing the government in exile to take decisive action in the placid Czech Lands. A gracious Edvard Beneš sits in his armchair in England smoking a pipe.

The village of Lidice, among others, is wiped out . . .

"It was Dr Beneš who decided the fate of this village," Ladislav Vaněk yells at his wife.

"Stop that nonsense," his wife replies calmly.

"That sure showed him! Hitler is now shaking in his boots."

Heydrich is dead. The retribution was predictable.

The gentlemen in London are rubbing their white-gloved hands. The world's eyes are on Prague. And on the government in exile.

"You see what the Nazis are like," says Beneš over lunch whenever someone brings up Lidice. "The whole world is talking about it."

"Many more villages have been burned down in the Soviet Union," his Soviet visitor cuts him down to size.

"But no one has heard about them," says Beneš, cutting him down in return.

He is pleased. He is pleased that I am allowed to stay with him. He presents me with a gift, a shawl.

"You are pleased."

"The Soviets are the ones who are pleased. They were putting us under pressure."

"I don't believe you."

"This is a political success."

"Your political success."

"It was a decisive act."

"Oh yes, and it's clearly made Hitler shake in his boots."

He takes the shawl and chucks it angrily into the box lined with tissue paper. He turns to face the window. A sign for me to leave. Another Edvard is reflected in the windowpane, cheekbones protruding, muscles on his cheeks rippling. I leave the room, go down to the first floor, find my coat. I take a stroll outside. I look up at the window and see a shadow standing there. I would have to climb a ladder to stand face to face with him. It's always the same. I must grant that he is divine. That is a precondition for having a conversation.

He still loves his academic gowns. He loves degrees. Just like everyone did in Austro-Hungary. How much is hidden in routine and ritual, my dear.

He is accustomed to observing schedules, stands on ceremony, and respects the protocol dictating who should ride in which car and with whom, who should be allowed to address him first, who should welcome the President's wife and her entourage. The successor to the Liberator Thomas Garrigue Masaryk. Fanfares and the national anthem. Solemn speeches. University deans addressing him, standing up while he is seated. The gentlemen kept separate from the ladies, ladies being an ornament.

All the deans are men. No use denying it. Don't even try. I've seen through the games that men play. When I mention that I'm writing a play with the working title *The Games That Men Play*, I am instantly advised to change it, in the spirit of political correctness, to *The Games That Men and Women Play*. Perhaps, in the spirit of political correctness, I should now reveal that a silk moth is hiding below the surface. People's lives rarely follow a politically correct path.

What kind of place was it where he was born? What kind of place is it where I was born? What has shaped the local mindset? We recognize one another like animals, by scent. He can't leave his Czechhood behind.

Does national affiliation seep into one's genetic makeup? Is it etched into every word the mother tongue has extracted? Is it passed on subconsciously from one generation to the next?

Beneš admires England. Beneš admires France. How long had England been a colonial power? How long had France been a colonial power?

Why can't I shake the feeling that, in order to understand the Czechs, Beneš is more important than Masaryk and Havel?

In his student days in France there was only one thing he admired: the aristocracy of language and demeanor, Beneš is an aristocrat. It is his choice.

Nobility.

Twenty-seven Czech noblemen were executed in June 1621, oh, the sweet month of June. The Battle of White Mountain was peculiar. Well, this is his country, where you don't turn your back on a battle. But its people don't really participate in the fighting, they just pretend to. Why can't they just admit that they would like to be neutral. Like Switzerland. They are close to the Swiss. Fence off your gardens. And observe the others.

And the Czech language, still so young and still growing. Not fully established yet, adorning itself with jewels, adding sentences and phrases modelled on German, French, and English. He would like to live long enough to see German and French and English adorn themselves with words taken from Czech. All those Austrian place names, hastily translated following the foundation of Czechoslovakia. Mozart's Salzburg becoming Solnohrad.

In London, separated from the Czech Lands, he surrounds himself with an elite circle. I am there to interpret his wise words. And yet, sometimes he roams the garden. He observes rituals religiously. Breakfast and five o'clock tea. Dealing with correspondence. What holds him together are his visits to the barber and the tailor, and his impeccable white suits. But the flesh under the corset is caving in, losing shape. There are moments now when Edvard can't see any point to what he is doing. Because the familiar world of which he used to be a part has disintegrated.

"You don't have to be president."

He gives me his hangdog look.

"Hana complains that I didn't spend enough time with her when we were young."

"She is tense and menopausal."

"She is long past menopause. But now, all of a sudden, she is complaining that I didn't sleep with her often enough. Even though we were together all the time."

"Leave her. You can stay in England and teach at a university."

He looks at me as if I were out of my mind. If he wasn't afraid of a scandal, he would sack me and our paths would part. He is anxious because no one knows what the future has in store. The only thing he knows how to do is rule. And it's the only thing he wants to do. That is what he wants. He wants to be a benevolent monarch. A benevolent scholar. A benevolent university professor. All these are well-established systems that he navigates safely and comfortably. But now, suddenly, his former life has been called into question, it's as if he was ashamed of his former self, no longer sure of who he was and what he should become.

How old is he? A personal crisis merges with an external one. He is reluctant to leave his wife, Hana, the idea frightens him, he'll never pluck up the courage, one doesn't leave one's mother. He has reached the top but that is now under threat. So he accepts decorations that validate his exceptionality. In the comfortable seclusion of London, the president accepts decorations for valor.

Everyone around him is pussyfooting, telling him that he is destined for greater things that are more important for the nation.

"You should save your own neck."

He is not used to being spoken to bluntly. He finds it unsettling and attractive by turns. He latches on to every cliché. Like a tick. My beloved tick.

"It is 1944, and all you care about is receiving awards from the London government in exile."

"I have deserved them."

"So many?"

"Yes, you heard the citation: the Czechoslovak War Cross for 1939, the Czechoslovak Medal of Valor and the Czechoslovak Order of Merit, first class."

"A war cross?"

"Yes, as the citation said: in his capacity as the supreme commander of the Czechoslovak army, thanks to his foresight and unflagging energy at the most critical time the troops were redeployed from France to Great Britain, where he swiftly negotiated all the prerequisites for further fighting."

"And the valor?"

"The citation went: the personal bravery he demonstrated by participating from the outset in the battle that flared up in 1939."

"And the merit?"

"The citation said: for his outstanding effort and unceasing endeavors to establish a Czechoslovak army abroad and for his continuous and effective impact on and vigorous support for the army's morale and materiel."

He is bewildered, doesn't know what to do with his life. He knows what he would do in peacetime. He would collect degrees and receive accolades. But now this man has found himself at the center of political and social turmoil, the sociologist in him is enraged and refuses to accept reality. Reality hasn't reached as far as his village, Aston Abbotts. A white suit with gloves and ironed creases, Mrs. Beneš's hat, and the smiles they disburse continue to matter more. His vanity hasn't faded away, fear has *only* added fuel to it. He is furious at the lack of adequate response to his decisions. I suggest that in his capacity as a sociologist, he should change the subject and write a book whose subtitle should be *An Individual Amid Chaos*. This is his lifelong topic, addressed to a healthy society still permeated by Austrian law.

Edvard is tripping over himself. He believes he will be sheltered by Masaryk's protective wing for the rest of his life. He feels he is an heir, not just an associate. As the chosen one, by virtue of being welcomed into Masaryk's family. In fact, what has always protected him is simply the fact that he has moved in circles that followed the rules of bourgeois humanism. But once these rules began to dissolve and disappear, he lost his bearings, became weak, and appeared cowardly. There was only one thing for him to do: avoid situations that he might not survive.

Edvard wants his peace and quiet. He escapes into illness.

He has remained a lifelong son. Hana's son. This has never been a relationship of equals, but rather a perfectly maternal relationship. How lovely.

There is no room for a child in a relationship of this kind. I found his appearance and impeccable attire confusing. Deep inside he was a sensitive man. He just lacked a key quality: manliness.

Something Mrs. Beneš had in spades.

Edvard will always remain elitist. An epicurean and utilitarian like him will never allow anyone to make his life difficult. He is not a man of action. His appearance is deceptive, he draws his strength from Hana. There is nothing that would throw her off balance. They share an interest in the history of ideas, art, religion, philosophy. Typical bourgeois predilections. *Only* those paintings that are inoffensive grace their walls. Biedermeier.

But the century he was born into is monstrous: Nazism in Germany, communist regimes, Russia and China, the resurgence of militant Islam. His approach to life has its advantages, as he manages to combine being dazzled by specific sensuous pleasures with a respect for higher spiritual goals. He will never succumb to fanaticism of any kind. The word asceticism is also missing from his vocabulary.

Looking back after all those years, and the moments we shared at a time when my body was young and resilient and resisted him, I wonder which of those memories I should convey. I fell in love with Edvard, which was forbidden. But he was civilized, smart, and gentle. Until this illusion was shattered. The strenuous effort to keep it all together. Edvard was ahead of his time. He lived in the present. This is how people live today, in the twenty-first century, when no one cares about the past. Or about the future. *Only* the present. He could always handle the present.

Edvard gets rid of everyone who is inferior. He gets rid of the Ukrainians because he regards them as savages, you just need to look at their faces. After the war, he gets rid of the Germans because they have been rendered inferior by disgracing themselves historically. And no one dares to protest for fear they might be suspected of standing up for the Nazis, and hence of being Nazis themselves.

Edvard was still at primary school when the first portent circled the globe. The theory known as phrenology. This mother of all racially-tinged pseudosciences and monstrous theories deduced a person's character from the shape of their skull, with snouts and receding foreheads relegated to the animal kingdom. It arose at the end of the nineteenth century, the time when Vincent van Gogh and Henri de Toulouse-Lautrec sipped absinthe together in Paris. Mixed with water, it would turn yellow and green. The narcotic of choice in the waning years of the nineteenth century. Mental institutions were full of syphilitics who had lost their minds. Fallen through the sieve.

Eugenics. It purports to cleanse humankind, to get rid of influences that cause the birth of defective individuals, and to perfect the genetic make-up of populations.

Edvard joins those who ponder the question of how to respond to the decay of humankind. He embraces these ideas. And once you accept an idea, you can't expunge it by banishing it from your mind. Edvard wonders how humankind can be refined. Why, by letting intelligent, educated people mate. It is a tempting idea. Like cultivating the roses he admires in the park. Or like breeding bulls. He is not alone, there are many in Europe who think that way. Nikola Tesla, for one. The idea is being seriously discussed. This elitist attitude never really goes away, having crept into people's minds, thrusting the population into pigeonholes where they remain confined forever.

In Europe it is known by a different name, for Europe sees itself as superior to the rest of humankind, as a highly cultivated rose. The division into castes proliferates across Europe in a gentle and peaceful guise, as handpicked ten-year-olds are sent to private boarding schools while access to education is made more difficult for others.

Edvard and people like him are in for a shock. The Nazis have adopted the noble idea of cultivating aristocrats of the mind and put it into practice. Ideas became reality and the reality was not shocked at all. The insane, the feeble-minded, and the crippled were eliminated. Beautiful women were expected to copulate with strapping young men. But the experiment went slightly awry as intelligence and shrewdness does not automatically inhabit perfect bodies. So bodies were prioritized.

Bodies have been prioritized.

The Nazis stole the idea from Edvard and others of a like mind. It can no longer be discussed aloud without leaving a foul taste in the mouth. Edvard and others of a like mind ponder the question of how to arrest the decline of humanity. They hold their discussions in the drawing rooms of England. When those who discussed these ideas before the war meet again, they know they will stick together and won't give away or betray one another. They also know they're under threat. And that they have to build a fortress of decisive deeds. So that, should anyone mention that Edvard and other people of a like mind once supported eugenics, it would look like absolute, crazy nonsense in light of their noble and resolute actions.

Edvard is an elitist. And elitists are a group that sticks together more than any other. To divide and rule comes naturally to them. They believe that the occasional glitch in history is only temporary. They are convinced that they know better, and that the world belongs to them. They validate one another in this belief. They are above the crowd. And the crowd is a waste of time, a bunch of nobodies, human trash. Trash must be swept aside.

Humankind will be forever befouled and contaminated by these ideas. They are passed from one generation to the next. Anyone who is socially disadvantaged is inferior. Gypsies are inferior because the racial theory says so. So are the Jews. And women, of course.

Women are inferior. In fact, who isn't? An empty husk, all it needs is a wrapper. A wrapper made of what? Of university degrees. Of uniforms made of expensive cloth. Custom-made shoes. Blue blood. Why are you so terrified, Edvard, why are you staring at me in such despair, why are you not saying anything, talk to me, please, talk to me, what are you scared of, don't go, don't run away, talk to me, do you hear me?

Well, when Edvard Beneš was growing up, his capital city was Vienna and Franz Ferdinand was set to accede to the throne. Fin-de-siècle Vienna, a magnet for large numbers of Czechs hoping to find work, like Prague, is an aesthetic, erotic and intellectual world unto itself. Sigmund Freud's psychoanalysis emerges to the rhythm of the waltz and Austrians are reading a certain book, an incendiary study by an author who has discovered and foreseen darker contexts that will lead up to the moment when Austria gives Hitler an ecstatic welcome, and it will be the German Nazis who will have to rein in the cruelty of their Austrian associates. Describing the world he grew up in, Otto Weininger gave his controversial work the title *Geschlecht und Charakter* (*Sex and Character*). The philosopher was born in 1880, and committed suicide at the age of twenty-three, shortly after the book's publication. In it he claimed that women and the Jews are merely sexual beings who lack a distinct individuality. It became a bestseller, which turned into a weapon in the hands of thugs.

Edvard is familiar with the book.

"It is the product of an immature mind."

"But it is in your library. And you have read it. Why?"

"A book not read to the end is like a journey not completed."

"But you've never spoken out against it. And yet, so many Czechs came to Vienna."

"Vienna was built by Czech bricklayers; it was Czech cooks who brought pancakes and plum dumplings to Vienna."

"That was the end of Vienna, the Czechs have wrecked it."

He is furious, but I want him to be furious.

"The book is alive. It is still here. You served it to Hitler on a silver platter. You have let these ideas out into the open and Hitler inhaled them with the air. You were a student of phrenology."

Vienna, Weininger's home city, gave Hitler this book. This was the original *Mein Kampf*, Hitler's *Mein Kampf* is only part two. He got rid of the Jews.

He couldn't get rid of women.

Women who go to university, women who get a divorce, women who are capable of critical thinking. According to Edvard's ideas, too, they are defective human beings who live truncated lives. Sometimes I think that, faced with the choice, he would choose women to be the first to be sent to the death camps. Edvard is perceptive, he is oh so considerate to the ladies. But he is incapable of treating me as an equal sparring partner, not even in a critical conversation. In his world, women are not entitled to such a role. He stiffens and observes the woman as if she were some strange insect. An insect that needs to be refined. In his world, a woman can play the maid, wife, mother, or sister. She is not supposed to take on any other role.

"Edvard, I am fluent in over thirty languages."

"You are an exception."

"I am not."

How long have I lived. How long Edvard has been dead. And how much has changed. It all seems so strange to me now. Each group boasts about being the greatest victim of the twentieth century. Yet for thousands of years, one half of humanity has been quietly prevented from living freely, thinking freely and moving about freely. Whose idea was this? And who accepted it? Who has allowed this to happen? And who has approved this topsy-turvy genocide that has inundated the world, ratified by every religion? And even accepted by women as a fact of life. Muzzles are handed out in the delivery room. You are born. And this is how the world will see you and there's nothing you can do about it.

Birgit's Notes Written at Night, Torn up, and Thrown Away, Variations on the Same Theme, Bolstered by Erika's Playlist.

He is welcomed by the hotel staff on arrival in London. The city may be pummeled by air raids every night, but decorum is maintained. He is ushered into a room with polished mahogany furniture, vast walnut-colored surfaces with inlaid mother-of-pearl daisies and delicate dark lines, some straight, some curved. The windowsills are made of marble. The dark-blue rugs boast a pattern of yellow roses, forming an intricate web. The rugs can muffle one's steps, but they can't cope with the bombs. Between the walls covered with blue-and-white flock wallpaper, there are black leather armchairs in a variety of sizes, a desk that has many drawers with golden handles, a lamp ablaze with gold and adorned with two golden hounds; there are bedside lamps with plump golden bases and pleated lampshades, and the bedroom is shuttered off by metal ironwork with golden flowers, as are the enormous windows. The golden drapes are decorated with dusty blue motifs of flowers and amphoras. Two black columns stand in the middle of the room. The bathroom is of greenish marble, with a double vanity, a bathtub, and a separate shower. Snow-white towels. On a glass-topped coffee table with golden legs stands a glass vase holding a gorgeous bouquet of yellow roses and chrysanthemums.

The secretary knocks on the door.

"Everything all right, Mr. President?"

"I have requested two separate bedrooms for myself and my wife. I work until late at night."

"I'll see what I can do."

The secretary tries to oblige, but to no avail. The hotel manager is summoned. He squirms, unable to fathom what the problem might be.

"I am very sorry, Mr. President, but this is our best suite."

"I need two rooms."

"I am truly sorry, but we are fully booked. May I remind you that we're in the middle of a war?"

The President controls himself, he is friendly, but he stares into the middle distance. He disappears into the bedroom. Mrs. Beneš comes in immediately. The hotel manager listens poker-faced as Mrs. Beneš explains, clearly and emphatically, that he simply has to find a solution, it's *only* for a short time, until they find accommodations outside London, it is not just a question of security for the two of them; the future of the war itself is at stake, a war Czechoslovakia did her best to prevent, but which, unfortunately, led to injudicious consequences due to the unwise intervention by England and France. The hotel manager stands motionless while the chambermaids are busy in the underground garage, ripping up sheets and winding them into bandages. One of the laundry rooms has been turned into a temporary shelter for the wounded. Soap is in short supply and is used only to disinfect wounds. The hotel manager stands impassive. As he leaves the room and takes the elevator down to reception to run over the guest list, a chambermaid rides up to the best suite, hastily putting on her little bonnet. She knocks on the door, Mrs. Beneš opens up and hands her a white suit on a hanger.

"Please make sure this is cleaned by tonight."

The chambermaid curtseys and dashes down to the laundry room, while two others go hunting for soap and gasoline to clean the suit.

The hotel is in a fighting mood. Ladies who have congregated in the lounge to organize a support group for the wounded are horrified to learn that an American woman staying at the hotel—with her son but without her husband—wants to join the effort. Gentlemen in the cigar lounge have gathered over a map.

Mrs. Beneš joins the ladies for afternoon tea, she has been expected and arrives beaming, full of smiles, as always. She is showered with names, titles, and invitations, and her own name is added to the list of the newly established *Ladies' Association for the Support of Victims of War.* The American lady enters and Mrs. Beneš knows immediately whose side she will take. She greets the ten-year-old boy with a noncommittal expression. The American speaks.

"I *only* came to say hello, I think it was a cowardly thing, for the English as well as, Americans, to sacrifice you."

The ladies are horrified.

"I hope you don't suffocate in those corsets of yours."

She turns on her heels and disappears, her son who was playing with the globe in the corner in tow.

"A divorcée. And she writes poetry," one of the ladies tells Mrs. Beneš by way of explanation.

The hotel manager is discussing the tricky situation with a receptionist. The American woman approaches, takes off her gloves, and asks for a form: she would like to send a telegram. She overhears the hotel manager and the receptionist whispering.

"If it's any help, I can let you have my suite."

"Madam, but the *only* room left is a single room on the top floor."

"Surely you must have a camp bed? I prefer people who defy the dyad of victim and transgressor and are capable of discarding this simplistic anthropological mindset," the woman says somewhat cryptically.

Decades before, in the late nineteenth century, the same hotel hosted an English viceroy under whose rule thirty million people died in the Great Famine of India. Thirty million Indians, not a single English person among them. He is careful not to touch the locals. He takes off his jacket and holds it at arm's length.

"A famine has broken out."

"There's nothing we can do about it."

"There are supplies in the harbor."

"They are meant for England, God Save Queen Victoria, the Queen of Great Britain, and the House of Hanover."

"We could . . ."

"It's very sad but that is what the Lord has decreed. As has nature. Have you not read Mr. Darwin?"

"Yes, sir."

"*Only* the fittest survive."

This holocaust was forgotten. The groundwork for the Great War was laid in India. And Ukraine. And Namibia. The groundwork for World War II has been laid for as long as mankind has been in existence. The totalitarian system has been explored and developed to perfection. By the religious churches. For *nonreligious* churches also exist. That is a fact. Why do people need a church to have faith? Why do they believe that a Pope knows more about God than a daisy or a seagull? Why do popes have to be elected for life? Why not let a daisy or a seagull be Pope?

He knows exactly what the other man at his table is thinking. He will make use of every chink. He is not interested in anything. The *only* thing he wants is to stay in power. Autocracy. He likes himself. He is an English viceroy.

He has a suit tailor-made, a white one. As the tailor takes the Viceroy's measurements, he wears a strip of material stuffed with cotton wool wrapped around his wrist in which to stick the pins. He looks like a gladiator. A pin sticks out of the corner of his mouth. The English Viceroy is pleasant enough, but he gazes into the middle distance. He can't bear the sight of the pin inserted between the tailor's teeth. He can't stand the idea that the same pin will be inserted into the pristine white material. When the finished suit is delivered, the Viceroy has it thoroughly cleaned. The thought of the pin drenched in saliva makes him queasy.

Along with the suit the tailor supplies a handkerchief for the breast pocket and a tie of the same color, both wrapped in tissue paper. He presses a fresh shirt and makes arrangements with a shoemaker, the finest in London. The Viceroy has his mustache trimmed and his hair done. He is pleasant enough to the barber but gazes into the middle distance, speaking to the barber's reflection in the mirror or looking down at his lap as he lowers his head to let the barber run a razor across the nape of his neck. The barber takes a close look at the neck and blows on it gently as if about to kiss the skin. A whiff of warm breath on the back of the neck, the little hairs fly off, the neck tenses in disgust, the body stands up abruptly. He is the English Viceroy.

He hasn't always been Viceroy.

It's June again, oh the sweet month of June. How much is hidden in routine and ritual, my dear.

A silk moth. Come, and let us listen to the sound it makes.

ACKNOWLEDGMENTS

Lukas Spinner, the island of Amrum
Rolf Seelige Steinhoff, the island of Usedom
Slobodanka Radun, an island

Franz Brunner, Markus Hiesleitner (Galerie Kulturdrogerie Vídeň)
The Czech Literary Foundation

Coffee House Press began as a small letterpress operation in 1972 and has grown into an internationally renowned nonprofit publisher of literary fiction, essay, poetry, and other work that doesn't fit neatly into genre categories.

LITERATURE
is not the same thing as
PUBLISHING

FUNDER ACKNOWLEDGMENTS

Coffee House Press is an internationally renowned independent book publisher and arts nonprofit based in Minneapolis, MN; through its literary publications, Coffee House acts as a catalyst and connector—between authors and readers, ideas and resources, creativity and community, inspiration and action.

Coffee House Press books are made possible through the generous support of grants and donations from corporations, state and federal grant programs, family foundations, and the many individuals who believe in the transformational power of literature. This activity is made possible by the voters of Minnesota through a Minnesota State Arts Board Operating Support grant, thanks to the legislative appropriation from the Arts and Cultural Heritage Fund. Coffee House also receives major operating support from the Amazon Literary Partnership, and the McKnight Foundation.

Coffee House Press receives additional support from Bookmobile; Dorsey & Whitney LLP; and the Schwab Charitable Fund.

The publication of this book was supported by the Ministry of Culture of the Czech Republic.

MINNESOTA STATE ARTS BOARD
CLEAN WATER LAND & LEGACY AMENDMENT
MINISTRY OF CULTURE CZECH REPUBLIC
amazon literary partnership
MCKNIGHT FOUNDATION

THE PUBLISHER'S CIRCLE OF COFFEE HOUSE PRESS

Publisher's Circle members make significant contributions to Coffee House Press's annual giving campaign. Understanding that a strong financial base is necessary for the press to meet the challenges and opportunities that arise each year, this group plays a crucial part in the success of Coffee House's mission.

Recent Publisher's Circle members include many anonymous donors, Patricia A. Beithon, Theodore Cornwell, Jane Dalrymple-Hollo, Mary Ebert and Paul Stembler, Kamilah Foreman, Eva Galiber, Bryan Garrett, Roger Hale and Nor Hall, William Hardacker, Randy Hartten and Ron Lotz, Carl and Heidi Horsch, Amy L. Hubbard and Geoffrey J. Kehoe Fund of the St. Paul & Minnesota Foundation, Hyde Family Charitable Fund, Kenneth & Susan Kahn, the Kenneth Koch Literary Estate, Cinda Kornblum, the Lenfestey Family Foundation, Carol and Aaron Mack, Gillian McCain, Mary and Malcolm McDermid, Daniel N. Smith III and Maureen Millea Smith, Vance Opperman, Mr. Pancks' Fund in memory of Graham Kimpton, Alan Polsky, Robin Preble, Ronald Restrepo and Candace S. Baggett, Steve Smith, Jeffrey Sugerman and Sarah Schultz, Paul Thissen, Grant Wood, Margaret Wurtele, Jeremy M. Davies, Robin Chemers Neustein, Dorsey and Whitney Foundation, Elizabeth Schnieders, Allyson Tucker, and Aptara Inc.

For more information about the Publisher's Circle and other ways to support Coffee House Press books, authors, and activities, please visit www.coffeehousepress.org/pages/donate or contact us at info@coffeehousepress.org.

RADKA DENEMARKOVÁ is a celebrated Czech novelist, dramatist, screenwriter, translator, and essayist. She has written nine books. Denemarková is the only Czech writer who has received the Magnesia Litera Award four times, and has received international awards such as the Styria Literature Prize, the Brücke Berlin Award, the Franz Kafka Prize from the ÖGfL, and the European Prize for Tolerance, among others. Her works have been translated into twenty-three languages. *A Contribution to the History of Joy* won the Spycher Leuk Literature Award 2019, and is her second book to be published in English. She lives in Prague.

JULIA AND PETER SHERWOOD are literary translators based in London. Julia Sherwood took up literary translation after working in the NGO sector for over twenty years; she is also the editor of Seagull Books' Slovak List. Peter Sherwood taught Hungarian at the School of Slavonic and East European Studies in London and in the University of North Carolina at Chapel Hill. Together, they have translated into English some thirty books by mostly contemporary Slovak and Czech writers.

A Contribution to the History of Joy was designed by Coffee House Press. Text set in Adobe Caslon Pro.